Peter de Lissovoy

Wisconsin

YouArePerfectPress

My thanks to Geoff de Lissovoy for his reading of *Wisconsin* and his many helpful insights and suggestions.

With gratitude to Patsy Felch and Ed Sachs for their help.

All names and characters in this novel are fictitious.

ISBN: 978-0-9844139-2-8

Library of Congress Control Number: 2015900464

YouArePerfectPress, Lancaster, NH

It's often been told,
Don't lose your soul,
When ol' midnight
Creeps 'round your door.

—'Round Midnight

Two steps inside Jackie's joint on 43rd Street, sight of an evil face sliced off twenty years like brain surgery with a straight razor. The cop was sixteen years old again, full of hate. Hastily he turned his back on the booths (made from old car seats) and ducked toward a rickety barstool.

Bobby the Fist had spruced up some since the days, and he looked old, like he'd seen plenty, but the cop recognized him. The Fist was sleeker looking, wearing a purple shirt with sparkles all over it and a babyblue suit with lacey white embroidered lapels, his forty dollar hair dripping greasy ringlets over his ears like he was in show business. He was black and ugly as ever. Next to him in the booth was a white girl about half his age with a presumptuous look in her eyes like she owned the place. *Jackie's.*

His heart pounding like a straight arrow kid again stung by the gang leader's taunts, the cop accepted a scotch from Jackie without exchanging a glance with the little man, sucked it down, the ice rattling against his teeth as he communed with soul. Superimposed over the faded Country Club Malt Liquor logo embossed in the murky bar mirror, to one side of a picture of Muhammed Ali cut out from a magazine, a dim vision of the Fist raising his hand to make little scooping motions in the air twisted the knife in his brain. Either he was shooing flies—no, he was being welcomed over!

Seeing the cop approach, the Fist sang out, "Jesus, looka the boy! Look good, man! Shooter Teagarden! Hey Rita, ya know the basketball star I was tellin ya he was my homeboy back when? Hear ya the law now, Shooter, got the star, bad tan suit! Ha ha, yeah, y'always listen to Coach. You right, Shooter! You the man now. Siddown I buy ya one for ol times."

1

"Old times, shit! Sound coked like a motherfucker. Stand up, Fist!"

It was old times all right. The sneer on Bobby's face brought back a fearful long suppressed memory on hot waves of shame full of blood as then, an evening after basketball practice, when the cop had lingered with his girl friend, a cheerleader, the loveliest thing in class. They'd made passionate love on the gritty floor of a little used tunnel between the gym and the boilerroom. When the moment had come, sneering laughter had rung out from the unsuspected shadows and the Fist's commentary on the girl's performance. She had never spoken to the basketball star again, though she'd cheered for him. The best he'd been able to do for her was allow fifty dollars to be extorted from him in several installments by the gang leader who threatened to tell her mother and his Baptist deacon daddy. The Fist had accepted every payment with his patented sneer.

"Turn out your pockets like they was every shitty memory, nigger!"

He made him turn out every pocket and pull off his shoes.

"Whachu think, boy, ya think I'm a fool?" The Fist slammed his wallet, keys, change on the table. "There punk, sniff it!"

The cop flipped open the wallet, thumbed its crevices. With his grim look unchanged, he turned to the girl. "Now you."

"Really basketball player, you uncouth as ya turned out, aincha?" sneered the Fist.

She stared past him, or gazed inward, her bland look of ownership all gone from her eyes, raising a cigarette to her lips to hide raw fear now, a skinny, not-very-expensive-looking blonde in tight glitter jeans, scuffed red spikeheels, and a blacksilk shirt which encased her upper body from trembling chin to silver fingernails like she was trying for an impossible blend of styles— gaudy hip and provocative discreet in the same wild shot—or her arms were full of holes. In her face was something blurred, scattered, the elements of beauty—nice cheekbones, bowed pink lips, Slavic slanted blue eyes reflecting a mass of platinum curls— without quite getting it together in an actual beautiful look. Behind the cigarette dangling, she hid. He made her guilty, though maybe only of being alive.

"Dump your bag, bitch!"

2

The members on their barstools heh-hehed at that. Swallowed their drink. Something irreducible in her expression now, she wouldn't do it herself, so he did it for her, upended her bag and spilled out the sundry cosmetics, combs, lipgloss, tissues, crumpled cigarette packs, loose breathmints, several soiled-looking twenties in a wad, and—with the murmur of the crowd rising, on a Christmas vacation high, an all-Chicago tournament roll, the hero of the King High kids' worlds again, he had stolen the ball and run the length of the gleaming hardwood floor to lay it in effortlessly—framed on the backboard of the scarred tabletop by her compacts and kleenex and things, the shot went home, a glassine packet of pure white snow glistened, not very large, in truth, but big as a basketball to the cop.

"Fist, you dope, you walk right in!"

It was 10:30 on an August morning in a sultry Southside tavern, already hot and bound to get much hotter, and none of them were kids anymore. A jukebox blues was left wailing in the air as conversations dropped straight off around the room. At the bar the members discreetly turned their backs, all ears. A man got up and with his hands thrust deep in his pockets skulked unsteadily out. Others followed one by one, careful not to hurry. Behind the bar Jackie paused in the work he was doing with a bottle of Beefeater and a carton of orange juice. His bland face had grown a shade blander.

"I don't believe this ten cent heat! Jackie!" In righteous anger the Fist appealed to the barkeep as to a repository of higher culture. Had they been searched, how many other purses and pockets in this room and in many other rooms in Chicagoland this morning would have held a friendly taste? No thought like that occurring to them! However, one after another, the members were slipping out of the place, until finally the last one was gone. Anyway it looked like a private party from now on.

> *There may be a new tomorrow, baby,*
> *I hope you'll find a love to hold you spellbound,*
> *Then you'll be oh so happy,*
> *When ol' midnight comes around ...*

crooned the jukebox and went silent.

Behind the unvarnished somewhat lopsided bar the little pokerface squinting into a new clear panel of mirror provided by the distributor of Colt 45 Malt Liquor like it was a dubious crystal ball, Jackie sought the cop's eye, but didn't find it.

"Whachu doin on the *block,* Fist?" taunted the cop.

In his whim of a return to the neighborhood from his life in New York, Bobby was victim of the avid heart: what we once imagined ourselves to be around here we still are. But he only sneered.

More and more lately it was the cop's habit to stop in Jackie's this time of morning. What exactly his weariness of life consisted in he couldn't exactly have said but there was no denying how weary he had become. No scotch on the market could have given him the kick he was experiencing just now, damn near joy.

"Talk to me, Bobby! Ha ha! Make it easy on yourself an say somethin er other. Ha ha ha!"

Once the gang leader had been more than a match for the basketball star, the team player, cut him like a surgeon and at will, laughed at him for listening to Coach and his Baptist deacon daddy, laughed at his daddy too, an easy target in his worn and shiny Sunday suit and frayed starched collar or his nightwatchman's uniform made to resemble—but failing ludicrously to do so—a policeman's blues.

He hardly knew which way to savor it best. He reached into the little bag with a finger and stuck a tad up his nose. He snorted and laughed and got another fingerful which he took over to Jackie and stuck up the little man's nose. As if they had been boys again. They all laughed like evil boys, Jackie a trifle hesitantly, even the Fist in remonstrative fits of disbelief.

His palms outstretched luxuriating in the windfall if minor affair, bag of coke pinched between thumb and forefinger, the cop indulged in a shrug.

"Candy for the baby! But we fuckin f'real here, baby!"

Everybody around here knew who was the law, who was behind Jackie. Jackie's joint was his home away from home. The Fist must have heard that. And now he stood (he hadn't sat back down after the cop made him stand up) with a hurt and wrathful look mixed up in his patented sneers and his back couldn't have had more shoulder blades to the wall in the deepest dungeon in the District station. He wanted to buy him one for old times. Now that was funny!

The erstwhile basketball player thought to play with his old enemy a little and stick the glassine bag into the sidepocket of the babyblue jacket, who was a fool if he thought the woman carrying it for him let him out. He reached for the pocket—

"Come on Shooter, damn copper! Les do it will ya! They had a pass ya the ball four times fore ya had the nerve to shoot. If ya a had more *balls* we woulda won state championship but y'always listen to Coach an let the damn play overdevelop. Ya was slick as slow shit, so get on with it, motherfucker!"

All the Fist had to do was say something and it stung like truth even when it wasn't quite. He had always been a team player but he never had been slow or unwilling to take a chance. The inaccurate critique rankled like all the Fist's barbs in the old days, poison-tipped even if glancing blows. What kernel of truth had Bobby's commentaries contained that they rankled so? He was behaving like it was no big deal!

He would be back on the street in a day, if not hours, wouldn't he. The truth was he had been enjoying the moment so much he hadn't pictured the actual arrest at all. He'd only wanted the moment to go on and on. But however and whatever else Bobby seemed, he looked flush. It was only a dimebag. In the end the only tangible result might be some boomerang heat and attention on Jackie, whose endeavor in the half legit zone always risked losing its image as a window on trouble and gaining one as the opportunity and setting for it. The place was not really a "tavern." It was a "social club," an ill-defined legal entity. An afterhours joint no matter what the time of day or night, the backdrop for so many of his happiest hours beyond the call of duty, it operated without a liquor license on the cop's sayso. The usual scenario at Jackie's was peep the show now, dig the actors later.

He tried to catch Jackie's eye, but the little man was no longer seeking his. He couldn't even see the little man any more, sunk down on a wooden crate behind the bar, only the top of his head showing its premature sprigs of gray, suddenly touching in the cop an adolescent sense of wild inadequacy.

Instead of Jackie the cop found himself exchanging glances with the late Mayor Harold Washington, at one end of the bar a portrait of His Honor displayed prominently, all jutting gray eyebrows and confident ex-prizefighter's grin, first and only

5

African American mayor of Chicago, radiant, beloved, so recently having reigned over the city with regal high spirits, grace and beneficence, giving to every tawdry street corner, every subway ride, every routine duty its measure of pride and joy sufficient to the day—all of that over too soon, the great man dead and gone in office. As if it had been only yesterday, that golden era cut short, when hope had understandably soared, the breath stopped whenever the glance fell over the late Mayor's portrait. Actually it had been more than a year by now since he had had been stricken by a heart attack shortly into his second term. Too much partaking of the rich fare at the tables of Chicago's finest restaurants it was whispered by some bitterly. A promise of goodness unfulfilled, a courageous story foreshortened, dashed hopes afflicted everyone. It wasn't as if the cop's recent disgust with life had been *caused* by those dashed hopes, no, but the untimely death of the good and glowing man had not helped any. Like everyone else he couldn't help taking it personally. Whatever was hard in your life became worse.

He hadn't *squeezed* the Fist yet, hadn't robbed a clue why the dude was back in Chicago either. For Christ sake what did it matter? At best he'd be talked about, doing a homeboy for a lousy dimebag he'd never stretch to intent to sell. Brought back to earth, he sighed heavily, his resignation toward the morning and life in general returning. At least he could ruin their day.

"Fist, I'm gonna lock her in a funky cell!"

"Do your worstest basketball player," sneered the Fist knowingly, unchivalrous just the same.

"Were ya really a basketball star, Shooter?" she asked suddenly in a whispery singsong that seemed to shock them both. The cop had the distinct sensation that she was reaching for a sexy tone in addressing him. Apparently the Fist was alarmed by a similar perception.

"Shut up, Rita!"

"Ya still look . . . in great shape, Shooter. Like an athlete."

"Hey girl, ya wanna know his real name? Pageant! *Pageant,* baby! His daddy give him ol time religion, an Coach make him a square player, but his mammy lay a Pageant on his ass! Ha ha! Pageant Teagarden! Ya ever hear a name like that?"

"I think that's kinda *pretty.* I really do. It *is* pretty!"

6

What was this? She was gazing at him with frank admiration. She didn't feature a funky cell, did she! She meant to play her way out of this and throw the Fist over, didn't she? And Bobby didn't like it a bit. Why would he, he was about to lose his freedom (if only for a day) and his girlfriend in one swoop. The sense of a poetic if lowdown justice evening out the scales between them after all these years came over the cop like a powerful spell, like an aphrodisiac. My, it was hardly worth the trouble, but it would be sweet! The Fist was about hopping he saw out of the corner of his eye. She had opened her arms, leaving her face unclouded by fingered smoke. Her lips parted in a lovely smile, revealing a sizable gap between her front teeth. Damn but it was kind of cute. This earthy detail, which she'd kept modestly or cautiously hidden, she knew how to play. Unaccountably that hole between her front teeth was charming, it brought her whole face together suddenly in an integrated ordinary beauty, made her look like a spindly sweet kid.

"Fist, go back to New York! Hear? I give ya a pass! Jackie, ya hear? I aint do no homeboy for no dimebag. Fist, go on an git! Forty-Third Street too short for us both. This aint where you belong no more, so *go*, boy!"

But the Fist was man enough not to just cut and run or anything. In fact he stood there looking at the two of them steadily and very sourly.

"Fist, I tol ya! Take your greasy head an git!"

Instead Bobby reached over and placed his hand on the back of her neck. "Les go, baby."

"No, she stays!"

"Get up, baby."

"She don't want no parts a *you* no more, Fist! You land her in this mess? Plus she like me, don't ya, Rita? Ask her, Bobby—you gonna stay an have a drink with me, Rita? Ya better get on outa here now, Bobby, while ya can."

She had closed her lips again and was smiling a closedlips dreamy smile. She parted her lips just enough to insert a new cigarette between them and waited expectantly. The cop drew out his lighter gentlemanly, searching Bobby's eyes as he did so, and as if it had been a blade, thrust his hand with the lighter in it straight at Bobby's heart. He flicked on the flame and sought her lips.

7

Smiling, she bent to it. The Fist grabbed her from behind and hauled her straight out of her chair.

She kept stabbing the tip of her cigarette for the light as the cop jumped up and followed after. He held the flame out and his thumb was burning. The guttering flame made little circles in the air as Rita's head bobbed this way and that as she was dragged backward toward the door. When he finally got her cigarette ignited, he threw the Bic lighter down so hard it bounced six feet in the air. Rita took a drag and released a sexy puff of smoke from between her gap teeth with some style under the circumstances.

The Fist was hauling her backward and her red highheels scraped the dirty floor with a faint protest the only sound now as the cop stalked them wordlessly. Here was the devil—and not altered so much by the years, not altered beyond recognition—the very devil his Baptist deacon daddy had denounced as the personification of all youthful temptations and the awful results of succumbing to them, warned the basketball star against while scoffing at the gang leader as nothing, less than nothing. The vehemence of this contradiction (a warning at nothing) had piqued his interest in the gangster life though his athletic talent had enabled him to hold out. Between his daddy and his Coach, in the beneficent sway of these men, bugged half to death he had thought by both, he was not likely to have joined a gang. But in the kids' world the Fist had wielded a compelling influence, a charisma that couldn't have been matched by any adult, and when the old man had railed against the gangs it had only made his trumpedup watchman's uniform appear the more pathetic, almost overcoming the ballplayer with the ludicrousness and sorrow of it. It had almost succeeded in producing a seed of sympathy or even admiration for the notorious gang leader. Had there ever been such a seed, before it had blossomed into a poisonous flower?

His father, for all his heartbreaking insignificance and Christian longsuffering, had told him something of life's iron progressions that had sunk in after all, and here was living proof he had been right. The Fist was a disgrace and a joke dragging this girl! The cop almost laughed out loud watching him haul Rita backward toward the door like his manhood, his very soul, depended on it. He was clutching to the skanky white girl as if losing grasp of her would be to lose dignity and face, stripped of a prize possession, a dubious trophy.

Fist's forehead had sprouted seeds of perspiration. His eyeballs flamed. Momentarily he let Rita slip, the better to get a new grip on her. He bent over her collapsing form. Seeing his chance the cop skipped behind him and delivered a vicious kick. With a war shriek Bobby let her fall altogether to the floor and swung on the cop, but missed. The cop slapped his face twice and butted him against the wall and manhandled him straight out the door into the street, outweighing his old nemesis by thirty pounds at least, not to say he was in far better shape than the Fist in spite of his drinking habit and no matter Rita's doubtful flattery. When he came back in, panting from the exertion in the late morning summer heat, straight on his heels followed the Fist as if he had been his evil shadow. But Bobby lingered in the door and did not again enter.

Staggering once, gripping the door frame, silhouetted painfully against the sunlight, ringlets trembling violently, seeming to drip dark drips, Bobby sang scornfully out, "Believe me Jackie, I *understan* your position, I just keep the good memories in mind. I jus come back here today to say hi boys, that's all I did. It aint like I'm gon take an fry up your place or nothin one night, Jackie, so don't *worry!* Nary one a my boys gonna sneak up behind Shooter about a year from now an—no, don't you worry none neither, copper, you half-white motherfucker. I aint study no revenge, boys. I got you so bad in the old days, *Pageant,* you never catch up no way! *An you bitch,* you aint gonna get yo ass whupped when I catch you, is you? No, actually, believe it or not, I aint study nary one a y'all. Ya aint worth it! So don'chall worry about *nothin,* hear? I'm a let y'all be, an forget about yo sorry asses, an go about my business!"

Having delivered himself of this oration unexpectedly culminating in admirable wisdom, the Fist languished in the doorway, black and craggy looking and hard to see because of the hard yellow glare coming over his shoulder. With a manful show of dignity, not hardly hurrying or anything to get away, at last he slowly disappeared from the doorway into the bright street with a shred of honor intact it seemed, but at the last moment succumbing to temptation and spoiling the effect after all by calling spitefully over his shoulder, "Don'chall motherfuckers worry bout nothin, hear? Cuz dead motherfuckers caint worry, an y'all is *dead motherfuckers, hear?*" His livid voice trailed away beyond the door's black shadow into the grinning blaze of nearly noonday sunlight, and he was gone.

How good to hear him holler, thought the cop, a little spent and even pleasantly relaxed after the struggle with Bobby. By this last hilarious, defeated outburst from the relic of his old adversary, he was entirely satisfied. He let him go, who departed from his thoughts at once. Savoring his triumph in the relative coolness and absolute saving dimness of the social club, in his home away from home, not quite daring to glance at Jackie, however, the cop walked back up the room, smiling with satisfaction at symmetries of fate, what goes around coming around. About the only thing he had neglected to do was take fifty bucks off the dude for old times' sake before slapping him and letting him go, but you couldn't think of everything. It was good enough and would have to do, and the man's plaintive howls had showed it.

Catching sight of Rita, who had gotten up off the floor and taken a chair again, and was from all appearances calmly smoking her cigarette, he looked at her without recognition. He had nearly forgotten her. For God's sake, what had he won? She parted her lips coyly, revealing the semi-enchanting gap a little, looking as good as she could. It only made him uncomfortable.

Dutifully he sat down beside smalltime, sad Rita, with an imperceptible shudder, understanding he had a job to do. It was a job of truly minimal importance and for this reason threatened to plunge him down into a brand new level of gloom. Who was she anyway? It wouldn't matter. Jackie came over and set a bottle and two glasses at his elbow. He regretted chasing away all of Jackie's familiar paying customers. He would rather have had witnesses of his correct and straightforward manner from now on. Without the friendly chatter and laughter, the room seemed cavernous and forlorn. As he swung around to face her, his eyes brushed once again the late Mayor Washington's portrait and he caught his breath. The great and glowing man so full of life and promise must not be gone. Realization that it was so was always a fresh blow.

10

At a pretty fair cultural distance, for real, from the scene in Jackie's club, a despair nevertheless oddly similar to the cop's afflicted a very different character at the opposite end of metropolitan Chicago this morning, a cab driver working the far northern town of Greenshores, so recently carved out of farmers' fields, an exurb of the city as creamy white as a bushel of silver queen corn, a foreign country probably to Southsiders, yet directly connected to the rest of the metropolis and even the Southside by the Tri-State Tollway, the Northwest Highway, the Kennedy, and other implacable thoroughfares. There, a cab driver on the Greenshores Hilton Hotel cabpost was suffering, too, through the slowest, hottest, midmost of the morning in the middle of the slowest, hottest month of the summer, and his parallel gloom was soon to drive him to a nearby tavern for a midmorning drink also.

Cab drivers and cops, working alike the underbelly of the city, are natural adversaries, the one the prey of the other, or at least wary cousins who suspect the worst of each other and dislike each other on sight. Like the cop the cab driver was also about to have his world disturbed by a strange girl, in fact, none other than Rita. But being a weak denizen of the city jungle, the cab driver must have a very different first impression of Rita than a cop who by function as well as by nature is a predatory creature. As unlikely as it must have been, from alien planes, and miles apart, inhabiting nearly polar ends of the urban wilderness, shortly these two would get to know each other, as guys do, that is, mix their misperceptions of each other dramatically and violently. It was the last thing Rita would have wished to happen, although women are often judged as aiming to create conflict and confusion. She had plenty of problems of her own.

On the hotel cabstand this slow morning the cab driver was enduring boredom so excruciating it verged on paranoia. Weird insights were glinting through his brain like dying salmon fighting their way upstream to spawn only to be blocked by a dam. His mind was like a drunken fisherman who can't get his boots on and can't find his pole. He'd been sitting in front of the Greenshores Hilton hotel for more than two hours as the day grew hotter without a call, and it must have set a record, seemed like damn near forever. He could have gone fishing, except that he was forever about two years away from having saved enough for his little coho boat. He couldn't even go home, for he had no home, his girl friend having thrown him out six weeks ago, and although he kept intending to find an apartment he'd been too depressed to put out the effort, and instead had been sleeping in motels, yes, even in his cab, which after all was very plush and comfortable.

He stifled a desire to moan by shoving a cigarette between his parched lips. "I am *dying* here," he thought, even his inmost thoughts apt to arrive in cab driver's lingo. "To die," cab driver's parlance for being thus becalmed on a post, was taking on lurid new depths of meaning. His flesh seemed to stick to the red velour seats of his prized Cadillac converted cab like meat to a campfire's embers. His tongue was smoked like a sausage by cigarettes. Before he'd sucked it halfway down he removed the unfiltered last from his trembling lips, leaving bits of paper stuck to them, and tossed it out the window to the ground with the overhand futile violence of a Chicago Cubs outfielder throwing at yet another runner making successfully for home, where giving off a faint blue wisp it lay in a ragged line of two hours' worth of butts.

All that would save his day now, as the cab drivers liked to romantically put it, was a very long ride with a very beautiful woman! On a corporate expense account. Might as well dream. A nuclear attack would be preferable to these dogday doldrums! If only something would happen—anything!

And then amazingly it did. Sirens howled distantly, and got louder, and louder. Fire trucks were bearing down on something around here, and even seemed to be heading for the hotel. This woke him out of his stupor and sent hope pulsing through his veins. Maybe the hotel was on fire and about to burn down! The silver snouts of two red fire engines burst onto the hotel's circular tarmac.

Thank God, heavensent entertainment—a tragedy for someone perhaps, but to him the most welcome diversion. The shining red engines rolled past him and pulled up at the hotel's front door. He reached for his Polaroid camera on the seat and headed straight after them. Firemen in heavy rubber coats despite the heat raced into the lobby. Others unfurled a hose. He sniffed the air, and as a matter of fact, smelled something burning, smelled smoke, and not cigarette smoke, of which he had just been producing an inordinate amount. There was a trace of smoke in the air but strangely it smelled like woodsmoke, like a campfire. Searching the horizon he saw nothing in a hopeful state of conflagration.

There was nothing wrong about the hotel that you could see, nothing visibly burning but the summer sky. Of course that was the way with big building fires. They smoldered in the seams before leaping into the open like volcanoes.

The firemen who had gone into the lobby came out again with puzzled looks and moved deliberately onto the grounds as if searching for something. Camera poised, he followed them. There was nothing around here but an acre of parched lawn unless a tree in this terrible August heat had gone up in spontaneous combustion. One of the firemen waved his hand and the guys with the hose came trotting up with it. They had stopped right by his cab on the cabstand. What the Jesus, was his car on fire?

Camera dropping to his side, he watched this activity with alarm. If this didn't beat everything he didn't know what did, but what was it? When the silver hose went stiff with water it jumped like a snake and slapped the rear bumper of his Cadillac with a metallic *whamp!*

The firemen were hosing down the ground around his cab, hard sprays of water hitting its bright prow and sides. Extinguished completely was his happy excitement at the prospect of the Hilton burning down, replaced by wonderment that the day was so hot the very ground had caught fire and ominous sensations of guilt that such a phenomenon should have transpired so close to him. Through the shimmering sunlight he glimpsed a wisp of blue smoke before it vanished in the plume of water from the hose. Peering closer he saw something he had never noticed before in all the hours on all the days he had been crucified to this cab post. The edging of the hotel marquee was not grass at all but those brown chips of wood that he associated with children's school playgrounds called "tanbark." Here and there it still smoked as the firemen aimed their hose. Could this be? He had caught the ground on fire with his cigarette butts!

An overwhelming wave of embarrassment threatened to wash him away as if the firemen had turned their hose on him. Accosted by a trivial nightmare which could take place only in reality, and only he was sure to him, the ludicrousness of it beyond your worst dreams, he wished desperately to slink inside the hotel bar, into the darkest corner possible, but obviously he couldn't run away since any moment the cops were going to show up and arrest him for arson. The firemen, who must have been sweating in their black raincoats even with their helmets off, laughed easily among themselves as they soaked the ground around his cab. Who could have dreamed up so pitiful a thing?

They never said a word to him, at their periphery, a lank, hesitant figure, unable to move forward or back. The right tone to take had he wanted to joke with them eluded him completely. The ordeal lasted ten minutes as they found more and more charcoals to put out. He couldn't have smoked that many cigarettes, could he? The fire must have spread. It was that dry a summer. Hours, lifetimes, seemed to pass. Perhaps they didn't mean to punish him with kindness or their indifference, but he felt their discretion hotly.

Once having satisfied themselves that they had extinguished every danger, the firemen, who had dumped their coats and were finally working in their T-shirts, took their time coiling up the hose and putting away items of equipment. He was glued to the spot like a crazy snowman who had not melted in hell after all. They were discreet and took no stock of him. What good guys. Gratefully, he effaced himself, a rake-thin shadow, though he was tall. The public servants, about his own age, performed their ritual of packing up carefully and didn't glance his way.

When they had finally rolled away, leaving puddles of steaming coals, his relief knew no bounds not to have been written a ticket of some kind, to have been spared a visit to the courthouse, a cause for rejoicing. There was no worse way, not even sitting dying on this cab post forever, to spend a morning than a visit to the halls of justice. His spirit soared at having beaten the rap, and joy transformed humiliation into self-deprecating amusement. Something like this could only happen to him. His car was moist around the edges but unhurt. He gazed at it with awe before getting inside, as if it had barely missed obliteration by a cyclone. His Cadillac was his pride and joy. Once back inside it, he unbent further to the point he regretted not having taken a picture or two of the incident. It might have been an affront to those good boys, the firemen.

It was the sort of shadowy unnatural experience you wanted to be rid of at once by speaking about it to somebody, having a laugh publicly, so as to neutralize the dire effect and reenter the company of living men. Around him the black puddles accosted his senses with little chunks of charred "tanbark" swimming in them. The acrid odor of drenched embers clung to the superheated air sending their message of futility and nightmare. He gunned the motor, and the Cadillac lurched off the stand, raced round the circle, finessed the stop sign and lurched into the stream, traveled four blocks in one burst, nicking a red light and briefly topping sixty before cutting off oncoming traffic and diving into a parking spot in front of the Pair a Dice Bar and Grille. The bartender, if not a good friend, was a familiar acquaintance. Probably it was well he had been too preoccupied (to put it mildly) to take a photograph or his sense of a burden he needed to share would have been intense. That was a game his girl friend and he had played and once enjoyed so much, smiling at the funny things he had seen in the day over their drinks at night, and looking at a photograph or two he'd taken with his Polaroid camera. But now of course he had no girl friend. He deeply missed her it was true.

Those were the days when she had thought him so charming and a little crazy and the funny things he had seen on the streets a delight. They'd been in love. By the end, she was saying strange accusing things like, "You are happy for no reason!" When he had pointed out he was happy because he was with her, she'd glared at him like she wanted to kick him in the teeth.

Yes, it was true, he was subject to spells of happiness which seemed to come from nowhere or everywhere, as if on the breeze through the windows of his car, without justification, she began to insinuate, when she understood that driving cabs was not a phase for him. She had thought every cab driver meant to be doing something else. By the same token bouts of gloom came on deep and unprovoked sometimes, futility of driving around the city in circles all day only to come back to the place where he'd started, or like today, unable to begin the circle at all.

At the bar he closed his eyes and drank off a bottle of Leinenkugel beer at once. Drinking Leinenkugel reminded him of fishing in Wisconsin and since they had started selling the brand in Chicagoland he always drank it for that reason, aside from the fact he liked it. It brought close the North Woods joys of sitting in a little lakeside tavern listening to a polka on the juke box with his buddies or a girl after a day on the water. Happiness trembled in him like moonlight on the waves. They didn't play many polkas in the Pair a Dice bar in the old part of Greenshores, but that was cool. It was someplace to sit and indulge fantasies of escape to the North Woods.

He clanked the bottle down on the bar, said Ah! inwardly, and considered another. Then he positively decided on it. On his second wind, he tipped back the bottle and a little more slowly finished this 'Kugel. Enjoying the shimmering cavelike shadows of the Pair a Dice bar now so much, he opened his mouth to tell the bartender of his recent experience as a near arsonist and the story stuck in his throat. Suddenly he wondered how it would sound. The bartender was more of an acquaintance than a dear friend, although that could change if he had the third beer to which he was addressing profound consideration, while his story lingered on his lips. But he wondered how he would have reacted if even the most regular passenger in the backseat of his cab had told him a pathetic story like that about setting the ground on fire.

He thought better of drinking a third beer just yet in the day and summoned up willpower to keep his ridiculous if compelling story to himself and arose and left the pleasant shadows of the tavern. It was too early to start drinking in earnest. It would be all too easy to call it a day. Maybe business would be picking up pretty soon, since it couldn't get worse. He left the Pair a Dice bar blinking at the annoying sunshine. It was nearly highnoon, the time of day for terrible confrontations if only with oneself. He knew he had to go back to the Hilton hotel cabstand, scene of the crime. He had to go straight back there right now and face it down or he might never go back there in his life, and how would that be for a cabdriver needing a cabpost? Maybe somebody from one of the tech companies or other corporations would be wanting to go to lunch somewhere fairly far away, like the Loop or Milwaukee.

He was disappointed to find another Bull's-eye cab pulled onto the Hilton stand and he would now be second up in this desert. But then he saw it was his friend Armchair. His spirits rose. To Armchair he could tell his story! Buoyant with the prospect of getting it off his chest, he pulled in with high feeling, although he was always glad to see Armchair, who was settled in behind the wheel comfortably, characteristically reading a book. He drove up stealthily behind him and gave him a little "love tap" as the drivers called it—ran into his rear bumper hard.

Both cars rocked wildly on their springs. Armchair looked up from his reading irritably into the mirror until he saw it was the Cadillac. He laid his book aside and waved at his friend urgently to come and have a seat in the back of his cab. He had few friends, and the Cadillac was maybe the only one. The cab driver got out of his Cadillac and made himself comfortable in the backseat of Armchair's ratty car, as drivers do who are friends. Not the frontseat, until the back is filled with friends. Armchair did not own his own cab but rented the heap. In Armchair's car few friends gathered, as Armchair did not suffer fools. "You see any papers I might have lost on the floor back there?" he asked, as he always did, in greeting. No, he didn't. Armchair was writing a novel and didn't want to lose any notes. To Armchair he could tell all, who had a way of understanding as from Olympian heights whatever it might be, and what a tale, involving the Greenshores fire department. At once he launched into his sorry and incredible story about having lit the cabstand on fire with cigarette butts a short while ago, and shaking his head, laughed self-deprecatingly.

Armchair sniffed the air suspiciously and peered haughtily out his window. "I thought something smelled funny around here. I wondered what these puddles were. It wasn't rain for sure. Hey, I woulda gone up to em with a cigarette and asked em for a light— *'Hey, got a light?'*—ha ha ha ha ha ha!"

That made him smile with embarrassment all over again. What a thought, to have asked the firecrew for a light. Only Armchair to think of something like that. He shuddered, but at once

17

felt so much better, sober and calm. It was unbelievable what even a short talk with Armchair would do for you. Armchair was good as gold, better than alcohol, with his gift of making your troubles small in light of his appalling imagination. The cab driver was aware of the profound gulf that separated his own from his friend Armchair's outlook on the world, and was consoled by the sense of his own relative sanity that his friend's antic attitude induced.

The cop, alone with semi-pretty Rita in the Southside clubroom made overample and strange by the absence of any members, studied his purported prize, trying to work up an inkling of professional interest. She almost looked good, flushed and animated as if his triumph whipping Bobby had excited her and she was glad to be rid of the ugly dude herself. She had pointedly the air about her she was with *him* now, God forbid. She smiled up at him, vulnerable and expectant, lips parted, revealing the friendly gap in her front teeth. The charm was gone.

Behind the bar Jackie performed his customary chores, although his clientele had departed. The presence of his friend was enough and made Jackie content.

"Look here, Rita, all I want from ya is a little bit of information an ya can go." The cop poured them both a drink, compassionately.

"What makes ya think I wanna go? I like it here, with you." She shivered and hugged herself despite the heat of the morning.

She thought she was still in trouble. "Relax. Don't worry, Rita. This aint quite the bright lights. You're okay, I just want to know somethin about Bobby. I don't know why I'm givin you a drink. I oughta card you first."

"Dealin cards?"

"Look at your driver's license, girl, see how old you are."

"I don't *got* no driver's license," she shot back, "in case you wanna start pawin through my purse again. Don't waste your time."

She *was* a cute kid, the way she delivered her lines. He wasn't even curious.

"How old *are* ya?"

"Old enough to know better. Don't worry, I'm old enough."

All he wanted was a little story, so he would have something to cover his ass with in case the Fist did anything outlandish while in town. But naturally she couldn't see it. He regarded her grimly, aware how far beneath him this sorry business was.

"Rita . . . how ya know Bobby?"

"I don know why I should be nice to you if you won't be nice to me. We could be friends."

A miserable memory deviled him unaccountably, like a pesky fly buzzing up and landing on him. One evening on the way home from a church meeting which his Daddy had obliged him to attend, the two of them had run into the Fist and a couple of his buddies on the corner. After some carefree exchanges, on no account including the old man at first whose huge bulk had been about as significant to these boys as a passing truck's, a profanity of the gang leader's had ignited him though, and the older man had challenged the Fist, who had suggested the Deacon do something totally unimaginable with his Bible, who had delivered a couple of swift kicks, the first one connecting glancingly, but the second missing so wildly the older man had wound up lying flat on his back on the pavement, the Fist hooting as he escaped up the street.

Why had this horror struck afresh? The cop tasted briefly the ancient and profound mortification. Even stealing this girl Rita from him couldn't make up for that memory. In fact it made it worse and she even seemed to have produced it somehow. He just wanted to be rid of her. He was glad his Daddy could not see him with her right now.

"You from New York too, Rita?"

19

"Anything ya wanna know. But we could have fun while ya was knowin it. Do I talk like New York?"

"Pure Chicago."

"Fraid so."

"What part?"

"Elk Grove Village."

He pictured the rows on rows of light industries tucked in next to O'Hare Airport, the dusty, treeless streets giving off a smoky orange glow on the clearest days. In the residential sections out that way, the sorts of tickytack developments he thought of as whitefolks ghettos, there was another sort of industry, behind the obvious strip joints and peep shows and adult bookstores on Mannheim Road.

"How the elk?"

There was a forest preserve out there where the municipality kept an actual herd of elk like village mascots. It had made the papers recently when somebody had gone in there by night and slaughtered half of them. She gave him a sideways glance.

"My Dad took me by there when I was little to see em," she said. "They were real pretty. He fed one a cigarette an it ate it. He threw his whole pack on the ground. I wonder if the elk got a buzz. They were Pall Malls, you know, no filter."

The thought that Rita had had a Dad too gave him a sinking feeling of sorrow and disgust. "No, some guy went in there butchered half of em. Really knew what he was doin. Dressed em out, took off just the best cuts a meat."

"Thanks a lot!"

"Sometimes I wonder how the people live."

"With a little help from my friends. That what ya gettin at?"

"Bobby?"

"Sure. I met him at a party on the Northside. I met him at the Green Mill tavern. He's loaded, okay? Don't talk business, if that's what ya want. But if ya ask me, a deal went down, ya know? He got the dough, an he got the snow. He thinks he likes me, you know, so we been partyin. He's goin around lookin for old friends, turn em on. I think he made a bundle on whatever cuz his pockets are full. That what ya want? He must see the past different than you. I don't know what ya got against him or nothin, but believe it or not, he admired ya, a basketball star an all. He actually talked about ya like

20

ya were friends or somethin. I mean, Jesus, before ya came in an . . . Jesus! He aint so bad, if ya ask me."

"Yeah, so tell me bout Bobby the Fist," the cop said icily, experiencing a new and unexpectedly sharp stab of hate. "He aint shit, never was shit, an never will be shit!"

"Yeah? Well, I'm sure you're right. So fuck both a you niggers," she said dryly. "You don't care about me, ya just want to hurt him." She scowled at him disapprovingly, and stood up.

That made him laugh. "Oh, so ya dig me," he remarked sardonically. As soon as he had said this, he wondered why in the world he had.

"Yeah, *fuck you!*"

It almost did him in, her standing there. Unexpectedly her beauty had come together. This chick was not his cup of tea in a month of Mondays. He would rather be caught dead with a skunk than leave Jackie's out on 43rd Street with the dudes watching him with this moonbeam. The back door of the joint? His old lady was going to hear.

"Oh yeah?" he grinned. But he could enjoy it in here.

She looked down at him steadily. "I think Pageant is a *beautiful* name." She sat down again, flopping in the chair. Her lower lip quavered with some misguided emotion. "I *do.*"

No, this was all wrong. It was out of the question. He couldn't help laughing a little more anyway, to which she seemed to pay no attention. Her expression had grown serious. He glanced over at Jackie, shook his head. But Jackie, impassive, didn't register. The face of his mother came before his eyes, who had given him the name.

"Skins are like *masks,* you know?" she said softly, from someplace deep in her throat, bending toward him across the table. A light had come into her eyes, which she threw his way. "But every second we wear *some* kinda mask anyway, usually the wrong one." Her voice was intimate now, full of intention, and she was smiling her cunning gap-toothed smile. "Did ya ever think the fun in life comes from choosin the right mask instead of the wrong one, *the mask for the moment?*"

If only it had been something controllable like a mask that you could just take off, he wouldn't have the feeling he was going off the deep end. Wherever they were heading, it was unprofessional of

21

him, to say the least, and it even somehow brought Bobby back into the picture almost as an equal, all traces of whom he wanted to be rid of. His girl friend would hear, the handsome mother of one of the boys he was weaning away from the gangs with a hope of a goodpaying job, she would hear of this on the grapevine. Yet she was part of his despair of his life too, wasn't she? It angered him suddenly. It seemed to him that he was a pitiful character indeed. Where did this pale broad get off thinking she could talk to him like this and turn him on? He might be a morning drinker who made his living keeping tabs on thirdrate hoods and mentally deficient gang leaders, but he knew the score.

He suddenly had the urge to bring her down as cruelly as he knew how. Following his impulse, he took her silkmasked wrists in his hands. They were soft and fineboned, and felt good under his thumbs. They looked all wrong, hidden in black ruffles down to the knuckles on such a hot day. She thought he was caressing her. She submitted to it, looked down. He rubbed his thumbs round and round. Her lips parted in a sharp grimace as if that hurt. If she was clean it would hardly matter since his intent was purely to put an end to her nonsense. She'd get the point. But you never knew. Hell, masks were for hiding, weren't they? What was she hiding? It seemed to hurt her wrists. He smiled insinuatingly as he glanced up from the fragile curves of her sleeves into her suddenly wide-open eyes.

"Tracks? Junkie?"

In the created intimacy, the gesture was effectively crude. The way she cringed, with the sick stricken look in her eyes, he must be onto the worst, as he had been with the dimebag in her purse. Her eager looks dissolving, he almost didn't go through with it, peeled back a sleeve with the bold distaste the way you'd flay an animal you'd hunted down. Flay it alive! She was quivering violently.

"What the hell!"

He felt like he'd been slapped in the face. His fingers, sliding past the pallid inner arm where the needles would have mostly been, encountered no common puncture marks but violet swellings at the wristbone. He let her drop, afraid he was hurting her, as if his hand had touched fire. For a moment her arm lay on the tabletop blue and tortured in spilled liquor and rings of condensation from icefilled glasses, until she pulled it back, drew it back under black silk. He couldn't stop himself reaching for her neck, pulling down the high collar. The purple scars he saw there made him wish he hadn't.

She looked at him with despair and hatred to soak up every mediating drop of whiskey in his bloodstream. The masks had slipped far down. It blew his mind with pity and disgust. All her invitation to high times, had she planned on doing it with her shirt on? He felt deceived, or gypped out of something, what he couldn't say, since he'd decided against having her. As a woman this woman hadn't really interested him, until this moment perhaps, when he realized she was a human being, who had been injured, and she had gone far away from him. Grief flickered across her face, then accusation. Some similar emotions must have been reflected in his own. He wished for nothing but some impossible innocence of his own lost long ago.

"Bobby?" he muttered hoarsely, his eyes bulging, his mind settling on the likely culprit, full of hate once more. He'd just given the dirty dude a pass.

"No." She dropped her eyes, her body slumping. "Just business."

"Business!"

Her features knocked out in limbo again, scattered, her hair streaked into her face, deliberately she stood up, as if there was nothing much else to do. She hesitated as if finding her bearings, took a step aimlessly, slinging her purse over her shoulder. Shooting the cop no kind of look, her gaze wavering toward the bright doorway, she slowly made her way, shuffled defeatedly out into the street.

A spasm of terrible weariness went through him as he watched her stumble out. He glanced back at Jackie. Nothing resonated from that corner but cold caution. The weirder the shit, the stonier Jackie's face. High above that deadpan look, which he remembered since forever it seemed, the little man's survival weapon, Mayor Harold Washington beamed down from his honored place on the wall, competent, confident, a winner, cut down in the prime of life.

He stood in the doorway and watched her at curbside listlessly flag down a Jimmy Morgan taxi. He watched the car take off in the direction of the Dan Ryan Expressway, he supposed. He took an involuntary stride after her before catching a grip on himself, with a groan, and stepping back inside. He walked to the bar, picking up the bottle from the table as he passed.

"Fist took me back, Jackie. Didn't it take ya back?"

Jackie didn't say.

"We *okay*, Jackie."

"Shee-it!"

"We *here.*"

"Gonna be here!" This type of conversation made Jackie nervous.

"Wonder if a time come, say, where the hell it go—ya know?"

"Shee-it, you make Lieutenant next year for real."

"Lieutenant . . . Jackie . . . Say, that some shit the Fist come in with, aint it? Wouldn't ya know he'd come in with some shit like that?"

Not his morning custom, certainly, but Jackie poured himself a small drink, frowning.

"If we aint somebody at least we a *right* somebody!" the cop went on protesting.

"Shee-it, somebody! You got the star, shit!"

"Jackie, sometimes I wanna escape my own damn skull, man," said the cop.

Jackie began to polish a spot on the bar hard. Without looking at the spot and not looking at the cop, he rubbed his towel back and forth.

"Somethin don't count up right about that pale girl, man," said the cop. He stared at Jackie, and finally Jackie returned the look, with his own peculiar one blank and knowing.

Making it for the door, the cop mumbled over his shoulder, "If they call after me, tell em—*somethin,* Jackie!"

Jackie stared at the empty doorway for a long time, as if he expected his friend to have second thoughts and come back in again. He stared with this hope. When they called from the precinct or the tactical squad, trying to reach the cop, he was going to have to think up a lie to tell. The cop hadn't even had the goodness to give him a hint what direction the lie should take. Jackie knew enough to make an effort to let it go, but a friend's problems are as difficult to be shut of as your own. The problems of his friend were not so unusual, of course, but he was a very special friend. Behind his pokerface, Jackie worried. Maybe he would gain something chasing after a sick white girl he had caught with a little coke in her purse, let him try. But he doubted it very much.

The cop was walking fast, and with every step the idea gnawed at him that he'd missed something about the girl and the Fist whom he'd allowed to walk. Through the windows of a barber shop, from the raised chairs of a shoeshine palace, men observed him. Someone called out a greeting to which he didn't respond. Already the story of his run-in with the Fist would have filtered down the street farther than these storefronts. In his mind he had it the way he would have liked it to be told. The point was he hadn't done a homey for a lousy dimebag, now had he? But anybody who knew the street knew that the up-from-under history wasn't always told from the point of view of the guy who thought that he had won.

His plaingreen car was blocking a crosswalk. The tires screamed making a U. On the Dan Ryan Expressway, his speed briefly touched ninety. He picked up the Jimmy Morgan cab at Ohio Street. She wasn't going to a Rush Street club. The cab didn't take a Loop exit. She wasn't heading out for Elk Grove Village either. The driver swung off hard from a center lane at North Avenue like she'd given him last second instructions. They were eastbound.

The cab made another impulsive turn on Clark Street, and went north, at Diversey veering onto Broadway. For about a mile they struggled up narrow, semitrendy, congested Broadway. A block beyond Addison the cab made a sudden stop and held up traffic while she got out. She started ambling up the street, close along the curb, one foot in the gutter, weaving around the parking meters, swinging by one hand on them. The cab she'd gotten out of didn't move, her cab driver counting his money or whatever, being an asshole, stopped dead in traffic causing brakes to squeal.

He had lost sight of her. He stomped the gas, then the brakes, then horn as he realized the Jimmy Morgan cabby was going to sit there. Cursing him and craning his neck, he spotted her once more at the corner. Assaying the traffic over her shoulder, suddenly she stuck out her thumb. Could he believe this? She would score some fast change? This would about do it, for him. Again all the weariness of his morning came over him worse than any hangover and he drew his hand over his face. It was just about right. A little nothing streetsign, battered by the traffic. A fitting end of a mad dash.

Too fitting. She slipped between cars across the street. He lost her in the crowd and sizzle on funky Broadway, carnival of flesh and chrome, urban rainforest of boutiques with kaleidoscopic windows and overflowing trashcans, parade of gays tripping holding hands, hipsters cruising knowingly, senior citizens shuffling to lunch, Koreans sweeping their shop doorways assiduously, everybody crushed together, pushing past, no letup, in noon's heat and blinding light. Traffic southbound in the other lane backed up for a red light. She popped into sight almost in front of him between parked cars and hopped into a Flash cab with the bolt of yellow lightning on its door. The red light changed and the Flash cab rolled away past him with her in the backseat. The lightning bolt seemed to mock him paralyzed in the wrong lane. He twisted his face away. Yanking the wheel he forced his way into the oncoming stream of traffic, not looking, backed up, causing horns to blare.

The light turned red again and he went into the parking lane and gingerly picked his way through the cross traffic. Ahead the street was clear. Way ahead he thought he saw the Flash cab cut left on Belmont, its creamy top giving it away. He finally caught up on Lake Shore Drive. The Flash rolled off the Drive onto Michigan Avenue and cut left on Oak Street. In front of the Drake Hotel Rita jumped out and walked under the canopy. He paused just long enough to catch the doorman's eye. Circling the block, he pulled in behind the hotel where he could see the Walton Street rear entrance and the hotel's loading dock. He counted off the seconds it would take her to walk through the long lobby and waited another sixty but no more. He eased up rich Walton Street into Michigan Avenue traffic again and came back around once more on wealthy Oak. The doorman told him she was drinking in the Cricket Room.

He cruised up the street a little way past the estimable facades of the Drake Hotel and parked in a driveway. The image of Jackie's joint superimposed itself in his mind's eye over the gray stone and black shining windows of the landmark Drake and adjoining unknown gray eminences. Jackie's little hangout had no window, shining or otherwise, only a piece of redpainted plywood where the glass should have been, adorned with peeling ads for Kool

Cigarettes and Old English Malt Liquor, and the ragged legend, "43d St. neighbors Club."

"Nary a matched set a chairs in the joint," he muttered to himself, picturing in his mind's eye Jackie's, but staring through his windshield at a granitelike promontory of either the side of the hotel or one of the buildings next to it, he couldn't tell which block of granite it was. If he were to walk into the lobby of the Drake right now, he would have had to deal with the ugly sensation that splinters from Jackie's funky chairs might be sticking out of the seat of his pants.

By some association, a poignant sorrow bit him. He remembered once standing in the caverns of the Loop on LaSalle Street and seeing beneath the looming skyscrapers in the street a little lost dog darting. Nobody was threatening the dog, nobody was even noticing it, as it avoided the cars this way and that. Its microscopic pitiful furry little body beneath the shadows of the towers that touched the sky and blotted out the sun had created in him an overpowering sadness and it had seemed to him that tiny lost dog flitting between the wheels was the only spot of life in a monstrous machine and it was doomed for this reason. To crush the dog would not be illegal if anybody ever even noticed it. It would be inevitable, not illegal. It would be run over under the wheels of the ceaseless traffic without ever being noticed he had realized as he had watched it. It would be killed without witness, and so he watched. There was no point in trying to help, for the list of life's little tragedies preoccupying you was so long already. That's how it made him feel now, he realized, to sit by the Drake, and wait for Rita who was drinking in the Cricket Room, and think of Jackie. It was almost as if however this adventure all turned out, it was Jackie who was going to fare worst in it, like that little doomed dog, and he didn't know why he ever was getting such a thought as that, but that was what he felt.

There was no way you'd ever lump them all together, no way. But there they were, and here he was. He felt in his soul the immense distance that separated the Southside and Jackie's joint from this Gold Coast scene and the Drake, a stark distance he and Rita had just traversed. The chasm between his side of town and this one was so deep, it was like an abyss into which you could holler and there would be no sound coming back, like the Grand

Canyon, or outer space. He was staring into the endless chasm. He contemplated the unmarked yet powerful boundary he had crossed, barren and crude rubblestrewn no-man's land between sectors of the city, invisible and potent—that was crossed *only for a purpose.*

He thought of that *masked* move of hers with the cabs on Broadway. Was that what she had said to him? Masks was it? He thought back on the whole morning with Rita and the Fist, and suddenly he wondered what *hadn't* been a mask. What had she said? "If ya ask me, a deal went down." *Went* down?

No, not *went* down, but going *to go* down for real, he was certain! Even the little glassine packet of cocaine, now in his inside breast pocket, had played him false, concentrating his mind on its charming self, as if it were a leftover and not a taste of things to come. He was on to something and he was sure of it. Rita's dance with the cabs was a dead marker something was coming. Had she figured on his seeing her scars? What would he have learned if he'd gone with her? She was after leading him to slaughter like the guy with the elk. He wouldn't have found out that she drank at the Drake, that's for sure. What was real was the simple wrongness of the Fist and her together in Jackie's that half of America could have seen, which he'd missed, being consumed with ancient rage against Bobby. Reality was a mindblowing equation with Bobby the Fist and the Drake Hotel on the two ends of it, with Rita as the streetsign in between, leading to all the wrong conclusions.

He heard again Bobby's ridiculous remonstrance after being tossed on his can into the street about how he didn't seek no vengeance. He had been taken in royally by the boy with that sly act, hadn't he? Rita sitting there telling him he had a pretty name and how skins were masks, and the Fist acting like he was a sore loser. They were some slick actors, and he'd come that close to being taken in by it and never guessing the score. They'd been out to show him they were nothing and nobodies and if they had a game it was a funky one, and he had bought it, he had wanted to believe it, in fact nothing else could have possibly crossed his mind. And maybe they were nothing and nobodies, but nobodies tried for big scores sometimes. Why else would she have jumped cabs like that on Broadway, and what could a girl like he had thought Rita was be doing at the Drake? She was not what she seemed. The Fist

28

in town with a big load was weak enough to start partying with the ladies and looking for homeboys to impress *before* he'd taken care of business—

Hearing a low whistle, the cop looked around in time to see the doorman's nod. Rita emerged from the hotel doorway, hesitated under the canopy, looking proud. Trying anyway. Tossed her golden head. With a second whistle the doorman brought her a fresh cab. Not so fresh. Another patron the doorman would have waved this one away. Battered vehicle belonging to V.S. Rathmawakat Co.— probably the entire fleet—rattled past the cop's ear. Rita tipped the doorman and entered her car, which took off with a lurch toward Michigan Avenue.

On Michigan the battered cab went north, veered onto the inner drive. Shortly it turned west on Schiller leaning hard on its springs and immediately took a right on State. At the park it cut right again, then right once more past the Cardinal's Residence onto Astor Street. In the first block of Astor, Rita alighted, and V. S. Rathmawakat livery disappeared into the noonday brilliance. At the corner of Astor and the park, the cop slouched down in his small plain sedan.

He'd been almost too close. There'd been no place to pull over but against the very corner. Rathmawakat was almost as unmarked and twice as nondescript as his own vehicle, and the way the dude had taken the corners of the narrow Gold Coast streets, he'd been afraid of losing him, and dangerously closed the gap.

He didn't think she'd spot him at the angle from her window, whichever window it was. He would be the last somebody she'd be worrying about right now anyway. But there was too much green space around him for comfort. To his right, the imposing, fortresslike Cardinal's Residence, with its slightly littered lawn. On his left, the open park with a few trees and an old green statue of a seated man reading a book on his lap. From the Cardinal's mansion emanated a hallowed vibration of the ages and sanctities unassailable that made him feel vulnerable and the more visible by contrast. The verdigrised statue of the man with the book in spite of its peaceful thoughtful pose afflicted him with a thought of Chicago's and America's evil past.

He didn't like the past, even the immediate past, the last five minutes, which always chafed, let alone the centuries. Bobby had shown up bringing the past with him. Today the past seemed to catch up to him from every angle and he felt swallowed by it, drowning in it. The expression on the statue's face was at peace, farseeing. A man who had made his mark and made his peace. Imagine a statue of a guy reading a book, but there it was. You could easily be fooled by history's poses though, drained of anger and passion. Confronted by American icons, the cop played his mental game. A lyncher or not? By peering intently he was able to make out the name on the statue's base, Greene Vardiman Black. That was from the days when white people, other than southerners, had names like that.

If anything, Astor Street was more impressive than the Drake Hotel, which after all was a public facility. In spite of the morning's heat the tasteful facades of Astor suggested an absolute lack of sweat and irritation—and plenty of cold cash. Even the shrubbery seemed to coolly glisten as if every leaf had been polished. The black doors with their brass knockers were lustrous and closed, locked up like vaults. As the minutes went by a kind of relief and peace began to descend on him, as if they were the unavoidable essence of Astor Street. He seemed to catch his breath, so rare these days, to breathe it in. Professionally, like all cops, he liked neighborhoods like this one, or at least found them tolerable. They paid his salary. Tentatively he decided in favor of Greene Vardiman Black, a thoughtful icon with the book, a merciful man, not a lyncher, probably, and the Cardinal's Residence was so calming and reassuring, blessing from the Lord. He forgot himself for a moment, almost forgot what he was about, as if his innermost being demanded this respite, the way a thirsty man must acquire drink. He drank in the rectitude and order of the environs. He even forgot her for a second, so that when she appeared again in the doorway that she had entered but a moment ago it was like a bad memory tearing his guts out in the painful present.

When Rita came out of the Astor Street townhouse she had transformed into a walking masquerade of a powerhouse female professional in a chic conservative darkblue pinstripe suit over an elegant highnecked whitesilk blouse that made him gasp. Her curls were pulled back tight and straight over her skull and whatever was in her earlobes gave off flashes of white light that made him blink. She looked like a LaSalle Street female lawyer or banker if you didn't know better. She looked older, as such accoutrements will do. With a sick dropping feeling he wondered how he could have been so mistaken about her, not her new look, but the genius behind the switch between looks. Which was the real Rita made him think how much more of her was yet to show.

She glanced his way, but only for a new cab. Seeing none, she began to walk, taking short swift steps on sexy, teetering, unbusinesslike highheels, which were all that was left of the old Rita, the high heels and how the ruffled cuffs of her white blouse went discreetly down to her fingertips. She looked like she was about to pitch onto her face, making her awfully easy to follow at a distance of a block almost. She had walked nearly to the cabline at the Ambassador West Hotel when an old bigfendered Yellow cab swooped down on her and stopped with its front wheel going up on the curb. It must have been one of the last of those oldstyle balloonfendered Yellow taxis left in the city in 1989 and would be a pleasure to tail. She too seemed struck by it and smiled tentatively and doubtfully. She wouldn't have to walk any farther on those highheels. She got in and they headed south on State, and swung west on Division.

With the surreal speed with which one neighborhood in the city violently turned inside out revealing its opposite, they left the oasis of the Gold Coast and entered the desert sands of the Cabrini Green Housing Projects. Division Street got ugly fast, like all the city's streets if you followed them long enough or even for a short distance. The projects looked stonier and funkier than a prison where the inmates at least were somewhat secure and well fed, where anyway many of the younger male residents of the projects were soon heading so they might as well get used to it. This was familiar, nearly invisible scenery to the cop, who barely glanced at the kids playing idle games in the street, the gang signs on the walls, the winos and junkies on the corners. Just before the dank underpass at Halsted, a boy ran into the street right in front of him bent double in a burst of speed, a bigger kid after him.

The cop slammed his brakes for the first, narrowly missing hitting him, unavoidably cutting off the chaser, who slapped his fender, cursed him, and ran around him. The Yellow cab already dangerously out of sight through the underpass, he couldn't stop to read the kid the riot act like he would have liked to. He felt he owed that to the least of them, the worst of them, to try to tell them the score at any opportunity. The politicians and do-gooders said these kids were beaten down and should be pitied and uplifted. The problem was their spirits were too high. A lot of them were so high they never looked down to notice the page the score was written on. He jumped out of his car.

"Hey, boy, don't you slap my car!! I'll slap your head! Go back to school! Get your diploma! You're going straight to hell, hear? To hell! You too small to be slapping cars! I'll slap your skinny behind! Don't you see where you headed? I see ya *in jail*, boy. Hear?"

The kid was out of sight and the Yellow cab was too. He realized he was sounding just like his Daddy, raving and pointlessly fulminating to doubtful and no effect. But in the end his blessed Daddy had had his effect even so. He knew that now. His Daddy was remembered. He had better ways to talk to the boys, but there was no time for this one. The thing was to keep talking to them. They needed talking to, and punishing too. The marginal ones you sometimes could get to, those not hopelessly drawn by the siren song of the "life," the glittering deathgrip of that gun madness. The Fist had been such a one lost to false dreams. He ducked back behind the wheel and seethed at having his fender slapped. He had to let an errant boy go he had no chance to straighten out just now.

A vast carnivorous penal system awaited that child like a river full of alligators their rightful prey and he would be eaten up with his baggy pants on. Eons and centuries had gone by while that prison system had grown fat and perfected itself in the swamps and backwoods and cornfields of the United States, branching out from slavery, spawning new replicas of itself in every clearing, and the boy who had just flown by and slapped his fender had no more prospect of escaping it than a newhatched mosquito of being missed by a hungry lizard already adjusting its sticky tongue to flick the child back into the churning gullet of state prison. The fleet and winsome boy who had just missed his chance to be lectured by the cop no more understood that he was to be the meat of a monstrous god than he could have performed calculus or recited the Psalms. They didn't get a Christian education as he had from his Daddy to give them some grip on reality, whom he had once thought pretentious until he had understood he was guardian of a vanishing wisdom and cunning which would be all that would save the race, especially wayward boys who needed the sharpest stick possible to be applied to their backside—figuratively speaking, for it was a blow to their *imagination* that was called for—before they were locked away and dissolved in the inconceivable bowels of a devil he knew intimately, as he was one of its keepers and henchmen, whose terrors he felt his calling was to make vivid to as many small boys as possible, even the worst of them, for now and then he reached one and plucked him from the gangs.

He spotted the Yellow. It hadn't gone far. You couldn't miss an old Marathon car like that one. The Yellow cab crossed the river, turned onto the Kennedy Expressway, and floated clear the hell out of town, like a hotair balloon that had broken its tether. The cop felt like a wayward kid himself, chasing a bouncing basketball of a Yellow cab careening up the teeming highway. Why was he doing it? Why wasn't he sticking to business like he knew? There weren't too many fatfendered old-fashioned Marathon cabs like this one left around the city, this had to be about the last of them, or he rarely saw any any more, and it was easy to pick out in traffic. Rita was in it. He let it drift way ahead as you couldn't lose a car like that, past the junction, past Harlem, past Mannheim. They didn't turn off at Elk Grove Village. Past O'Hare airport they dipped around and got on the Northwest Tollway.

The Yellow cab driver must be thinking he had hit the jackpot, the way those hustlers doubled their meters when you passed certain boundaries and even when you didn't. Mile after green mile they rolled through the established suburbs and far beyond, eventually entering lands that looked like they had only recently left off farming. Then he saw around him farms, cows, distant barns, dramatic endless cornfields racing to the horizon. No, he suddenly *was* in the country, in the middle of agriculture, in the midst of the green cornfields the occasional shining corporate highrise like a Mayan temple in the jungle of an Indiana Jones movie. He gaped like a street kid. He hadn't been this far from the city in a long time. Not since his mother had sent him to her folks in Alabama one summer for the experience and because something strange had been going on that summer between her and his Daddy, which had gotten straightened out somehow. Life had resumed normally after that childhood sojourn to the country. There were no high-tech towers in rural Alabama that summer.

It was not where he would have imagined Rita leading him. But he hadn't dreamed the Drake Hotel when he had been with her in Jackie's either. What next? Something evil was his hunch, as he contemplated some fluttering inner compass fleetingly one more time, therefore potentially profitable to himself professionally or what else was he doing? he wondered faintly. This was strange natural turf out here not every inner-Chicagoan had even heard about, let alone ever seen, where the powers that be had taken to hiding their new technology towers and info switching links. The unaccustomed vast and dusty hot greenness of the scenery suddenly dominated by awesome black mirrorfaced corporate obelisks now favored the cop with a vaulting, soaring sensation, a twinge of some completely unrecognizable ineffable joy.

Past the fields, into stands of lush forest, punctuated by smooth squares of green cleared for security purposes around the corporate spires gleaming like Egyptian temples, the Yellow cab pushed relentlessly, exploring it seemed. When it turned off the highway into country roads that ambled past barnyards alternating with car dealerships, into the outlying streets of a fairsize town, the driver, and Rita, obviously got lost right away, the cab going round and round a few blocks past the same blinding strip malls, mega gas stations, and halfbuilt condo developments, as if looking for something without much hope of finding it, floating round and round like a yellow balloon led by a kid on a string. Even the cop, who was lost himself by now in the unfamiliar scenery, could tell they were going in a circle. She didn't seem to know where she was going.

He checked his watch for the tenth time, with a mixture of exhilaration and guilt. He was way out on his lonesome ownsome with this one and frankly he was very late for work. It was a long shot if he'd ever justify this day without extensive effort of the imagination. He could have just as well put a tail on the Fist on the Southside. The Fist would have been no mystery to find again. That was just it. None of this feeling of novelty, of freefall fascination. Let's face it, he wouldn't phrase it this way when the time came to tender his explanation of his day to his superiors, but Rita was a whole lot more fun to follow than damn Bobby. He reached out tentatively with his right hand and opened the glove compartment and pulled out a pint bottle of Johnny Walker Red. He was pleased and even shocked to find it nearly full. He had a long pull on it and rolled the liquor around in his mouth satisfactorily.

The cab stumbled onto the main drag, and drove up and down it for better than a quarter of an hour, passing and repassing the same fastfood franchises, tractor parts suppliers, tire barns, patio furnishers, home fixit omnicenters, in sudden green groves discreet entrances to the corporate parks marked by no more than little tasteful gilded signs like billionaires' embossed calling cards, and a Hilton Hotel with a flagpole and a circular drive, repassed for the third time, into which the Yellow cab finally ducked most likely out of sheer desperation, eliciting a low cry of relief from the trailing cop. There was a local cab parked in the Hilton's circle drive.

The Yellow cab driver, an Indian or Pakistani, jumped out and ran to the window of the local taxi, gesticulating with both hands as he probably asked directions. After half a minute the local's door opened, slowly pushing him back, and a country boy got out stretching like he'd been woken up from a nap. He was a lanky punk, with ragged blonde hair that looked like it had been blowing in the wind all summer. Looking from one of these cab drivers to the other, the cop was unable to decide which of them he would likely detest more. Some of these immigrant drivers could truly be annoying. They could be more prejudiced than the average cracker. The mental game they sometimes played was to look at you like as a black man you had less standing than they did, who barely spoke English while your ancestors had built the whole damn country from the ground up including the White House. Or if they did speak English, like some kind of yakety-yak English English, they pretended you were the one talking funny. Which brand of ignorance irritated him more, the immigrant's or the cracker's, was a sad puzzle he regarded obsessively like running your tongue around a sore tooth caressing the pain. For the moment he sat on the outside of the Hilton circle morosely looking from one to the other of these detestable and pathetic morons.

In general he did not like cab drivers, shiftless, no-account, unfulfilled, unjustified, unappealing, smirking motherfuckers, at least the ones who did not own their cabs but were just getting by. Their game was they were so marginal there was nothing the law could do to them anyhow, and they had a way of sneering at you in that regard, especially the Russians you ran into these days, they could make you boil with their impudence, and particularly any white trash cracker drivers, too, from Uptown, who had come to the city maybe from down South someplace, racists all of them, or now and then petty hoods with a record, for whom he felt a twinge of regret sometimes, as they had never known what hit them, or the occasional out-of-work professional or even college graduate who could not get a job and looked down on you or even had a real chip on their shoulder because they had to drive a hack that the cop never knew whether he should knock off or not. Black drivers were not much better, junkies, homeless, drive-for-a-day bastards who when they made fifty dollars thought there was no tomorrow. They all sneered and would all lie to you about everything and anything for no reason at all other than you were a cop, and if you were a *black* cop their contempt was plain (or if they were black they were familiar and stupidly prevailed on you), and all that did was give them another reason to despise you, since they regarded you as a slave or a guardian of a culture they could barely get a toehold in but had every right to and had more right to than you whose ancestors had built this country.

The beanpole local white boy moseyed over to the Yellow cab apparently to take a gander at Rita is what it looked like, and he must have liked what he saw, because he aced the Yellow driver out, and Rita switched cabs again, loudly berating the Hindu as she paid him off and imploring the blonde cabby to get moving. He forgot the sorry drivers for a moment and his hatred of them dissipated in lovely amazement at Rita in that business suit cursing and lambasting them in a shrill voice. He loved it!

The Chicago cab headed back to its territory, or probably to get lost some more. No, no circles, without the meter rolling it would travel straight there. The local cab with Rita in it pulled away from the hotel without haste, and he could hear Rita urging the farmboy driver to hurry up clear across the Hilton's lawn. These guys skimped on gas by not running the air conditioning until the passenger demanded it and the windows of the cab were wide open. The cab was a sight to behold, a garishly converted Cadillac El Dorado with a big number 17 on its trunk lid, and red, white, and blue bull's-eyes painted on its doors. What a wagon. Farmhand's notion of a sharp ride, looked like something out of a hicksville pimps' parade.

These big roads out here in the far suburbs had been laid out nice and wide but the traffic was worse than in the city. The cop felt himself flailing up a steaming river of glass and chrome and steel whose banks were only more glass and chrome and steel, car dealer showroom windows, a thousand mirrored office complexes, Red Lobster and Olive Garden restaurants no end, up the gleaming main drag that led away from the mirrored windows of the Hilton. The sunlight was coming at him in blinding waves off the bumpers of the cars, the white back of the Cadillac cab, the asphalt parking lots of restaurants and stripmalls. There were none of the darkened brick recesses of doorways and cavelike mouths of alleys as in the city to absorb some of the awful light.

And of course everybody on the sidewalks and in all the cars was white, real white. Not just white either but the sort of chicly farmery overalled, designer-blue-jeaned, or pink-exercise-gear-clad babes who might never ever go to the city any more, ever. They probably never saw a black person but their maid. When the traffic backed up at the fantastically long red lights they had out here he felt himself being eyeballed a little from the other lanes. In the city the murder rate would go up if the lights were timed on such ungodly long intervals. He had the weird feeling the people in the other cars might suddenly prevent his progress.

Then, something like this happened. Moments after coming to a stop at a redlight, the red-white-and-blue cab with bull's-eyes on its doors suddenly cut around the cars in front of it and blew straight through the redlight, a trick as old as the history of the automobile. A fully loaded eighteen-wheeler grinding slowly the other way in low gear had created an easy chance in crosstraffic through which the bull's-eyed flag-painted cab ducked but so barely the truck driver had to hit his airbrakes and the big rig shimmied to an awkward stop in the intersection. The trucker laid on his triplebarreled horn in triple irritation.

He had been following in the right lane. Her riding in a wildly painted, easily spottable cab had put him to sleep. The cabs must be few and far between up here, where everyone had cars, he hadn't seen another. How could you lose a Cadillac with big bull's-eyes?

The traffic and parked cars and the eighteen-wheeler in the intersection pinned him in from all sides. When he sounded his own horn and edged his car toward a crack, the other drivers packed tighter vindictively, giving him uneasy stares like who did this black guy think he was, they had places to go themselves. He had a small emergency siren, which he could clip on the window, which he thought better of using.

He was overcome by an ancient emotion, a bad racial claustrophobia that came at him from his core, and the bottleneck became an ordeal at more than one level. He was surrounded by these ofay crowds who would tolerate him so long as he did just like they did and otherwise never moved a little finger or made a sound except to grin. He had to freeze and hold a rigid pose at the wheel, and above all appear cheerful and pleased about it. There were so damn many of them. There was no way out of them. He was trapped in by the thousands.

Weird how the numbing sensation of being outnumbered, of being in the "minority," as old as consciousness itself, could come at him out of the blue, with almost the same sad force as when he first understood such things as a child, or perhaps even like when the equally strange meaning of "mortality" had first hit his adolescent soul, the suppressed, inadmissable dread. He couldn't now imagine having any such an impractical emotion, not since he had made detective anyway, but there it was coming down on him. Becoming aware of his unpleasant mood, dangerously close to self-pity, he threw it off with a firm inner shrug.

In a traffic jam of this magnitude in the ghetto the people would have been sounding on each other and passing remarks through the windows, and even getting out in the street to talk and walk over to visit in one another's cars, but this one was proceeding in total tomblike silence—except for the shrieking of horns like weird birdcalls under an empty sky. Up ahead, the trucker finally rolled his big rig out of the intersection, the light changed, and traffic began to move once more. Another minute, and the cop was passing under the traffic light hanging on a wire whose dead chemical greenness leered at him—too late now!

In the clear he blazed on and at once came to a fork in the road. No longer certain of the lay of the land, or that confident in his reading of the personalities of the players he was tailing, he had a choice to make. A narrow old lane veered off the highway to the right and an instinct told him to take it. He cruised down under a viaduct supporting a rusty railroad spar from an inconceivable past, and immediately soared up a hill. He wondered if anyone had ever been lynched out this way. He was pretty sure they had.

He had a hunch that the cab driver would have cut off on this old road with the intention of getting him thoroughly lost. He felt this to his bones. For an instant, he held the hope that from the top of the hill he would catch a glimpse of the Cadillac. But it was long gone of course, and the downslope was too gentle anyway, the road curved and meandered through an old part of town with big old leafy trees and rambling rundown houses blocking off any view. Hope was replaced by throbbing indignation stiff as a toothache. Like something dropping over the edge of a cliff, the sight of the Cadillac cab running the redlight came back to him with terrible finality, a trick that wouldn't have fooled your mother.

Two old ladies came out the door of the Greenshores Hilton hotel restaurant and peered severely in the direction of the cab line, populated by two cars, Armchair's and the Cadillac. They stared straight at the driver of the head-up cab, Armchair, who had picked up his book. It was obvious they wanted a cab, but on the other hand old ladies like these were notoriously bad tippers and took unbelievably short rides. One of them waved her umbrella, and it wasn't too hard to figure out she wasn't trying to unfurl it since there wasn't a cloud in the bitter blue sky.

"You're up," said the cab driver in the back seat mildly to his friend Armchair, trying to hide in his voice his pleasure that it was not he who was head-up. Armchair who was deep into his book by now hadn't noticed a thing. "Aw, hell, they're gonna go six blocks an give me a quarter," complained Armchair, looking up and blinking, nonetheless resigned to his fate as signaled by his placing a bookmark in the pages and laying the volume on the dashboard rather carefully and dolefully. This was deceiving as resignation was never one of Armchair's true attitudes. He cleared his throat and leaned toward the passenger window, the side toward the hotel.

In his special voice he had for such occasions, like the sonorous honk of a barge cutting through fog, Armchair cried, *"Caaaaaaaaa!"*

"Cab!" rejoined the old lady weakly, but dropping her umbrella.

"Caaaaaa! Caaaaaw!" He leaned closer to the open window to be heard better.

Her friend took her arm. The ladies lurched backward into the hotel. Actually, it was lucky for them they hadn't had to ride even a short way with the Armchair. The cab driver said no more about the incident. He would have been head-up cab if Armchair had gone off the post, but on the other hand there were things not worth worrying about, and into that category fell Armchair and his ways. In lots of ways he was a good friend and always so in a pinch. This could be let pass. The dispatcher might be going to hear about this from the old ladies over the phone, and then he'd scream about it a little over the radio, trying to find out which driver was the offender. His rantings would be cut short when the culprit became known. There was no hope of disciplining the Armchair, everyone knew. Well, complaining about cab service was futile, wasn't it, on a par with griping about the weather? But old ladies would never learn.

Business was picking up. Some Japanese gentlemen came out of the hotel and hesitated. They put down their bags, waved at the cabs, and waited. Their air was of hoping for the best, of faith in the proper thing happening. It was Armchair's turn out of the gates, however. Sensing a good load for his friend, the cab driver instantly jumped clear, and Armchair's car lurched forward, one wheel on the sidewalk, nearly running into his fares. His prospective passengers took a step back, smiling at exotic American behavior determinedly. Armchair got out of his cab, and actually took one of their bags to the rear of his car, leaving the rest, thinking he'd done his part, but it was unusually solicitous of him, they had no idea. Often he merely handed the trunk key through the window. So much of what passes from man to man is lost, in the interpretation, as it were. No doubt he wanted to make a good impression on visitors to America, the cab driver indulged in black humor, hopefully.

But the luggage they had with them on the sidewalk wasn't all. A bellhop suddenly came trundling out of the hotel under a burden of more suitcases and golfbags. Armchair's spine arched back, his neck drew up straight, his head achieved a lofty height, as he was quite tall, and he surveyed the scene down his nose, as if unsure whether to take it or leave it. The thing that made the cab driver hold his breath was that Armchair might leave, he'd seen him do it. Then an obviously good ride would be his, so it wouldn't be all bad. Seeing how it was, laughing among themselves, the party began lugging their things to the back of his car, grinning at each other. They were goodnatured, or at least resigned, and efficient, travelers. As far as Armchair was concerned, these people had too many bags. They were making demands on his good will. Good cabriders traveled light. At this moment he looked like a flustered college instructor, extremely down at the heels, to be sure, reluctant to admit unruly students to class. By his manner he seemed to suggest they should part with some of their luggage if they wanted to ride in his car. He was eyeing their golfbags like they held snakes not clubs. The standoff had the Japanese guys muttering wry obscenitites to each other no doubt and laughing up their sleeves. Finally Armchair looked back at the cab driver and shrugged in an exaggerated way, as if he were now going to attempt the impossible, namely to pack his trunk.

Armchair bent over his trunk fiddling with the key in the lock. The lid didn't seem to want to open. The reason was his trunk was already crammed with all kinds of junk. By leaning on the lid as he turned the key, he finally got it to pop up. He hauled out an extra spare tire, and after glancing back once sort of shyly at the cab driver as if hoping he would take it off his hands, leaned it against the bumper. He peered back into the trunk and smacked his forehead with his palm in amazement. He reached in and hoisted out a full brownpaper bag.

He walked straight back with it and exclaimed to the cab driver, "Jesus, I wondered what happened to this bag! I was cursing the kid at the supermarket for misplacing it. Here it is in my trunk of all places. My groceries, damnit! I forgot."

He was standing outside the window with the expression of a lost puppy on his face. The cab driver, who had been smiling at all of this, and was laughing even now, was adamant. "I aint holdin no bag a groceries for you, man! I don't have room for your groceries!"

"I tried to get you a load too Cadillac! I tried to get em to hire two cabs. I told em they should hire a second cab for their stuff, that was the way we did it in the States. But they didn't go for it."

Remembering the dismal experience with the firecrew, which seemed long ago already, thanks partly to Armchair's listening to his story, finally he gave in and took his bag of groceries for him, stuck it on the floor of the frontseat under the radio. He loaned him some tiedowns for his trunk lid, because naturally Armchair, among all the junk in his car, didn't have as much as a piece of rope.

Armchair stumbled back to his cab, and noticed his extra tire leaning against the bumper. He glanced back again at the cab driver, but put the idea out of mind. He shrugged and just rolled the thing out onto the green lawn under the flagpole. He confronted the enigma of his full trunk once more, even without the tire and the groceries. He began rearranging things in his trunk, eyeing the possessions of the Japanese businessmen piled up at his feet. Suddenly he pulled out of his trunk a bag of golf clubs and went running with it into the hotel. It happened so fast that his passengers looked down at their own golfbags to make sure it wasn't one of theirs.

After a couple of minutes, Armchair came out of the hotel and walked back to his friend the cab driver. He ignored his fares completely, but seeing him gave them hope, and they began packing his trunk. He stuck his head in the window of the Cadillac and said, "I just want you to know that son of a bitch bellboy insisted on two dollars *in advance* to hold my clubs! I didn't mention my tire because he would have charged me double. Do me a favor, if you see him out here, run his ass over!"

Armchair absently observed his passengers complete the loading of his trunk, after which he attached the tiedowns to the bumper. There were still some items on the ground they would have to hold on their laps. With all his own junk underneath their bags, the trunk lid didn't come within a foot of closing. With forbearing smiles the Japanese party piled into the car, but Armchair still wasn't ready. He got out a rag and squirt bottle and began polishing the windshield. He cupped his hand and called back to his friend, "They're going to the Loop. Big deal! I got to clean up this buggy."

The Loop, thought the cab driver, a huge ride from up here, and Armchair was dithering. When he was done with the windshield, he opened the hood and pulled out the dip stick.

"I'm a quart low!"

"I would kill the fucker," thought the cab driver, thinking of the excellent ride his friend had in the car waiting for him.

"You don't have a quart, do you?" he called back at his friend. He put the dipstick back in the engine, left the hood open, and walked toward the hotel. He had reached the big glass doors. He was looking for something on which to wipe his oily hands. There was nothing. Suddenly the cab driver jumped out of his car with a shout. With his Polaroid he caught a shot of Armchair seizing the glass door in his oily mitts, a wild grin lighting up his face.

Armchair's antics had taken him far away. Somehow or other, Armchair cooled you down and mellowed you out. But you had to be ready for it. Having been trying to take off now for ten minutes, the businessmen of course were having the opposite reaction and understandably getting nervous and were no longer able to hide their alarm. But in the end, down in the Loop, when the ride was over, they too would probably experience a catharsis. The thing was, out here in the extreme suburban boonies, cabs didn't exactly grow on the trees. The Cadillac might be the only other one for all they knew. They approached the El Dorado.

"Beautiful car!" said one, smiling urgently.

"Thanks." Look out, flattery would get them everywhere!

"Maybe you will take us?" Edgy grins all around. To the Loop from out here was a fabulous ride, the kind to make your day, and the way his morning had been, it would have been a Godsend. The average cab driver would hear "Loop" and be going too fast for the people to change their minds before they got the doors closed. There were guys who would have stolen the load from Armchair, offended by his cavalier attitude, justifying it that the customers were getting delayed. Armchair, after his style, had wandered off into the hotel, God knew where. These good fellows didn't deserve this, but he couldn't steal Armchair's load.

"Listen, he's all right. It's a long trip, and he just wants to be sure everything's okay," he lied.

Their faces fell. They knew a baldfaced lie!

He had a soft spot for Japanese visitors. There were a lot of them around these days. They were decent tippers. Some worked for American corporations and others for Japanese companies that did business around here. A couple of them had been his "regulars." One guy who was in Greenshores for a long posting had been trying to get his driver's license and the cab driver had taken him to driving school twice a week for about six months. Then he had taken him for his exam at the Motor Vehicles Department, which he kept failing. One day on the front page of the *Sun Times* had appeared a story about a terrible scandal in Japan. Some cases of mercury poisoning had been traced to a particular Japanese company, and there was a photo of an executive actually crawling on his knees to the doorway of a victim. Another executive had committed suicide. The cab driver had remarked on it to his "regular" that day, going to the driving school. He had been dumbstruck by the extreme contrition and acts of expiation of the executives. No American executive would remotely respond to his company's errors or crimes in such a moral way.

"It's a damn shame, but to take responsibility like that and kind of do penance like that, it's impressive. An American would just hire a lawyer. I can hardly believe the goodness of it! But I mean one guy killed himself out of honor or something. What a culture."

"Hmm, good for culture," his regular had opined, "not so good for executive!"

Just now the Japanese travelers were crowded hopefully by his window. His Cadillac must look inviting and luxurious next to Armchair's rattletrap. Plus, he was available, he was just sitting here, the main thing. But it wasn't his turn up. Armchair was up.

"Really, he's coming right now!" He gave his voice an optimistic ring. They shot him looks of horror. Amazingly, here he did come, bursting through the Hilton's front door, taking long strides, making little outstretched palm gestures of incredulity.

"Can you believe this joint? Not a can of oil in the place! So they say. I think they save it for the limos!"

With his thumb he motioned his passengers into his car. With sly looks all around, they took out after him. He jumped into the driver's seat and began revving the engine while they piled in. It had been brave and gentle stock like this that had produced the Kamikazes, mused the cab driver. At this point Armchair was asking them to check if there were any papers of his on the floor by any chance. He watched Armchair's car careen around the circle and out into the road. It was an old jalopy and tilted viciously on its bad springs. *"BANZAI!"* shrieked Armchair, waving his arm wildly.

The shameful episode had at least been a diversion, and he was almost sorry to see them go. He was happy Armchair would make some money, and maybe the fellows would get where they hoped to. A calm fell upon the hotel pavilion in Armchair's wake. Unaccountably a surge of promise came from somewhere, some angel hinting of better things, and he was content to wait patiently in the sunshine. Damn if he wasn't experiencing sensations just as pleasant as if he were in a little boat on a Wisconsin lake fishing, it was so peaceful, as if a motorboat had just rocketed past and was now gone. The quietude was almost supportable, demanding nothing, not even a nibble. Armchair was so crazy he neutralized your own craziness, and made you feel peaceful and in control, by contrast. He soothed your soul. He picked up the day's newspaper from the seat and read Mike Royko's column and was entertained.

He must have dozed. He was disturbed by a car pulling up directly beside his own. He was afraid it was Armchair come back mischievously on some obnoxious errand like because he had forgotten to buy cigarettes for the ride or even sincerely fearful that the old wreck he drove would not make it to the Loop. He wouldn't have been able to bear the looks on the faces of his longsuffering passengers. Cautiously he opened his eyes a crack to see who it was.

But what it was, when he raised up gingerly and glanced offhandedly to his side, was another sort of old crate, a real old city of Chicago cab, one of the big old Marathon Yellows of yesteryear, must be about the last of its kind, like DeNiro drove in *Taxi Driver,* like the one that appeared out of the city's mists at the start of that movie. Man, it must be one of the last in that old line of cabs, he

45

hadn't seen one in quite a while and had thought they were all gone, and he couldn't help sitting straight up and admiring it. But abruptly the moment was compromised by the driver jumping out and walking around to talk to him through his window, sticking his head too close to his own, halfway through the window.

"Good morning to you, sir!" he exclaimed in heavily accented but impeccable English. "I say! Are you an American?"

"You talkin to me?"

If there was one thing he hated, it was someone sticking his head inside his car like it was a public place. It wasn't public until it was hired. It was just like somebody opening the door uninvited and sticking his head inside your house! Was he an American! He understood the spirit of the question even as his momentary irritation passed and his usual good humor and willingness to see the other guy's side inexorably reasserted itself. Professionally, he liked to see people get to where they wanted to go, however they got there. Rubbing his eyes, sighing, he turned lightheartedly to the city cab far from home to be helpful if he could.

"I say, old man!" persisted the Indian. "I'm a bit lost! I say! Can you direct me to the Avenue of the White Stallion?"

White Stallion was where they wanted to go? It was going to be hard to explain all the twists and turns to get over there. The foreign guy was never going to get his fare over there without getting lost again. The cab driver glanced at the fat Yellow cab. There was a girl in the back seat. If it was the Avenue of the White Stallion they were looking for, they really were lost. That street lay in one of the glitzier corners of Greenshores clear across town, in some fancy estates where all the streets had names like that. The Avenue of the Colorado. The Avenue of the Lonesome Pine. The Avenue of the Golden Buttes.

"You are way on the wrong side of town."

"She told me that she knew the way once we got out here!" complained the Chicago cabby. "I say—"

"Hold on, I'm tryin to think how to send ya without gettin ya lost even worse. That's clear on the other end of town."

"My passenger is in a terrible hurry, I'm afraid."

"She is?"

As little money as he'd made today, he ought to take her over there himself. He didn't want to hijack the guy's load, but maybe he'd made his money already and would be glad to be out of it and if he took the fare from here it would be the happiest outcome for all concerned.

His nap had spaced him out, or maybe the insane interlude with Armchair had mellowed him out and drained the day of false urgency. Relaxed, he slid out and stretched. He took a curious gander at the big old Yellow rig and checked out the fare. He glanced in discreetly. There she sat on high behind glass, like a princess on an elephant. She was beautiful. She was too beautiful, actually, he quickly calculated, not that it mattered.

She returned him a haughty, blinding stare. He was taken aback by the inappropriate force of it. Her golden hair drawn tight over her skull made her highboned features stand out unsmilingly and commandingly. She looked awfully young though. She was sophisticatedly dressed in an expensive-looking business suit, a smartass lady junior executive, apparently, or trying to be anyway, because she looked hardly more than a teenager. The effect on him of some vaguely sensed contradictions couldn't have been more disturbing if she had planned it that way.

Seeing him reluctantly start to retreat, she dropped her mask and stuck her head out the window, and yelled in the toughest Chicago accent, "Hey, pal, ya know where dat street is at? I'manna pay off dis turkey an good riddance. Take me by dere will ya, guy? I'll take care a ya, chief, don't worry!"

She then flashed him the nicest come-on grin, and he was won over. The Hindu put up only a short facesaving squawk about losing his fare before muttering his profound gratitude to the cab driver, and left gleefully counting his money. While she paid him she berated him wildly, "No tip since ya never got me where I was goin, bud! Turkey!" But in fact he did receive a tip in spite of it, the Chicago driver discovered counting his money, and remarked to himself about his strange passenger, so young, tough, and handsome. He glanced back but she was already in the American's car. There had been something fraught and suspicious about her, she had been muttering and raving all the time, and he had wondered if he was going to lose his time and money, kids like that ran out on you sometimes, and now he had his excellent money, more than he had expected, and he felt she was in some trouble, and wished her well.

47

As soon as she was in the backseat of the Cadillac, she leaned forward so close to him they were almost cheek to cheek. "Hey, step on it, please, will ya, friend?" she begged the cab driver. She was distractedly glancing out the window and then into his mirror into his eyes. Her accent had softened up dramatically.

"Please, hurry! Jesus, I'm glad I found ya, an American an all."

"Thank you."

"That turkeystan run me aroun out here an hour. We been out here as long as it took to get from the Loop. We never woulda got to White Stallion."

"Hi ho, Silver, away!" he remarked, and they were rolling away from the Hilton hotel.

"Very funny. Hey don't fuck with me, okay, man? We drove by that hotel three times. I tol him, go in that hotel, ask another cab driver. But the numbskull won't do it. He keeps goin, 'We will find, Miss! We will find!' I told him, I been in that hotel, there's always a cab in front. With an American in it."

"Thank you so much."

"What?"

"Never mind."

"Yeah? Hurry up, will ya? Ya sure we're goin the right way? Don't worry, if ya get me there fast, I'm gonna take care a ya, guy. Don't be runnin up the meter on me, pal! Just cuz I got tits don't mean I'm deaf, dumb, and blind, okay?"

He looked in the mirror while she talked and noticed a hole between her front teeth, which, while it blurred her attempt at a classy image, did not detract from her beauty. On the contrary, the flaw made her allure vivid in the mirror, when he glanced her way, as did her whole animated conversation, and she was not so perfectly turned out like an apprentice executive manager all of a sudden, but was real people to him. She no longer seemed all that young either. She must be twenty, anyway. She was trying to sound streetwise. He felt she was dressed up for some role. Maybe she was going for a job interview. He didn't think she belonged in a pinstripe suit any more than he did himself.

"Listen, kid," he said, "look out the window. We're goin in a straight line. Can I be runnin ya around?"

"Yeah, don't think just cuz I don't know how to get there I don't know where I'm at. I'll see the neighborhood. In fact, I'll see the whole goddamn section when we get near it. That jagoff tells me, 'Well, Miss, you must get some directions before you start out into the country like this.' Listen you idiot, I told him, this aint no country. This is just more a the same damn city, there aint no end to it. I should know, I was born in a joint like this. Well, not exactly like this, but in the suburbs. I come out here all the time, to see my friend. Ya never see how to go if you're not the one doin the driving, know what I mean? I mean, if a cab driver don't know how to go, whacha spose to do! Ya sure we're goin right, buddy? I don't recognize a thing out here."

He shot her another look in the mirror. There were tiny jewels of perspiration on her temples, and she was actually wringing her hands together. She was talking nonstop to keep herself together, he imagined. She was so wound up, she seemed ready to jump out the window. She sounded coked up, really, high on something.

"Hey, does your friend wear spurs?"

"*What?*" she whispered fragiley, like glass shattering.

Jesus, he gulped, he hadn't meant it like that, however she had taken it. White Stallion, all that. He ducked his head, embarrassed. When he raised it again to look in the mirror, he couldn't find her at first. She had sunk way down in a corner.

"Hey, no offense, but do they gotta come up with names for these new streets like that? I'm sorry! Cowboys and Indians names. What'sa matter with regular old names? Say, is somethin bothering you? Are ya sure ya want to go through with this?"

"What in the hell are you *talkin* about!"

"Excuse me. I don't mean to get personal. But, honest, I get the feeling ya aint exactly lookin forward to whatever I'm taking ya to."

"Well, you're awful observant, aint ya? Awful *talkative!* You're right, I'm not looking forward to nothin! I definitely aint enjoyin this ride neither, okay? I don't believe this conversation."

"Hey, I don't mean to butt in. But if I had business that made me feel the way you seem to, I would cancel it an no delay, lady, I wouldn't do it, believe me!"

"Yeah? Listen, buddy, just drive, would ya? Would ya mind, speakin of business, just drive your cab, okay?"

The subtle undermining effect of intimacy she had been having steadily and unconsciously on him since she'd jumped in his car he had lost the capacity to recognize as false and hardly knew he was talking out of turn. He lost control and spontaneously bubbled over, "Hey, dig it, girl, let's go have a picnic! I know a spot!"

"I thought that coolie was somethin."

"Right near here. That guy wasn't wrong about this being the country. It still is. You might not believe the old farms an stuff nearby. I know an old red barn in a meadow, friend of mine's. We pick up some sandwiches at the deli, some cold wine. Curl your toes in the wildflowers, forget your troubles, sit in the shade beside that pretty ol red barn."

"Oh my God . . . a picnic. . . . Okay, listen, honest, that sounds nice, man, damn if it don't," she said in a suddenly yielding voice, a tired, fading, even yearning voice that gave him a falling sensation in the pit of his stomach like maybe she was going for it. Either that or she was just humoring him desperately so as to get to her destination. He certainly had to admit that possibility to himself. But then, "It does, guy, ya know?" she added, convincingly.

He had just been talking and having fun. He became acutely aware he had crossed a line unwittingly. Pangs of exquisite hope gripped his heart like hungry demons. He wondered if she was actually about to say yes. Without warning, hopes he hadn't known he had were up. He suspected he would pay for this.

"I'd love to," she went on dreamily, "I really, really would."

He stared at her in the mirror. She was drooping like a flower too long out of water. Something complex about her beyond loveliness transfixed him. She was leaning on her knees, with her chin almost resting on the frontseat next to him, then it did, her chin propped on the seatback next to his shoulder, an unladylike posture, just like a little kid. It didn't go with the business suit at all. He didn't look at her in the mirror any longer, just turned his head a little. She was rubbing her temples with her fingertips.

"Say yes and we'll go," he continued foolishly. "This minute! There's a pretty little pond up nearby there, too. Sometimes nobody around. Afterwards we throw off our clothes an go for a dip, ha ha ha."

Something disturbing of energies at cross purposes in her had touched off lilting possibilities in himself. He was on a roll. He found her face almost nestled into his shoulder, with dreamy half-closed eyes looking up through the windshield. She seemed taken by his conversation.

She sat up, blinking, looking around like remembering where she was. He wondered if he had gone too far. He had a firm rule: Don't mess with the fares. But he'd broken it this time. She now had a somber waking-up look in her staring eyes. He sensed a shadow had fallen across her being, and in her expression a sharp seriousness had appeared. Her whole body was trembling and even shaking. In the mirror again something in her seemed to compress, then flare up in anger. She exploded.

He had made an impulsive professional move in traffic—she was now sitting straight up wildeyed and pointing her finger accusingly out the side, then the rear window.

"Hey! Ya ran that redlight, man! That truck nearly cut us in half! Ya tryin to kill us?"

"The opposite, believe me."

"Ya just blew off that light!" She was staring back through the rear glass. "He's jumped out of his truck. He's screamin at ya! Ya nearly killed him too."

"Oh man, don't let the traffic get to ya. Once it gets to ya, you're finished. You won't get very far that way!"

"We coulda got hung up there with the cops forever if he hit us. How far are we?"

"Tell me."

"Oh shit, look, honey, your meter reads twelve dollars already, don't ya think that's about enough? Would ya let up a little? Here!" She was shifting around on the back seat as if it were hot and fishing in her pocketbook.

"Here's a twenty! No, thirty! Now just get me there! But don't get us in trouble! That's all ya get if it takes all day. Listen, I'm late, gimme a break, will ya? Okay, here's another ten."

The green bills floated over the seatback from her fingertips and lay beside him offensively. He didn't like to be paid in advance as if he might cheat somebody. And overpaid at that! The meter reported the fare when the ride was over. He didn't even want her money suddenly. The money he hadn't made today which was obsessing him a few minutes ago no longer meant anything to him. What he was interested in was—well, not her money. (What *was* he interested in? What was he *doing?*) He couldn't stand people telling him how to drive. It was no business of theirs if he ran a hundred redlights, if he got them where they were going. They weren't going

51

to court, if he ran a light. She was crying because she was late and now she was crying because he saved time at that light and got her there sooner. From the way she was going on it was obvious she had enough problems of her own without sounding off at him.

He turned onto a sideroad and drove under a low viaduct where he knew a shortcut if she had to get there fast and where there were also some bad potholes. He felt like shaking her up a little. On the other side was a hill and then a descent. The road meandered off toward their destination actually shorter on the meter but might take a minute or two longer and give him time to think. (Think about *what?*) He wouldn't take somebody this way normally because they would suspect they were being run around, even though it was a shortcut. That truck had been fifty feet away and barely moving. He had almost gotten over with her, when she had gotten excited about that light.

He snuck a glance in the mirror to see her bounce off the seat a few times clear to the roof of the car when they hit potholes. She leaned forward and clutched the seatback next to him as they crested the hill at high speed. He decided to go around even more, so he could mull this over. (Mull *what* over?) She'd already paid, so it didn't matter. He was zigzaging as the spirit moved him. These were some old side streets he hadn't been on for a while. He'd clicked off the meter since she'd already paid but still he didn't want her to get the idea he was "running her around." He was racing through the streets in a personal, moody way. The drive had become a meditation, a trance, a means of purging himself of the enchanted and sullen mood he'd fallen into. He felt blindsided by her and by his whole day. It was irrational, but he couldn't shake the idea that she was being awfully contrary. This was ridiculous, since they'd only barely met, if riding in the cab together could by any stretch of the imagination be called meeting. He found her eyes in the mirror, round, searing, blank, and blue. She was holding onto the seatback with both hands.

Yes, he'd broken his rule. He was getting involved. And he couldn't stop. The last thing he wished was to stop and become uninvolved.

"You're not happy! Ya think ya got it together but ya don't!" he cried. "I see you're into a certain money an power level, the way you're dressed, the address you're goin to. I tell ya what, I can sense ya got a little corner of your life open for somethin *different,* somethin just for *you* an pure *fun* for a change! You're too young to be so serious! Ya know I'm for real, anyway, don't you? I think we're the same, in spite of your suit."

He spoke directly, forthrightly and at the top of his voice. He didn't know how he could do it much better. And it was hopeless, he knew. What did she want with a cab driver when she had a rich friend on White Stallion? His heart was about to do a disastrous, foolhardy number on him.

Her mouth fell open, the corners of her lips turning up in a coy grin. Her chin was drifting toward the seatback again. In her blue eyes was a bold twinkle of recognition, an inner sparkle as though she had just had a new thought, a revelation.

"I'll tell ya one thing, you're a maniac, aint ya? Ya drive this crate like there's no damn tomorrow, buddy."

"I knew after we got the formalities out of the way we'd be on the same wavelength."

She muttered aside thoughtfully, "At least you didn't tell me your damn sign yet." Turning to stare out the window, she seemed to go away from the ride, from him, from her problems, even her destination. A cunning intelligence had come into her bearing, no longer slouched but arced upward alert, staring aside. He was no longer watching where he was going but steadily watching her in the mirror in fascination and driving by a cab driver's sixth sense. She appeared far away in her thoughts and yet for the first time she seemed actively and wholly present with him in the car. Her air had focused, and she had become accessible to him.

"Shit, no jive signs!" he assured her. "The picnic?"

"Tonight, maybe. Yeah, sure, honey, why not, tonight, *by moonlight.* Really, I'd go for a picnic!" She actually appeared to be picturing it to herself. By moonlight! If it wasn't cloudy, there would be a sliver of moon. "Later, when I get somethin out of the way," on a practical note. "Tonight. Maybe. I do like you. Maybe we *are* alike. You're sort of, uh, remarkable, mm, *okay.* Say, what part a town we in anyway? What is this old stuff? Look at those old houses. God, where've you taken me? I never seen any a this before an I been out here a million times."

"We're not far, really. I'm sorry you're late. This is a shortcut. It's just off the main road. This was what was here before the fancy part where you're going an the corporations' headquarters an laboratories an all got here. This part is still a country town. We're just around the corner now from where you are going. Don't look like it though, does it?"

"Look at those old ladies on that porch with the fans in their hands! Look at those little kids playin on that swing, that old tire on a tree limb! That coolie wasn't lyin. Oh man, I always wanted to swing on a tire by a rope like that hanging from a tree limb. We didn't have no tire like that when I was little."

She turned her head and watched it recede through the rear window.

"Yeah, it has its charm."

They left the old neighborhood with its ramshackle front porches and shade trees from one of whose limbs a swing made of an automobile tire hung by a rope. The street opened up. The big old trees disappeared. On either side of this road were littered, open construction sites with half-completed structures that would become new Dollar Stores and the like. At a stop sign, he pulled up for the cars whizzing past, then forced his way into Northwest Highway traffic. The air was full of smoke and dust and reflected light after the shadedappled side streets. Car dealers with "Acres of Cars" alternated with every fastfood franchise known to man. Fresh saplings stuck out of the bare earth like cocktail toothpicks in front of new condo developments festooned with plastic pennants and billboards announcing "Adventures in Elegance" and so on.

Greenshores was one of those sleepy little towns lying along the corridors of the Tollroad and all the big highways west and north of the city which had woken up one morning not long ago exurbs and even unlikely competitors of the city of Chicago. At first if you were a businessman or an accountant, you could live out here in your McMansion and enjoy the rural scene and get downtown in fifty minutes or so, and then when the corporations and businesses began moving out here you never had to leave at all. Its name had been changed, the old one having been Green Junction. There were actually no green "shores" around here except for those on a few small ponds and perhaps those of time itself, which was coming faster and faster. The milestone newly laid, the achievement far from complete, just outside of town, farmers' fields made an unstable truce with the campuses and parking lots of the new corporations and the blossoming harvest of new and expensive housing tracts.

"Hope I'll really see ya again," said the cab driver in a low urgent voice, somberly, humbly, afraid of breaking the spell, but saying what he felt had to be said, reaching out to her, aware there was no more to be said now, but something must be said, surely, as they were nearing the entrance of the Old West development.

"Yeah? I said, by moonlight."

"Don't kid me. I can take it."

"Why not? Tonight. You said it, a picnic. Like ya said. Only we have to go far, man, far—*much farther than this.*"

Far? Much farther? He gulped with improbable success. He was hearing her say yes! He could sense it in her bright attention concentrated inward on some vision. She had taken his invitation and imposed some idea of her own on it, forming a plan. What it would be exactly he couldn't know and didn't care, since it seemed to include him. He'd find out. You had to meet halfway in this life or not at all. What her angle was was her own business. We all have our reasons. He was only overjoyed that she had hers! Not only was she saying yes to him, she was far ahead of him. He found his thoughts struggling to catch up to her animated ones, not wishing to be left behind. But he'd have to take them on faith, he thought with a hope that is indistinguishable from a sort of pain.

"Tonight, *for real?* Really?"

"Hey—see that pickup truck? *There.*"

It took him a moment to find what she pointed at, though floating directly ahead of them in traffic. Even after seeing it, it was hard to see, just a battered tan pickup drifting ahead.

"See that bumper sticker?"

Yes, he saw. On the bumper of the pickup was the familiar torn and dusty ESCAPE TO WISCONSIN sticker put out by the Wisconsin tourist industry in the 1980s, like on half the bumpers in Chicago.

"The whole damn city dyin to get away out of the ratrace to the peace of the lakes up north," she said. "We have to go far, man, far up north."

"For real. The farther north the better, as far as I'm concerned, believe me."

His heart turned right over and was in his words. With her lips near his ear she was talking about heading for the North Woods. He smiled deep inside. Could such a thing be? Talk about a dream ride. God's country and this fox. The smell of lost lakes hit him that special pang, a stand of white birch mirrored in black waters, the look of the ages in the big lustrous eyes and primeval spines of a walleye flopping in the bottom of the boat, dark brown beer bottles on the table and "Echo Lake Polka" or some crazy old tune ringing in the rafters of a cozy roadside joint. A deep embrace, a beer or a brandy, their bodies shivering together under the stars of the northern heavens. They'd get free.

"I'm your guide baby. The North Woods!"

"Hey," she groaned. "Ohhh, that name."

He heard the catch in her voice and when he looked at her he saw her staring away with tears in her eyes as if she could see all the way up there in her own special way. He loved it up there on a fishing trip, nothing better, but she was being carried away by the mere thought. He suddenly couldn't believe it or quite understand it either. He could see she was overcome by some dear dream of her own. He kept staring at her in the mirror so he almost forgot he was driving. And now she stared back into his eyes in the mirror.

"That name . . . so simple for so much."

"You like it up there, huh?"

"We useta go up summers before my dad died. I was only twelve, when he died. But I remember it like yesterday. I never been up there since. Always in the city."

"I know the trail."

"We went up in the fall the last time, I remember."

"Fall starts in August up there."

"The fall was so beautiful. The trees turning . . ."

"The girls churning." Just to keep it light.

"Churning?"

"Butter. The Dairy State!"

"What kinda mask am I wearing?" she mumbled to herself. "Every sonofabitch wants to stick it to me."

"No, no, I'm kidding. But I mean it!" He turned right around in the seat and stared into her eyes. "I can hardly believe all we have in common. I feel like we know each other down deep. I don't even know your name yet."

She paused before replying. "Rita," she whispered. "I'll call you 'Wisconsin.' You went by my address a ways back, Wisconsin."

They had entered the development with the Old West names. The streets were broad and the big houses well spaced. They were on White Stallion, apparently. He glanced around distractedly unable to recognize anything. He had hardly noticed when they'd swung into the lush lariats estates. He put it in reverse, the transmission whining. He never looked back, hitting forty, fifty going backward. Actually it was a piece of cake, because every house around here had a big circular drive in front of it to hold the owners' cars and there was practically nothing on the street.

"You can drive," she observed dryly. Her eyes glittered.

"You shoulda hollered. All the houses look the same."

"The moment hadn't quite arrived."

"Rita . . . how'll we meet again?"

"I'll call ya later—*tonight*. For our picnic. Right? What's your number? Yes, I will call you tonight, Wisconsin. I *will* call you. Will you be ready when I call?"

"I'll be ready. But, uh, well, I don't exactly, at the moment . . ." He wasn't about to let on he was living out of his cab right now and had no phone.

"I mean your cab number," she rejoined tactfully. "Your dispatcher will give ya a message, won't he?"

"Yeah, he will of course. Here's my card. Just call number 17, okay? Listen, Rita, I hope I get to earn that nickname."

"Ya wear the right mask, Wisconsin. Keep your radio on."

Discreetly, or cautiously, he hadn't pulled right in the drive. She didn't walk up the drive but took the shortest angle straight over the grass. He watched her step briskly across the lawn, even taking a running step, as if to emphasize to whoever was waiting for her that she'd been trying to get there. On the doorstep she fished in her purse, couldn't seem to find a key, then tried the door and it was open. Before she went in she turned and looked back at him for one moment. No expression on her face, just the limpid, masklike beauty. What a change in her demeanor from how the ride had started out. (And what about *his* demeanor?) She was just looking at him. Then she smiled so slightly. He leaned out the window and snapped her picture with the Polaroid. That made her go in and slam the door behind her.

The picture was developing. She'd formed some happy notion on the way over, he was sure, with him in the plan. He'd seen her

57

come to an intention in the mirror. Bliss faced with delay crossed with doubt. After another minute he stopped the car and peeled off the print. Behind him a car honked. He hadn't bothered to pull over. There was plenty of room on either side to go around. He barely glanced up as a white Mercedes hurtled past driven by a housewife in a white sunsuit. Her twisted, livid features contrasted cool Rita in the picture, who peered at him presciently and unreadably.

His mood swung upward studying the picture he'd just taken. Somehow a picture of anything creates a heightened and hopeful reality. It implies a bond. In some way they were the same kind, disabused, outsiders. One thing that he was sure he was right about—her life was no fun trip, no picnic. With this, his heart clouded over as fast as a midwestern sky with a storm blowing up. Everybody's life was no picnic, that didn't mean they were going to do anything about it, nor do it with him. As if the process of developing had gone on apace, she seemed to look back at him in the picture with the relief of one who's barely escaped danger.

He counseled himself, let it go. But philosophy was not up to its task, and his spirit stewed in the glitzy diamond valley heat. When he had first seen her in that Chicago yellow cab, he couldn't have imagined her seductive power. As usual, he'd broken his rule: Don't get involved with the fares! Especially a knockout one like Rita. Sometimes the world seemed full of beautiful devils, who swerved close to destroy his peace the way a stray spike mangles a tire. It was another ride. His heart was swinging wildly out of orbit. But hey, happiness was a catch-as-catch-can business, wasn't it? She might call. They had the North Woods between them.

Having once formed a conception of her as smalltime and sad back at Jackie's, despite the interlude in front of the Drake Hotel and then the Cardinal's Residence when his mind had labored to catch up, and then her reappearance masked in tailored pinstripes that had taken his breath away, and then the ride clear across Chicagoland, the cop was still having a hard time getting his earliest perception of her out of his head or at least into sync with unfolding events. Amazing how first impressions stuck. Finally, the redlight she had paid the guy to run, it was time to wise up. As of now, blown off at that light by a hick cab driver, what he had was to scout up an El Dorado painted flagrantly with red, white, and blue bull's-eyes on its doors, despite which it was going to be looking for a needle in a far exurban haystack. He couldn't chance leaning on the Bull's-eye cab dispatcher. Tipped off, cool number 17 might dig a hole, and there wasn't time.

The miragelike corporate towers on the horizon reflecting in their black windows green pines and yellow corn glittered like the redoubts of evil robber barons. Not his turf, he reflected dryly. Flying after Rita on the expressway it had excited him to be leaving familiar ground. He'd even managed somehow to maintain a knowing feeling of being in control, at least until that redlight, but now there was an undercurrent of having been lured out here, of being encircled by blankfaced alien powers. With Rita vanished into thin air, the entire metropolis, his whole morning, wore a mask.

God, but these suburbs ran together with far less rhyme or reason than the sprawling neighborhoods of the city, and he had to find his way through them to the tavern, poolroom, motel, or green glade where a wouldbe slick driver might hide after a move like that at that redlight. Plenty of tall grass in these parts. Had she thrown a C-note or something over the front seat at him to make that move? Cab drivers were notoriously greedy, but also lazy and stupid, why they were cab drivers. The cabby might just pull onto a cabstand and be bragging about it to his buddies.

The amount of roadside green meadowland rambling to the horizon, rank unchecked overgrowth between new settlements, lush cattails suggesting streams and swamps, bright acres of tall corn, bona fide working farmland with tractors and cows stuck in among condo developments, car dealers, shopping strips, and hightech spires disoriented him and added to his suckered feeling of being out in the Euroheartlands where they practiced rituals both too old and too new for a city boy such as himself. When he found that redlight running smartguy he would bring him down to earth and rattle his spine for him when he hit ground. Someplace in the crazy corn he was sneering at him right now.

For a half hour the cop cruised the winding roads randomly in the direction they had been headed. The cornstalks plastered to roadside made ornate walls of green taller than a man like driving through a tunnel. Everything must grow by leaps and bounds in a heatwave like Illinois had been suffering through this summer with soaking storms that brought no relief. His airconditioning always weak had run out altogether. He was on the list to get it fixed. The thunderstorms drenched the earth but did not cool things down. After the rains, it got hotter. The city was bad, but this was worse. His nose began to itch, and his eyes smarted. There was nothing to be seen except the liquid tar road and the man-high corn plants undulating in suffocating blasts like they were under water. The ovenlike heat heavy with pollen cut off his breath, and gave him a new perspective on how lost he was.

He turned back the way he'd come. At a shopping center he picked up a Chamber of Commerce map in one of those mega-drugcenters that sell you everything, even the maps gas stations no longer carry. Inside the acres of airconditioning he lingered. The air on his car was broken, compressor or something, and he was well down on the police mechanic's list. He had another week to wait for it to get fixed, and the fine way it felt in the coolness in the big drug store, he could wait right here the whole week.

Back in his hot green car, with the help of the map eventually he found his way back to the Hilton Hotel where all this had started and saw no cabs there. He waited a while in a corner of the parking lot but none showed. He headed for Depot Street, which didn't materialize as shown on the map. He unfolded the map again as he drove. The breeze caught the map making it billow up in his face like something malevolent and alive, and he smacked it down with a crack like a gunshot.

When he found Depot Street, there were no cabs at the train station either. It was deserted this time of day. He pulled up by an ancient wooden baggage wagon, not in its shade, because it didn't give off any, but in the refracted sunlight and patterns of shadow that poured past its tall frame and big rusty iron wheels. He tried to think, but mind was devoured by the midday light. He gazed through slitted eyes at the dusty station yard, the crude plank station building. It was an unimproved rural station except for a quaint new sign put up with a new generation of commuters in mind. In the distance a blackglass corporate tower was being circled again and again by hundreds of swooping birds, like persistent jobseekers, no bigger than tiny gray moths, disappearing into the azure sky like showers of ash.

The picturesque old baggage wagon with its primitive iron wheels loomed beside him with an indifferent sunbaked horror. Everything grim and unredeemed about the relic repelled him, as such artifacts usually did. If the hoops and canvas rotted off a pioneer wagon this might be left—or worse, it was the sort of rude old cart slaves must have had to ride around in unwillingly as so much baggage. Soon the up and coming whitefolks who were populating this rural stretch of track would build a modern station, one in which he might feel more comfortable too, if only to a degree. With their sense that history was "good" they might save the old wagon and spruce it up some as an antique. The idea that such a thing had charm to some people turned his stomach. For him history was not good, it was bad, even if his faith was that it was redeemable.

Over the station's metal rooftop, a few miles off, jutted up the black spire, creating winds that attracted the birds, near its peak a corporate hieroglyph of a luminous blue—not a funky neon sort of blue but a mild and living chemical blue as if the scientists had captured a piece of the sky itself and injected it into plastic tubing or that the tower was so tall the sky seemed to occupy a top floor. Weird, well, breathtaking, what the richfolks could hire the

61

scientists to do. A view across the tracks? He shuddered, suddenly lost, alone, a poor boy gaping. A paroxysm of wonder came over him why he had come out here. Things happened for secret reasons he had been taught in his Daddy's church and he was old enough to know it was true. Was he no more than his Dad had ever been, a watchman for these people?

He rubbed his forehead furiously with the heels of his hands to erase these sorry thoughts. Violently he pulled himself together out of his funky reverie and slipped the car into gear, sure he must have some idea where to go now. But he didn't. What was he self-indulgently thinking of anyway? What was he doing out here? What he was doing was tracking some people, something he was supposed to be good at, and he'd screwed up, that was the problem.

A Bull's-eye cab pulled in and drove past him. Not the one he was looking for. Some other one, a heap, more badly battered even than Rathmawakat's, and badly needing a wash, too. The cab driver made for the opposite corner of the station, where there was a shady nook under the eaves. Right above where the cab parked in the shade, on the station roof was the big new station sign in gilded lettering. GREENSHORES. The cop drove slowly over and pulled up next to the cab and after what he meant to be an impressive pause talked through the window to the cabby who glanced back at him through a pair of owlish tortoiseshell glasses, giving him an adamant, disapproving glare—at whoever was daring to disturb him. It gave the cop a shock and he stopped talking and stared back inquisitively. There was something wellbred and patrician in the cab driver's expression like a lawyer or schoolteacher into whose office he had butted without knocking. Plenty of cab drivers were really doing something else, or had been, or planned to be. Might be out of work, laidoff manager or something, this one, why he was driving a cab. Pay to be diplomatic.

"I beg your pardon! Excuse me for disturbing you, sir. You'll never get a fare in this place, in my opinion."

"I hope not. I intend to do some reading, as soon as you leave me alone."

"I'm sorry. I won't disturb ya a minute. I'm looking for an acquaintance of mine, cab number seventeen. You seen him around lately?"

"I'm not sure what you mean by lately but the answer is no."

"Real lately. The past hour."

"No, I haven't," said Armchair firmly, sticking a marker now in the book he'd opened and laying it on top of the dashboard. The way he did it, thought the cop, was remarkable, not like the guy was in a cab at all, the way a dignified and even important person would make a point of marking then laying his book down, in a library or a classroom maybe, so he could give you his undivided attention at the same time making you know you probably weren't worth it, the gesture so decorous, putting in the placemark, waving the book through the air deliberately aside. It put him in mind of something—nothing else than that mildewed old statue of the man with the book by Rita's place on Astor Street. That statue's name on its base was Greene Vardiman Black, remembered the cop. This train of thought reminded him he needed a drink. This cab driver was having a very odd effect on him, making everything even more unreal than it already was. It was ludicrous for a guy in a cab painted up like an archery target to act as if his studies had been interrupted, and he bit his lip to keep from grinning and blowing the interview completely. As soon as he got something out of him he would have a sip or two of Johnny Red, he promised himself.

"Where does he generally hang out? Seventeen. Where would I find him right now?"

"I would try the erotic movie at the edge of town. The town fathers or police may have finally closed it up for all I know, but if it still exists, I mean it did yesterday, maybe you'll find him there, in the airconditioning, watching the fuck flicks."

The cop chuckled, trying to make it sound appreciative of the fellow's droll sense of humor or whatever it was, while inwardly registering eccentricity he might still exploit somehow. "Where else would he be if not there? Where would he go for lunch?"

"Lunch? Where would he lunch? I really wouldn't know where he'd be lunching, truthfully. I've never lunched with the man, in that sense of, you know, where he would lunch. I think I've told you everything I possibly can now, in spite of your shitting me about being the Cadillac's friend."

"No, I aint shittin ya, guy, I see you really do know him too, his nickname Cadillac. I really got business with him, okay? I owe him money. Think, will you—"

63

"Don't insult my intelligence, officer. You're a black man and so initially have my sympathy, but I have to say you haven't done much to increase or justify it so far."

Sympathy? Officer? For a black man? He felt despair come over him in an itchy wave. He might have misjudged this screwball. He had an instinct he was talking to a wall. He threw the car into reverse. Time to get away from this funny guy before it got worse.

"Wait, *wait!*" Armchair with his whole arm waved him back in.

Reluctantly, against his better judgment which told him his depression was going to be total, that the next thing was going to be really and truly off the wall, he couldn't help himself but rolled back up next to him, unable to hold off an awkward grin.

"Hey, I'm sorry," said Armchair. "I shouldn't have said that. You think I'm a liberal turd. Right? Look, no offense, really.—Say, did you see any papers on the ground around here when you pulled in? No? Listen, I'd like to ask you something. What's your true opinion of affirmative action, as a successful police officer I mean?"

He knew he should have pulled out. And he was sitting there.

"No really, it's a question that concerns me a lot. Do you think the Republicans are right that welfare has destroyed the souls of millions of black people? Is there some truth to it? What's your view? Or are they just a bunch of racists?"

Something in him must be heading for the gloom with a will, speaking of destroying your soul. He had sensed this coming. Slowly, almost relaxed now that he had heard enough, he began to back out again. Strangely, he had suddenly regained complete control over himself. The guy's conversation had snapped him back into focus.

The "professor" jumped out of his cab with his hands out. He walked rapidly after him making genteel sort of calming or assuaging motions with his two hands, signaling him to stop. The cop watched him approach the way a dying man watches the vulture of his fate descend. Yet an idea took hold unaccountably that if he took it all, drained this encounter to the dregs, his luck might somehow turn around. He waited. The guy's buttondown light blue shirt, his preppy khaki pants, and penny loafers were wrinkled, soiled and worn.

"Say," said Armchair, "you don't have a spare can of oil do you by any chance?"

They looked at each other warily, cagily. It was a strange moment when each knew he might suddenly break into mad laughter. The cop drove slowly out of the station. On the other hand he was surprised to find he did not feel worse than before he'd pulled into the train station, but completely together somehow. Chafing at his acute apprehension of his lostness, in various places his skin seemed to have broken out in a rash. But his head was no longer spinning. His nose was clogged up and his eyelids smarted from all the pollen and things in the air. How did people breathe out here? Paradoxically he felt easier. It made him wonder whether he was getting ready to give up and go home. But no, he felt like was about to get a second wind. He was optimistic again for no reason, as if the interchange with the guy had invigorated him.

He wondered vaguely if he should try to locate the dirty movie outside of town. The cop, like others before him, had a moment of reprieve, a gift of grace, from Armchair. His mind wandered. He thought of the call he should make to his watch commander with some story. He must call his woman, and talk to her boy. By now, they all might have tried to reach him at Jackie's, where he was known to tarry. As soon as he saw a pay phone, if there was such a thing in all this vegetation and modern architecture, he'd stop and make the call.

He was hungry. He hadn't eaten anything all day but coffee and Johnny Walker. Last but not least, he had a full bladder. He spotted a Chinese joint. In the parking lot was a pay phone in a cubicle against a light pole, and despite his bladder, his impulse was to stick in some coins and make his call right away. But there was no receiver. The whole thing was ripped off, metal cord and all. The phone box was blackened, singed. It had been burnt out. Weird on this wellkept corner. They didn't have gangs out here in far north suburbia, or soulbreaking poverty, did they? Maybe they did. They needed phones for drug calls, maybe this was one the phone company had wired to take no incoming calls, so as to foil the drug pushers. They burnt up those out of spite. The Chinese joint and the destroyed pay phone made him feel somewhat at home.

There was another call he should have made this morning. There was a kid he'd gotten a job for recently, a gang kid he'd taken an interest in, been weaning away from the gang, the Black Stone Nation, and once a week at least he made sure to see him, and also

65

talk to his mother of course with whom he had begun a relationship. She hadn't called him this week, and he was several days late finding out why. He'd been meaning to get by to see her only he'd been somewhat out of spirits of late. He hadn't gotten by to rap with the kid. He'd been putting off this routine act of checking in on the kid which was really chief among his pleasures. Not just to see his old lady. This was a critical time, because it was essential the kid kept the job.

It was not hard to be saner than the gangs, yet the gangs drew the talent to them in the ghetto like electromagnets. Sanity was not in demand. You had to appeal to what was terribly faint in a 17-year-old, mostly nonexistent in all but the best, the moral indignation, for lack of a better way to describe it, in a child, the ability to think to the future, very weak in the boy, to imagine something that had to be called forth, the high and secret visions of the race which must be carried over to the new generation. This was the duty of the man to the child. It was a responsibility he cherished beyond even liking any particular kid. You had to strike a romantic chord. Otherwise the pay differential was too stark. If they stuck it out at MacDonald's for six months, and never missed a day, he would find them something better, that was his promise to them. Six months didn't seem so long, but it was an eternity for that kind of kid. Not missing a day, or he added a week for each day. Long enough to mean something to a kid. They still had their old friends to contend with. For the particular kid of the cop's thoughts this morning, that six months was almost up, and the cop was negotiating a job with a painting contractor who would pay the kid nine dollars an hour. MacDonald's was the trial by fire for the intelligent and sensitive ones. They came out welldone by the meat monotony, but they had shown they had the determination to put up with the worst that the real world threw your way, the funky mindless routine. Then the jump in pay could set their feet on the straight path. Not that it compared to what the gangs might pay.

The cop looked back over his shoulder at the firebombed phone booth, then ahead at the bright red door of the New China Doll restaurant and felt sharp regret that he had not talked to the boy. There was something so familiar about the kid which made him think, "But for the grace of God." There was high optimism in jeopardy as his own had nearly been at that age in spite of or because of his father. A worldly success the old man had not been, a night watchman at a factory. He'd communicated his opinions a lot. Now that the cop looked back on it, that had meant everything. The old man had always been there for him, bugging him, as he'd thought then. It hadn't been what he'd ever said but that he'd been always saying it. The kid on the cop's mind this morning had no father to bug him, to embarrass him, to give him a sense of what a man had to deal with. The kid who would soon learn the painting trade if he flipped hamburgers another month and a half had risen to a corner-managerial level in the dope business and had a coke habit that would fill a paint bucket when he was caught on the street making a sale. The kid's uncle had called a friend who knew Jackie, who knew the cop—who knew the assistant D.A. There was something fishy about the bust to the cop right away. Not that the kid had been set up but that he was too smart to be, and had been too successful at what he'd been doing to have gone down in that way on a street corner. So he viewed it as a call for help, from a child who half consciously knew life was bottoming out. It had proved a good working hypothesis. A vision of that prison cell, which the cop was most adept at instilling, an evocative gift he had from his hellpreaching father, had hit the boy's ready and sensitive soul like a different sort of snort up the nostrils.

He'd talked to the assistant D.A. he knew socially and arranged for the charges to be dropped if the kid kept a job for a year. The irony was that the cop and the D.A. had met across a line of coke at a party on the Near Southside. People like the cop, the assistant D.A., were worldly enough to suffer such ironies. Often the kids had such intelligence and imagination, it was easy to convey the hell of prison, but on the other hand difficult to point the way to a solid goal. The problem was to paint a convincingly attractive portrait of not the survival value (they weren't that interested in survival necessarily) but the transcendent possibilities in swimming in the mainstream, whose ethos and billboards and airwaves touted always the supreme virtue of *flying*, which had gone into making the cocaine habits of the kids in the first place. If they knew anything, the advertisers of America knew the kids, and black kids in particular, wanted to fly. That you had to walk before you could run, and that flying without a pilot's license was a sucker's game, was a hard argument to make with a kid whose imagination had been in the habit of roaming freely *everywhere* while his practical sense had been stunted and his intellectual habit of rejection encouraged by the racist residuum, the racist constant. It was nothing less than instilling race pride, which it was the cop's theory was in decline. What was needed was to speak of black aviators! He told them about the Tuskegee airmen. And, yes, there must have been moral giants among the slaves! He did his best to paint an epic picture whose premise (long ago slavery endured) was abhorrent and unrecognizable to a kid. He gave them an education. You never knew when one loaded with fool'sgold might have a mind to hear.

The kids were a responsibility which in a little superconscious part of himself he supposed came down to him from God, which he had always assumed was a part of his duty, if not the core of his job, which had elevated him, restored him, given his days their sure flavor, and the thought that he was letting his burden slip made him break out in a dank sweat in spite of the heat. He had always known because of what his Dad had told him how the salt could not, should not, be let to lose its savor. He really couldn't have said how he had let slip that which maintained and restored him.

One fact was for sure, at this hazy disappointing hour, he liked Chinese food. Also he was heading for the urinal with a purpose like the tides. He entered the typical threadbare redplush Chinese restaurant with a bar at the front and so many empty tables at lunchtime you wondered how they kept it going, secret of the Chinese. Same cynical looking smiling mama and courteous youngsters running the place and waiting on tables as in the city. He entered the redwalled hallway with faded watercolors of nature, mountains, valleys, bamboo groves, exotic birds, calendars from a Kung Fu academy, a tire warehouse. A door flung open and he had a glimpse of the kitchen. He appreciated the kitchens of Chinese restaurants, the old guys in there really cooking, lots of stainless steel pots, utensils flashing, lot of Chinese banter. One thing blacks and the Chinese had in common, they got down with some cooking. He had a faith in the kitchens of Chinese restaurants. It wasn't like a lot of places, you wondered what was really going on in there. You were just certain, they had this culinary culture, they were honestly cooking, trying to make a buck of course, cutting corners no doubt, but no dicking around, spitting in the food and that, like in lots of joints. His gladness at being in the usual

Chinese restaurant in the middle of this alien territory was sincere and overflowing.

In the hallway, on the way to the restroom, on the wall with the watercolors, was a pay phone. He marked it but didn't slow down. With the imminence of release, all the muscles were letting go, the floodgates collapsing. Ahead was the sign on the door—no lettering, just a little picture in that new universal stick figurism, as if everybody were either Spanish or illiterate. It was the little guy with two legs stretched apart but no thing hanging down! What if you were really illiterate. You'd look at that sign, see the little gingerbread man, with his arms outstretched, think to yourself, whatever this room is, it can't be the john, little guy aint got no thing! Ha ha ha! He started laughing so it was going to kill him. He just barely got there, and as it burned out of him, he wondered what in hell he was doing out here in a fortunecookie restaurant in the middle of the midwestern prairie on this wild goose chase anyway. It was uncanny and totally ridiculous. The futility of it came over him. As if emptying the bladder had left room for all of it. He glanced at his watch. Two hours! It was hard to believe that two hours had passed since he had lost them. The minutes were frozen together in a bad green flash. He couldn't just keep drifting around lost in this territory. Maybe it was time to admit defeat, head for home, and salvage some of his day, nobody the wiser. Except the Fist, who would hear from Rita. Never mind a halfslick cab driver.

He stood at the wash basin and threw cold water onto his face, grabbed for paper towels and rubbed dry. He squinted at himself in the chipped mirror through the greenish light, breathed the acrid waste disguising perfume of sanitary chemicals, and finally was moved by the disagreeableness of staying where he was to step out the door. For a second, relieved, he lacked all purpose. Now what? Well, eat, eat and drink, then think. Just outside in the hall was the telephone. The kid had taken a lot of razzing from his erstwhile friends over the idea of a job at MacDonald's. It was an act of raw courage and defiance every morning when the kid put on his little suit and packed off to MacDonald's the cop knew, and it was his job to keep him fired up, but he had let him down.

First he would call the stationhouse with a story. It was getting late. He stuck coins in the slot. He cast about in his mind for the story. Affixed to the casing of the phone box was a stained but barely legible Bull's-eye Cab Co. sticker with the number. Little printed semicircular slogans embedded in the red, white, and blue concentric circles of the target pierced by a feathered shaft promised ARROW FAST SERVICE!   24 HOURS!   CLEAN CABS! EXPERT DRIVERS!

After six rings, he got music. That wasn't bad enough, he got a commercial. They were playing a radio station. No cabs on the street that he had seen, except a dirty, sneaky bastard and a dirty, insane one (those were the EXPERTS!), and he could picture the dispatcher's office—same stonedout guy calling the cabs, answering the phone, bullshitting some sleepy chick from down the hall, cigarette butts everywhere, stirred his coffee with a ballpoint pen—

"Bull's-eye! where ya going?"

"Hello! I want to go to . . . Midway Airport!" That ought to be far away enough to get the dude's salivary glands going! Almost to Indiana. That ought to classify as a "good load"!

The dispatcher didn't seem impressed. "Name?"

"Teagarden."

"Very good, Mr. Teagarden, your address please?"

"Uh, I'm at a restaurant. The New China Doll on Northwest Highway in Greenshores. You know where I mean?"

"Are you ready now?"

"Wait! What's it run down there?"

"Seventy-dollar flatrate."

"Okay! I thought it would be more. Listen, I wanna ride in that Cadillac you got—you know which one I mean? Number seventeen, I'll wait for him."

"Hang on."

Actually this conversation with the cab guy had progressed with astonishing efficiency, and a trace of optimism reentered the cop's vision of his day, who cradled the receiver against his shoulder, lit a cigarette, and drew hard. But instantly he yanked the smoke away from his face and pressed the receiver to his ear. He could hear the radio transmissions. The guy hadn't put him on hold or anything.

"*Shut up Bull's-eye!* Give me some clear air. Stand by everybody. Seventeen? *Seventeen,* you read?"

A garble of voices came back in response, guys talking at once.

"Bull's-eye, stand-uh by-uh! You all deaf? How many seventeens we got in this company?"

"One-fifty-seven at Half-Day an Prairie"—"Sixty-nine wanna have breakfast with thirty-four?"—"Nobody's comin out! She says she called the cab for tomorrow"—"I don't see no forty-two-forty on"—"Hey Mike, I got a no-load—"

Crackle of voices nonstop. What animals, thought the cop, comparing this lack of protocol to the discipline of the police radio.

"I said stand by Bull's-eye! *Stand by!* Does anybody know the meaning of those words. *'Stand-uh by-uh?'* How about some radio courtesy? It's startin to get a little busy up here. I don't know why, considering who we got for drivers. Now! I'm gonna try again. Quiet, please! Seventeen? One-seven?"

"Shut up,you bastards!" muttered the cop under his breath. He listened intently, along with the dispatcher, to a moment of silence. The moment elongated, became precarious, and then broke, the cackle of voices started up again worse than ever.

"Shut up, thirty-four! Shut up, you guys! Seventeen, you read? Are you out there? This is the last time. Seventeen?"

"Answer, seventeen, punk!" cried the cop.

"Yeah, I hear ya, whadaya want?" The voice came in faint and breathless.

The cop jammed the receiver hard to his ear, and grabbed the top of his head with his cigarette hand as though he could suck in smoke there. The butt stuck out between his knuckles, bent and glowing red, almost catching his hair on fire. That would be the Cadillac all right, absorbed with his escape act with the girl, dug in someplace to hide, not hearing the call at first, more likely shrewdly wondering whether to answer at all.

"Is that you mumbling, Cadillac?" cried the dispatcher. "You got a powerful radio, but don't mumble please. You sound far away. Where are ya?"

"Why where?"

"Not why, *where?*"

"Havin chicken at an Uncle Remus on—"

"Spare me the gory details and just gimme a *location.* I got a guy askin for ya wants to go to *Midway!* What's your twenty?"

"Midway! No way, I'm on the Westside."

"Of the city?"

71

"No, of your . . . of course the Westside of the city. Forget it."

"Wait a minute! Stand by, seventeen. Stand by, Bull's-eye!"

Then at this crucial moment, the transmission went off, or the dispatcher must have realized he hadn't put Mr. Teagarden on hold, and the loud music came on again, overdistilled whitefolks' superheavy metal rock sounds, and then commercials for a used car lot and the local supermarket. The effect on the cop having to wait through these blasts was to throw him into a rage at the particular driver he was after. When he ever caught up with Cadillac number 17, he was going to kick the slick right out of him!

He flung his cigarette onto the floor, stamped on it twice, and banged the receiver against the wall, staring guiltily down the hallway in case mama had seen this. This was probably how the phone had gotten broken out front. Somebody had tried to call a cab.

The dispatcher came back on. "Listen, sir, he's too far away. I'll send you another car."

"No! I got all day! I want to ride in the Cadillac or nothin. My plane doesn't actually leave till tonight, see?"

"I see," said the dispatcher doubtfully as if he wished he didn't. "Okay, wait one more second then, please." Again he left the phone line connected and didn't even bother turning his face away so he was shouting at his drivers and into Mr. Teagarden's ear at once, but the cop was fascinated.

"Seventeen—"

"Thirty-four, hey there's no one at the Partridge Ridge address, there's no one home, you sure they want a cab today, a little kid says they wanted one last week."

"Thirty-four, do you hear me tryin to call seventeen? How many times ya gotta call me an tell me there's no one home. So there's no one home. Am I supposed to go over there an create a customer an take them to be home? I should find them an make them go home so they can leave again in your cab? Ya got a no-load, is that your problem? I'll see if I can get ya three no-loads! Ya got that? Your next three calls are gonna be no-loads, ya got that, thirty-four? Shut your mouth. You make no money! Got that thirty-four? *You make no money!* Thirty-four, ya got that? Answer me!"

"Ten-four," said thirty-four sullenly.

"Sixty-nine, ask thirty-four if he wants to have breakfast, sixty-nine," came a new blast from somewhere, innocent of all that had just transpired in the case of thirty-four, or indifferent to it.

"Oh Jesus God!" whispered the cop.

"Sixty-nine, didn't you just hear me talkin to thirty-four? Didn't you hear me tell him he makes no money? Sixty-nine, if you open your mouth once more, you take it home."

"Sixty-nine, just ask thirty-four—"

"Take it home, sixty-nine—"

"I'll come up there an kill ya."

"No, *you're* dead! You are 10Xed, sixty-nine, till tomorrow, I mean that."

There followed some general cowed silence, but the dispatcher didn't fill it.

"Hey!" said the cop after a while. The dispatcher seemed to have gotten up from his board and forgotten about everything. Anyway the phone had gone dead. The cop began to walk around the small arc allowed by the length of the cord. He reflected upon his wisdom having visited the men's room before placing this call, thank God. He saw mama peering at him from her cash register and motioning as if he held a glass, called, "Scotch! Scotch!"

After about a minute the dispatcher came back on and very mildly said, "Seventeen, *please,* do you read?"

"One-fifty-seven, did you give me ten-eleven Peahen Place or eleven-ten Peacock Circle?"

"One-fifty-seven take it home! You're 10Xed for the rest of my shift. You make no money. Go home."

"Go home? You go home! Just tell me, am I on Peahen—"

"Okay, one-fifty-seven, you never drive for me again. You're 10Xed for *the resta my life.* An I'm a young man. Oh great! Somebody's jammin my air now!"

"Oh my God, good Jesus!" muttered the cop in exquisite empathy but now he had a Scotch and could wait.

"Listen, Mr. Teagarden?"

"No, I'll wait! I want to ride in the Cadillac!"

"One second, I got clear air again. Seventeen?"

"I hear you, an I told you I'm too far away!"

All impatient hell broke loose again. The dispatcher over the din of queries and complaints from drivers all too like the pitiful pleas of inmates in Cook County jail through the bars to the cop's ears explained that number 17 with the Cadillac was simply too far away. "It could be an hour before he gets back in the territory. I can get ya a nice car—"

"I told you my flight isn't till eight o'clock tonight. I got all day to kill. I haven't even finished lunch yet. I haven't even ordered yet. An hour, even two hours will be fine. I want to ride in the Cadillac, okay? Nothing else will do. A business acquaintance told me it's your nicest car okay? For seventy bucks! I'm going to wait!"

"Just a minute," sighed the dispatcher in a terminally beleaguered tone.

"Seventeen, do you read?"

"Read an write."

"He's gonna wait, okay? What's your e.t.a.?"

"I don't believe it. It'll take me an hour. Did you read my twenty? He wants to go to Midway? I don't believe it. I can't get back there—"

"What are you mumbling, seventeen? You comin back or not? Party wants to ride in the Cadillac. Nothing else will do, they say! They'll wait. How long?"

"All right! Tell em half an hour!"

To Mr. Teagarden at the New China Doll, the dispatcher said, "He's on his way," and hung up.

The last thing the cab driver could have expected was a handwaver at the entrance of the Old West developments. Out here people called cabs on the phone or not at all. There weren't enough cabs around here for people to hope one would pass on the street just any time, not like the city.

But there one was, a black woman waving her hand, a maid probably, waving at him. Then she dropped her hand, as though she'd thought better of it. She turned her back. She was drunk. He could tell that at a glance. Her body was exhibiting that tendency to form an *S*, with bends at the knees and neck. But he stopped anyway. No sooner had he stopped, than she denied having waved at him.

"I aint got but five dollar!" she added cagily.

"Look here, I can take ya to the train station. These buses don't run at all in the middle part of the day. Ya can get a train in about an hour. I'll take ya over to the train station for nine dollars."

"*Nine!* Lord, *nine* dollar! Don't be talkin you cab driver game at me boy, cuz I'm onto it. I ain wave you down. I was swattin a fly."

"Yeah, you did. I saw you wave. You're gonna stand here on this corner all afternoon an die in this heat waitin for a bus."

"Thas what you say. But time I be gettin in your cab, here come that ol bus. I got all day, thank you! Thank the Lord. I ain in no hurry."

"What's the matter? How come you're goin home so early? Aint it a little early?"

"Don't ask! Go drive your cab please. Puh-lease, mister, go drive yo cab an leave me be. With my nine dollars! Hoo! Shee-it! I aint wave at you, boy. That damn train aint be runnin much this time a day neither. I can wait, goddamn it! I aint goin back to that bitch house no way no how no more anyhoo. I don care if she beg me! 'Mattie Lou, honey, I'm sorry. I didn' mean it, I don know what got into me! Everybody deserve a little drink now an then. It human nature! You the bes cleanin woman I ever had. I don trust them other ones. Them Polacks an Mesicans. Some of em steal, Mattie! All you did was take a *little drink!*'"

As if to illustrate just how clean her conscience was, she pulled out of her big handbag a fifth of gin that was about half full and had a slug. She ran it around her mouth one time and swallowed it down, giving a nod of satisfaction. She returned the bottle to her bag, and cupped her hand over her eyes to gaze up the street and see if the bus was coming.

"Listen, ma'am, where exactly are you tryin to get to, know what I mean? I saw you wave at me. No need to change your mind." He was leaning over talking to her out the passenger window.

"Well, I'll tell ya," she said, opening the rear door of the cab and falling heavily into the backseat. "Since we gonna have a discussion bout it, I may as well sit down. You seem to want to talk. But don't pull that meter. I jump outa here so fast! Woo, it hot! You like a drink, cab driver? I see you a right sort really. I like a good ol American white man driver. Mos a these cab drivers talk so funny, caint hardly speak English nohow. Say somethin to em plain as day, they be goin 'Huh? Huh? What you say?' Where they get all these funny peoples drivin cabs? What happen to the good ol American white man?"

The cab driver ignored this somewhat offensive question. "Listen, you goin down the Southside, that where ya goin?"

"Don fast talk me! Ha ha!"

"Really, I'll make ya a deal."

"Shee-it."

"I gotta go in the city anyway next hour is why," he lied.

"Yeah? I'm goin more west, more'n south, matter of fact. Westside."

"Okay, you know the fare from way out here, the meter gonna run sixty, seventy dollars to the Westside, at least, right?"

"Lemme outa here!" She struggled up on an elbow, and caught hold of the door and began hauling herself out to the street. *"Sixty!—who?"*

"Wait! I said the *meter!* What the meter reads. I aint gonna pull no *meter,* I already told ya that. Ya work in here with all the phony cowboy names for the streets? I'd be takin a few drinks myself. Ya wanna go home an put your feet up, right? I'm gonna take ya over the Westside for forty-five dollars flat rate, all inclusive, I mean, no tip. That's half price! Nobody gonna make that run in a hundred years for that price. How about it? I think we understand each other."

"No, we do not!" Hey, look in your mirror, see if that ol bus comin. I'm gonna get on up out a here." She groaned.

"Come on, Mattie. That's your name, aint it? That bus aint comin. You can be in your home sweet home in less than an hour. Have your feet up. Hell, put your feet up in the cab, if you want, relax, have a nice ride. Forty, an we're gone. Hell, thirty-five."

"You jus about a fool aint you boy, talk to a maid bout thirty-five dollars to get home! These bitches out here be payin twenty-five slave for em all day long, they aint give no carfare. Listen. Ten dollars take me home, no more."

"*Ten!* Jesus Christ." Just the mention of such a ridiculously and impossibly low figure depressed him acutely and he rubbed his head in pain. She might as well have said ten cents. He wanted a long, cleansing ride not to commit suicide and drive off a cliff.

"That aint even gas money, for God's sake, an you know it, that is an insult, a dead loss. I don't know how you can say such a thing!"

"Twelve. High as I go."

"Okay. Thirty-four." She didn't know it but he was practically sobbing to say thirty-four dollars, he'd be better off to go to the Pair a Dice and have a beer.

"Look here, fifteen bucks, that's all I got, you cab driver. Fifteen bucks! Good God on High. I don't have no more I tell you. I slave half a day for fifteen dollar!"

"I may as well lay down in the grass an sleep for less than thirty, an that's the truth."

"Well sleep then, I aint blame ya. I aint got no more. Is that bus comin yet? I tell ya what, I give ya fifty cent if I can set here inside in the shade till he come."

He wanted to ride. Rush hour was still a couple of hours away. He didn't want to sit on the cabstand thinking about Rita. He took a breath and cranked it up once more. "Okay. Mattie. I'm gonna take a ride. You can put your feet up an enjoy. Let's compromise, okay? We're right close to a deal. Come on now, you're really gonna have to get outa my car for less than thirty."

"Thirty, ho ho, oh me."

"Twenty-nine. I'll go for twenty-nine, but that's the rock bottom, now!"

At this she might have heard the catch in his voice and she knew that she had him and he had gone too far. "Thas the rock, eh?" She frowned. She gave his face a surreptitious squint. "Twenty-eight," she whispered in a tone like sealing her doom.

"Okay!" groaned the cab driver.

Mattie swung in her feet and hauled in her bag. "Home, James!"

He gunned the motor and hung a fast U turn barely glancing into traffic before either of them could have the chance to think further. He really was suicidal to take this trip for twenty-eight bucks, but then Mattie probably thought she was crazy, too, on her pay. Life was hard on people like them. He was going for gas money, maybe some lunch besides, but a guy like him had to keep moving, luck was always in the motion, and he couldn't sit on the stand any more. He took people where they needed to go, even if he had to figure it out for them, and make them see it and lead them there. The people knew where they were supposed to be, they could even express it, only sometimes they had to be helped and shown the way. It was almost a sacred function, this taking the people to their points A and B, as he had once tried to explain to Armchair, who had stared at him blankly. Anyway that was why he was riding with Mattie, and taking her home, it was his life.

It was good to be rolling. Just like that his spirit kicked into high gear. Even the billboards struck him as strange and colorful. One needed so little to be happy. So what if he was going for gas money and lunch money? Once you were rolling you never knew.

Mattie had dropped the bills over the seat straight off so there would be no misunderstanding later and gone to sleep. He forgot all about her. His cares washed away, his consciousness set in rapid motion in the light breeze. *Gas money plus lunch money.* But the air bathed his temples. It was in his lank blonde hair. It ran across his narrow body and washed away all traces of the grim morning. Hell, he liked driving, he did. Sometimes it was enough in and of itself, an answer in itself, enough. Maybe down in the city afterward he would "play" a little, as the drivers said, that is, pick up down there, illegally, until one took him back north a ways.

After a summer's driving, his was a striking example of a "cab driver's tan"—left arm and leftside of his face burned brown, rightside poolroom pale. His car, pushing through traffic with unhurried ease, the five miles an hour over the speed limit that got you there but ensured peace of mind, although it would go some, when he wanted to, with its big V-8, was an unusual cab, to say the least, and to his eye an unusually handsome one. He had searched far and wide for an old El Dorado with the elegant lines of years past but in good condition and had blown money making it perfect. The cab colors were festive as a Fourth of July skyrocket. The emblem on the door, meant to suggest promptness of service probably, not the literal treatment of the customer one hoped, was a series of concentric rings with an arrow through the bull's-eye.

He headed for the outskirts of town toward the nearest Tri-State Tollway access. The Tollway would take him partway to the Westside of the city. He would pick up the Kennedy at O'Hare, or if he cared to, he could keep going and enter the city on the Eisenhower, a longer route but more exhilarating, and since he was making this run with Mattie practically for free, and she had already paid, he could go any way he pleased, and take what was the scenic route for himself.

The road he was traveling was a page out of standardized and multifranchised 1989 USA, only recently imported into old Green Junction, minimalls and office furniture warehouses, car dealers and video rental stores, Checker gas stations, McDonald's and Popeye's, and new corporate complexes adorned with saplings that refused to take hold and really grow, but that must be an illusion, one day they would be tall and give the buildings an established look. All this along with a tractor dealer, seed stores, a last Dairy Queen and other touches of the past. Right off the highway were old country roads that plunged into a dizzy mixture of past and future, in the cornfields sudden hidden drives that led to nodes of high technology and finance, oil and loan and pharmaceuticals companies, and clusters of generic high-rise offices.

Like the other natives of these parts, the cab driver vaguely disapproved of the changes and improvements to the countryside. He remembered when he could have parked his car and gone fishing in a brook or plinked at a groundhog or wild turkey right out the car window and without a license and nobody would have noticed but you could get arrested now. That was but a scant ten years ago or so. Without thinking much about it he shared a general feeling against the loss of farmland and woodland along with more scrutiny by the law that progress had brought. On the other hand, he would have been quick to defend the newcomers had he been asked, since the cab business around here would have dried up without the daily influx of office workers who got here on the train and took cabs to the corporate towers. He had grown up here, but the new businesses were what had allowed him to return from the city, where he'd lived for a while. He approved of the new tall buildings and was persuaded of their magnificence since they put people in the backseat, although he wouldn't have wanted to work in one himself.

All the sights gleamed and came alive through his window, with their quality of being "just so," as he flew by, of being what they incredibly were, while as long as he was stuck on the cabpost and was part of the scenery himself, they oppressed him. It was being in motion brought out their special life and beauty—yes, beauty was the right word, the beauty of what simply is and no other. The trick he pulled off when he slowed or stopped to photograph something, as he'd used to do for his girl and him to look at over drinks, as their game had been, was to capture this common beauty before it relapsed into motionlessness and hid itself once more.

At the corner of his eye shimmered the black towers of a pharmaceuticals plant known to everyone as "the Labs," about which it was rumored they were sending out poisonous or radioactive dust into the air. The Labs made him uneasy and if he sometimes gave a customer a long ride around it, it was only to give the place a wide berth. He sped by and soon hurtled up the ramp onto the Tri-State Tollway. In the backseat, Mattie slept like a self-medicated baby. Once on the Tollway, which descended from Wisconsin, circuited Chicago, and wound into Indiana, the cab driver marveled at the wonder of the big road, multilaned, cosmic ribbon that almost persuaded you the earth was flat and vaster than you ever dreamed.

Suddenly Mattie sat straight up, blinking. In the mirror he watched her check out the plush red interior of the car as if seeing it for the first time.

"Hey, this a taxi? No wonder you so 'spensive, got this to keep up! Wooo, this a pretty taxi though, ride me home in style. . . . Well I'm goin home an take a *rest.*"

After that she could do no wrong. She propped her feet up on the seat and began to sing. What the hell, he dug the blues, and Mattie was really the blues. If her voice was raw and rough with drink, too loud, and wobbly, he made a point of getting a kick out of it. You got a kick out of things, or they got a kick out of you.

"*Bring it on home, baby,*
To me!

"Hey, ya don mind me singin, do ya cab driver? Have a drink! Thas the onliest thing I stole from that bitch, this here bottle, since she accused me already, hear?"

"You bought the ticket, enjoy the ride. No, I don't drink when I drive."

"I unnerstand. Hey, ya ever been to the funky Blue Ridge mountains?"

"No. I never been to that part a the country."

"Ya haven't? Oh my! Thas the mos prettiest part a this land I do believe! Where I was born, there. Oh, I'm so tired a this city—

> *Las night I dreamed*
> *My mama spoke to me.*
> *She was standin in the Blue Hills.*
> *Her head was wreathed in clover.*
> *She tol me, Mattie, say, well,*
> *You better get back—*
> *You better change your tune, honey,*
> *An come on home to the*
> *Funky Blue Ridge mountains."*

Just south beyond O'Hare Airport, a mighty bend in the freeway riding high into the blue heavens on webs of steel girders traversed great freightyards very tiny down below under the infinite sky, where sudden rising air currents were ridden by massive flocks of common swifts or starlings, wheeling awesomely, by the tens of thousands, above the square miles of the trainyards, a noble and breathtaking sight, both squads of diving birds and way below them the dozens of ranks of gray freightcars on the shining rails going off in straight lines into the prairie distance.

The rectitude of the yards, origin and enabler of a vast sustaining network of trade, reminding of man's remarkable practicality by which the long trains of cars would start their journeys of hundreds or thousands of miles from point A to point B and get there, always gave him a strange shock of mystery and promise. The sundering explosions of the birds, freesoaring and suddenly swooping like schools of fishes, made nature's lighthearted comment on this stark human endeavor, his own included. The whole contrast, silver rails and dark lumps of miniature freightcars far below like a child's scattered toys, the orchestration of birds rising up on the waves of air suggesting, beyond, unseen worlds to redeem this poor one, the precision and freedom, impulse and grace—such visionary moments afforded by the driving made it worth it. Add to it the soundtrack of soulful

Mattie in the backseat singing snatches of the blues in her ginrough tones and he felt drunk on the ordinary overflowing magnificence of it all—just this and no other.

Mattie didn't notice or care that he had taken the long way around on the Eisenhower, it was his gas, and she was nodding out, only to suddenly wake up and look out the window with a wonder of her own. Streetwise, she had paid upfront, and they had an understanding, just as there was an understanding among the African American citizens of the city and all cab drivers that the former did not tip, and thus had to stand around and wait a bit longer for a ride when they wanted one. Or maybe it was racism and fear. Life was a shameful standoff, a desperate game. And he didn't care if it was, for he had taken this ride for twenty-eight bucks.

Mattie lived somewhere in the area of Roosevelt and St. Louis on the Westside. Those were the last street signs he saw as she guided him dazedly into her territory, with a word, and pointing her finger, still singing in snatches, abstractedly. Her song which had been eerie and jarring had become poignant. He could tell she was thinking about rest and home now. He was halfway happy with the highroad blues himself. Sad or happy, who could tell any more, and did it matter? He was glad he'd given Mattie a ride, for gas money. It had made him forget his ex-girl friend, his futile hopes about Rita, his lack of a domicile, his wishes for a fishing boat, and his whole predicament in life, whatever it amounted to.

The street signs were ripped off in this area, or they were hidden by trees whose boughs flowed down and touched the earth like the folds of curtains. For blocks the streets were deep in shade, forested so unusually for the city. No city crews came in here to do any trimming, so much the better. The weeping willows were wild women whose hair had never been cut. The top of the occasional cottonwood shone white like the crown of a lonely patriarch. The little old weatherbeaten bungalows smiled solemnly under the thick green canopy.

For some reason it surprised him to see big trees like these down here in the ghetto. You couldn't pay money for such trees, you had to let them grow, as people in ritzy Greenshores knew well, whose recently planted saplings went silver in the sunshine and threw no shade at all. There were no lawns, no grass would

82

grow under such foliage, or nobody could afford a lawn on the Westside. Here and there, beyond the broken curbstones, the dark earth was neatly raked. It took a while for his eyes to get used to the wavery dim light in this glen.

On the uneven sidewalk in a green cleft, an entrepreneur had set up a refreshment stand. Children dashed here and there around it, women sat in chairs beside it fanning themselves. A mound of ice behind a glass pane gave off sparkling assurance that here was provided summer's relief, and for only a quarter—25 ₡ said a cardboard sign on top. On a packing crate tottered a tower of paper cups and gallon bottles of flavored syrup glimmered a submerged rainbow in the vague light filtering through chinks in the treeleaves, grape, lemon, cherry, root beer . . .

Mattie the maid had come home to be healed. Against all odds, the strongest idea that came to him was not of poverty and despair but of modesty and peace. In its way, the ghetto street seemed as secluded and removed from outside influences and invasive billboards as any rich Northshore neighborhood. Probably it was an outsider's privileged impression. Maybe every other dude, and the chicks too, were all winos and junkies. Anyway, it was home to Mattie.

Her house had frontstairs that went right straight up to the secondfloor nonstop. They just skipped the firstfloor altogether. It was the funniest looking little home. It looked like the old woman who lived in a shoe. Belonging more to the unknown past than a forlorn present—and more to dreams than to memory—having these qualities in common with many odd structures in old Chicago—Mattie's home seemed to give them a storybook welcome (in the straits she was in) in the moment before she alighted.

Mattie hesitated. There was a crowd of women and children on the street all staring at Mattie and the cab driver. Whatever they had been doing before the cab pulled up, the people in the street and around the refreshment stand stopped and stared. All of a sudden it was him and her against the street.

"Would ya mind givin me a hand, cab driver? I think I overdone it a little," whispered Mattie.

Having been caught in the act of a midday return by her neighbors she must have decided to grab his unlikely stage presence to help her sneak past. Was that what it was? Or was it

83

that unlikely as it might seem, in the transforming interlude of the cab ride, as sometimes strangely happened, they had become comrades?

"Look here, I think I'll have that drink you offered me."

"Oh yeah . . . oh, yes, surely."

She pawed around blindly in her bag and came up with the gin bottle which she handed to the cab driver. He held it a moment, looking at the people in the street, all of them gazing at the two of them in the cab. He tipped back the bottle and had a long slug of the gin, handed her back the bottle, and ran it around in his mouth and waited for it to have its mellowing effect. After a second the stark lines of the watchers softened and smoothed to normal, and whatever ambivalent or even hostile vibes they were giving out retreated into plain old curiosity.

He did his best to carry off his part and helped her all the way up the exceedingly tall set of stairs. Poor Mattie was damn near staggering and losing her balance and leaning on him heavily. It was hard to keep his eyes from the watchers'. They were blank with a dull sheen and had an attracting power like magnets. He felt he was in danger of being drawn out of himself into an uncharted melancholy zone by the looks they were giving him. The gin had worn off in a second. The empty sky itself might have been staring at him out of those expressionless eyes, the colorless, humorless, scorchedout, highsummer's sky. They mumbled their goodbyes and Mattie was finally home.

The crowd were looking up at him up there like he came from the moon. He was in the wrong neighborhood in Chicago was all, he reminded himself as he stepped back down. He was glad he had had that shot of gin from Mattie's bottle, otherwise he would have been paranoid to be here. But it had worn off already. He had the disturbing feeling of having strayed close to the limits of things. It put a dull ache in his heart. He did not delay his departure

A kid threw a rock at his cab and ran up the street. He was lucky it wasn't aimed at his head. "Po-lice!" the kid shouted indignantly over his shoulder. The cab colors were unfortunately very similar to those of Chicago squads, but awareness of this didn't soften the message. Heat waves shimmered off his car in all directions. The rock thunked against his fender and careened in the street. He didn't pause to inspect the damage.

He cruised around lost for a while in these lost streets on the bad Westside. For some reason he was in no particular hurry to find his way out again, as if he liked being at the far edge of things. Before he left the Westside, he got a little reward for his waywardness. Maybe only he would have thought of it as a reward and so it was his because he recognized it. He found a new street— new to him, an absolutely brand new street, near as old as the city itself probably, but one he'd never remotely heard of before. He had a hunch that plenty of people might have lived out their lives in Chicago, even cabbies, policemen, truck drivers, gridworkers like himself, and never heard of it.

He was somewhere in the thirty hundreds west about to pass through a low dank tunnel under what appeared to be an abandoned spar of the Chicago and Northwestern railroad. The shade in that hole had the layered stained look of a pass through the solid rock of the funky Blue Ridge mountains. Before driving through it, he looked up.

Governor's Parkway in rust-reddened letters. The sign pointed vaguely into the sky, a crooked cross against the sundazzled embankment of the railway. He hit the brakes and turned into a dirt lane, no more than a rut back of the tracks, Governor's Parkway. It was pretty rich all right, and as he headed down it, with one wheel running up the yellow bank and the other climbing in and out of pits, dodging boulders, going a safe speed of four miles an hour, he couldn't help laughing with pleasure. But he instantly shut up. It was too weirdly beautiful to be staring at the windpeeled shacks, with their little treasures of broken machines lying in the raked dust, their vegetable plots in one of which he surprised an old man on his hands and knees digging, who looked up at him with a face as round and craggy as a distant planet, with his right eye staring straight up heavenwards, and his left eye fixed on the intruder in wonderment.

He couldn't refrain from taking a few pictures, and he stopped long enough to do so and to look at his map. It was real all right, for a map makes things real, doesn't it? a tiny blue capillary in the immense circulatory system of the city. Governor's Parkway. The name was longer than the street. He felt like a diver who has found a pearl. To imagine the reason for its name, the obscure history of such a name for a farflung back street, to glance from map to unpaved reality, gave him a pure, clear thrill, no doubt childish, like a kid's stroking a precious little toy on Christmas morning. It was too intense to sustain. It threatened to become ridiculous, and so did he. He rolled out of the place, having intruded upon it four or five minutes.

The pictures lay incubating in their chemicalized shells. He touched them as he drove. In a few moments they would further confirm what he'd just seen, and redefine it. To whom could he show them? He would have liked to tell somebody about Governor's Parkway, a dirt road in the heart of the city perhaps ironically or historically named. He had a feeling Rita, whom he'd probably never see again, whose picture he'd recently taken lay on the seat with the others, would have been enchanted. His old girl friend would have lambasted him merrily, breaking into tears. He would have liked to pick up the microphone right now and tell the cab dispatcher he was on a street he had never heard of, make a bet with him that he hadn't heard of it. He could imagine the reaction. Bringing the dispatcher's attention to a little old street would pack all the charm of holding up a grain of sand for somebody's attention on a crowded Chicago beach.

Anyway he was discreet on the radio. He didn't jam the air with comments and questions like the other drivers did. He had his standing and reputation as a pro in the cab service. So he would not mention it to his friend the dispatcher. Chicago was populated by people who were just doing their jobs, who were very busy all the time doing them, who had healthy sober attitudes about life, who weren't about to lose their minds and get captivated by something sort of out of the way. Look here, check out this crazy grain of sand here! Yeah!

Once upon a time, not long ago, his ex-girlfriend would have enjoyed a story about a lost little dirt lane with a grandiose name and vegetable plots in the middle of a busy Chicago that didn't know or care. She would have smiled and marveled when he told her about it. But then all of a sudden she had grown up, as she had crudely put it. She'd told him he was like a little kid who collected bottlecaps, in whose eyes the bottlecaps with their endlessly varied colors and patterns had a genuine and important value. Driving his cab around he was like a kid who hadn't sufficiently grown up to be able to recognize that bottlecaps and photographs weren't money.

Well, enough of this! He ran his hands through his hair as if to clear his head of thoughts. It was about time to be getting back to business. He was capable of doing that, in his way. He should eat first. He stumbled onto West Madison Street and went east. He passed the United Center where the Chicago Bulls played basketball. Sociologically observed, this was one weird sports palace, where multimillion-dollar black athletes performed before middle-class white crowds surrounded on all sides by abject black poverty. At the same time this was the height of normality, nobody thought twice about it, it was the American way, the way of the world, and maybe of Nature, and it made him dizzier and tireder to even notice it. People were strange, as every cab driver knew. The accepted setup was weird, really. So was life. A driver had the time to see this and meditate on it—too much.

He badly needed that lunch he was going to buy with Mattie's cash. He was thirsty, he was hungry, his mind wandering aimlessly. He had to eat before going back to work, and if he headed toward the Loop he was sure before he got there to find a hotdog stand.

Then a memory of the last time he had been here on West Madison Street came to him, something comical though distasteful. Suburban cabs weren't supposed to pick up in the city, and there were enough undercover "taxi cops" on the street that it was somewhat risky to do so. There was an ordinance against it. Like all the drivers, he did it anyway, since you were down here. Once, a guy looked like Serpico with hair down to his waist and a diamond-studded crucifix in his earlobe had jumped out of a storefront and arrested him and he'd spent several hours in jail. Bond was only fifty bucks, and he'd had that on him, but that had cured him of "playing" in the city for a while. The essence of cab driving was to keep warm bodies in the backseat so it was very hard to resist the temptation to stop for a handwaver although you weren't licensed to do it. This time a lanky white dude with big glasses tottering on a West Madison Street corner had almost jumped in front of the cab, so he had let him in with misgivings, glancing in every mirror paranoidly as he did so. Immediately he regretted letting the white guy in. He wondered what he was doing down here anyway, on West Madison in the black neighborhood. He found out he had been so drunk the night before while bar hopping around here on the black side of town that he had forgotten where he parked his car, he said, and wanted the cab driver to drive around and help him look for it. Last night, he never had found it, he said.

This was one of those junk rides where the passenger seemed to get farther from his destination every minute. The money seemed tainted after all. But each time the cab driver urged him to give up or call a cop, the hillbilly thrust another bill at him over the seatback and before long he had handed him close to a hundred dollars, so round and round West Madison Street and the general territory they went, and it looked like it was turning out all right after all if only for the cab driver.

It almost seemed to amuse the guy to cruise around like this. The only thing was when they passed any black women on the street, the crazy dude would lean his head out the window, ogle them through his spectacles, and call loudly, *"Smoked bacon, yeah!"*

"Don't do that!" he had told him. "Don't do that again."

"Okay, okay, keep goin'!" And he handed over another tenspot. "It's got to be around here someplace."

So around and around they had gone, weaving through all the back streets around here and it was a wonder they didn't get shot because he wouldn't stop shouting.

"Smoke bacon, yaaaay!"

"If you say that once more, I'll put you out!"

"Okay, okay."

They passed a luridly handpainted storefront church in whose doorway some church ladies were lingering, sweeping the stoop and socializing.

"Smoke bacon, yay!"

That did it. He stopped the car, opened the door, and pulled the guy out by one of his long arms, and sent him reeling toward the church door.

"Pray for this asshole!" He ran up to the women, gave them some of his money, and took off leaving the guy squinting at the women in front of the church.

The cab driver pushed down this unsavory memory into forgetfulness again along with any others and dwelt on his hunger and how to sate it. He had to get something to eat soon or he would begin to lose consciousness. He was starving.

There were enough juicedup winos and junkies on West Madison, if they gave out light, the place would be floodlit all hours. A bunch of undercover cops crossed right in front of him and he had to slow down to let them pass. There were five or six of them, all white, a tactical team, wearing baseball caps backward, white T-shirts, one of them had on Bermuda shorts. They were some hit squad heading for a desolate building across the way—on what mission of terror? The winos leaning on the window ledges watched the bulls come without looking at them. They were like guys on a fence, ready to jump off and run from the animal.

On a corner he spotted just what he was looking for—a chicken shack. He was halfway out of the cab and going for it when he registered the name of the place, Uncle Remus Chicken House. The social or literary implications of that name made him crouch by his cab a moment, and then actually sit back down behind the wheel. He had passed an Uncle Remus chicken shack before down here but not when he was hungry so had not had to reflect on it. He had a hard time imagining that in this day and age Uncle Remus could be a cultural icon among African Americans, enough so that somebody would name a chicken shack after him, and that black people would be streaming in and out of the place as they were presently.

The signage Uncle Remus Chicken House was quite aged and well-worn. So the past met the present thoughtlessly and quixotically, it seemed. The Uncle Remus figure looked faded, and perhaps there had been such a day when such had been the norm and the institution had lingered. Or had this area once been white, a white (people, not meat) chicken shack? Neighborhoods changed and with it came weird inheritances. The mysteries and depths of American culture and history absorbed him momentarily.

He had the irrational feeling that somebody would physically bar his way inside a place called "Uncle Remus Chicken House," that whites would not be wanted, though whites had always probably been the main fans of Uncle Remus, but perhaps to think so was merely a race-centric shortcoming of his own. No, surely that had not always been true, before somebody or other had written down the old tales. At one time they had been African folktales. Nowadays admiration or even approbation might be resented, though. He really didn't know.

Still he had only the happiest associations with Uncle Remus, personally. The backstreet chicken shack tribute jogged a warm childhood memory of an old codger who told stories about cagey animal creatures who lived close to the ground outwitting the more powerful. He related to that. It reminded him of his pleasant school library in grade school where they had books like that you never saw anymore when you grew up, the books that were true to the life you now led.

If he might have had a vague and perhaps mistaken idea that black people might object to Uncle Remus in some way, that was obviously in the presence of the overwhelming evidence of the busy chicken shack in front of his eyes just another white person's misconception in the face of a richer reality. Then he thought, what it was, if they had a problem, it was only with white people *fucking with* Uncle Remus. Puzzling it out in this way, he felt again his hunger, was released from paralysis, and went inside.

He took the chicken "to go" only because he always ate in his cab. A cab driver always likes to stay close to his radio. Should an order come over the radio now in the Loop, say, from some Greenshoresite far from home who didn't trust Chicago cabbies, it would save his day. It would make up for the financial soaking he had taken from Mattie, which had put him way behind. But he was never hoping for such a thing, the odds were way against it. Still, miracles did happen. Professionally, you played the chance.

So he was sitting behind the wheel slurping chicken and biscuits when the dispatcher called his number, and he heard it. It wasn't bad chicken, but nothing special considering it was genuine Uncle Remus's. He heard the dispatcher calling his number, but his fingers were so greasy he hated to pick up the mike. He knew he wasn't going to be lucky enough to get a call down here and for that matter the dispatcher had no idea where he was. He would think he was in Greenshores. Somebody asking for him back home probably.

So he didn't care if he answered the dispatcher or not, and frankly preferred not to answer and be bothered by the dispatcher while he was eating fried chicken. Whatever business it was, it was not going to be favorable for him, since he was way down here on West Madison Street and not in the territory. Had it been a call like "Anybody near the Loop?" he would have grabbed the mike like it was a hundred dollar bill greasy fingers or not.

He even thought maybe he was just hearing things, at first. His radio was a powerful top-of-the-line Motorola, and the signal came in loud and clear. Dispatcher kept asking him to answer. He just didn't feel like answering, although it was tying up cab business because the dispatcher kept calling him for some reason. By now he should have decided number seventeen was not on the air.

He was deep into his fried chicken and let the increasingly testy and annoyed dispatcher call him several times. The other guys out there with problems of their own interrupted him and the dispatcher began yelling at them, and it was causing havoc on the airwaves. It started to be funny to the cab driver and he sat there and enjoyed it. What could be so important? People got so worked up about nothing, about business, they called it. The drivers with their little problems were chiming in oblivious. He heartily enjoyed hearing the dispatcher calling and calling him, and the other guys trying to butt in. As usual it sounded like they were all going to kill each other, but later they'd have a beer together after work.

It was all greed as usual. Then it occurred to him it might be a message from Rita and he hastily wiped off his hands on the bag the chicken came in and grabbed the mike.

When he finally picked up the mike and keyed it to respond, he noticed that the radio's red transmission bulb was still burned out—naturally, since he'd never replaced it. It had been burned out for weeks. The green receiving light went off when he keyed up the mike, but the red one didn't come on. He had been too lazy to replace it. It bothered him every time he transmitted. He liked things to be right. But he'd had a lot on his mind lately.

It wasn't Rita calling. He couldn't believe what the dispatcher was trying to tell him. What he had for him was the opposite of his vague hopes for a ride back from the Loop to the territory. It really was one of those wrong place, wrong time situations. Somebody up in Greenshores wanted to go to Midway Airport on the Southside and had requested "the Cadillac." Of all the damn things to hear. It would have been a wonderful ride but he was already in the city, too far away to take it. He had given Mattie this cutrate deal for twenty-eight dollars and the caller would have paid him the flatrate of seventy dollars to Midway plus a nice tip, let's call it eighty bucks, maybe more. Incredibly, the dispatcher said the customer would wait. That didn't sound right. By the time he raced back, it would be a no-load. In the first place, nobody went to Midway Airport from the far Northwest suburbs. That made no sense right there. You'd go by O'Hare getting there. Then wait an hour for a cab first? But the dispatcher wouldn't lie to him, although without saying so the dispatcher obviously read a no-load, too.

Could it just maybe, possibly, be Rita, hiding her identity? A chill of hope touched the cab driver but he disbelieved it. Why would she have said Midway Airport? No, she wouldn't have dreamed that up, or bothered with it, would she? He sorely wished it would be Rita but he couldn't kid himself. He glanced down at her photo on the seat beside him. He noticed that he hadn't eaten his potato salad.

Somebody wanted to ride in the Cadillac that was all. That was understandable! People did like riding in it. Perhaps this touched his vanity in just the right way for he suddenly went for it. Yes, they might just wait for the Cadillac. They did wait often enough, if not an hour. His was the prettiest car in all the Bull's-eye fleet. People especially liked to ride in it. He had had business cards printed up advertising it, which he'd given out to passengers and placed in restaurants. Of course his charming personality had something to do with it! He gave himself a grin in the mirror and wiped his hands again on the paper bag (these places never gave out napkins voluntarily, you had to hunt them up, and he hadn't seen any), and then on his pantsleg. Maybe it was an old customer who had called for the Cadillac, in which case they'd wait.

Just before he turned the wheel and headed for the Kennedy to blaze back to Greenshores, a kid standing in front of the chicken shack threw a bottle at him and took off running. The bottle missed his head and hit his car. That made two chips out of his pretty fenders. It felt worse than if it had been his shins. "Po-lice!" yelled the kid. To the kid, he was the cops.

The cop ordered lunch on the basis of speed. First, a Johnny Walker on the rocks. A shrimp kow, he was told, would take only ten minutes (as would everything else probably).

The guy wasn't on any Westside. He was right nearby, maybe the next block, the next street. Was he going to show? If not, why tell the dispatcher he would? Cab drivers would lie any time as soon as not. Just out of habit. They were all "independent" and shiftless. He would get his ass chewed out later, if he, Mr. Teagarden, called back and complained.

He'd been told he had an hour to wait. He drained the scotch. The shrimp kow came. The cabby would lose the benefit of whatever fat tip Rita had laid on him if out of fear he didn't take any other orders for the rest of the day, or even for a few hours, or if he blew off this order, a good ride clear to Midway Airport.

There were two types of cabbies in this situation. If he was the greedy type, he just might show, if he was greedy enough. This was likely. Or he could be the type that got a good load and took a vacation afterward. The lazy type. Depended on which type he was the more, greedy or lazy. It would be one or the other.

Suspecting who was calling, he'd probably agreed to come just to stall him. He'd take the heat from his dispatcher. Eating chicken at an Uncle Remus, the punk had said. The cop misswallowed a water chestnut, had a coughing fit, poured some tea. Yeah, on the Westside—a thumb in your eye, nigger!

So he wasn't going to show—but he bolted down his meal anyway. Never underestimate minor-league greed, it could get people to do more than you would ever believe. The punk had said

93

half an hour, or the dispatcher had said that, he couldn't remember. No, the dispatcher had been more realistic. He arose anyway, feeling desperate again, but replete and refreshed, applied his napkin a last time and dropped same. Bowed slightly to mama his hostess after paying. She grinned cautiously at this, two well-meant masks. He liked her food. Who he was, she didn't know. He was almost sorry to leave the Chinese restaurant whose customary appointments had given him a sense of the familiar and a moment of respite.

Light on his feet in spite of the full meal, the admixture of raging adrenaline and Johnny Walker Red seeing to that, reading his blood chemistry, he realized he was expecting the guy. He *needed* the guy to show. What a crack to have been put in, by a cab driver, when he was as good at shadowing people as the basketball guard he once had been. He felt like he had been fouled and the punk had gotten away with it. He'd make the sucker's teeth chatter.

In his car he studied the blue veins of the map. He studied the map because it was the only information available. He gazed at it hungrily trying to drink in its secrets. The cab driver, if he showed up, would be an expert in these streets. It wasn't like Chicago, where you could say how many hundreds west, or south, and know everything, regardless of the street names. The roads on the map of Greenshores crossed each other at random and twisted around all over the place. Once they must have been cow paths, farm roads, if by now some of them were highways. Still, there was a county trunk that ran pretty straight and seemed the basis of the east-west coordinates. In fact, there was a vague hint of a modern grid. Apparently the numbers increased to the east and south, as the town had been growing in that direction since being hit by the northern and western rush of the city.

He concentrated on the region beyond the general spot where, as near as he could tell, he'd lost them at that light. At the far southeastern end of town in the direction they'd been headed was a circular development that had to be new and rich, all the streets with preposterous names like Avenue of the Eagle Feather, Avenue of the Indian Maiden, Avenue of the Prairie Seas.

He could picture a semi-elegant subdivision, with a lot of phony names like that. Out here, where the developers were carving out new suburbs, new probably had to equal upscale, particularly when they bothered to dream up such street names. Dressed as she had been when last spied, definitely she was heading for the money. Or she could be with some fast players way up in one of the intimidating corporate high-rises that did not show up on the map, but towered over the green countryside, who knew which one? The cab driver would know.

The El Dorado, number 17, with the big archery target on the side, came up unexpectedly, from the wrong direction, the back of the parking lot. The car had barely lurched to a stop before the cab driver bounded out with the pentup emotion of the chase clear across Chicagoland, something telling him it was completely nuts, a certain no-load, that he wanted to get behind him as soon as possible, if that was the case. Yet he was hopeful.

Disguising his peaking anticipation, fending off the expected disappointment with a wise cool smile, the cab driver strolled toward the front door of the New China Doll with exaggerated nonchalance. Just business, he told himself, it didn't matter in the big picture (*greed,* as he liked to say). On the other hand, he'd gotten back so fast, if the call had been for real, there was a fighting chance the party would still be in there. (Was he secretly hoping that it might be Rita?)

In front of the hotel earlier when he had watched her switch cabs, the cop had gotten a glimpse of a mop of blond hair on a stringbean body. As the guy sauntered up and casually flung open the door of the New China Doll, he checked out his closeup arrogant good looks. Yes, a smart guy he made him, a halftough punk, with a cool smirk on his face like he was above everything since he was a cab driver and didn't give a shit, just the type to pull off that redlight stunt without thinking twice. With Rita's C-note or whatever it was in his pocket, now he was going in to look for his nice ride to Midway Airport like it was his just deserts for being the cool punk he thought he was. Sucker must think it was his day.

As soon as he disappeared through the New China Doll front door, the cop got out of his car and walked over to the cab. He restrained himself from planting his foot in the bull's-eye. He climbed into the back seat and made himself comfortable, easy to do, the interior wildly luxurious, punk liked to ride in style, sort of dimpled supervelour, soft as your sofa, in a shade one purple tone louder than screaming fire engine red. He slouched down as far as he could in the corner so he could give the guy a good scare when he came out and got in.

After making his fruitless inquiries of the proprietress by her cash register, who glared at him askance, scolding, "No cab! No cab!" peering into all the dim corners, and even making a trip to the men's room and calling "Cab! Taxi?" in case his fare could be in there, the cab driver trudged dejectedly back out the front door. Well, so be it. Going out, his eye took in the glittering liquor bottles behind the small circular bar in the corner, where no one sat, and he told himself too early, too early. But holy God, after such a disappointing mad chase home, he could use a drink. He'd raced back clear across the city for a no-load, what else was new. But no, he wouldn't. He walked out. Anyway, he was back in the territory and the afternoon rush had to be starting up soon. But instantly his expression lightened. So familiar was he with his car, he saw right away that it was sitting down that inch on its springs that proved he had somebody in the backseat. His fare!

Elated beyond measure, behind the wheel, with the help of the mirror, located the guy slumped comfortably in the corner. He approved of his posture, ready to roll, kicked back for a nice long ride. This was the one who had called and he had actually waited. Miracles did happen. It was a black guy, so that explained everything. Whatever was anomalous in the situation was given added incongruousness by the load being a black guy up here on the purewhite far Northside that pushed everything into the zone of the completely improbable making him comfortable with it as an explainable outlier. It made complete sense that a black guy would go to Midway from up here, for he would be as much a foreigner as those Japanese businessmen the Armchair had carted off to the Loop and wouldn't know better. He would pay too much to get to the wrong airport but after that he would not tip, or if he did, maybe being a professional of some kind, the bare minimum, the exact proper tip. He turned his head and smiled cordially at him.

He adjusted his attitude to being extra nice, which was the only way to handle African American fares, since they took the position that every cab driver always cheated them outright. Naturally they didn't tip after that, who would? It was just a matter of being pleasant and mellow, without limit, since their conviction that they were being stolen from in plain sight was unassailable, because of slavery. You had a lot to prove. He understood all that. He didn't mind a bit, and even approved of it. It was life.

All in all the cab driver was proud of his store of such cultural knowledge, confident in the tools of his trade, and sure of himself. At any rate, he liked jazz and blues. In terms of music, like most white Americans, he was quite black himself. He was well disposed. The grin of greeting the cab driver was giving into the mirror was natural and broad and as far as it went sincere.

In the backseat the cop braced himself suspiciously at this, in case any kind of baloney soulbrotherly business was about to come sailing his way, as no doubt from such a one as this it might. He had no illusion about the larcenous ill feeling a punk like this would have for him. Were he going to take the ride, he'd be talking brotherly jive to him while he turned on the extra fast meter.

It was just crazy enough to be all too real. Every job had its little mysticalities. Types of cab fares came in peculiar bunches sometimes. Say one morning he'd have two pregnant women in a row and then not again for six months. Or maybe twice in one year he'd make a delivery run from O'Hare of some part needed at the nuclear power plant in Joliet and both those times would be within a few days of each other. It happened that way.

So today was his day for black loads out of all-white Greenshores. Long rides too, the kind blacks, who knew how to hug a dollar, did not ever take. First Mattie the maid to the Westside, and now this man to Midway. It made sense, in this way, in the sense that it made no sense whatsoever. Nobody went to Midway Airport from Greenshores. You had to go right by O'Hare Airport on your way to Midway. Whatever you saved on the airfare you'd lose on the cabfare. But it was the day for it. Travelers and out-of-towners did strange things, either out of ignorance or because for some reason they had to. A black guy would easily qualify, definitely an out-of-towner around here. Probably there was an overwhelming reason, an unavoidable circumstance the cause of it. In any case, to the cab driver, his fare at this moment was a prince of a fellow. He had waited for him, hadn't he?

He waited for him to tell him where he was going, Midway. He didn't presume to know for sure until the passenger told him. Usually the dispatcher did not mention a destination, although this case was different. He glanced at his fare back there ensconced in the corner and approved of him. Hey, make yourself comfortable! It was not up to him to tell him the lay of the land or give him advice, which would be first resented, and then never believed, but if you had to get to the Southside from up here and you had the time there were better ways to do it than jumping in a Greenshores cab for the whole trip. His job was to take him where he wished to go. Any advice would just make him suspicious, which blacks were on principle with cab drivers. They had their guard up even if they asked you the time. Advice would be scrutinized for that angle. He had the feeling he was being studied from behind.

The whole way he would act as if riding to Midway (almost in Indiana) from Greenshores (almost in Wisconsin) was the most ordinary thing in the world and completely sensible. However he was giving him no break on the fare no matter what heartbreaking story he told, and blacks could come up with some wrenching tales, if they did decide to talk to you. He was short of sympathy after Mattie, who had used up the day's whole supply. Not only was it possible to lose the tip, but to get the price of the ride pared down too, if you got too chummy. He smiled in the mirror professionally.

Maybe seventy bucks was nothing to this guy because he was on an expense account, which his suit suggested was the case. Seventy bucks from up here was a good rate actually for the customer. Even though he was on an expense account there would be no tip no matter how friendly they got on the way there. In fact the less likely the tip the more friendly they might become, he knew from experience, by some logic he did not understand. Except that blacks were the only people in Chicago, except of course the wonderful Spanish, God love their Latin selves, who did not strictly view every cab driver as categorically beneath them. So he loved them, even without a tip. Actually the Spanish tipped handsomely, respecting cab drivers. African Americans respected them rather as thieves are respected, at least watched carefully.

Finally, as the fare was silent, he said brightly, "You called, huh? Goin to Midway, right?" There was no reply.

The guy was wearing a suit, thank heavens. No tie, but he looked a well-heeled sort and worked for one of the corporations, the Labs or one of the data gathering companies. That was good. Anyway Mattie's was the last break he was giving anybody today, black, white, yellow, or green. The guy was observing him, it

seemed, or maybe waiting for an associate? Jesus, he wanted this
ride though, having raced clear across the city for it.

"Midway, right, sir?" he tried again, enthusiastically.

Eager and breathless, but no longer out of fear his load would
be stolen before he could get back, doing eighty all the way, peering
fearfully around overpasses for cops, now he was breathless and
flush with success and couldn't help grinning with goodwill to all in
the backseat.

"No, asshole, I aint goin to Midway," said the cop, at last.

"Oh. . . . You're not?"

"No, I'm not!"

"Where *are* ya going?" Disappointment gaped.

"Don't play dumb with me, farmboy! Where ya take her?"

"Who? Mattie?" he gulped, putting two and two together. She
had been his last ride, she was still on his mind, and this guy was
black too. As soon as he said it, he regretted it.

"Mattie! Mattie?" said the cop. "Your *mama!*"

His mama! He supposed it made him a racist to have put two
and two together like that, but who was he talking about anyway if
not Mattie? and what would he want to know about her? The back
of the cab driver's head now received an annoying push forward
from the guy's hand the way some unwanted object might be
shoved off a tabletop in a pique, only it was attached to his neck
which registered some minor whiplash. This was very unpleasant
with the best will in the world and actually unbelievable to have his
head pushed by a fare, if he thought about it.

The descending elevator of his disappointment went down a
couple more floors and stopped with a thud. He gave one more
glance in the mirror at his ostensible fare and then just gazed
gloomily ahead over the steering wheel and waited, not replying.
Whoa, farmboy, dumb! This didn't fit into any category except that
broad one for all junk rides and insane occurrences, a wide enough
category, worse than no-loads. People freaked out in the cab,
sometimes, not infrequently, if that was it. Sat in the back and
talked to their phantoms. Decided you were the right audience for,
if not entirely the cause of, all their tale of woe, went into
paroxysms of violent muttering and pounding on the seatback in
their protest at the world. Happened constantly, no problem, but
usually you didn't have to drive home from the Westside at 80

miles an hour to enjoy the experience instead of going to Midway. He had an eighteen-inch piece of angle iron under the seat by his feet if it came to that, which it never did. Patience was always the answer. Sometimes he reasoned softly to desperate people who asked questions of him about the meaning of life.

Such things happened often enough. Just the other day a self-proclaimed Vietnam vet (as if that explained everything) had opened the backdoor and threatened to jump out while they were doing 45 miles an hour on Milwaukee Boulevard, even stuck his legs out and dragged his boot heels on the pavement. There had been no reason stated for this, or why it was the cab rather than a tall building he was going to jump from. It was just something insane and desperate to do for the sheer perverse joy of it for such guys. He didn't pay him any attention and didn't slow down until they hit a redlight and then he had pulled over and parked. The guy's feet were bouncing up in the air as his heels struck bumps in the pavement and he was yelling incoherently. After he parked he just sat there while the guy stuck his feet out of the now parked car. His way of handling these fares was to sit there and remain calm and let them do their thing. Then when they had got it out of their system, he would wait some more.

So he stared through the windshield and waited for this one to play out, as the crazies always did eventually. Cops thought they saw the worst side of humanity, but he wasn't ready to concede that. Cab drivers were treated to many displays of hysterical, violent, self-indulgent, and destructive behavior, also from cops. Could this guy be a *cop* by any chance? Asking him questions.

It sounded like it. Had he been following him? He could hardly have seen him speeding home on the Tollway, could he? No, it had to be Mattie. Sighing, he gazed through the windshield waiting patiently for the bad news whatever exactly it would be.

"Hey look, wise guy! *Where ya drop her?*"

The cab driver felt himself nudged hard at the base of the neck, and turned apprehensively. Something sinister and silvery gleamed at him as if from underwater, maybe a knife. He turned his head sharply and shot a hard look—no, there it was, the badge, Chicago star. Shit, he knew it, should have seen it coming, Mattie the maid, had to be. Detective must not even know her name. What had she actually done to get fired this morning? They'd found him fast enough. Now he was going to have to be a rat and tell a cop where she lived. But he wasn't going to do it. This cop sure had a nice, engaging way about him. He had thought he was a black guy—but he wasn't a black guy at all—he was a fucking *cop*, of all the damn things. Nothing like a brush with the law to make your day. What had she had in that purse besides that gin bottle? "Did she steal something valuable, officer?"

"Steal somethin! Yeah, bout half my day. You want the rest? Hey, I'm gonna tow your pretty car. Tow guy's gonna drop it six times on the railroad tracks. Get it? Guy's greasy mechanic overalls, roll aroun good on these nice clean purple seat cushions."

His *car?* What *for?* "Don't even talk about my *car*, man! Don't even have a second thought about my *car!* Okay, mister?"

The threat to his car freaked him out. Dropping his car on the railroad tracks? What a thing to say! Of all the—! Things had proceeded to the exact dangerous edge, when somebody started talking about damaging his car. With the crazy loads it came to that sometimes, when they were going to beat his car with chains and whatnot if he didn't solve the riddle of life for them.

It was just like a cop to sense somebody's weakspot and know how to threaten him with it. Plus since he was white, and the cop was black, he had a world of problems to unload on him. White guy to blame for whatever was bothering him this morning, most especially a cab driver. Cops always knew how to pick on a cab driver, they were the cause of all their problems, since they were vulnerable to the law in every respect, being common-carrier vehicles on the road and also socially and classwise totally beneath them. You weren't driving a cab if you had any pull in this world. Black cop and a white hack and it was obviously a world of trouble from all directions. What did he want out of him really? He wanted Mattie but he didn't even seem to know her name. Oh, old Mattie! What could he ever tell him about Mattie, poor thing, who was really the blues.

The cop laughed softly to himself—smugly and ugly to the cab driver's ear. It tickled the cop to have gotten a rise out of him, as he knew he would. One glance at this ridiculously trickedout taxicab and you had the guy's whole story in a nutshell to say nothing of where you had his nuts. Such stonewalling from an impudent punk was amusing in itself. He laughed long and low.

101

"What she give ya to run that redlight, buster? *C'mon!*" he said cold and insinuatingly.

"What light."

Mention of a redlight naturally struck a chord in the cab driver. It produced generic guilt. Professionally speaking, with the best will, you had to lose one occasionally. Redlights were for the citizens. The detective's remarks touched on an everpresent halfconscious stream of guilt, but as far as any particular offense went, he drew a blank. He was sure he had not run a redlight taking Mattie home. How could he? He'd been on the Tollway practically the whole way. Maybe he had. He'd been flying, thoughtless, so glad to have a long ride, even for gas money. Or on the way back.

The light he'd run with Rita he'd never registered. He'd never noticed it in the first place, in spite of Rita's exclamations. That redlight had been a surge of hope, a ruby glimmer, a black gush of the heart, no redlight at all, unremembered now.

A new suspicion suddenly took hold of the cop. It could be deeper than he thought. There was a whole lot he didn't know and he meant to find out all about it. He let a silence build. He knew how to make a punk like this wait in anguish.

The cab driver suddenly recalled a redlight—embarrassing, yesterday evening in fact. He'd picked up a harried businessman from one of the office complexes. The guy was really wired. At the first redlight they had hit on the way to the airport he had stuck his head out the window and shouted to the pretty woman driving the car in the next lane, "Hey I want to eat your pussy!" Fortunately the light changed and traffic intervened, but a mile farther on they again sat next to the same woman in her car at a redlight, and his passenger had yelled, "Hey, I want to eat your pussy *so bad!*" He had cut into the oncoming lane and run the redlight, after a couple blocks pulled over hard, and made the guy promise not to do that again. Maybe the cop had seen that redlight from yesterday? But he didn't think that could be.

After a long pause, the cop asked him in a low, signifying tone, "How long ya know her, guy?"

"*What,* how long?" the cab driver boiled over with frustration, thinking vaguely of the woman in the next lane yesterday, then of course Mattie again. "Be serious! How long would I *know* her? How *would* I know her? No offense, I mean, I never seen her before in my

102

life! She's not a regular or nothin. I don't think she been in a cab in the last twenty years to tell the truth. I seen her waving over by the Lush Lariats. I picked her up at the bus stop. She was drunk. She couldn't wait on her bus. She said she got fired. I just *met* her!"

He was blabbing too much. That was all he was going to say. He felt a stab of loyalty to Mattie. He felt guilty about how he'd hustled her, lied to her about the train schedule, even though she'd turned the tables and totally outhustled him in the end and beaten him down on the price till he'd taken her for gas money, all the while she'd had her employer's silver or something worse in that big purse. No wonder she wanted to go home to the Blue Hills. He knew he shouldn't have taken her to the Westside for twenty-eight dollars. It was asking for trouble. Still he liked her. She was a fond memory. It was one of those strange sweet rides that came along. She'd sung her songs with such raggedy soul. She had expressed admiration for his car! How he loved her for that. He'd helped her up the stairs with that hostile crowd staring at them. He'd taken her home, had a slug of her stolen gin, been invited to walk her right up to her door. They had become, for a moment, close.

The cop's imagination was seized by the cab driver's revelation he'd been over to that section of town with the cowboy names that he had spied on the map, Lush Lariats he called it, the Red River Road and the Sierra Trail and all. He'd *guessed* she might have headed for such a nice part of town. It sounded fancy and new. He was proud of his intuition, and flush with the new knowledge, he had one of those winning moments when he felt like he had climbed right inside the guy's head. He *knew* he had taken her over there. That was where he had left Rita off, even though he claimed he'd *picked her up* there waving. The truth was reversed in his bullshit about his having picked her up there, the way people's lies often doubled back on the facts like that for lack of imagination. He *knew* he had dropped her that end of town.

"That so, a bus stop, *that so!*" hissed the cop, like a fuse burning fast. "She's waitin on a bus!" Exploding, he reached out and grabbed the cab driver's shirt collar and hauled him halfway into the back seat by it. "That where ya take her, dude?" he wheezed in his ear. "To them cowboy name streets? What address exactly?"

The cop had yanked the cab driver's shirt so hard he was just about wearing it inside out. He had pulled it out of his belt and half pulled it over his head, who now got the impression this whole business meant far more to the cop than he had imagined.

"The city," he admitted.

Patience was at last exhausted, for them both.

"The *city?*" How could he lie to him blandly? How stupid was he? It was a brazen lie, the cop knew, but it was worse than that, it was outrageous and insulting, since Rita had just come *from* the city. He lunged forward and got his forearm under the cab driver's chin, who supposed he was now being asked for specifics.

"Westside," he gasped. That was all he was going to spill.

"Westside!" There was that *Westside* again.

"That's right."

"Where? What street?" Against his better judgment, the cop suddenly wondered if it could be true. Rita was that cagey she had run all the way back to the city again, doubled back? It could be that bad, it was possible, from what he'd seen of her, especially if she had spotted him. Could she have made a move like that?

"I don't know those streets," said the cab driver.

Why was this cop trying to put a scare in him? What had she done, strangled her employer before leaving as he was presently being strangled? It wasn't his job to inquire into the moral character of his fares. He was just a cab driver. He took people where they wanted to go. That was all and it was enough. The cops were always ready to let you know they could shove you around if you drove a hack, since they needed *somebody* to shove around. They figured any guy that drove a hack they could certainly shove around to their heart's content. He remembered Mattie's crazy lovely song, the compliments she'd paid his cab. Mattie didn't think he was the cause of slavery and everything. In fact she had spoken endearingly of "good old white American" cab drivers, of whom there were fewer and fewer, to be sure. Where had they gone? she had wondered. This fuzz had heard all he was going to from him.

"Gimme some truth!"

Using his knees against the seatback as a fulcrum the cop pulled him up and levered him back over the headrest threatening to break him in half. Their temples ground together, intimately but not affectionately. They remained in this embrace and he held him like this for twenty seconds, pinching his windpipe and cutting off his air. Using all his neck strength to keep his back from breaking, the cab driver stared up at the red velour headliner of his cab an inch away.

"You think I think you're my problem," said the cop enigmatically, dropping his hold. He yanked his arm away so hard the fabric of his coat seared the cab driver's throat.

The only truth the cop ever got now was the blackest look of fixed refusal. He stared at the side of the cab driver's head, then looked around at everything he could see. He inspected everything from the cab license on the dash with the punk's vainglorious photo to some notes and addresses on a pad next to the cupholder. He gazed down at the addresses but the guy's handwriting was awful. On the seat next to the cab driver were some photographs, which he fingered. One after another, he riffled the photos, and found one he seemed struck by. He didn't wait around for any more lies. Just like that he opened the door and got out without another word. He walked to a plaingreen car. The cab driver sliding back down into the seat behind the wheel followed him another moment in the mirror, then lost him as his car slipped into traffic.

"Fucking law!" said the cab driver to the air. "Where do they recruit these sadistic *maniacs?*"

He sat there with some evil blues coming on. He thought he'd get a breath of relief as the moments passed, same as you always got when the bulls let you go, but instead came a rush of heavy anxiety, tinged with strangeness and loneliness, because of the objectionable mystery of it. It was just like a cop—to have put him through that and left with no explanation. This had not been a good day. Imagine that he had thought it was a flush black dude taking a nice ride after a Chinese meal. His heart began to smoke, his blood came to an unholy boil. What was the meaning of it? Cab drivers were always being pushed around by the law, but this had the ugly feeling of something almost personal. He had the idea he had been watched or followed for some unimaginable reason, and he must have been. It was all on account of that loser ride with Mattie, poor Mattie, what trouble she must be in. He had helped her escape, apparently. A ride he never should have taken. The cab driver, a.k.a. "Wisconsin," felt suddenly overwhelmed and consumed by the central dilemma of his trade—lots of openings, few middles, and no conclusions to the stories. Sore and frightened, his thoughts turned to Rita hungrily and he wished mightily to see her again.

Thank heaven the busy time of day was coming up, let's hope! In the heatwaves of lust and carbon that signaled evening's release, in the shining eyes of the crowds in flight down the unribboning roads to those destinations where all sorts of fares went for love or money, he'd forget this. There was nothing but to drown himself in what was trying to send him under, more trips, more fares, new faces and voices, their dates with destiny, if only the Liquor Store, more trials, everybody else's hopefully, more half stories, traces or seeds of high hopes for all, however seamy, in the rush hour traffic, in the steamy hazy summer afternoon's finale that was coming up, common fleeting nirvana, "Happy Hour," when a few people might be finally calling for a cab!

The cop had found the photograph the cab driver had taken of Rita. Above her shoulder, the house number had jumped out at him bold and black against new white paint. He had committed every detail of the picture to memory, from the unstable minglement of competence and terror in Rita's eyes suggestive (to him) of unpredictable repercussions, to the long shapes of black shutters and a high arched front doorway that peered out behind white pillars, and a statue of a girl with a vase on her shoulder.

He had dropped the picture back onto the cab's frontseat and dismissed the cab driver from his mind. He had the professional investigator's knack for concentrating on the promising matter come to hand and instantly letting go (for the moment) of up-to-now compelling concerns that had suddenly turned into irrelevant

106

details, and now the cab driver was but an irrelevant nuisance. Why he was both photographing and protecting Rita it was hard to say, but the straight line to her no longer ran through him. Maybe he'd find out in time, but it didn't matter right now. He pulled out of the China Doll parking lot and headed toward the "cowboy" streets, reorienting himself on the way with sharp glances at the map to be sure he was headed the right direction.

His study of the map had proved supremely worthwhile, as had his interview with the cab driver because of the photo, for it seemed to him the house number might show up at that end of town (toward which they'd certainly been traveling) and he was convinced that there would be no more than half a dozen streets with the cowboy names that would have the number 2232, if he read the map right. You wouldn't spot a house like that with pillars like a bank's and a Grecian statue of a girl with a vase, it would practically run you over.

A pair of giant old oaks that had somehow survived a century's worth of man's devices marked the ingress to the development. The first street curved more exaggeratedly than it appeared to on the map. The Avenue of the Big Sky expanding voluptuously as if to better show off vistas of "stately" homes set off by the skinniest saplings seemed to open up all around him. Despite the Old West names, the style of the houses was generically Big, New, and Rich only, with an acre or two of land apiece. A porcelain glint from one of them—a statue. He stopped the car with a lurch and grabbed his binoculars, pressed the eyepieces against his brows till they hurt while he studied the white facade fifty yards ahead, the wide pillars, the Grecian statue. It was hard to believe he'd found the place so fast, but damned if he wasn't looking at exactly the picture in his memory. He was fortunate not to have driven straight up on it—he'd known it was going to jump right on top of him like this. He checked the numbers nearby and counted down to the house. Lord almighty, it would be the one. Could it? He couldn't tell what was happening with his heart, whether it was soaring in delight or sinking with suspicion. Realizing he was parked in plain view in the middle of the street, he pulled up forty feet, and parked behind a painter's van, momentarily blocking his view. Never taking the glasses from his eyes, he one-handedly backed the car up six feet, adjusting his angle.

Her breasts were bare. That was different. He was certain he would have made at least an unconscious note of it if the watercarrier in the photograph had been half naked. No, definitely she'd been clothed in some fluted frock. And she was shiny white, and the statue in the picture had been metallic green. Something else, something about the trim under the gutters, it seemed to be not the house after all, but another bearing a mighty close resemblance. Throwing caution to the winds, he started the motor and drove straight up to it. His curiosity was as pure and intense as a scientist's spotting an unheard of cousin of some rare creature. It was incredible that there could be two of these mansions outfitted so nearly the same, and yet as he approached it he caught other ambiguous details. He'd just convinced himself it was not the right house when he saw the brass knocker without question that had been in the picture. He slowed a little to catch the black numerals. Yes, his arithmetic was right on, 2232.

He drove past the house to look at it from the other side. The more he stared, the less sure he was that it was not the one. To the left and right were homes which though not cut from identical molds bore striking similarities to each other, and must have been put up by the same developer. Surely not every house around here could have been dreamed up by the same outfit? That would be a disaster for himself. They began to look more and more alike to him till he could no longer distinguish any of them, and by contrast this number 2232 merged with the picture in his head. Unbelievably, it had not been enough to memorize the salient features in the photograph, which were now blending and blurring with all the houses on this street.

No, no, he bore down on memory. None of them was the house. His hand moved to the right through the air and punched the button on the glove compartment. Deftly it plucked out the bottle, and he had a long slug of the scotch. Something in him that had tightened up like a snake around a frog began to uncoil. No, he was sure it was not the right house.

He glanced at his map to trace the shortest route to the next street with a possible 2232 on it, Avenue of the Tall Grass. Was that really the unpleasant name? A few minutes later, turning onto it, the 2200s came up as fast on this street as on the one before and he experienced again sharp hope. He overshot the mark before he could slow down, but it didn't matter. He saw the numbers make a leap from 2212 to 2240.

He decided to forget the map and just dive into the place as into a nest of concrete cobras and fight it out in the winding lanes. He drove on aimlessly and after five minutes found himself again in the 2200s, now on the Avenue of the Continental Divide. A tall neo-Victorian structure that was happily unmistakably different with crazy turrets and gables and "eyebrow" windows was number 2232 all right. This one he easily ticked off as it whipped past his elbow.

On the Avenue of Pike's Peak, his spirits were on the rise. With naked eye he spied pillars like silos, black shutters peering out. Was 2232 coming at him? Was there a brass knocker on the door? The vision wavered in the heat. There it was again, everything that belonged to it, even a statue. The photograph seemed to superimpose itself on the air and dissolve sadly.

Wrong statue! A hollow whiskey laugh formed in his throat. A lush circle of arms and limbs figured famously under the porcheaves of the affluent homesteaders, a facsimile of Rodin's Kissing Couple or whatever it was properly called. Was there no limit to which these people would not go? Rodin was one of his favorites. He always stopped for a moment or two with Rodin when, with his girl friend on a rainy Sunday afternoon once a year or so, he made a pilgrimage to the Art Institute. On somebody's porch, it was like art theft. He felt the culture of the city had been hijacked. There was truer, more honest figuration in the elevators of the city's housing projects, at least it genuinely belonged, if only to a hell.

What the fuck! All this ersatz art purgatory out here in whiteyville suggested criminal copyright violations—they should all be arrested for bad taste! His sense of triumph, as he had memorized the water carrier in the cab driver's photo in the parking lot of the China Doll restaurant, faded to futility once more.

With only an occasional meditative swallow of Johnny Walker Red to cool him, his anguished efforts at the wheel in the peak heat of the afternoon in the deceptively winding streets had him sweating heavily and heading into a deep funk again. A sullen glance out of the corner of his eye at the map condemned its deceiving scale. Coiling back on themselves, the wide streets were much longer than he had guessed. This place was a vaster development than it looked like on the map. He had a lot more territory to explore than he'd figured. He reached out to the glove box and had another hefty sip.

The street names were beginning to grate on him. He crossed the Avenue of the Black Panther on a signpost, and chose not to turn down that one, regardless. He didn't want to think about that one. The name gave him a new jolt of alienation and aversion. His face, or rather the side of and back of the cab driver's head, flashed before his eyes. He might've been too quick to dispense with the cornhaired punk.

He'd been so pissed off about that redlight, he'd taken the wrong tack—he should have straight out bribed him like Rita must have done. It'd been a mistake to take that redlight personally. Nothing made sense to a cab driver until you waved some green. He wondered if he wasn't looking like the fool in the cowboy movie who fired the Indian scout on a bad bet. The guy could've guided him straight to the house. He might've refused though—why? Wrangling with him might've cost him more delay he couldn't afford. But why would he have refused? Why had that white boy stonewalled him like he had?

He was involved in some way with Rita and the Fist that was sure. That cabby might be the key to their game, and he had taken that key out here to try to fit it in the wrong door! The cop found his thoughts, like the streets, circled back on themselves and fixated on the cab driver, whom he had let slip away. It reminded him of how he'd let Rita and the Fist go this morning.

He caught the sign on the next street—White Stallion—and groaned. Each name was worse than the last. Up ahead one more house with a statue in front of it made its predictable appearance at about the right number. He brought the car to a stop, cursed roundly and generally, and raised his glasses. Same guy sold richfolks these homes out of a catalog.

Into a dazzling portrait of a white facade, with the right pillars, statue of an urnbearing maiden, but a frontdoor with questionable panels, hurtled the dark blur of an oncoming car, a black Lincoln, big as a house, seeming to have pulled out from the very drive, with Rita in the picture window, heading straight at him, aiming for a spot between his stinging eyes. He dropped the glasses.

Her brow was pinched up like she had a problem, her eyes were shut, and her head turned away. The collar of her white silk blouse was turned up high. It was too late for the cop to duck. The moment stretched to a gleaming transparency. He forced himself to observe without flinching. The gray eyes of a silvermaned gentleman driving, jaw jutting confidently, his mouth a grim line, momentarily touched his own. You wanted to reach for your wallet and invest money with a man with a chin like that. In the suicide seat, the girl cradled herself in her arms, as if trying to rock herself to sleep in a realm as far away as possible without actually opening the door and rolling out onto somebody's lawn. She looked even more spaced than when he'd first seen her in Jackie's. Behind her pained expression was she thinking just as hard?

The cop watched the black Lincoln recede in his rear view mirror. For an instant before disappearing around the bend, it made a shadow blacker than fresh tar, shimmering devilishly against the green of an ornamental grove of tortured looking miniature shrubs and dwarf trees adorning somebody's garage. He swung his car around, not cutting the wheel sharply enough and digging a trench in a showcase lawn. So he had made the right move after all and his guess about the cab driver's picture had been confirmed. It made him so happy he pounded the wheel again and again with joy and affirmation as he accelerated. He caught sight of the Lincoln as it was turning out of the wild west homes to the south on the highway without signaling. They headed straight away from town into the cornbelt.

After a few miles, they hung a left on Plainfields Road, a twolane crumbling blacktop. Way ahead of him he could see the Lincoln swerving from side to side to miss the potholes as he too was having to do. He had to keep his eyes on the road to avoid the missing chunks of asphalt. They crossed a meager creek. Two boys fished from the top of a culvert. A gas station–liquor store and a green highway sign announced the village of Grass Lake, the last the cop saw of it. They turned north on Diamond Lake Road, which after a crossing became county trunk M. Here and there the farmland and cornfields gave way to scrub woods. The pockmarked road curved and sank and he caught a glimpse through trees of a pond. Maybe the man had a cabin someplace out here. He lost sight of them momentarily but for a dust plume.

111

They were moving somewhere ahead, at a leisurely pace. He took care to hang back but not too far. The terrain opened up wide. It seemed to him there was no place out here where a big Lincoln could pull off and hide. On the horizon tall black towers appeared, violating the blue heavens. That's where they were going. The road straightened, new subdivisions appeared on either side, under construction. Bands of green corn and scrub woods alternated with streets of partially built houses, stretches of bare brown earth, yellow frontloaders and bulldozers, stacks of palegold lumber and building materials under tarps. The Lincoln was heading for the looming black towers. Feeling himself out in the open, he hung back more and let them go on.

At the intersection with Fox Glove Road, the Lincoln no larger than a black beetle was turning at the stop sign like a drop of blood on the green grass. Fox Glove between tall ranks of corn was a tunnel like the ones he'd gone down fruitlessly all morning. The light at the end of this tunnel after a mile or so was Laboratory Drive, two broad lanes newly paved, leading through vast manicured grounds around three black towers. Tiny dark figures wearing cowboy hats and carrying sacks and gardening tools moved in the green depths. Joggers in bright running attire dotted pathways along the corporate campus like little red and blue wildflowers blowing in the wind. The towers were ringed immediately by parking lots in which hundreds of cars gleamed in the heat, bisected by groves of trees appointed with picnic tables and trash receptacles. Small groups of workers or managers were taking their lunches there.

Outside its several hundred acres, the outfit was surrounded by cornfields on all sides. The cop lingered on Fox Glove Road in the corn and watched the Lincoln move unhurriedly up the Laboratory Drive through the campus reaching the towers after about a quarter mile. It made a turn and disappeared.

He pulled onto the shoulder, grabbed his field glasses, and waded a little way into the corn rows, up and down furrows, till he came to a vantage point from which, through the groves, beyond the security guard's shack and picnic tables, the glass door of the first tower loomed up under magnification. The Lincoln had pulled up directly in front of it. Rita and her banker friend must have gone inside through that door.

In spite of garden artifices, the impression that came over him of the huge campus was only the raw power. The contrast with the funky cornfields in which he stood affected him weirdly. It seemed to him he'd been taken to the outer rim of a thoroughly confused though supremely virile civilization. Of course, to the farmers of these fields and the owners of the hundreds of parked cars, the massive mixed-up juxtapositions of things must look completely normal and everyday.

He felt lost in a jungle grown up outside a temple wall. The headquarters and grounds carved out of the jungle might as well belong to another planet. He thought he saw a brother in the security box and checked him out inside his walls of glass. He let his fieldglasses float up jogging paths, past the parties of technicians in the green groves on their lunchbreak. Inside the tower like a castle behind a moat, the man was in his world with Rita.

The air was heavy with fine green dust, and he dropped the glasses on their strap and grabbed his nose, sneezing violently. There was no one to hear him but mice and bugs. The awkward snort seemed to have disappeared into the silence of eternity. The vegetative silence was awesome, and the sun baked down. Through a gap in the timeless leaves of the maize plants, he gazed at the banks upon banks of sunblazed black windows in the towers. The automatic sprinklers peck-pecking furtively around the lawns in scores injected not moisture but a sinister rhythmic tension into the burning stillness. Standing in the dirt, he felt his smallness, his outsideness, an insignificant watchman for the vast organization of American society. About on a par with that cat in the guardbox, no more.

He sneezed five times in a row. To hell with this. His nose was killing him. He couldn't find a spot where his feet weren't on two different levels in the earth making a comfortable stance impossible. He turned around and picked his way back. As he ducked onto the road, a pickup truck swerved dangerously, the farmer ogling him. At the red and white barrier, through the glass he met the glance of the security guard in his goldfishbowl. The token Negro at the gate, glorified parking attendant. He dealt with little guys like this every day of his life. His father had been a guard like this one.

"Hello, good brother!" he smiled friendly as the glass slid open.

"What's to it."

"Everything is everything.... May I enter?"

"Who ya here to see?"

"Nobody, really. I need your help, man."

The guy's eyes came up from the star. The look in them was more than respect. It was total identification.

"... What's goin down?"

He slipped him one of Jackie's smudged and dog-eared purple *43d St Neighbor Club* cards.

"Look me up I can do ya somethin in the city. Somethin hot went in your gate an I need to cool in your lot awhile."

"Ya need help?"

"My man. I be right over there. If I make a move ... what they make in there anyhow?"

"Medicines, hospital supplies."

"Pills an powders."

"Not hardly. Ya bout go to the moon with what they does in there!"

"Shee-it!"

The cop grinned and put it in gear, and the barrier rose in a salute. In seconds he was lost in the gleaming mass of parked cars, but close enough where they could keep an eye on each other. Just talking to the dude in his little uniform had depressed him, for no good reason. It was probably a fair paying job, and the cat would never fathom any pity. The black Lincoln was parked in a line of limos and Cadillacs at the front door. In the sharp sunlight everything seemed close and bit into his eyes. It would be a wait now, in the heat. He was glad enough to stop cruising, to stop hunting, for he had found his people, but a wait would be hard. He wondered if the guard would alert anyone inside, but there must be a thousand people in those towers and he would never think of Rita, would he? He might, because nobody much was going in or out at this time of day, and she and her banker man might have been the last ones.

From the sea of cars stretching in every direction, waves of dusty light rolled at him, and he put his hand over his face. When he removed it, he glanced back at the guardshack. Windowed on all sides, the guardshack was hit one way by the sun and in the other by the reflected light from the cars and towers. The poor dude was in a pit of light, his form seemed to shrivel in it. He was staring expectantly in the cop's direction like he was waiting for something to happen. Man, but it showed you could get used to anything. His ancestors in the cotton patch would have raised a fuss at working in front of what amounted to a giant mirror. His uniform with its fresh creases must be treated with some miracle starch they made in there along with the pills. Air conditioning must be turned up high, thought the cop enviously. But as he watched him, he raised his hand . . . to mop his face from ear to ear with a big handkerchief. No way he'd connect him up with Rita and that man, who would never themselves have registered a little guard existed. The cop's heart sank as he suddenly thought of that sorry little dog again he had once seen chasing from curb to curb on LaSalle Street.

What brought the top dogs and the bottom dogs together, what bound up the city's ragged wounds and reconciled black and white, rich and poor, the scorched low buildings of the Southside and these shining corporate towers of the far north suburbs was *business,* coldhearted business, business as usual, that's all it was. A homeboy like Bobby the Fist who came back to town from New York and socialized at Jackie's juke joint and knew a man or knew a broad who knew a man like the owner of the Lincoln, it was sex and drugs, what it was, pure and simple—just plain business. In the pitiless afternoon light baking him to a cinder in his airless parked car, he saw it all clearly.

It was a home truth how people like Bobby needed people like Rita's man to make a dollar and how the likes of silverhair would need some help from the likes of Bobby in order to sin in the way he'd grown accustomed. Of course, to hear Rita tell it, the Fist had wound up all his business *already.* Sure, that's why she'd been walking a tightrope through time and towns. That's why she'd switched cabs five times, and now the Lincoln, and here.

The peace of the countryside bore on him like a drug. The afternoon grew long and got hotter. Everything rippled with sun's gold. The tower rose like a cliff heavily veined with precious yellow metal. The limousines stationed at the front door were splashed bumper to bumper with the liquid gold. His dashboard was baking like a stove. To his back there was nothing but a cornfield to speed the evening's shadows. His eyes hurt and he shut them.

He took deep breaths of the air which might have been laced with enough powders and chemicals from the Labs to cross the booze with a different buzz. It must have been all downers, and the green soporific powers from the fields were heavy. His body was rebelling. He couldn't get out of the car and take even a few steps without calling attention to himself. Whew, God, it was never the occasional danger but sitting hours in the car made the job rough. If it was his job he was still doing. He had another flash of the way his superiors would view the way he was spending his afternoon out here, and shrugged it off.

Yet he felt a stir of a strange satisfaction, as if he had accomplished some deep thing already, and a promise of something fine he was going to do now. Fortunately, there was something to buoy up anticipation and ease conditions. He reached into the glove compartment for his bottle. There was still a reassuring level left in it. He held it up to the sunlight before rolling the first amber swallow around his mouth, and had another.

He relaxed and got into the spirit of the heat. Got behind it and entered into it. Once you accepted it and let it wash over you without fighting it, it wasn't so bad. The minutes passed in a steaming orange haze that felt all right. He must've nodded out. Motors starting and the chatter of people getting off work roused him. His jacket was soaked with sweat, and bunched up under his shoulders. He grabbed the steering wheel and raised himself with a grimace. The dashboard clock said 5:04. The shift was letting out. He rubbed his eyes at the jump in time and the unfortunate disruption of his thought process. Men and women were coming out the front door and from around both sides of the tower, and heading for their cars. Two lanes were exiting past the security shack. The guard had donned a bright orange vest and was waving cars on. In ten minutes, half of the cars around the cop had pulled out. Nobody looked at him twice. A few of the slots had been taken by new arrivals, a smaller evening workforce coming in at the same time.

The possibility that he had missed something accused him and he let his annoyed gaze roam helplessly everywhere. A wave of gut fear came up and bottomed in incredulous disappointment that he had slept. The Lincoln was still there. Then he thought he saw her by the teetering way she walked more than anything as if she might stumble. Just a tremulous not quite yet seen presence in the middle of the crush with the last of the two shifts pushing past each other, she was coming from behind with other women toward the front of the tower. They had come out a side or back doorway, not through the magnificent glass front door she had entered with the man. He grabbed his glasses. One of the women was pulling a white smock over her head, blocking his view. Rita was right beside her, behind her from his angle, he thought, but when the white garment came down, she was gone. Maybe he'd been seeing things. The lenses of his glasses fogged over with sweat, and he wiped them with the lining of his jacket, and passed his sleeve over his sleepdamp eyes. He scanned the whole crowd of women. He'd had a long wait, and must've checked out for a while, but he wasn't ready to conclude he'd started seeing things. He knew he'd seen her. He stabbed the glasses again and again at the female lab workers thrusting forward, homebound, and there she was walking shoulder to shoulder with them. She wasn't with them exactly, she was hiding among them, he thought, matching their fast pace, stride for stride, staying deliberately in their middle, her big purse swinging, giving her away.

His jaw had dropped and he was breathing through his mouth which helped keep the glasses from steaming again. In step with the others, she passed down the rank of limousines and came abreast of the black Lincoln she'd arrived in. He glimpsed her impassive red mouth, her bright fixed eyes, suddenly blurring as she ducked her head and made a move out of his field of vision. He had to drop the glasses to find her again. She had slipped to the side of the car, opened the driver's door, and stooped to reach the hood release. He felt it pop clear across the lot.

In front of the big car she worked the tips of her fingers under the hood trying to trip the latch but she couldn't get it. Through the glasses he could see her poor fingers poking mightily and the pain in her eyes. Over her shoulder her big purse hung heavily and awkwardly while she struggled to trigger the mechanism, her body rigid and a vein in her neck just under her ear standing out, on her face panic and rage, probably not the mask she'd intended for the occasion.

A man stopped and spoke to her, probably asking if she needed help. Her reaction was shocking. She glared at him redfaced as if he'd propositioned her and retreated to the other side of the car spitting like a cat. Slinking off with hurt feelings, he cast her an indignant backward frown. He might remember this. A handsome girl in a pin-striped suit with her hair drawn back in a platinum helmet with a violently twisted mouth.

She went smack down on her knees in front of the car and peered through the crack while she poked with her fingers at the latch, where she supposed it must be. She no longer cared what passersby thought. In this awkward and abandoned pose her essential dangerous beauty blazed like a signal fire to him who would see. The high collar of her blouse stood up behind her bent head like a plume, concealing the signs of a crime, and the white ruffles at her wrists had grease on them by now. He winced thinking of the painful blue welts hidden beneath those ruffles.

"C'mon, baby!" the cop heard himself anxiously whisper.

Whatever it was.

Whatever she was doing, she had wanted to get it over with fast in the anonymity of the day's-end rush. Having marched watchful and ghostlike with the crowd she'd thrown herself on the hoodlatch, not dreaming it would present a bizarre puzzle. Nothing really had gone wrong yet. Even the rejected helper had probably already forgotten her, and all the others streaming by were looking right through her to their own evening dreams and immediate plans. This excellent cover wouldn't last long. People were moving along and the shift was over. Everything was organized to let the people and their cars pour out and the new shift come in quickly. The guard in his orange vest who had been signaling them out was back in his glass shack now. The workers had seemed to all but run to their cars to get away homeward.

The heavy slab of metal went up six inches suddenly on the heels of her thin hands. She staggered to her feet, fighting the thing upward. The cop blew out a blast of relief through his lips. His whole soul and body urged her not to falter. The Lincoln was no tin box. Her face was livid with the effort. He was rooting for her. Whatever it was.

"Go, baby!" he muttered.

His glasses fogged. He had a blurred look at her deliberately pull a large brown package out of her big purse holding it in two hands. He wiped the lenses, squinted again too late. She'd pushed the package down out of sight into the engine compartment. All he had was a longshot of her tautskirt ass bending over. It was a pretty ass but he would have traded the next sixty seconds of it for two more of the package, which she'd held gingerly in her hands.

She worked down in there. At last, she straightened up, with a triumphant spasm of her whole body. With a strength that belied her slim frame she slammed the black hood down. He watched it fall in terror, grimacing at the crash as if his own fingers might get caught. She wasted no time splitting the scene on those precarious highheels. Her suit was twisted around on her shoulders and her fingers plucked at it to straighten it. Her empty purse no longer obstructed her free movement but swung vacantly behind her.

He felt a catch in his throat that became a lump of some obscure emotion. There was no one on the walk for her to blend in with any more. The change of shifts was over, and her act had been as painfully visible from all angles as if she'd been in a spotlight. She glanced back over her shoulder with eyes that showed burntout fear and a smoldering contempt that was pure bravado. What a look she cast the Lincoln! Whatever it was, she had packed in all her hopes. This was not the spacey skulking little girl he'd met at Jackie's this morning, long ago. Not hardly, this grown woman was bad, bold and beautiful. When she disappeared again behind the tower, he no longer knew what he felt.

The hiding darkness was a balm. In the rich darkness, the cab driver stretched out in his car. He pressed the button and all four windows of the Cadillac opened all the way down. The evening was still hot but the air was soft. He was "hiding" (as the dispatcher would have put it) in the unlit back parking lot of the Athen's

119

Restaurant (that's how they spelled it). He liked the nighttime the best. It was why he did not work at night, he liked it too much to work in it if he didn't have to. He reached up and touched his sore Adam's apple, remembering the cop choking him. In many ways it had been an evil day but now it was over at last. Couple of glasses of retsina had assuaged his hurt feelings. Behind this corner of the Greek joint, even the spectral glow in the sky from the nearby Tollway was cut off. The whole idea of traffic, obstreperous fares, and any kind of unwanted motion was obliterated, and he was as much in his castle as any man. A dim hum from inside Athen's Restaurant murmured unheard in his ears like the undulant sea.

The green emerald eye of the radio threw its underwater glimmer through the interior of the car, turning the plush red seats to royal purple. The radio turned way down, but not off, whispered its half meanings to him in a faint echo of the turbulent life to which he no longer owed allegiance, for this day anyhow. It was lovely to just barely hear this business chatter he'd left behind, what no longer needed listening to and couldn't touch him.

All at once, he was so gratefully distanced from the day's jumble of events, painful or otherwise. He didn't know how he'd suddenly acquired such a feeling of distance. He couldn't have forced it to come. The peace of the night just slid into him of its own volition. He'd been on the wrong track all day. Getting involved with the loads. Jesus, he did not want to start remembering. Mattie. That cop. He did not believe for a moment he'd ever see Rita again. He was resigned about that. What a job driving a hack was anyway. What a soul satisfier to let it all drift away in the dark, like black ripples widening and disappearing on the surface of a big lake leaving this blessed calm. You grabbed in this life, and got or missed, and it all amounted to the same thing when the wonderful moment came to let go.

Amazingly, he'd made a little money today, enough. Rush hour had been that good. After gas and radio fees, he'd cleared a hundred bucks, not bad for a day with so absolutely miserable a beginning. He might have been a fisherman resting in the dock shadows, with his fair catch at his feet, eyes lingering on the black, propitious waters. From his corner in the imponderable scheme of things, he looked out past the green gemglow of the radio's incoming signal on the fertile night that was restoring him and considered the web of life in which there would always be rides to chase, as long as you kept your motor humming, and fish to haul in, if you kept your hooks sharp, and new girls to meet, forget about Rita.

"Seventeen? Seventeen, read?"

Maybe because the radio was turned way down, it didn't register for the threat to his peace that it was. He'd had enough for today. Somehow or other he'd made a few bucks this evil afternoon and enough was enough. His number seemed to slip in through the windows on the gentle air. So deep was his reverie, or so complete was his resignation, after a while he picked up the mike unsuspiciously.

"What do you want?"

"Cadillac, somebody askin for ya—Pratt?"

"Ten-nine?"

Pressing the transmission button on the mike, he noticed distractedly the green receiving light go out but the red transmitting light on the face of the radio did not go on, as he'd still forgotten to replace the burned-out bulb. The face of the radio was black and blank when he transmitted. How disagreeable. He promised himself for the hundredth time he'd fix it.

"Pratt? At the Labs?"

"Yeah? What? Ten-nine?"

He had been so exquisitely relaxed after such a trying day and the nice meal and wine provided by Athen that he completely and uncharacteristically lost all grip on this meaningless conversation with the dispatcher.

"Get Pratt at the Labs, seventeen."

What had just happened? He had taken a call? How could that have happened? How could he have agreed? He hadn't agreed, he was just asking! A second later, he couldn't figure how, but it had certainly happened. The dispatcher had misunderstood him, but it was too late. Somebody named Pratt asking for him? He'd never heard of any Pratt. It was all because of those business cards he'd handed out at restaurants, places like the Hilton hotel, even the Labs, apparently. What had gotten into him handing out cards like that, especially at the Labs, a place that gave him the creeps? *Greed*, he accused himself, and it must have been unconscious greed that had made him pick up the mike and take the call too. Never enough! Armchair would have had a sly laugh. Armchair would have had the sense to turn the radio clear off not just down low. When Armchair wanted to read his book, for instance, he made sure that his radio was *off.* Why hadn't he turned it off? It was too late now to change his mind and every second that passed stuck in the mud of amazement at himself it got even more too late. The longer an order cooled off, the less inclined the dispatcher was to take it back and put it out again. Anyway it was unprofessional to give it back.

Clouds had rolled in, the stars in the heavens seemed shocked dumb, half awake. The road flowing beneath his tires was half made, full of black pits and pools. He could hardly see. His eyes wouldn't adjust. How many glasses of wine had he had? His headlights were swallowed up in the gloom, and he checked twice to see they were really on. The road that led out to the Labs parted waves on waves of corn rippling like the sea, revealing yawning depths.

At first he drove slowly, afraid he might go off the road, but as his eyes finally got habituated, he began to speed, to get it over with. Halfway there, excuses that might have covered an escape were still running through his brain. A flat tire? A speeding ticket? The dispatcher had heard them all. Down this same road, seven or eight miles past the Labs, was a roadhouse, the Treetop, where a lot of girls came from all over to dance, and he was tempted to keep on sailing and blow off the load. Yes, turn off his radio and blow it off, something he was constitutionally and professionally incapable of doing, unfortunately. He did not blow off loads, one reason why he stayed in good graces with the dispatchers. His peace and happiness in the darkness after a couple of beers at the Pair a Dice tavern, nice dinner and drinks at the Athen's, mellow as a m-f, when this crazy call had come in he could no longer even remember in the untoward exigency of another crazy ride which he did not want when he had had enough today, all dissipated like a forgotten unrecoverable melody.

On the horizon, beyond the lonely fields, the yellow radiation of the Labs towers lit up the sky. He could have wished the order were for someplace other than the radiant Labs, for real. The place gave him the chills on a hot night. Medicines and chemicals in semitrailer loads rumbling into the blackgreen night made you wonder what strange byproducts laced the air. Once he'd taken a poisoned technician from the Labs to Greenshores–St. Mary's Hospital. He was a walking skeleton with chalky white skin. He had a degenerative disease from handling certain chemical ingredients in the Labs, so he'd claimed. That is what he had told the cab driver. Or perhaps the story had been about radiation poisoning. Something they did or made there in the Labs. He told the cab driver all about it, as people often did, all the gory details. A lot of people in Greenshores were apprehensive about the Labs. You were afraid you could be poisoned just by driving past this place.

Speeding to get it over with, slowing to make it all stop, as at last the cab driver emerged from a sparse woods that bordered the Labs grounds on the backside, from which angle few visitors knew how to approach the place, along a truck route to the loading docks, the chemical gold light of the towers flooded over him distressingly. The windows were lit up all night always and the vast parking lots illuminated from every angle by monstrous banks of arclights, like some max prison or isolation facility for lunatics or people with contagious diseases. The security guard for this back entryway slid open his glass window to ask for a name and the cab driver said Pratt in a listless tone and waited at the barrier. It was a long wait. Speaking into his phone the guard did not seem to get the right response. The cab driver could care less and looked away.

Late that afternoon he had caught a nice fare from the Hilton to O'Hare Airport. The load was a commodities speculator of some sort, what he was doing up in these parts was anybody's guess, instead of downtown in the Loop, and the cab driver hadn't asked. He claimed to have just lost a whole lot of money, and the way he wanted to talk and talk, it was probably true. Misfortune made people lose control and talk their heads off, and after misfortune they often called cabs too.

This guy wound up telling jokes from the backseat, what was worse, cab driver jokes, lewd jokes featuring cab drivers and women in the back seat with nothing on under their coats, and so on. She pulls back her coat and says, "Will this pay for it?" "Got anything smaller?" Pretty bad, and the cab driver had heard all those, and didn't respond in any way.

Then the garrulous commodities broker told an unusual joke. Seems a Chicago cabby picked up a rich Texan in the Loop, and Texan took a shine to him. He took him around for a couple days while he did business. Then he told him he had to go to London and he was taking the cab driver and his cab with him. What a ride, a dream ride, right? (In the back seat the speculator waited for a response but upfront the cab driver said nothing.) They went over on a boat, cab and all, and the cab driver took the Texan all around London for a week. When it came time to return to Chicago, the Texan gave him an address on the Southside, told the cabby that when they got back to Chicago, he had to go to the Southside. Cabby responds, "I don't go to that part of town."

After this punch line, when this joke also got no response from the front seat, the guy in back finally said, *"Get it?* He has this dream ride paying him to go back home as well—he don't go to that part a town! Haw haw haw!"

"No, I don't get it. It makes no sense. From London, he won't take a load to the Southside? No, it's not logical, let alone funny."

"It's not logical! It's a *joke!"*

"Well it's not funny."

"You don't get it? You guys go to the Southside?"

"I go anywhere."

"You go to the Southside, like at night? You don't care? You're not afraid?" The guy in back had wound up speaking to him in an exasperated, hysterical tone, outraged that he didn't get the joke. He was very strained, he must really have lost a lot of money today.

"No, I'm not afraid. I go anywhere, anytime."

Anywhere but the Labs, in Greenshores. These towers full of the ingredients of designer drugs and cures for cancer and the common cold, and the masked people in their caps and gowns brewing them up and shipping them out, made him uneasy. But here he was.

Eventually the obvious fact that he couldn't care less if he was let in or not and had almost gone to sleep made the Labs guard think it must be okay and he let him pass, figuring somebody must want a cab, whoever it was, otherwise a cab wouldn't be here. The guard never could get the response he wanted, but the name made sense, the name was an important one and probably the caller had left the office and not informed the front desk. On the strength of the name alone, and a cab was a cab, the guard finally waved him through disdainfully. The cab driver dutifully rolled on never noticing anything of this process.

By now he was almost in a trance and just ready to get this ride over with which he hadn't wanted and hadn't even actually accepted either. He came around the towers from the back and overshot the main entrance to the first tower, but he didn't back up. The people would see him and they could walk over.

In fact the people were not at the door anyway, they were standing by a black Lincoln and they began to move toward him. He didn't look at them. He didn't say to himself it was his load, but it must be. Whoever showed up and walked over was okay by him, or not. He could sense them coming near.

It was unusual for self-important people from the Labs to be waiting for him outside. It must be the nice night or some other reason. Thank God he hadn't had to go inside and roust them out. A few minutes inside the cold foyer of the building and you could taste the chemical dust in the back of your throat. He didn't look at them. A woman and man sat down in back, and a tall guy got in front with him without asking.

The cab driver had studiously avoided glancing at them so that he would experience as little of this ride as possible which he had never intended to take at all. He would have expected all three to sit in back and would have preferred that. The back seat of the Cadillac was plenty ample for three. The guy would have actually sat down on his maps and camera and things if the cab driver hadn't hastily raked them all toward him at the last second. He hadn't asked if he could sit in front, which was the proper thing to do. This really annoyed him and set him off. He realized he'd lost his cool slightly. He hadn't meant to take this call and he resented their presences around him when his night off had already begun. He particularly didn't appreciate the guy getting in front with him uninvited. Didn't they realize he was doing them a favor letting them in the car at all? Of course not. How would they know or care about his personal life. It wasn't their fault.

He was overcome with irritation, at himself. He stared ahead indifferently. He wanted only to get this ride over with, and hoped it wouldn't be a long one. Even a simple "Where to?" was more than he could manage and he was silent and didn't glance their way. It was one load too many, and they were, in the drivers' parlance, "bodies." Apparently they felt the same way about him because they were chattering at each other about the fact that their car would not start. That was always an unbelievable, amazing and earthshaking fact for people when their car would not start.

When people called a cab and told the operator or dispatcher where they wanted to go they assumed the dispatcher told the driver. That was no doubt what people thought. But the dispatcher didn't use up the airwaves for nonessentials like destinations. Cab drivers were told where to find the people but never told where the ride was going. The drivers were out there to take people wherever they wanted to go, period. It didn't matter where they wanted to go. That way the whole issue of which driver was getting a good ride and which one was getting a poor ride would never come up. Luck of the draw. People didn't imagine this though. When they called on the phone they assumed the driver knew already, and so they got in the cab and continued their conversations and sometimes said nothing to the driver at all.

This is what happened now, and after the two men went on talking for a few moments after getting in, speculating pointlessly about the surprising problem with their car, and finally stopped, their conversation running down, they all sat there in a weird silence that grew until finally the cab driver said to himself, this will never do. He had better snap out of it. So he finally asked them where they wanted to go.

It seemed to take them by surprise, that he didn't know already. They had been talking among themselves idly and now they all looked at him at once, like, didn't he know?

"Luminati's restaurant, you know it?" growled the guy next to him staring at him like he didn't get it. "Turn on your air, will you? It's warm tonight. Roll up the windows."

As he pulled out of the parking lot, he grew even more irritated at himself. What had happened to his professional cool, which made time fly? He might have said a pleasant word to them, just one would have been enough, to ease tensions, inside himself at least. He could still say something pleasant about the hot weather or something, and turn on the air. He was ranking them out with his surly silence and doing himself no favor. It was only a ten or fifteen minute trip to the restaurant, but at this rate it was going to seem forever. With him bad vibing the people. But it was already too late to fake a pleasantry. To make it worse, he refused to turn on the air conditioning. He had the windows locked open.

126

Completely oblivious, the man in back began a monologue. He talked in cool, ironic, business tones, gossiping, naming names, as if they were completely alone, or mellow with Luminati's cocktails already. The cab driver raised his head and sighed in gratitude. The guy next to him laughed once or twice. Thank heaven, they were at separate levels, in different worlds. The last thing that would have been expected from him was a pleasant word. He appreciated a fare like this one that kept to themselves. He thought better of them. He got a little of his spirit back and sped on taking them where they wanted to go. In a minute he would get his own life back. He sank into his own thoughts and heard nothing more than meaningless chatter.

The gleaming big frontentranceguard's capsule vanished like some piece of hightech junk lost in outer space as they left the towers and descended to earth. The wide black lane bordered by a few inky trees gave onto the country road through shadowy silver cornfields, oblivion. The cab driver was more outside the car than in it, and his hands controlled the wheel by instinct.

Making the sharp turn onto the Tollway ramp must have woken him up from his own trance. He heard from in back the man's voice which intoned a sense of easy mastery and power. Or it was that peculiar tone, so outrageously cold it caught his attention.

". . . the 'company image,' he says, if you please! Harland, I told him, your life is at stake not any of ours. We got a warehouseful of Romodon to get rid of, and in your territory they're writing Prozene. You want a little sales advice? You like to talk the doctor talk to em, and they're pissing on you. You think they went to medical school six years to listen to your presumptuous sophomore chemistry bullshit? Pull off your tie an open your damn shirt. Bare your breast an show em what it means to you personally. You got pictures of your kids, Harland, to show em, why they should write Romodon? It's time to bring out your goddam kids' pictures, Harland, believe me, boy, don't hesitate another moment. . . ."

Whatever this was about made the big guy in front next to him laugh in a sycophantic way but the cab driver could also tell how deeply he was amused by that poor Harland's lot. The cab driver glanced at him. He was real beefy, in his late twenties, about the cab driver's age. The man in back was much older, the boss. It was surprising, and kind of shocking, that medicines should be sordidly pushed like any other product line. Of course they were, just look at TV. But by the crying of salesmen in the doctors' offices?

The conversation of the old man in the backseat was unholy, indiscreet, and shocking. You heard a lot of things from the backseat. Sometimes it was amazing how people let their hair down and talked in the cab, just like the driver didn't exist or didn't matter. The cab driver sometimes felt as though he had an idea how the slaves had felt, simply not existing beyond some bloody job they were doing like parts of machines. He glanced in the mirror. After such an anecdote, he expected to see a man's naked face. But the only face that was suddenly naked was his own, because before he could locate the old man in the mirror, he saw Rita.

Awkward intimacy suffused the shock. He felt hot with embarrassment, like his fantasy was hanging out. He had never glanced at the people and certainly not at her when they got in the car. Was that why he'd picked up the mike, with last hopes for some violent disturbance of his heart? Her eyes held a merry, wiseacre look. She'd called after all, like she'd promised. It was a good thing the road was straight. For several seconds he completely stopped driving. His eyes refocused on the road, he hunched his shoulders, and got a grip on the wheel.

"Hey, Wisconsin! Ya musta had a long day I think."

How was he supposed to play this? Finally, he smiled too. "Hi, Rita."

After a measured pause, the man in back finally said, "You know this guy?"

"Wisconsin's the cab driver finally found your house, J.A., an he's not only a nice guy but a *very good driver*, if ya get me."

"You called this guy? Rita, let's not talk."

"The fuck! Is it my deal or not? Bobby's gonna show, an how'm I gonna do it? I need somebody I can trust."

The silence from in back got heavy. The cab driver had heard his share of arguments between men and women, and it was partly the silence a man resorts to at a certain point. But there was way more in it than that. The thing was, the cab driver was suddenly not invisible, not part of the machine, the scenery. He was being marked, center of everybody's attention. A novel sensation and not welcome. Finally the man decided to go ahead and talk again. They usually finally did.

"How will you do what, Rita?" he said quietly.

"J.A., Bobby aint gonna carry back until they call him, or maybe he calls them. He's gonna sit with us, with the bread."

"Sit with us."

"Until they call. He holds the bread. They seriously insist. They have to see the product, taste it. Then Bobby hands me, us, the cash. They don't trust his judgment, you know. You think they would? They say, send it in a fuckin cab, man, 'special delivery,' ha ha, you know how they talk. Or maybe you don't. The Spanish do a deal for, you know, thousands, but if they ride in a cab that means something! They have to be satisfied and then they phone Bobby and then he pays. In the meantime, he has a drink with us. You see the cash. The cash is on the table."

"Rita, I have no idea what you're talking about . . . I thought you were all . . . friends. Your friend . . . can't do the . . . quality control?"

"With Bobby I'm friends. I don't know the Mexicans. I met them once. They don't trust nobody. Wisconsin's gonna make the run, J.A., he's cool—and dependable."

"Wisconsin?" drawled the big guy next to the cab driver in the frontseat, as if waking up to something, looking sideways at him, as if catching on. "Wisconsin?"

"You called this . . . guy . . . when . . ." The man in back went on spelling it out with the abstracted air of trying to make two and two be four-and-a-half but not quite getting there. "Your deal. It is your arrangement, baby, and I assume you know what you're up to. We'll assume so. I'm done talking."

His mouth hanging open, the cab driver was not doing the speed limit. He was blocking the fast lane and cars were pulling around him angrily. Was he trying to prolong this interlude with Rita's friends? Learn about their business? He was being enlisted as a wheelman by her in some scheme. She was telling them all about it, and it sounded like the man in back was as startled by what she was saying as he was. Just like that he knew way more about their business than he would ever have wanted to know, sort of a cab driver's nightmare. He was in the middle of it. He felt like laughing to show them how out-to-lunch it was. Except Rita had proposed it.

He'd been trusting to her plan, that it would include him. It did. His throat was too dry to laugh. He pressed the pedal and quickly got back in the flow at seventy-five.

"Wiscon—"

"Nice car," the guy in front interrupted Rita.

"Wis—"

"Very nice!"

If the man in back was serious about no more talk, the guy in front meant to enforce it. The old guy had sounded baffled by what Rita had just told him, and that about made three of them. He didn't want to hear anymore either. He did his job and tried to find her eyes in the mirror. A few mixed feelings were threatening to blow the top of his head off. He wanted her bad enough, but the rest of it was completely out there, whatever it was. He was professional, he would go anywhere, anywhere that was legal, he was not afraid, but he was not a fool. She'd called after all, it was more than wonderful. He wanted her very much—and here she was. He needed to talk to her alone. What was she doing with these people? She was in trouble and needed help. He drove, barely, squeezing the wheel hard, the car swerving over the lanes.

The guy next to him had gotten in a groove. *"Very* nice," he said one time too many.

The cab driver felt like telling him to shut the fuck up.

"El Dorado. Nice, cabby."

The cab driver let it pass.

"Nice seats."

The guy ran his hand over the seat, then the dash. The cab driver felt like telling him to fucking not bother.

"Real nice. Unusual. A Cadillac cab . . . like somethin a nigger pimp would drive."

The way he felt about his car, it was almost a vice. He threw money at it. And it *was* pretty. Many people admired it, or at least knew enough to keep their mouths shut and enjoy the luxury of the ride. That the guy thought a racial slur would bother him made him despise him in a new way and was the last straw.

He dropped an eye on the clock and saw he was edging over eighty. The wind was whipping hard through the open windows. The green glow of approaching tollbooths was in the sky, and he took his foot off the pedal and coasted down. There were four or five cars ahead of them in the line, and as they crept forward, the cab driver fishing in his pocket for change was doing a slow burn.

"Want to visit em in the booth over there?" he said out of the side of his mouth to the guy next to him.

That made the guy laugh. He was satisfied to have gotten under the cab driver's skin. It made him comfortable.

"Hey, turn on the air. Roll up the windows. Don't your air work? What's this?" His shin was rubbing Armchair's groceries.

"Walk?" The cab driver finally looked directly at him. "Want to walk? That guy in the booth will call you another cab, okay?"

The guy laughed some more, happily, like this was getting real pleasant. It was good. He glanced back to include his boss.

"Otherwise I'm gonna take ya where ya goin." The cab driver tossed the correct change into the basket, and the barrier rose.

The big boat couldn't accelerate that fast, but there was no telling where she'd stop. He'd never had cause to try for the very top before. Never had Rita in the backseat before let alone an asshole like this one in the front at the very same time. The guy on his right was still chuckling at ninety, but at ninety-five his throat must have gone dry.

Bidding for the century mark, the car was trembling all over. A hard jitter leapt bumper to bumper through the old metal in waves. A hammering buzzing like a dentist's drill attacked from under their feet. A hundred miles an hour she was eating up stray traffic like pac-man, rolling on the air. A wild frontwheel shimmy jarred his hands like a jackhammer when she bounced on a tarstrip and rose into the air, and he held on. She had new tires. He believed in good rubber. But if he'd had to swerve suddenly, he couldn't have vouched for her stability. With the needle jumping like a drop of water on a hot skillet back and forth across the 110 stripe he was steering by the stars.

A gentle curve of the road was almost too much to negotiate and the car drifted to the far right lane and onto the shoulder. Threading the needle through a tight bunch of cars in a deft stitch, the sensation they were all going to die almost froze his muscles briefly. He held on tight and narrowed his eyes until they shut completely and pierced through the knot of cars blind. She was twelve years old. It was gratifying to see she would go some. Beside him the guy's knuckles gripping the dashboard were white.

The guy let go of the dash and absurdly began to drum with his fingertips like he was passing the time. That did it. The cab driver let his foot all the way down and stood on the floor. The Caddy surged slightly, her nose rose, and she climbed. The needle was beating on the roof. Three o'clock straight out. There was no more. The wind roared in their ears galeforce and almost peeled the skin off their faces.

The cab driver glanced at the meter. What a roll it was on! It was funny to see the numbers hop like that changing nonstop, and he started laughing. He began to whistle a tune. He glanced at the guy. He had a cheekbone like a slab of beef but at this speed it was shaking like a bowl of jelly.

"Chump! *Slow down!*" said the guy through clenched teeth.

It was the cab driver's turn to laugh.

"Slow down or I'll kill ya!" cried the guy.

The next second the guy was massaging the windshield with his nose. The tires were screaming and smoking. The old man's breath was on the back of the cab driver's neck, and Rita's head was next to his own. He reached up and touched her cheek. She was gasping ecstatically as a kid at the fair. In a dead skid, rear end slapping the pavement, rising clear off the ground, it was costing him six months' rubber, but it was worth it.

He finally brought the car to a stop broadside to the road. They'd missed their exit and he had to go back. Cars streaked around them horns blaring. He caught a break in the traffic and headed back the wrong way, across the lanes. Oncomers hit their brights, horns screamed in outrage. What was the point honking at somebody coming the wrong way at you on the Tollway?

He dove down the offramp grinding his foot on the accelerator, tires wailing, car humping and skidding. In the mirror, a vision of distorted faces, purple mouths pulled out of focus, as on a roller coaster ride when the fun you paid for stops for a horrible moment and real terror takes hold. The old boss squashed her against the door. He was right on top of her. If it was up to the cab driver, it would be the last time.

Coming out of the butterfly, he scorched sideways into traffic without looking, the car whipping on its springs. He was going too fast to hit anything. In the backseat, Rita giggled again and again and exclaimed at the top of her voice. A big hand reached across and grabbed him by the throat and applied pressure. Second time today, and it hurt.

LUMINATI'S—the name of the place burned in hotpink script on its rooftop as though a girl's lipstick had scrawled it across the sky. It was all open around the restaurant, a field gave way to pavement, and rows of parked cars, and it was possible to drive into the place from any angle if you didn't mind running up a mound over a brushy verge before entering the grassy lot. Over the hill they sailed.

"Let him go," commanded the man in back in a choking voice bobbing up and down as they crested the rise and dropped onto the rough grass. Another second their bumpy ride smoothed out on black asphalt splashed with pink lights from the restaurant's rooftop and violet watermarks from a fountain under a spotlight.

Nothing could have been more blandly familiar and night-out routine than the long full parking lot of hugely popular Luminati's restaurant through which they rolled. The air was full of evening perfumes and the sounds of family fun. A common peace abruptly enveloped them. He could taste the moisture from the illuminated splashing fountain by the frontdoor. When the door opened, a din of diners and canned country music poured forth. A wave of food smells from the famous menu came out the door with satisfied customers and wafted over them like a curtain dropping on the violence that had just been. This disastrous ride which he never should have taken was finally over. Or was it? He hoped not. He touched the brakes and brought them to a stop in front of the place as smooth as a kiss that don't mean a thing.

133

Was it a drop? Or maybe it made the man nervous to ride with that much powdered fun in plain view, and he had her hide it in the Lincoln's engine compartment. Shortly they would come out and go somewhere again, probably to party. The cop lurking in the Labs towers' parking lot had nothing more to do than speculate on the strange scene he'd just witnessed with Rita fighting the heavy hood of the big black Lincoln town car. No, it was not likely that slick man was in on this. More than amateurish, crazy, out in plain view. Desperate scheme, whatever it was. All hers.

The question insinuated itself—could it be a cockamamy *bomb,* meant for the man who'd tortured her? She'd stayed under there long enough to hook one to the coil wire if somebody had fixed it up for her and told her how to do it. She'd been struggling with something down in there. He remembered her eyes when he'd found the swollen scars on her wrists and neck, how they'd gone black and deep as pools. Fathoms of crazy hate could swim around in deep dead eyes like those. Black hate coiled like electric eels in a cave in an abused woman's heart ready to strike.

There must be the ingredients for a simple car bomb back in these towers and maybe a little lovestarved chemist or somebody who could make one for her and give her the instructions. What had the guard said? They could go to the moon. Was it farfetched? He had thought her a pathetic little lowdown no-account thing back in Jackie's before this ride she had taken him on.

The adrenaline burning through him made the prospect of another long interlude of waiting unsupportable. Time passed, somehow, intolerably. Behind him the sun fell lower and the whole building was burning. A peculiar thrill was coursing heavily through his body very close to physical pain. Not only that he really might have a serious bag in his sights to vindicate his day, with the offchance that it was some kind of testtube rigged to sky the man's ass when he touched the ignition, not only having seen her act in delightful, precocious stealth, her highwire act was affecting him through the air as vividly as though he'd been her boon companion.

A deep quietude reigned, with the change of shifts long accomplished, the drowsy hush of the country evening fallen down. It could have been peaceful and probably was for somebody somewhere. It only heightened the nervous ache of expectancy and the sting of each empty passing moment. Nothing yet had been revealed and the night would soon cover all. He feared the night as a new player in the game. The huge round orange sun was smoldering through low clouds and seemed to be emitting a regretful last gasp of white steam.

The wide cornfield sky relinquishing the day trailing white vapors against the immanent pale gold void drained him of any tactic against the building pressure of the waiting. His mood turned, and flattened out, as shadows grew, and as he could see less and less, he suspected that in some profound way beyond imagining he did not know what in the hell he was doing here. He no longer knew what he was feeling. An hour passed, and another, and came the night. A green light was filtering down over the cars from the tall arclights, which emitted a steady drone, and a crackle of swarms of moths flapping and dying against them. The last sunset-rose had long ago fled the windows of the Labs towers, whose yellow-gold radiance now was steady and artificial. The Lincoln was a lump of coal gleaming in silhouette in front of the first bright tower.

He pushed open the door—in the direction away from the guard shack—and extended his legs, letting out a sigh. He bent and unbent his knees again and again and wiggled his toes. He felt like taking off his shoes.

The guardshift had changed. Had his friend said something to the nightshift? No. The new guy was white. It had not gotten any cooler, and he wished he could've had a stroll in the picnic grove and shaken off this weird mood. He hadn't needed to park so close to the guardshack. He might have had more confidence in the dull gleam his star had produced in the eyes of the guard—if not in the loyalties of a brother. It was too late to move now without calling attention to himself sitting in his plaingreen car.

His hand went to the glove compartment, but the short finger of booze left in the bottle made him reluctant to finish it. He wanted something though. His mind was vague and muddled, and his nerves were throbbing. A tingling objectless loneliness rose from his dammed up blood demanding action. No action but wait. Soon his thoughts were going to be robbed of all their freedom and elasticity. It was all he could do not to make some violent motion. He might have jogged fast to the Lincoln to yank it open and look under the hood. He moved his legs in the shadows and waited.

He remembered the Fist's little glassine packet of cocaine in his breast pocket and decided to do a couple of lines. When was the last time he'd done any coke? Must have been last year at that party at the hip assistant district attorney's crib near the University of Chicago. He spread the packet open between his thumb and forefinger and eyeballed it. Plenty in there to cheat a little from. Anyway, what was he going to do with it now? There was something cool and refreshing in the white powder. The irritating heat which had diminished with nightfall cooked in his brain. Nice as ice, Bobby's cocaine glittered.

Shit got your thoughts together a taste and he could sure use that. With his pocket knife he set out lines in a crease on the map of Greenshores. He rolled up a dollar bill, stuck it in his nose, and leaned down. A mirror flicker caught the corner of his eye—the rippling forward of the big glass door of the Lab tower—he jerked his head to watch the door opening. The sleek owner of the Lincoln appeared on the top step, followed like a shadow by an athletically built younger man. He almost wiped the coke off the map. The powder slid scale miles to some other part of town. In his anxiety he wanted to toss the whole thing out the window. But what the hell, it would clean up his senses. He spread down the map once more and brought his nose over to the new neighborhood. It was no longer in easily snortable lines, but more as if it had been snowing over one end of town. The effort sucking it up was sort of the reverse action of how you'd move your head to blow out birthday candles.

Letting out a gasp he brushed map, dollar, and Bobby's glassine packet to the floor. The gemlike lucidity that the drug imparts came on immediately. Cautiously he brought his fieldglasses up over the dash. The man had looked swank and sturdy in his car, but he was fatter than that, prosperous and suave. His silvergray continental suit was smooth and creaseless as a skin. It flashed darkly in the yellow tower light as he shifted his bulk.

The young guy next to him was wearing a tan blazer and jeans. He was cleancut and looked tough in a football sort of way, built like a big tight-end, rangy and tall. His eyes swept the parking lot warily, looking for the play. For a moment his gaze seemed to rest on the cop's green car a hundred yards away. Come again? Was the man a captain in this outfit of the magnitude that needed protection? He only looked like a standard issue swinger salesman, vice president, or lawyer who featured a little blow on the coffeetable alongside the lovely cocktails, not one who attracted serious threats.

The cop's thoughts jumped a square. If Bobby was the man, who exactly was this fancy customer of his who needed a bodyguard? Silvertop executive wasn't *dealing* to this northern territory from the Fist's connection, was he? To his social set, perchance, to support a Big Habit or a lavish lifestyle? To professional acquaintances in these laboratory towers? technicians needing a buzz? neighbors on chic White Stallion avenue who behind their circular drives and garden statuary were spilling powder all over the little polo players and alligators on their breasts? the affluent on Astor Street? patrons of the Drake? A body guard suggested all of that, but maybe more. Could Bobby the Fist have come so far?

Rita squeezed backward through the Labs' glass door a few moments after them, pushing the door out with her ass, turning and stumbling through sideways, as though it weighed a ton, looking preoccupied. Her heavy shoulder bag looked full again, swinging pendulously, banging the glass slab awkwardly. Nobody had held the door open for her any more than they had held open the hood of the black car while she did that thing. She was under the radar or not worth considering. In their powerful company she looked as small and alone as ever. They weren't studying on Rita. Moving with paradoxical gliding grace for a fat man, silversuit had reached the door of the Lincoln. He might have glanced back at her expressionlessly over the top of the car as he got behind the wheel. After one more sweep of the eyeballs, the bodyguard sat down in the backseat directly behind him. The big car rocked a little under their weight. The hard, earnest expression on bodyguard's face reminded the cop of those hotshot private guys who cut a figure giving the bad stare to the crowd while the man being protected caught it from the other angle.

Rita was still up there at pavilion level looking sullen and self-important. She came down one step with seeming reluctance, and on the next twisted an ankle. Her shoe flew off. She knelt down, rubbing her leg, reaching around for the shoe. She appeared to duck, she crouched.

The stillness in the parking lot rang in the cop's ears deafeningly, relentless chirping of grasshoppers or some kind of bugs in the fields, the lethal-sounding lawn sprinklers' bright rhythmic spurts. A distant unintelligible voice spoke out of nowhere, through some crack in the sealed glass towers. He wondered if it was the cocaine weirding him out a little as it inevitably did after a while. An oily gleam flew to his eye off the hood of the black Lincoln. Something swelled and ticked. His ears were straining for any sound, but bracing for a monstrous fiery blast. Listlessly she fished for the wayward shoe. Damn if she wasn't ducking!

He'd as soon see him die. For a second the cop indulged envy and contempt for the man, who used his wealth and leisure to play at drug dealing, at sadistic sex games with Rita. If he had his money he'd—never mind what he'd do. He caught himself in the distasteful role reversing mood of a servant evilly gazing at a master. He, the cop, and his sort, not the man's sidekick, were the real protectors of the likes of the fat man. Did the Laboratories support ghetto charities, no doubt? The chance even in a thousand of an appalling explosion followed by pieces of metal and body parts raining down probably made it his duty to honk or yell or do anything to warn them, but he wasn't kidding himself he wouldn't enjoy seeing the occupants of the Lincoln blow all over the parking lot in bitesize chunks.

The starter motor of the Lincoln ground over piercing the silence and sending the blood pounding through his veins as he ducked too. The car didn't explode. It didn't fire up either.

Annoyed, the man kept his hand on the key for a whole minute, let it cool, and tried again. The starter ground over and over but the motor refused to start. After another minute of it he gave up, and the two of them got out of the car. They stood together in front of it hesitantly, looking at the car accusingly. The sidekick fished around for the latch, taking even longer to find it than Rita, pushed up the hood, with more ease than she, and they examined the engine malevolently but helplessly in the manner of guys who may be looking at it for the first time and haven't a clue. Rita was staring hard in another direction rubbing her toe.

The cop wiped the sweat off his brow with a finger. His skin felt feverish and raw. A side-effect of the drug was that he felt clear but was practically twitching. The two of them studied the engine compartment the way people do who don't know what they are looking at but are hoping forlornly. The two men were squinting at the engine futilely, not wanting to have to finally do something about it. The fat man gazed abstractedly at it, his mind elsewhere, thinking of his next plans, the cop felt sure, while the bodyguard glared with suspicion at it. Abruptly the man stared at Rita.

Rita didn't notice. She was cool. She stepped down seeming to concentrate all her attention on how her highheel was fitting now she had found it. She looked pissed off but in general, not at the car which apparently she hadn't registered because she started to get inside it.

Silvermane waddled and glided fast around to Rita whose legs dangled out of the open passengerdoor and said something close to her ear. The cop studied them intently through his glasses as if they had been actors in a play. The bodyguard shot the motor a last scowl and slammed the hood down. The bland confidence on the fat man's face suggested he understood everything perfectly. Anybody on the level and not a player with a play to make tonight would have been ticked off and agitated, the cop thought. The man's farseeing glance and control in light of big plans were evident. So were Rita's for that matter, insofar as she was hiding them, who got out of the car, casting a sidelong look at it, climbed back up the steps, and walked back into the tower, struggling with the door again.

When she came out again, she leaned back with her ass against the rear fender of the car and searched her purse for a cigarette. She said quite a bit carping out of the side of her mouth to them. Nobody listened to her or came to light her cigarette. She shut up and smoked. Her big purse, which had held that brown parcel the size of a box of poisoned candy, slung over her shoulder as it had been all day starting in Jackie's this morning, bulged and sagged once more. Her hands lay flat against the shiny black metal of the long, dead car and the cigarette dangled from her lips. Her gaze flicked upward at the hidden stars or focused inward.

No, it would have been dumb to fricassee the man in his automobile. What she was about was picking him clean. That package of hers was a nice scrapeoff she hoped he wouldn't notice, at least not right away. The crazy chick had refilled some secret laboratory jar with powdered sugar or something after she'd stolen it. After hiding maybe fifty or a hundred thousand worth in the man's own engine compartment, she must have yanked the coil wire.

He sat straight up. She was going to run! Tonight! The stashed parcel was her nut, her getaway. She'd be back for it soon, or somebody would. Who, Bobby? It was too large a piece, she couldn't stick around long after stealing that. Spunky lady, she'd hidden it under his nose! She was going to take a powder on the fat man. He grabbed the Johnny Walker and before he could stop himself, killed the bottle. *Go baby!* he whispered vehemently to her. The fat dude probably thought he had her down so far, he'd never conceive she was capable of it. Heart of hearts, the one he loved to beat on, but what was she going to do, steal his car too?

She took the keys to my Cadillac car,
Jumped in my Kitty
And drove afar!

His heart sang. He knew her far better than they did, like his own dear kind. In his soul he felt a thrill of recognition—more than that, a secret sympathy.

Rita's eyes narrowed, and the angle of her head changed. She tossed away her cigarette. All heads turned. The cop swung his glasses, a Bull's-eye cab was coming around from the back of the campus someplace. Number 17, that farmboy, the Cadillac, the lying fucker.

The cab pulled up beside the row of limousines, looking like a circus nag among stallions. This was not chance, of course, that of all the cab fleet it would be him. Who was he working for, the fat man, or Rita, or them both? The cab rolled too far and they had to walk up to it. That was him all right, the punk, making them walk.

He would strangle him if he was the fat man. They piled in, Rita and the man in back, the bodyguard in the sport coat in front next to the cab driver. The notion of his mind as a lightning swift instrument that the coke had given him left him abruptly.

It was a weird thing about the lucidity of the drug. It cast its light in all directions, making alternatives burn with agonizingly equal intensity. The cab 17 waited a long minute or two in front of the illuminated tower for some reason after they got in it and then at last it made the circle slowly to the gate. Why were they moving so slow? Did they have things to talk about, were they making plans? He wanted to know them. He wanted nothing further from life than to make the move and follow them and see what those plans were, yet he was loath to leave the package in the engine unattended.

She would come back here for it, or probably the cab driver would, or Bobby, or *somebody* would, soon. He didn't want to miss that event either and to see where it led. As much as he had been depressed lately and one man's disgust with life been too much to carry, he wished he were two, he had enough excitement and curiosity now for two. The bag in the Lincoln was no small deal by the size of it. The package might fly away to anywhere if left alone. Right now it was everything he had. The cab was pulling away past the guard shack. Suddenly he understood nothing about anything.

The cab had passed the guardshack and turned out of the gate. It was like being ripped apart by two magnets, a powerful one hidden in the engine compartment of the disabled Lincoln and another planted in a ridiculously painted bull's-eye rolling farther and farther away from the poised arrow of his blunted mind. He didn't have time to ask the guard in his glass shack to keep an eye on the Lincoln for him, and it might not be a good idea anyway, the nightguard was a white dude.

No way was he interested in Rita alone, except for herself, of course, as a woman, a friend. He became excruciatingly conscious of his desire to snatch the fat man's ass out of the tall tower, out of his long car, out of cab 17, right out of his silver suit. He felt he could leave the package, her secret stash, under the hood of the Lincoln, to Rita's own plan. He freed her in his mind to fly with it how she would, her secret nut, her getaway stash, God bless her if it meant escape from her tortured life with these evil motherfuckers.

141

Her alone, he'd let her to go with God's grace. Who he wanted were the three guys with her in the cab—plus Bobby, of course.

A sudden panic gripped him. The cab had been moving slow enough—too slow—number 17 must know some shortcut through the cornfields, now vanished around the bend. Would-be-slick cornhusker! He took off. They had completely disappeared up Fox Glove Road when he emerged from the Labs' campus. They must have taken a sudden turnoff and slipped away, he surmised with a violent sinking pang. But as he came out of his dark nod, half a mile ahead of him up Fox Glove Road, it was amazing to see how little distance they'd actually covered. The taillights of the cab picking up speed winked at him complacently. The cab driver 17 was giving a nice VIP ride to him wasn't he, while Rita suckered the fat man.

Fox Glove crossed the Northwest Highway, and they turned east on Northwest Highway. On the horizon, a ribbon of light announced the Tollway ahead. After a minute, he caught the irridescent glimmer of a green and white Tri-State Tollway sign. The Cadillac cab turned up the ramp and disappeared for a moment behind roadside scrub. He followed its firefly ascent to the top of the ramp where it gleamed long and white for an instant before disappearing into the speeding yellow swarm.

The cop's small plaingreen car skidded onto the runway with his foot to the metal and careened upward, tail shaking. It spun into traffic on the Tri-State topping seventy already. He couldn't see them anywhere, and kept accelerating. They were right in front of him in the adjacent lane. He had to stand on his brakes or he would have passed them, exposed. What was the guy doing tooling along at the most relaxed five miles an hour below the speed limit? He was driving the man like he was a big fragile egg. He slowed to forty-five to let them pull way ahead. He grabbed the glasses, banged them into his brows, and was slightly reassured. All heads faced forward, though you never knew what games cab driver 17 was playing in the mirror. He fell back allowing a dozen cars to intervene. Traffic was thick. He'd had too much to drink and on top of it the coke which was giving him blind spots. He was no longer in the best shape to drive. He was sleepy and nervously energized at once, and his sense of timing and distance was being affected. He sped up again, slowed down, sped so he almost came abreast of them, and fell back as they were creeping along. For God's sake you could not lose a red-white-and-blue El Dorado painted with bull's-eyes. But he had once today already!

He blacked out. A deep waking nod. A vortex of futility swirled up. His head must have drooped, and for a second he couldn't see a thing, like his brain had been cut off its blood supply for the space of one agonized, tissue weary heartbeat. He fought upward out of the blackness for air. Coming out of it, the road and traffic, the wide-open land to either side of the Tollway, in which the occasional corporate monolith seemed to aspire hungrily toward the sky in loneliness and despair like a rocket, all struck him after the broken continuity as lost and strange, as though he'd just dropped down onto this road in a dream. Where was he? It took a moment for focus and memory to reestablish themselves. Alienation was succeeded by alarm as he recalled the state of his mission. He couldn't find the cab again no matter how he searched, near or far, with bare eyes or glasses. It must be around here somewhere slow as they were going. It seemed the same unseen hand that had dropped him back down onto this road after his blackout had in its swift retraction taken the cab away with it. Rage chased eerie apprehension. That halfslick guy! He floored it and burst through traffic, shoving the glasses against his eyes and spying far ahead of him, and nearly grazing the cars in his path, his progress marked by the wails of horns.

The guy was making a run for it! He was doing ninety when he picked out the cab by the crest of its toplight, which was turned off, black crown against a battery of brightly lit tollbooths sending up their odd ordinary greenish glow. With relief he hit the brakes hard and decelerated down. The warningstrips barked like gunfire under his wheels, jarring him to the bone. Far from routine, the checkpoint with its attendants in the booths and roaming about in striped green-lit safety vests struck a chord of dread. He hadn't forgotten he was on the Tri-State Tollway, but this commonplace interlude was demonic. He was stacked up in a line with drivers he'd just cut off coming to rest around him and giving him the bad eye. The cab was a dozen cars ahead, just going through a gate, its driver laughing at him.

It was a funny thing about the cocaine, after a rush of cold and seductive clarity, a backwash of apprehension set in, like a wave combing a beach leaving a trail of silver litter. Probably doing it on

143

top of a pint of Johnny Walker didn't help much. He was going to have to do some more lines, just to get rid of this icy doubt that was probing his brain like fingers of black water. He reached inside his jacket for the glassine packet, searched all his pockets, but couldn't find it. The horrible light! The layers of greenyellow tollbooth light came down to him oppressively and terrifyingly as though he were a diver deep in the sea, very quickly running out of oxygen, his hands unable to find the controls. Toward the green lamps above the gates moths swarmed, their frying sounds background music for the up and down motion of the barriers, signaling obscurely every time somebody dropped in their forty cents. High above, the velvet sky hid gems, the pearly gleam of a crescent moon peeked through the drifting clouds, the benign, clear atmosphere reigned, where he might have breathed again.

He was almost to the gate when he realized he didn't have any change on him. The business of disengaging himself, forcing the snout of his car through the lines in front of the automatic gates toward the manned booths, was ghoulish, nightmarish. A crowd of scowlers, devils behind glass, opposed him every inch of the way. The guy in the booth gave him a queer, sympathetic smile and raised the barrier before he'd paid as they sometimes did. He thrust out a dollar and didn't wait for change. The speedometer on the plaingreen car stopped at ninety though he knew it would do better. He thought he saw the cab, rocking wildly, a half mile ahead, doing a C-note, at least, good God almighty.

Too late, he didn't know what he had seen. He was coming up on the Cadillac as fast as if it had been sitting still again. He couldn't brake hard enough. The Cadillac *was* sitting still, stopped dead in the fast lane! All the drivers caught between them were standing on their brakes, taillights flashing red. Smoking his tires, the cop swerved onto the shoulder to avoid a crackup. As if the whole highway had caught fire, brakelights blazed left and right as the cab driver pulled off a deathdefying feat, diving back up the highway, crossing all lanes. Horns moaned and bellowed like stampeding oxen coming to an unexpected fence. On the far shoulder, the cab driver drove the wrong way back to an exit the cop had never seen, and disappeared over the edge into the dark country below.

Caught in the long jam of cars pulled up sharply, then lingering to gape, more and more slowing and gaping, at nothing now, dozens, hundreds, pulling up and slowing, for a few seconds the cop was too wired to move. When he regained control, he began backing up the left shoulder. He was staring straight across at the exit ramp. He was as wired as a mile of cyclone fence, which was about what he'd need to create a space to slide through.

Looking away from the traffic bearing relentlessly down on him, he happened to see the glassine packet on the floor along with his map. From his raised station the guy in the tollbooth must have been able to see it. Was that what he'd leered at him about? He saw his chance and burned rubber to make it straight across the highway, drove back up the shoulder, and pulled over at the top of the ramp and stopped. He got out, stepped on the bumper, and climbed onto the roof of his car. There was a long view of the country below the elevated Tri-State.

They'd let it all hang out. The cab driver was silverhair's special delivery boy. They had a play to make, and cops weren't invited. He smelled deal in the air so strong, it was like something burning. No doubt in the world drugs and money were meant to change hands tonight, this hour, even. Rita's adventure with the Lincoln had only been a little sideshow all her own in the shadows. That might be the only secret left, the one between him and Rita, who had thought herself unseen. The main act was out there below in the twinkle of merry lights someplace.

Standing on top of his car, he swept the territory with his knowing glance. Of course they could have doubled back underneath the Tollway in the other direction. The dark countryside was dappled here and there with many mysterious lights. His eye was attracted to a hotspot of radiation—a huge restaurant or banquet hall bathed in wine colors not a mile away. He could read its big pink neon sign with ease from here with his bare eyes, it blazoned the sky.

LUMINATI'S was the grandest point of light in sight by far. That's where they'd gone. The man wasn't going to Burger King, was he? He brought his fieldglasses up to his eyes and made a quick study. There were two hundred cars in the parking lot around the joint. A blue fountain spouted spectacularly in front of illuminated Grecian statuary before the main door. In fact, the place looked just like the fat man's mansion, except bigger. He would be right at home.

The parking lot was part asphalt giving way to a grassy field. You could cut into it anywhere. He drove down a sidestreet that made a boundary, gingerly steered over the weedy verge, and found a place lost in the middle of the parked cars. Got out and peered over the tops of the cars. A deep blue flicker from the illuminated fountain picked out a pierced Bull's-eye on a white cab's door, an arrow to his eager heart, number 17.

He'd taken this guy for a punk, a nobody. What was his game? He'd mistaken him a couple of times today. At first, he'd thought he was just the type who'd take a few bucks to run a redlight. Then, without really thinking about it, he'd guessed he might have kept a camera with him hoping to see a fire or a crime, and sell a picture to the papers. He'd figured he'd been struck by her was all, a little guy with a camera, who'd seen a pretty girl and fired away. While squeezing his throat, he had glimpsed several more photos of streets and people, along with the portrait of Rita in front of the house on White Stallion Drive. Why had he taken her picture there? The cab driver didn't have a little insurance game going, did he? If he'd dug deeper, gone in the glove compartment, would he have come across the fat man doing something funky? One picture was of that other screwball, that crazy professor driver. Why would he have taken a shot of *that* guy? Why was he taking all these photos?

There had been a picture of a street from the black side of the city somewhere. A streetsign you could read in the photo had said Governor's Parkway. Never heard of that. Where the hell was that exactly? He didn't know the street, and he thought he knew them all. On an impulse he pulled out of his jacket his pocket street guide and looked it up, on the near Westside somewhere. What was the cab driver doing over *there?*

But he had no more time or inclination to speculate on these matters, because another cab pulled in, a Checker cab from Chicago, and out of it alighted Bobby the Fist, blinking in the pinkish light, who headed toward the restaurant door, holding tight to a fat briefcase. The look on his face said he was in foreign territory. The cop knew how he felt.

146

The big guy next to him in the front seat, whom the cab driver had the weird sensation of now seeing for the first time as if there were layers and layers of reality yet to peel back, pulled him with one hand toward the cocked fist of the other. But the projected short arc of the punch was arrested by a voice in back.

"Let him go, I said! Forget about it!"

The old man's dry command caused the fist to hesitate, and drop. A couple of crumpled graygreen bills sailed over seatback.

"Wisconsin, we got a run for ya to make in half an hour." Rita's voice was breathless with the ride they all had just taken. "Keep your meter on an wait, okay? Gonna make it worth your while—very much so, dig? Hear me, Wisconsin?"

The fat boss was already out of the car, gliding off businesslike in the violet light. For a second the cab driver watched him go in grudging admiration of such self-control. After a ride like that. There was a man used to assigning people and affairs to their places. So he'd gotten to his destination a little too fast, all the better. He could even discount what passed between his girl friend and the cab driver, option of the powerful. The old guy was a lesson in cold. Even if you yourself were the object of such disdain, you had to dig it.

The sidekick had to wrench himself away, but he did it, keeping his eyes on the cab driver whose head he'd like to smack, seized and lifted by the old man's terse words to another plane, where the money was, no doubt, hauled backward out of the cab by the force of his boss floating fast away in his metallic suit flashing in the fountainlight, smoothing down his silver hair with a hand, jaw muscles rippling over the bone in spite of his fatness.

147

Rita got out of the car but did not glance after her companions, like it really was her deal. Flinging her heavy purse backward over her shoulder, she slipped right back through the front door of the cab the bodyguard had left open and squeezed into the seat next to the cab driver and held him close now and whispered conspiratorially, "Wisconsin, wait for me, okay? I got somethin for ya to do that'll get us over, if you'll help me. We'll go *tonight,* baby—to them old *North Woods!*"

She laughed in nervous delight of their projected fun but also the expected reward of seeing through some danger he didn't understand yet. The soft interior light and the flickering fountain made it seem they were already huddling together on the open road in the moonlight through the trees under the eaves not of Luminati's sprawling operation but a little lost lakeside tavern. The cab driver told himself he was in control. He'd seen she was in trouble this morning, and knew she was nervy, but he had never guessed she was dangerous. She was in a state of high elation mixed with lowdown fear that had nothing to do with their ride over here, but what was coming next. The blood was high in her cheeks, and she was leaning into him. He was overcome with apprehension, indecision, and desire.

"Rita, I don't know what you're doin or what you *think* you're doin, but *don't do it.* Just leave this fucking bullshit and come with me right now!"

"No, Wisconsin, wait. We need money, man, I mean *real* money! Keep your meter running, honey. Just wait for me, I will be out again in just a while—it might be half an hour—don't worry, it's not what *they* think, an ya won't have to do a thing but *this!*"

She kissed him hard thrusting her face into his. Her heart was pounding next to his. She was trembling, rocking. His tongue stumbled on that gap in her teeth that went through to bliss.

"Listen, Wisconsin, I'm gonna bring a package out to ya, but it's—"

A large hand flew in, seized her by the collar, and yanked her violently out of the cab, her head striking the doorframe, knocking the notion and the breath out of her. She could not, or chose not to, say more. Her unfinished words hung in the air, like a promise, or a doom, he did not understand which. Her big purse nearly fell to the ground, and the guy reached down after it and set the strap of it

148

over her shoulder again. She was propelled toward the restaurant door by the overwhelming force of his one hand in the small of her back, the other guiding her by her shoulder, her blue suit twisted askew on her scrawny frame.

He reached out to touch her again, but she was gone, leaving him with strange happiness mixing through blackest fear and doubt. In the doorway she craned her neck to cast him a final fleeting backward precocious look around the guy's shoulder that sent a wave of tenderness through him. It was a look that told him she had called him all right. In spite of being manhandled, in her eyes smiled a brash determination and a defiance of her predicament whatever it was. In her look was an appeal, and confidence—in him.

He watched her shoved hard through the door on her high heels, her slender ass swaying. She might be somebody's sex object, but she was nobody's fool, and her brave look at this moment showed it. She was planning something, but he couldn't guess what it was, and truly he didn't want to know. That might put him and her old man in the same boat, by the sound of things. But then again he doubted he was in a boat with that man. He backed the car away from the front door a little way into the shadows and began to come down from the ride and her presence. He smoked a cigarette. The shape of things escaped him more and more. As the long minutes slid past, he knew he was in over his head, but he couldn't leave.

When he had pulled up speeding, flushed with righteous emotion, he had discounted the old man as much as he had been discounted by him. *He* was the boss. He was in his world, driving. In the swelling still of the night, mixed in with the wellfed chatter of Luminati's many fans and patrons echoing right through the walls vaguely derisive of outsiders in the parking lot, his respect for the man born of his dry, laconic departure intensified into a wall of fear, holding him back, not abject fear, but plain old wise *knowing* fear, the kind the lone wolf feels for the hunter as it backs away into the forest, never taking its eyes off the man with the gun till the moment it turns tail and scampers.

But he sat there. He smoked the cigarette, drawing deeply. Rita hadn't missed a beat. She'd dreamed up some use for him fast, damn if she hadn't. He wondered what it was going to be. She wanted them to escape the deadly city together and make that trip up to the beautiful North. Everything he wished for had come about. She'd been prevented from fully explaining things. He guessed he'd find out soon enough.

He was going to make a run for the gang of them! He sincerely doubted he was going to do such a thing, but who knows maybe he was. He wondered what he was going to do. When he prided himself on going anywhere anytime with anybody, that didn't mean he was crazy. Maybe he was going to do it, since he wanted her, if it meant getting her.

Something she had intended to tell him had been cut short. He smiled to himself as the obvious good reasons for splitting the scene pronto marched home to him. He must fade away into the forest. He could see Armchair wagging his head to go! just crank her up out of here! He had no intention of leaving, he wanted her too much. She had reappeared, it was what he had hoped for, and the last thing he'd expected. She needed his help and she wanted to be with him. The run he would make would spring her from those wrong characters she was with. That was her plan he felt sure. The longer she stayed inside the restaurant with the two of them, desire and impatience for it to begin glued him to the spot.

After thirty minutes, a green-and-yellow Checker cab from Chicago pulled up with a devilmaycare lurch. A tall black guy carrying a briefcase gingerly got out, taking some cautious glances in all directions. He paid off the driver and stood talking to him through the window for a few seconds. His shirt was purple with Milky Way swirls and blobs of light, open to the middle of his chest, and his babyblue jacket was embroidered with sort of lace. His face was not confident and bland like most Luminati's patrons, even the few black ones, but held a wary, inward expression of having been through wars. Deep creases around his coldly probing eyes attested to ordeals undergone not typical of the average restaurantgoer in these parts. In contrast to his rough features, his hair was extravagantly coiffed in loose curls oiled so liberally that seen from behind his head looked like a chandelier. Keeping a firm grip on the briefcase, he strode in an exaggeratedly casual manner toward the restaurant door. The cab driver had one mindnumbing idea. The heavy looking dude was going inside to meet Rita, he was the one she had been talking with the old man about. There could be no other explanation for a cat looked like the bad guy in a kung fu or *Shaft* movie walking in Luminati's with its wholesome clientele of farmers and agricultural equipment salesmen, Ozzie and Harriet nuclear families, corporate secretaries, data crunchers, and middle managers, and high school juniors on a hot date.

The Checker didn't budge from the spot at the restaurant's frontdoor where it had alighted. The Checker driver turned off his motor. The cab driver stared at the Checker for a minute, lit another cigarette, and clenching it between his lips, walked over. The Checker driver was listening to music through earphones. He was resting his elbow on the windowsill, with his hand over his eyes, head nodding. On the hand was a tan leather driving glove.

"Hey, wake up! You can't sit here."

The glove came down languidly, the earphones came away from one ear.

"Say what?"

"It's my post. You can't sit here."

"I aint steal none a yourn. I waitin for my man."

"What's he doin in there?"

"What who doin?"

"Your fare."

"What my fare be doin? What *your* fare be doin?"

"I mean, could ya tell what sort of people he was meeting here, what he's doing, you know?"

"Shee-it, you think he talk bout his business? What's it to you, anyhow?"

"I got my reasons. How long he gonna be in there?"

"Be in there! Hey, meter roll, I be chillin, can be tomorrow, what I care, hey cab driver? Ha ha! Am I right, cab driver? Ha ha! Roll, meter, roll! Ha ha."

"How long he say for you to wait?"

"Look, I aint steal none a yourn, I tol ya. He don't wanna get stuck out in these parts here, believe me. I got a right to wait on my passenger."

"You're in a no-parking zone. You're breaking the fire code."

"Listen here, I'ma go piss, watch my car for me, will ya?" The Checker driver got out, adjusting his Walkman earpieces.

"Hey, I aint got time to watch your car!" protested the cab driver. "You'll get towed!" he promised.

151

The Checker driver couldn't hear him. He had turned his back, maxed the volume, and gone into the restaurant. The cab driver threw his cigarette on the ground, then immediately jammed a fresh one between his lips, stared at the empty Checker cab another moment, and went back to his own car.

He sat behind the wheel and expelled smoke. He had gained nothing by his interrogation of the Checker cat. He felt he had some serious thinking to do, but couldn't find the first thought. He had no thoughts, only desire. He made up his mind he had nothing to think about at all. All he had was to indulge himself in his desire, it was all there was for it. Rita filled a hole in his soul completely that had been waiting for just her fine shape. That was that. It wasn't something that bore much thinking about. He dwelt on her.

After a while he thought he'd just go into the restaurant for a quick look around, and to take a leak, and enjoy the airconditioning for a minute. Just inside the door an instinctive glance over the top of the crowd found the bunch of them in the booth in the far corner and he knew all he needed to know. She was trying to get away from them, he was sure of that, but not just now, for she was badly outnumbered. Nothing he could do about her right now. She was trapped in the corner. It wasn't the time. It was her move to make. She was cool for now. She wanted him to help her escape! He didn't know when the moment would come, or what it would look like.

He turned the other way and kept on going and headed for the men's room. He'd attended to his bodily functions back at the Athen's after dinner, but he'd had a couple glasses of wine. There were two white guys standing at the urinals, no black guy. Maybe he could get something more out of him after all. He wanted to ask him some more about the fare he'd brought here, who had come to do business with Rita and her pals. Zipping up, he stared at the doors of the stalls, but none of them were fully closed. Where could he have gone to? He wasn't going to get more out of that guy anyway. He knew quite well the guy would not have asked his fare about the business he had come to conduct here, any more than he himself would have pried into the business of a fare of his own. Still, there was no one else to ask.

He lingered near the dance floor in back, picked up a menu. He thought it would be a good idea if they all saw he was waiting for her. Leaving the restaurant slowly and nonchalantly, he tried to catch Rita's eye or any of their eyes, but they were too far away at the end of the big place, and she must be scrunched down in the corner of the booth, he couldn't even see her now. He hoped she had at least caught sight of him and was sure she must have. Those guys had her buried. What else had he expected to see? He'd known very well it was futile to go in the restaurant. He didn't want it to appear that he was spying on them, just that she would see he was still here and ready. Ready for what? Back in his cab, realization that he had nowhere else he wanted to be but here hit him like a ton of concrete crushing him in his seat. He had no other thought that he wanted to think but of her. No other love to love or fear to fear. Life was a wasteland and all was darkness except burning bright Rita, and there was only one possible thing he was going to do and that was sit here and wait. He was going to wait for her all night if that's what it took. But it was not going to take all night.

Through the cloud of blue cigarette smoke he was emitting, he saw the big guy approaching, the old man's sidekick who'd had those nice things to say about his car and nearly broken Rita's neck hauling her out of it. Maybe he had some more compliments to pay him. This was all wrong. He had expected to see Rita again coming out to finish explaining things to him like she'd said. Not this jerk. He didn't like it. What was this asshole coming toward him for? He stiffened, watchful for a sucker punch. The guy was carrying something under his arm. What had they done with her? Standing at the passenger window the guy pushed a large package covered with brown paper at the cab driver.

"She tell ya where to take this, cabby?"

He didn't take the package, didn't move, didn't reply. He stared straight ahead not looking at him. The guy seemed to have forgotten about what had passed between them before. His voice was no longer angry or cocky, but low and dead serious.

"Huh? Look at me. The Rendezvous Lounge on Waukegan Road, before you come to them Caldwell woods, near the city. Know the joint? The Rendezvous, on Waukegan. Who you want—*Rodriguez*. He'll be at the bar."

The guy opened the backdoor and tossed the brown package onto the backseat.

"You're on your way. Ya never made the run, cab driver. Ya never seen me in your life."

153

The guy stared down at him evilly for a moment, wrinkling his nose, as if remembering how much he personally disliked this cab driver. He pulled out a crumpled hundred dollar bill and tossed it onto the seat next to the cab driver, who didn't pick it up.

"How much to there, forty bucks? A hundred aint bad, is it cab driver? On the other hand, if ya fuck up, the odds the other way are terrible."

The guy looked at him another moment, and suddenly broke into a knowing grin. A lewd twinkle in his eye, he reached all the way in and nudged the cab driver's shoulder hard with his fingertips. "Hey, Rita's a wet piece, aint she, guy?" He shoved his hands deep in his pockets, chuckling, and walked away.

The cab driver, who had not spoken a word during this interview, nor moved one finger of his hand poised on the wheel, and had agreed to nothing, watched the guy's slab of a back recede out of the corner of his eye. He saw again Rita's eager, frightened face before him. He believed she meant for them to be on their way tonight for the North Woods for real. But why hadn't she come out to talk to him as she'd said she would? He was sure she wanted to get away from those guys in there—with him! They'd prevented her from coming out to explain to him her plan of how she meant for him to help her to escape. But that didn't mean the plan was not still operative, whatever it was.

A C-note wouldn't get them to Wisconsin. It was way too much for a run down Waukegan Road, the guy was right about that. Everything was wrong about this, even wronger than it had seemed at first hearing of it on the ride over.

Sometimes, on a lonely late night, when the number you got turned out to be a darkened closed gas station with three shady looking dudes hunched over waiting for you with ugly faces, sometimes, you sped on by. On the backseat lay a package like a bomb that would maim you if you mishandled it.

He could imagine what was in it, coming from the Labs. Some fantastic designer drugs the kids would pay thousands of their parents' money for, or maybe a fortune of prescription pills, painkillers like oxycontin or something, headed for the black market. Maybe it was somebody's secret sample of some new drug and they were stealing industrial secrets. Maybe what was in it wasn't even illegal, but probably it was illegal. No, it was wrong, obviously, all he had to think of was the slimy dude who had just handed it to him, but that wasn't the real trouble. The trouble was it was not *Rita* who had handed it to him.

He would make the delivery and see what happened next. Nothing else to do now, if he wanted Rita. And he wanted her so much. Was that what she wanted him to do? Probably it would be what she wanted him to do even though she had not come out to tell him so. Minute after minute the night seemed to open out with a thousand unknowns and actually to grow hotter. There was no other way to make the chance they'd find each other again.

The question burned at the edge of consciousness, unfocused as a dancing flame, too hot to handle, essential as it was elusive— was he heading toward a ride with Rita more intense and real than anything he'd ever known, or was he about to blow his peace of mind completely?

Inside the restaurant, with her back against the corner of their booth, being warmly contrary and superbitchy to make up for raw feelings at being treated roughly in public by J.A.'s boy (never mind in private) and to persuade J.A. (and herself) all was well with "her deal" and good times were at hand (for her anyway), Rita kept an eye peeled and spotted Bobby the moment he walked in the door. She waved at him discreetly, halfway across the place, he was so tall—and pitch black. She had described the location of the booth they would be sitting in pretty well and he saw her wave and sauntered over with a businesslike expression congealing his rough features, swinging his briefcase through the people.

When it had been first built almost thirty years before in the 1960s, Luminati's restaurant had been surrounded by prairie and farms, miles out of town. The vision of its then and present owner had been that it should become a destination hangout for all Chicagoland, or at least the northern half of it, and this vision had been realized. By now it stood square in the middle of suburbia. It had been enlarged twice. It was an old institution, for these parts.

It could have been a huge old dance hall, a football field long. It was taking a while for Bobby to reach them in the booth. There was a space in the back clear for dancing. Big-name country and western bands played there on the weekends. Waitresses, high school girls, dashed efficiently among the tables, plying their trade. Customers drifted in and out incessantly, the place busy seven days a week, from noon till midnight. Everybody who was anybody or wished to be somebody in the territory came to Luminati's, and from far beyond, yet it was informal to the point of exhibiting a chaos at busiest times that must be under control of only a kind of faith.

A large party that had been seated at several tables pushed together rose all at once and milled around delaying Bobby's progress. The restaurant's menu had been experimented with over the years, reverting always to a quintessential midwestern one, with a touch of southern flair, featuring the best burgers in the northern suburbs and the freshest fish and sweet potato fries on Fridays. You could order walleye at Luminati's, on Friday nights, caught commercially on the Great Lake. The remains of such an overample meal littered the tables of the well-fed party that were holding up Bobby. He was smiling patiently at the satisfied people, who were taking their time getting themselves together. His tolerant smile made his expression particularly vicious and evil. Rita's companions had plenty of time to take his measure and to study the briefcase he had clutched to his breast.

When J.A. Pratt and his party had walked into Luminati's tonight, they had not waited to be seated by one of the several hostesses whose office it was to assist them, but moved on directly toward a booth that was empty, which they approached without hurry, not as patrons did hoping for the chance of capturing one.

Until they got about halfway there the younger and taller of her two associates helped Rita on, keeping a tight grip on her elbow, while Pratt, older and very prosperous looking, although his silver hair was messed up, standing on end as if he had been in a struggle, led the way casually through the crowd with an evident manner of aiming for a preordained niche, someplace he knew was awaiting him, to which he had an unquestioned right, as much as if he owned it. And so he did, for anything is possible and many things are desirable in the Big City, and the booth they headed for was on his permanent reserve, or he had a season ticket to it, you could say. It must have cost some.

There was way more than enough room in the booth for just the three of them, but they spread out and managed to take up the whole booth, making themselves comfortable, Rita going to the extreme corner and placing her bag down at arm's length between herself and the fat man. They did not talk, and stared about at the noisy crowd and not at each other. Had anyone been observing them, they might have been taken to be members of a family, or at least acquaintances well known to one another, who needed no words, who even needed a little space, as if in the nature of things they had just gotten on each other's nerves, or had even been arguing. All of this would have been quite true. Or perhaps, like family, dysfunctional at that, there was nothing needing saying. All three were a little disoriented from the wild cab ride they had just taken, and even still somewhat battered and seasick.

Of course, no one was observing them, that was the point of coming to Luminati's (or if it was not the point always, it was tonight). But if they had been, they would never have suspected that it was not the formidable looking older man in the silversuit whose presence dominated the booth, nor the bigger, younger man either, who was really the center of gravity, but the slender girl, overdressed, scrunched up in the corner, casting her baneful smoldering glance this way and that, wired and all but biting her nails, who was responsible for their being here at all. For it was her deal.

"Damn if I'll talk to a Southside nigger for an hour," muttered crudely the large athletic looking younger man wearing a college blazer in the matter of fact or unconscious way of uttering a truism. He looked around for a waitress, but did not see one.

"Don't put on airs, Mac," chided the older man in the tailored silversuit with more than a touch of sarcasm, who without looking at once found the eye of a waitress and ordered drinks.

Rita laughed viciously at his "airs," who looking surprised at what his boss had said glanced her way darkly and significantly.

"I'll talk!" she assured them both with smoking heat and glared at Mac in fury, perhaps still indignant at the treatment she had received at his hands a moment ago having been snatched out of the cab, and other things. "Nobody wants to hear *you* talk, moron! You don't got nothing you can talk about? I believe it!"

"Somebody better be keepin an eye on his money, if the package is going down to the city before he hands it over," opined the young man, not reacting, changing the subject cautiously, stating the obvious.

"Keep an eye on it, Mac! You'll be talking, all right," said the fat man to Rita, smiling.

"Of course, J.A.," she said coyly, unbending from her corner, extending her shapely though slight body over the space between them, and draping her masked arm on the man's silver one. "Bobby is cool. I like to talk to Bobby, he's a funny guy. He's got a good conversation if he cares to. You said yourself you can't deal with Lutherans and Irish every time. Wisconsin is ready too—he's going to take the ride downtown. Unless MacDougal wants to drive down to Mexicantown, ha ha ha!"

"Them boys," said MacDougal agreeably enough.

"All our *trust* is in *you,* doll," said the fat man, drolly, even cheerily, turning on her an enigmatic smile, it seemed to her, with a strange and knowing twinkle in his eye, as if it had seemed to him time to change the tone of the party, patting her arm hung on his own affectionately but gingerly. He exuded an air of command and well-being without trying, really without intending to. *Her* deal seemed to mean little enough to him, she wondered.

Trust would be shattered within the hour, she reflected, if there was any. Trust meant they knew just how to lean on her and torture her. And she was counting on trust to help her get away.

It had all started out as a normal little deal she had had the luck to initiate and from which she would get her cut of the action fair and square, as J.A. had been pleased to assure her. One night, a week ago, when he had been away someplace, and she had been left to her own devices (instead of J.A.'s), she had decided to go out and hear some jazz. She preferred a homey little joint on the Northside, the Green Mill on Broadway, to listen to jazz. Maybe the Blackstone Hotel was the nearer and classier venue, downtown, but there was something a little stiff about that place, and the players were formidable, famous bands, which was okay, but she liked the more downhome feel of the Green Mill, where she felt more at ease, an amateur, a jazz aficionado who didn't know much, just enough to enjoy, and the crowd was regular. She liked a local band called 'Round Midnight very much, and they were playing there this night, so she headed over expectantly.

How she'd wound up at a table with Bobby, this cat from New York, she no longer remembered, but she had, it was just the way things always happened to her, she never understood quite how they happened, no use wondering about it. She had never known anybody quite like Bobby, a very slick tough black dude who said he was from New York, who at once matter-of-factly invited her outside to his car to do some lines of coke, and she went along. Sitting there, showing off she had mentioned she had a connection to the best coke in town, very very pure, if he cared, all he might ever want or need, too, she added, and he had said, not missing a beat, how big a score could he make?

One thing led quickly to another, for J.A. was amenable and he liked to get things done fast. She informed Bobby they would make the switch in a family restaurant in the Farnorth suburbs. Bobby had told her the package would need to arrive downtown with his friends before he handed over the cash. She hadn't relayed this information to J.A. at once. Bobby had come on strong, and said did she want to go to Honolulu with him afterward? Because he was flush. She didn't know about Honolulu, which she envisioned as a phony palm tree place out of tourist posters, but just the thought made her keenly aware how much she hated her life with J.A., how miserable she was, and how she yearned to be free.

Why play the same dumb little number happy with the few thousand dollars J.A. would give her? Now was her chance. Why couldn't she steal all of it? With that she'd be rich and then she'd be free. She could stick something else in the bag in its place because she'd be the one handling it, and she decided to do it, the way she made all her decisions, when she was ever sober enough to make

159

any—just did it. Once she got away with the real snow she'd head for—if not Hawaii—someplace warm in the glossy travel brochure. Life was a gamble and it was time to deal the mean cards again. The details would take care of themselves as she went along, they always did—if she got that far. Before she realized it, in her despair, she saw she was going to run, ready or not. It was the way all the big events in her life went down.

Bobby was not forthcoming with her either. He failed to mention that he was going to walk with the money as soon as the goods went out the door, never mind waiting for his friends to call. He had no idea of course of her plans and assumed the stuff would be as pure as she had described and the Mexicans would be happy enough. Rita's boys would never be ready for him in the busy family restaurant, he believed, and couldn't stop him, not wanting to have to explain all that cash in his briefcase any more than he would. They were going to tell cops those bundles of hundreds and fifties in rubber bands were theirs? It seemed to him an easy play, to just walk out of the big family restaurant with his briefcase.

He was sincere in asking Rita to come to Honolulu with him, and he frankly figured she would come, after what he'd learned about her life. Otherwise she'd be left to a cold fate when he took off with their money. Finally, when she wouldn't give him a firm answer, concerning Honolulu, to persuade her, he told her his plan, and it blew her mind.

They both had the same idea, from opposite directions, like great minds think alike, she realized, and told him hers. Her plan was still somewhat unformed after the part she told him (which was all she knew yet). Because he was so nice, and had told her, and trusted her, and had invited her on a trip to Hawaii, he seemed her new ticket out of this life.

"You send a lame bag to my boys downtown, get me killed?"

"You run with J.A.'s money, get *my* butt ripped?"

It knocked them out. They had a laugh. They put one and one together, and had two. Instead of screwing each other over, they realized they'd be rich together in 48 hours. Budding friendship nearly lost was sealed instead.

"Walk with me when I go," he told her. "Lose them perverts. You can't hang with them no more, gotta go somewhere. Honolulu be nice."

"I don't run that fast. They'd catch me. Don't worry, I got my way to get away from them."

She told J.A. she was going shopping. They spent the time going around partying on the Southside and savoring the prospect and having double the fun. Bobby had taken her to meet his Mexican gangster friends, kind of showing her off, she thought, his pals they were going to rip off. They met in the backroom of a tiny grocery store, drinking beer surrounded by crates of fruit. She was drenched in cold fear in spite of the heat but it was a thrill. They discussed the protocol of the deal involving a cab to bring the goods to them for a taste to the grocery on 18th Street before the buy went down. She was going to be introducing Bobby to J.A. soon enough. Then they'd met that cop who had almost sidetracked them and ranked the whole deal, but they'd been too smart for him.

It became apparent to Rita that they'd have to go somewhere very far away, indeed, after what they planned to do, Honolulu might be a start, if they carried out their plan. They agreed to meet at the Green Mill bar afterward and settle on their next move.

For hours at a time during those two days after their eureka moment as they cruised around partying, she lived in a strange nether world, neither still here nor yet there, a delectable frozen state of having decided to change her life again and seen how she'd do it without making the final fearsome commitment. It was a familiar enough state of arrested decision, as much pain as pleasure. She was anticipating the new life without finally having had to ante up for it. But the time was at hand, the first card dealt, and the hours flew by. The deciding action would just float up and take her under like a waterfall a wayward boater. Still she held back her last bet, unable to embrace her desire.

She was still in the "lush life," the charmed plush life, still under J.A.'s sordid protection, still on his payroll. Not in danger, not on her own, and not yet free as a little bird. She could still back out, she told herself, even after hiding the real bag in the engine of the Lincoln that J.A. had given her this afternoon. This was her zoned out, delicious, "safe" state of mind till now, even after Bobby had walked in the restaurant and joined them in the booth.

In their booth, J.A. and MacDougal kept their promise of letting Rita do the talking, as the actual seated personage of Bobby with his hairdo and his scars if it did not evoke confidence, neither did it inspire conversation. The two men were visibly on their guard. J.A. had that bland look on his face of total control, almost remote control, a man with imponderable means, not to be underestimated. He seemed to have his mind on better things and bigger affairs, behind a private wall. MacDougal checked his side under his arm as if he must have a gun. She suddenly understood, as she never had exactly registered before, that J.A. must be richer than she had imagined, his dealings more vast, although she thought she knew as much already; she thought that she didn't know him at all well, though she had thought she knew him intimately; and the idea came to her that he had let her get this far with this little side deal of hers—her that he tied up and played with on a daily basis, casually, cruelly, creatively, and with impunity—because it was no big deal to him, a hundred K! This unsettling perception made her lose track of the conversation for a moment, and the four of them sat in awkward silence.

Wisconsin the cab driver walked into the restaurant and immediately glanced their way as if somehow he knew just where they'd be sitting. Without moving or even turning her head she tried to signal him a sign of love and faith with her eyes but it was too far. It was enough that he had come in to show that he was waiting. It made her glad and confident. She forgot everything for a moment. A little while later she saw him leave, again looking in her direction to show her that he would be waiting.

Bobby was not into small talk, either, so nobody needed fear overcoming cultural barriers to pass the hour, but after a long silence that seemed dramatic enough to him, he slid the briefcase over to J.A. next to him in the booth, flicked open its clasps, and opened it outward toward the man. He turned away and scowled into the moving mass of whitefolks. J.A. glanced with hooded eyes into the briefcase for five or six seconds. He reached in and touched the bundles of bills lightly, pulled one out, and riffled it under the table. Closing the lid of the briefcase, but not reclasping it, he picked up his drink.

"What're you drinking?"

"J&B straight up."

A J&B was ordered for the Fist by an apparently satisfied fat man. Bobby reached over and reclasped the briefcase, leaving it where it was on the boothseat halfway between them.

Rita's laden purse lay on the other side of J.A. between him and her. At this point, Rita glancing significantly at everybody lurched to her feet. She hauled up her heavy purse and slung it over her shoulder, and made a move to get past everybody, but as she leaning on them bumped past their knees into the clear, with her big bag knocking into things, almost clearing drinks off the table, MacDougal stuck out his foot and tripped her. He grasped her slim arm in his big hand as she nearly fell and squeezed hard.

"Hey, owww!"

"I'll deal with it," said MacDougal, sticking out his other hand for the package that was in her purse, which he proceeded to try to paw out of it. Unable to grip it, he peeled the purse off her shoulder.

"No, J.A.! I've got to persuade Wisconsin some more and explain things to him. We can't let any driver take this, it has to be him! I trust him. He's waiting for my word."

"Mac will explain it to him."

"He won't listen to him!"

"Yes, he will," said MacDougal, standing.

Bobby the Fist did not move a muscle or twitch an eyelid (which were nearly closed) at all this but enjoyed his scotch, relaxed visibly, and sat there like he belonged. Indeed he was in a booth that some of the kids in the place would have given something to be sitting in. He exhibited full confidence in his end of things, and a well-being almost to match Rita's boss. The particular arrangements on their side did not matter to him, his attitude said, all that mattered was the quality of the product, which would soon be verified by his friends, or not.

Rita, struggling, shoved back in the seat formerly occupied by MacDougal, lost her self-possession, mouthed off at them, and still fought MacDougal for her handbag, even after the long brown package of apparently 100 K of cocaine had been pulled out of it and taken from her, getting up again, reaching around his waist for it, thrown back again with just enough force by MacDougal, then her empty handbag after her. He strode off through the busy eatery.

He suddenly turned around and came back a few steps.

"He knows where he's taking this, right?"

"No, he don't! I told you. I have to tell him, fool!"

Hanging onto the tabletop she pulled herself out of the booth and made another lunge for the package, which MacDougal raised in the air out of her reach. He backed her up into the booth holding the package above her head temptingly. She stood balancing on her tiptoes with her arms outstretched for it. Placing the fingers of his free hand between her small breasts he exerted just sufficient force with the tips of them to topple her back into the booth. By now a number of other patrons at nearby tables and adjoining booths were beginning to follow this.

"Where's he taking it?"

"It's hard to explain!"

She had collapsed. She was half reclining in the booth holding herself up by the tabletop frowning up at him stubbornly, her chin trembling. She was almost losing it, Bobby couldn't help observing out of the corner of his eye. He hoped she'd keep it together till the "dope" was on its way. He calmly ignored the whole scene.

"The Rendezvous Lounge on Waukegan Road," said Bobby dryly out of the corner of his mouth, with a sneer.

MacDougal looked at him with interest for the first time. "Where's that? By Skokie?"

"No, west a there, south—you know them forest preserves, call em Caldwell Woods near Devon?"

MacDougal was apparently not familiar with those woods.

"It's before you get to them forest preserves, from up here, before that, on Waukegan, next to a bowling alley. 'The Rendezvous.' Cab driver find it," Bobby assured him.

As MacDougal turned away again, Bobby looking in the opposite direction growled, "He want a cat name *Rodriguez*. He be at the bar."

MacDougal cocked his head in acknowledgment of that but did not look back.

Without the fat parcel inside it, her big handbag was light as a feather and deflated empty when it touched her thigh thrown down on her by departing MacDougal. And this deflated emptiness now in her lap felt as big as the hole in her heart from which what was suddenly missing was her hopes, a deadly reminder she was a real lightweight after all and could be run over how and where they pleased—a little nothing.

She had better not make any more of a scene. They'd think she had something in mind. It wasn't herself she feared for. Those Mexican hoods might be crazy enough to think Wisconsin was in on it. It would be commonsense to see it that way, for Mexicans. She had not had a chance to tell him to hand it to them inside the Rendezvous bar and be done with it. Above all he should not take them from the bar to somewhere else, let them persuade him to do so. They might want a lift. Maybe she would have told him to throw it straight out the window and never make the run at all. She had not been thinking clearly, if she ever had. She wasn't now. She froze in the booth, awash in horror. It was all going wrong fast.

MacDougal sauntered off nonchalantly through the crowd with the parcel stuck out in one hand. Rita watched him and her package go like death approaching—Wisconsin. She would have no chance to warn him now. Their plans were down the tubes, their dreams together, and maybe his life.

At this dark moment, nevertheless, she realized with finality that she was not going to Hawaii with Bobby, but to the North Woods with Wisconsin, as they had promised each other, as she had suspected she would since meeting him this morning, but hadn't been sure, unless they killed him downtown first, for the Mexicans would even blame him for their loss, when they were unable to raise Bobby on the telephone in the restaurant at the number he had given them. Now with her plans in disarray and the bag stolen from her, she was sure where and with whom she was going to leave town. If she could save him, they'd be gone to the North Woods tonight, and nobody could catch them up there. If only she could save Wisconsin!

She no longer kept up her end of the banter, which rather awkwardly was taken up by J.A., wanting to know something about the Fist's habits and haunts, who responded monosyllabically after long silences. In answer to his question, Bobby allowed as he was from Hawaii. This alarmed her as much as if she was still going with him there. A strange notion formed in her mind that Bobby didn't know Hawaii and Honolulu were the same thing, one of them was in the other. It was the way he had said "Hawaii" like it had nothing to do with anything else on his mind, like Honolulu, for instance. He should never have given that away. Maybe he didn't know they were the same place. She found she had lost confidence in Bobby, though she liked him as much as ever, even though he could have refused to tell them where the package was to be delivered unless they had let her take it out to Wisconsin.

She tried to keep her wits about her but it was no use. Her head was swimming. Everything would depend on J.A.'s reaction when Bobby went out the door, which he would do any minute now, when the spirit moved him, when he felt enough time had elapsed for the cab driver to be on his way. What would happen then to Wisconsin was all that mattered to her.

She was overcome by her worst demons, the ones reminding her of her incompetence and guilt and shame, pushing her toward self-indulgent despair. Things had gotten away from her once more. But she had a chance to put things straight yet if she could only find that Mexican grocery store where Bobby had taken her to meet his friends, for if she couldn't raise Wisconsin on the cab radio when she got out of here, there'd be nowhere else to look for him.

When Bobby got up and walked out of the restaurant it would put her in more danger than she had ever known in her short desperate life, and yet be the start of her liberation that she dreamed of, because when Bobby ran, J.A. was going to make her go get the money or get the cocaine back one or the other, unless she missed her bet. And she was never coming back. But if she couldn't find Wisconsin, if something happened to him, there would be no freedom for the likes of her.

J.A. sat calmly sipping his drink like he had other plans and more important things on his mind and was just talking with Bobby and her to be polite. He appeared aloof and even uninterested, really. As usual he thought he had everything under control. *Not hardly this time!* she thought bitterly and vindictively. He was in for a surprise. Then unaccountably the paranoid thought came to her that it was more than that. She thought that he was watching it all, and her in particular, with detached amusement. This made her whole body grow cold as if she'd walked into a meat locker. A strange feeling took hold in her that this was not an act of his or his customary manner anymore either but that he was *not* going to be surprised by anything that happened next and he had guessed as much already and foresaw just what was coming.

This disturbing idea deepened like a bottomless pool in the sea of her soul in which she had suddenly lost her footing and slipped under completely. In the unfamiliar blue depths she found floating the paralyzing suspicion like a jellyfish ready to sting her to death that he was ready for her to swim away, he was expecting it, and had accepted it. It was part of *his* plan! She had always been transparent to him, like a jellyfish you could see through. How could she have ever supposed she would outmaneuver him? Then the clincher hit her, almost sending her flopping onto the floor, like a fish, under the table. By letting her set up "her own deal" (for the first and only time) and knowing she was going to rip him off, he was saying *good-bye* to her!

This premonition was too terrifying to sustain, like entering a freefall zone not freedom. It struck a new note of absurd dread. If she were wrong (and surely she was) and didn't watch her step it could be a hell of a mistake. She had to play it all out just as they had it planned. She needed to act her accustomed slavish part, and do what they asked her to, when Bobby ran. They would be examining her closely as soon as they recovered from their shock. Her fate and Wisconsin's depended on her getting away fast.

The huge amount of money involved struck her like a slap of reality across the face then, sobering her up and restoring her wits. J.A. wasn't giving that away to anybody, certainly not her! She was dreaming strange dreams. No, J.A. was not so prescient he could have guessed her scheme that she'd barely formed and only put in play a few hours ago. Well, the money they would break your arm for. What was real was the changes that were going down the moment Bobby suddenly took off running and the role she'd have to carry off immediately after, promising to make things right. She'd have to be convincing—if she hoped to rescue Wisconsin from whatever hell he was going to be in when the Mexicans saw what he had brought them.

MacDougal came back in after taking the package to the cab driver. Things must have gone okay, and Wisconsin agreed to take the package. When he sat down again in the booth, he said nothing but picked up his drink, as though it was all accomplished. They all sat there thinking their quite different secret thoughts, saying nothing, awaiting the phone call from Bobby's group, which should come in an hour or so. There was a desultory interlude to be suffered through now, they all seemed to acknowledge, grimly. Bobby changed his posture, sat up straight, seeming to gather himself together. They all stared at him.

Bobby was out on the same breaking limb she was. But a guy like him knew how to fall. They had decided to saw off the limb together. It was going to break off any second now. It was nothing to the danger Wisconsin was in. He wasn't heading for his freedom, but it must be their dream together. He was making the run—for her! She almost wept with shame at what she had set him up for, but she had to smile through her tears. She had to keep her cool for now.

Where Wisconsin was at this moment, what he was heading for, she didn't want to guess. But she was going to have to start guessing because if she couldn't find him and save him, no matter how her and Bobby's plans succeeded, it would all be over. Freedom at that price would be so hollow and bitter it would make the worst slavery preferable. She might collapse and go back to J.A. as though she had never had any other thought in her mind. She'd go back then to her nightmare and fall back in accustomed toils of her own sweet destruction. She'd beg for it. She'd forget she'd ever yearned to be free. She wouldn't be able to live with herself and go on, having harmed a nice guy like Wisconsin, a guy she'd loved at first sight. Of all the ways she had imagined her plans going wrong, it hadn't been this.

He didn't want to think what was on the backseat, where the package sat a mute and mysterious traveler. He didn't need to guess. The route for him and Rita to them old North Woods was to make the run and wait for her call, which might never come. But it might come. Danger surrounded him, like her enigmatic kiss. You couldn't fake what she'd had on her lips for him. There was no guessing about what that was and what was in her soul, her excitement and her desire, but the question came upon his heart: Was it really meant for *him?*

For that matter, all this he had burning up his soul, what was that exactly? It was way different than usual, what Rita had in the way of, call it adventure, maybe, allure, for him—but it was beyond question how she had suddenly made life seem worth living again. It was beyond understanding. You didn't want to and you couldn't understand. You were all but overcome by illusions at every step in this life, weren't you, but some were prettier than others. Hell, life was a catch-as-catch-can business.

There was nothing to understand, but as usual there had appeared this trade-off. Only this one was a monster. The run with this package he was about to make could lead to trouble. Was it worth it?

There was only one way to find out. Stop thinking, turn it on automatic, and get it over with. A nice resolve but his head had other ideas. It began producing them at a great rate. That name, Rodriguez, for instance. A phony. Like when somebody named Smith called a cab. Of course there really were people named Smith and Rodriguez. Hell, if he was mixed up in something like this he'd be Rodriguez or Smith too. But he was mixed up in it.

Vaguely he remembered passing the Rendezvous Lounge on Waukegan Road a few times, a blue neon figure flickering in shadow deeper than this or any night, announcing a dim neighborhood tavern, three-quarters of the way to the Loop from up here, someplace on the edge of the city, in the bungalow belt in Niles or Morton Grove. He was going to have half an hour or more to think about it, he realized, suddenly afraid of his own mind. He cut around the restaurant for the rear exit, stung by an urge to enter the backways in the shadows. He'd take the backroads all the way if it took two hours. That's how he'd find Rita again, practically through the alleys.

Round the corner of the long restaurant building, he spun the wheel close. Another coat of paint and he would have grazed the trim of the building. A man in the white apron and cocked hat of a cook's helper doing something in the shadow of the garbage bins behind the kitchen jumped a foot in the air as the Caddy's bumper nearly creased the seat of his pants. A long Spanish imprecation hung in the air, blossomed in the mournful night like a sad omen. He was on the edge of things and would stay there, creep through the shadows the whole way down.

Does everyone have a secret hope, a faith in some fateful rendezvous after which passion will not leave again? He was under such a spell. Speed on with it, stop thinking, get it behind him, so the trip with Rita could begin down moonlit North Woods roads.

All at once he was chilled through again that it was not Rita who had brought the bag out. His headlights picked out the rubblestrewn track down which meat and produce trucks roamed each morning. He wished he could stay in such delivery lanes and backalleys the whole way to the city. On both sides of the lane a jungle of tall weeds and saplings thick enough to hide in was just kept back by a rusty fence. A blue star shot through the clouds and fell down on his dashboard, pale and clear.

He hit the brakes and backed up fast. The cook's helper had gone inside. The kitchen door was open, letting out a shaft of yellow light along with the steady clatter of food preparation and busy cries. It was all wrong. He reached back and grabbed the package and jumped out. It didn't have far to drop. The bin was reeking. He climbed back into his car, head spinning. How help her now? Just go inside the place and bring her out, take her away from those guys, if she would come. He'd tell them where their package was.

Headlights in his mirror dazzled him coming round the corner of the restaurant at him. The car struck his, both rocking crazily like his and Armchair's for the fun of it, but this was not fun. A man jumped out and ran fast toward him in the white glare of the lights. It was that cop who'd hassled him this afternoon about Mattie the maid!

"Man, you still lookin for that maid?"

"Maid! Yeah, this is the cleaning service. Get out!"

The cab driver obeyed, but slowly, with dignity.

"That drunk maid Mattie, that stole her employer's silver or something, that I took to the Westside—"

"Fish it out!" The cop grabbed him by the back of the shirt and sent him sprawling against the bin. "You're goin in next!"

He reached into the bin, found it, dripping with coffee grounds.

"What a mess," complained the cop, as though it had been addressed to him personally. "Wipe it off on something."

"Look, I'm only a cab driver."

"Ya get a nice tip from the guy you take that to!"

The cab driver pulled out a rag from under his seat and wiped the package down. The cop grabbed it out of his hands, shoved him behind the wheel, and climbed in back. The cab driver heard a pocket knife snap open, and then the heavy paper being sliced. The way it felt, it might have been his tires, or his heart, being slashed.

"Mercy God, what have we here!"

A rustle of the plastic inner liner, some sniffing, smacking sounds, the cop groaned voluptuously with such satisfaction, the guy was having an orgasm. The cab driver glanced in the flickering rearview mirror. In the sad light a large plastic bag of white powder bulged down from the cop's hand. A white fingertip lingered on his open lips.

"I'm just a cab driver. I don't know what that is."

The first statement was true enough. The second was one of professional intent that would have been true a moment ago but not any longer.

"You say that once more, I kick your ass clear around the building. Okay, lemme think. You just run the delivery like you do every night, stuff from the liquor store, the drug store. In fact, you just met these people."

"I never met em."

"No shit. Well, so, ya get the delivery in the car, this ordinary run. Ya go straight around behind the joint, throw it in the trash! That how you do with deliveries usually? Must make cab driving work a lot easier."

"Somethin told me it wasn't right."

"Ya spot me, admit it, pal."

"I wish I had."

"I've listened to more outside jive from you today," said the cop with a puzzled look. "You must spend a lot a time in traffic court tellin stories." A strange insight took hold in his mind about the cab driver. How much did this guy not know, really?

"You got your choice now." The cop's voice was a soft bass insinuation, the very note of doom. "I book ya straight in on the felony charge or ya deliver this just like ya spose to."

Another glance in the mirror showed the cop leaning back in the corner, stonedout, a drunk's look of belligerent fantasy about him. He had smelled alcohol all over him when he threw him against the bins. His eyes glimmered snakishly through redslits as he brought his head forward now. It was like when he had choked him this afternoon. He got another whiff of his hellish breath.

"You deliver it, if you want to help Rita. They kill both a you motherfuckers. I want to help Rita, too. Ya got some tape?"

Rita. It was *Rita* the cop had been after when he'd grilled him by the China Doll. Rita, not Mattie. He wanted to *help* Rita. He could easily imagine the help this vicious cop would give Rita. He'd been tailing her. Poor Rita, they were closing in on her from all sides.

Retreating from paranoia, the cop's view of the cab driver had listlessly returned to the general category of shiftless rascals, ready to do anything for a dollar, but then it went a step further on its own. He was trying to tell him he'd never met Rita! But he wasn't working for them as a delivery boy either. He suddenly thought that he must be doing this just *for her.*

After a second, the cab driver fumbled in the glove compartment and found a roll of black electrician's tape and handed it to him.

"Don't drop it in no trash! Don't be takin no sniff on the way either! It's a precise weight."

"The tape looks great. It looks tampered with."

"The coffee grounds all over looks good, too, guy. Where you sposeta take this to?"

"Waukegan Road. Someplace called the Rendezvous."

"Who to?"

"Somebody named Rodriguez."

The cop got out, slamming the door hard behind him.

"Take it where it's sposeta go!"

The plaingreen car veered toward the front of the restaurant. After a minute, the cab driver picked his way slowly down the delivery track as if he'd never seen it before. What choice did he have now? He could smell the booking room ink. Not that a charge like that would stick, but he'd be in the tank overnight while Rita needed his help. How would he help her if not make the run?

He couldn't think of anything else. Surely she'd want him to. He solved every riddle every day by taking the ride, so he'd take the ride. What else, walk in the restaurant, throw the shit on the table, and drag her away with him? She might not come. They all had something on her, whatever it was. The story would be over then, and he didn't know the story, and he had to make the story spin out to be in on the happy ending.

He drove slowly down the delivery lane bordered by a jungle of tall yellowgreen weeds. Then he headed straight for the Tollway. There would no point taking the backroads now. Car dealers' floodlights and shoppingstrips' neon streaked his face like a child's by the lurid lights of a carnival. He was headed for the Rendezvous Lounge with the controls on automatic. It was a familiar enough route. The new territory he'd entered was in his soul.

He'd seen chumps in the trick bag, but that cab driver took the cake. The way she was playing him was a coldhearted shame. She was the only actor he was really interested in anymore, he realized. As a person, as a wonderful woman to be watched. He was waiting to see what she was going to do next. He was sure there was going to be much more. Somebody was going to get burned bad. He had seen what was inside that bag. Smart cab drivers that got in over their head deserved what they got. One thing he wasn't lying about, he must not know what was in *that* bag. The poor dude, she'd got him in love with her. He could understand that.

The deal had to go down like it was supposed to until he saw the whole game. He didn't see the play yet, the hole where he could get in and steal the ball. She would help him set them up, somehow. He'd get them all tonight, fat man and his sidekick, cab driver, and Bobby in the bargain. He didn't see how yet. Her he would let go and help her on her sweet way. The worthless waif of this morning in Jackie's place had become a handsome determined woman to be protected . . . and desired. He hadn't been kidding when he'd told the cab driver he wanted to help her. Whoa, she was beautiful and cold. Rita, far now from how she'd seemed in Jackie's, hustling them all. Somebody might be going to be unhappy with the delivery service though. Well, too damn bad. He could care less about a lovesick cab driver. It wasn't his job to hip slick cab drivers heading to their doom—especially one who had certainly spotted him—and wanted the same woman he did.

There was no time for pity. No sooner had he circled around the restaurant to resume his vigil than the Fist came flying out the frontdoor with his briefcase at a right angle to his body like a motorcycle with a sidecar and dove for his waiting cab. The problem that the Fist had was his Checker cab driver wasn't in his cab any more, had never come back again. The dude had bopped off someplace with those earphones blaring life's soundtrack at him and vanished. Maybe he was hitting on some chick he'd found inside. Knowing cab drivers, probably he had ordered dinner.

The cop, just coming even with Luminati's luminous facade, saw a babyblue blur change into the Fist alone and outraged staring about in the back seat of the Checker cab. Wide-eyed, rigid with dismay, he peered over the front seat, peering farther and farther, like one of those wooden birds that sip water, in case the driver had fallen asleep there, maybe even slid down on the floor. The Fist's astonishment at finding himself alone in the Checker cab with no driver was funny, and the cop started laughing.

As luck would have it another cab had just pulled up behind, one of the locals. For a bad moment, catching sight of the familiar archery target on its side, the cop feared driver number 17 had boldly and sensibly decided to return the package to its senders and come around the front door of the restaurant again. But it was a different Bull's-eye cab, not the Cadillac. He had a feeling he'd seen this one before, a battered ugly car.

The Fist jumped into the Bull's-eye cab, slamming the door behind him, as MacDougal the bodyguard burst out of the restaurant in pursuit. It looked like the Fist would make it because MacDougal ran to the side of the Checker. He also peered around inside and even opened the door.

But instead of taking off past him with tires screaming and the Fist's promise of a prince's ransom for a tip ringing in his ears, the Bull's-eye cabby got out of his car and began to polish his windshield with a rag. The cop knew he'd seen that narrow figure before. He'd seen that haughty and bespectacled face, frowning angrily in through the windshield at the fare in the backseat as he stretched over his car and moved his rag, as though he'd rather not be disturbed. The Fist stuck his head out the window and hissed something urgently at him, causing the guy to leave off with the rag and look sharply at him.

"*Sir!* First, you imply that I can be bought. Are you *threatening* me now?—Say, are there any papers lying on the floor by you?"

The Fist didn't know what he meant by "papers" but looked around absurdly before bolting out of the cab in a crouch down a row of cars. Armchair howled with laughter. He threw back his head, and his laments split the night like a coyote's. Patrons in the light and shadows turned sharply to look, including MacDougal the bodyguard, who caught sight of Bobby and took off after him. The cop cruised in his plaingreen car down an adjacent aisle.

The parking lot eventually faded into a sideroad with no tireblocks or curbstones just a brushy verge to mark the transition. Where did the Fist think he was going? Beyond the sideroad was an office park and some vacant scrubland awaiting development. This wasn't the city where you could duck through a doorway or an alley and find yourself someplace else altogether. They didn't have alleys around here. You'd have to be half rabbit and make a run through the blackberry bushes.

The man's bodyguard was younger, stronger, undoubtedly faster down the stretch than Bobby, who began to zigzag along the dark perimeter. For an instant he stopped, sort of stood on his hind legs, listening, and peering behind him. Was he trying to lose, or lure, the guy? The bodyguard hesitated behind a car.

The Fist started hopping again, two lanes this way, three lanes that way, heading toward the main drag. He might be setting him up. Drop him, and the next second run into traffic and commandeer a passing car.

The cop pulled through an empty slot and cut him off. He gave his old enemy a lazy smile. The Fist slid on his heels to a stop and a look of dull shock filled his widening eyes. The man's boy chasing him didn't worry him, but Shooter Teagarden did. Where the hell had Shooter come from! The cop reached in his breast, came out with his .38, and took aim at the Fist's kneecaps, where athletes and crooks alike feel vulnerable.

"Get in!" He motioned with his gun hand. Unheeding, the Fist now headed for the empty lot beyond the office park. He couldn't lose the cop in traffic, for sure, but he remembered Shooter as a boy had been allergic to a lot of stuff, always sneezing, even during games. He might lose him in that field ahead. The cop drove into the street and then turned into the sideroad in time to see Fist disappear into the tall grass and scrub.

For a while he could see his glycerinated head bobbing above the grasses and then it reached a place where the blackgreen weeds and whips were seven feet high and he disappeared. The bodyguard stood at the edge of the road gazing doubtfully into the tangle of brush and saplings. Not that tough, was he, or anyway he didn't seem too eager to go in there after him to mix it up in that jungle. He glanced twice at a plaingreen car at the corner which he might have made as a cop's and turned directly and beat it back to the restaurant, as if he had other plans.

The cop watched the tops of the tall weeds sway marking the Fist's crouching progress through them beyond the office park. Then they stopped moving. He got out of his car and, keeping his eyes on the spot where the Fist was resting, headed in waistdeep at first. All was still, Bobby hardly breathing. Like this morning at Jackie's, his idea was not to beat the cop, just get away. He had accomplished his escape very cunningly this morning. But unlike then, if he got beat this time, he might not outwit him. He heard Shooter crash toward him in spite of allergies and he took off running. If he got caught now, he wouldn't get away again.

The weeds and brush shuddered as like a big wild rat the Fist scrambled in deeper. The cop rushed in and pushed forward beginning to sneeze violently as the brambles closed around him. He parted their powdery tips with his hands, turning his head aside and trying to protect his nose. "Fist, it's me! Stop or it's gonna get worse for ya!" Thorns tore at his bare wrists.

The weeds were seized as by a gust of wind as Bobby ran flat out. The cop sprinted flailing at the vegetation. The ripple began veering in a circle. He turned on the speed and dove. His feet left the ground and he snagged the Fist by an ankle and bulldogged him down. He tore the briefcase out of the Fist's hand. His fingers went inside the babyblue jacket and sent a gun sailing. The two of them rolled over and over, as lost to view as a pair of riotous wagoneers on a virgin Illinois prairie. When the cop got the better of him, he didn't stop beating him. When his hands got tired, he stood up and used his feet on him. It was good as groceries to whip the Fist. Blind Lady Justice herself applauded every kick and blow.

That he could receive so much grief from a cause so far back at the beginning of things was a mystery to Bobby. A gang guy has his own brand of innocence and he'd never taken the measure of what his youthful style might have wrought. It had been his fate, never thinking twice about it, to torment goodygoodies and conscientious athletes beloved of Coach. It seemed incredible to him like a natural disaster that had singled him out that the basketball player had pursued him to this field and twenty years later he had to pay.

His suit stained and torn, soaked with sweat, his knuckles bloody, the cop hauled the Fist out of the grass into the back seat of the car and handcuffed him to the bracket on the floorboards. He went back into the weeds and found the briefcase after a short search. He tossed it on the front seat ahead of him, sneezing several times hard as he got behind the wheel. How did people breathe out here? It was so hot. He was suffering some kind of allergy attack.

"Teagarden muhfucker, kill me cuz if I got a drop a blood lef, I kill *you*, muhfucker. Where my case, man?"

The cop unclasped it—two loud snaps. He stared at stacks of worn hundred dollar bills bound with rubber bands. It was actually seeing the money made him understand. The Fist was *buying.* Or was supposed to be. The white man was the man! With this novel reversal of the current that had originally electrified the chase, all of a sudden his whole day was justified, sanctified, and downright golden. The poison was spreading from suburbia to the ghetto not the other way around, of all things. Not that anybody was going to get poisoned much by that bag they'd given the cab driver to

177

deliver unless it gave some hoods a heart attack. "Who is this money, chump?"

"Since when money illegal, prick law?"

The dope wasn't where it was supposed to be, and neither was the money. Rita and Bobby were crossing some gangsters and this captain of industry up here in one fell swoop. Bobby had walked out with the same briefcase he'd walked in with. He would like to have seen the man's face when he ran. Maybe even at such a moment, it had been a poker mask of cold confidence. He remembered when he'd let Fist walk this morning from Jackie's.

The dope was sidetracked under the hood of the Lincoln. She'd made up a talcum powder decoy. No matter how duplicitously paranoid the bad cats were, probably especially Mexican gangbangers, they were always deeply even morally shocked when their worst suspicions were confirmed. Well, greedy lovelorn cab drivers deserved all they got. So did captains of industry that sold dope to children in the ghetto. Bobby had walked out of the joint with all their green stamps.

"Bobby, I declare, you just run right out on them whiteboys. You outrun em, matter a fact. I didn't know you could run so fast like that, Bobby."

"They aint shit, basketball player. They think they is, like lots a folks I know."

"But you aint outrun me. Where you an Rita sposeta meet?"

The cop made a U turn, and after a minute drove back into the parking lot of the restaurant.

"Basketball bouncin muhfucker," said the Fist, "I like to know whacha think ya doin."

"I'm out-thinkin you, Bobby, like old times. . . . Yes, both them suckers gone," the cop muttered to himself.

"Both which suckers?" asked the Fist innocently, such was the daze he was in, as if events outside the back seat of the cop's car could still make a difference to him.

"Both them cab drivers, Fist. You know, that white-hair man and his boy gone one way in one of em an Rita gone another way in the other—after you, I guess, they hopes. They tol her, bring us our money or bring us the shit or else! Aint they! They think she just a wayward piece a pussy, don't they? You know better, don't ya, Bobby!"

"I stop in that restaurant for a drink is all. I don know them peoples. I don know that bitch be there. She lucky I don whip her ass." Lying about it was as easy as it was futile. What was hard was it looked like they wouldn't be going to Hawaii together tonight.

"Ha ha! You come up here in farmland for a drink, Bobby? Shit you did. You don know where you is no more'n I do. They aint no cabs here no more, man. Them two cab drivers. Ya know, the Checker cool ya lay a taste on, wait for your sorry ass. An that white boy like professor. Ha ha! Ya musta talk to him real right, Fist, he polish his windshield, ha ha ha ha, ho ho ho!"

Again, without effort, even unaware of it, Armchair had given real pleasure to someone.

"Damn if I don kill that nigger. I know his number. Where he go? He sposeta wait." The Fist began to cough, very liquid. He spat on the floor. "Teagarden, ya broke somethin inside. I'm spittin blood. I report yo ass for brutality, ya don let me up from here. Ya know what that crazy honky mother say? Say, he prefer read his book! I burn up his ass! Pull his license for discrimination, will ya?"

"You an Rita some *bad motherfuckers,* aint ya, Fist? Ha ha! Whoo! What a plan! You aint dumb as ya look, is ya, Bobby? Where you gonna meet her, man? Ha ha! Think of you in Jackie's this mornin. Hooo! Damn if you two aint some *bad motherfuckers!*"

The cop laughed in genuine admiration. He'd shaken the stiffness out, even if he had ruined a good suit. He was tired and sore, but his mind was clear. He drove fast out of the parking lot. Somewhere in front of him rode Rita. He had no doubt of it, as if he were following her by a fixed star. He'd catch up to her just before she reached the Labs, or coming back headed for the Tri-State Tollway after she had picked up her stash. So sure was he of her movements that he didn't peer ahead through the black mists of the night to spot the flicker of taillights of whichever cab she was riding in, the Checker or the professor's, though he sped to gain back the ground he'd lost indulging himself whipping the Fist so much.

Brave woman, they had her down as far as she could go, but they wouldn't keep her down now. She was on her way. She had been let loose to retrieve the cocaine or the cash, from Bobby or that sorry cab driver, but she wasn't ever coming back. How she'd planned it all the way, knowing how it would be, the fat man had let

179

her go, sent her out to fix things, thinking she was his slave. He had her down so far, he never thought she'd dare do different.

His soul trembled hearkening to her courage. His heart beat with joy in tune with her spirit. She was making herself new, and he admired her. He would catch up to her and protect and help her. With his help she'd get away all right. He'd be seeing to it from now on. He had that lighthearted selfless happiness like when he was going to find one of his kids a good job. He felt like he was going to be her friend.

He battled the temptation to veer off for anywhere. Throw the package in the bushes somewhere. Pull over and sleep. That black cop was one weird character and one moment he seemed like a cop all right and then the next, when he breathed alcohol over you, he didn't. He'd seen that mean Chicago star though. Not long ago, he'd had enough and called it a day. He had actually been at peace with the world, his special talent. He'd forgotten all about the cop as if it had happened to somebody else. He'd known he shouldn't take another ride. But then he wouldn't have found Rita, would he? They wouldn't have found each other. The only way to find her again was to keep going. What little chance he and Rita had together depended on it.

This seemed to be true, because he couldn't think of anything else. The deal, her plan, had to play out before she'd have the space to take a chance. It was the only angle he could see. The conviction of his necessary part in it deepened but it didn't get easier to bear. Once more it was the cab driver's peculiar lot to have only half of the story. Not even that.

When he left the Tollway at Dempster Street, he doubled back on River Road and stopped in Rosie's on River for a Jack Daniels for courage. He left the package on the backseat with the car unlocked to tempt fate. When he returned, he didn't look at it, hoping it was gone. Backing out, he saw it, reminding him with a jolt that the mission he was on was deadly real and the timetable somebody else's.

On Golf Road, he passed a restaurant called the **FARMHOUSE** modeled like a big yellow farmhouse advertising breakfast anytime in an atmosphere of artificial wholesomeness under a blaze of neon sunshine, and then he passed the **TROUT DUDE RANCH,** where you could pay to fish in the concrete pond, if you were that desperate or stoned to want to do that, or had an unsuspecting kid on your hands to entertain. In front of it a giant plastic fisherman hauled up a huge plastic red, silver, and blue trout.

The Golf Mill Mall was fronted by littered parking lots, here and there a few abandoned cars rotted away, a cheap old hotel stood across from the Mall where musicians from some of the clubs and the theater in the Mall liked to stay, then came a string of even cheaper motels, and the fast food joints and shoppingstrips on Milwaukee Road. The hokey spectacle of all this tawdry normal existence passing him by came at him through the gleaming night like dear possessions lost in deep water. Down Golf Road as far as the eye could see, the tacky everynightness submerged under pressure in the depths tantalizing and demoralizing him, the old acquaintances who could only sadly witness but not arrest his descent into the unknown, who were themselves drowning.

The business sector played out. Busy Golf Road going east was intersected by dozens of narrow dark residential streets with their hundreds of dim bungalows glimpsed obscurely, their curtained windows glowing cozily and discreetly. Bitterly he envied their anonymous afterdinner lethargies and TV desperations, something like a commonplace heaven, had the bungalows' inhabitants known it, compared to the hellish ride he was on.

On Waukegan Road he turned south toward the city. There were several funky motels on this strip flanked by straightforward neighborhood taverns featuring the same stale air, fat jukeboxes, scarred pool tables, and big color TVs above the bar, the *Admiral Oasis,* the **Jacks or Better**, the Prairie Schooner, the *Mark*

181

IV, and down farther toward the woods someplace, as he recalled, would be the Rendezvous. He could remember rides associated with each of these joints as he passed them, a trucker whose rig had broken down, a carload of drunken Mexican landscapers, a hooker buying her groceries for the week, a prim Jamaican woman who had just gotten a job at Avon headquarters up the street. All the smart guys, hard chicks, no-hopes, and high hopers blurred into each other, on this strip like every other. No mysteries here. He remembered the common sadness in them all with a violent shaking awe at the margin of luck and safety in such sweet standard sadnesses as had been theirs.

Greed! Stone burning greed. That's why he was making this no-brain run with the dangerous parcel on the backseat. In the first place, his own unwillingness to turn the radio absolutely off, when he had made enough, and had enough today. In the second instance, Rita's involvement in some get-rich scheme that was going wrong somehow. The greed of those guys she was hooked up with, from whom he must help her get free. An atmosphere of festering greed, a cloud of greasy greed hovering over and around everything, as it always did. It might be he would save her from herself, and save himself too, save them both from all the deadly greed by taking the package where it had to go, and waiting for her call afterward. From what she had said it was the key to their escape to peace and love in the North Woods tonight, and he had to believe—he did believe—that it was so. He had nothing else to believe at the moment.

Passing Dempster Street going south he thought of the Skokie Swift train station just east of here where he had used to sit when he worked for Red Top Taxi before he'd bought his own cab up in the Far North. One of the drivers, the oldest among them who sat on that cabstand, had said something amusing one day on the subject of greed, or perhaps it was about envy, same thing really.The drivers at the Skokie Swift at that time had been all Jewish guys, Russian immigrants, Israelis, but mostly plain old Americans, as Mattie would have put it. There were a few Haitian drivers. Because of the mix of nationalities, the conversation took a geopolitical turn and was wide ranging. An Israeli driver told how he had been stabbed one time on a ride in the Arab part of Jerusalem. A Russian recounted how the KGB used to grab cabs on the streets of Moscow as they couldn't afford their own cars. One of the wildest characters who drove a hack in Skokie in those days, a Russian guy called Mikey Israel, had picked up a Chinese national at O'Hare. Coming to a tollbooth, Mikey told the Chinese they were passing into the next "province" and he must come up with a hundred bucks to pay off the official in the tollbooth. At the Russian nightclub in Rogers Park that night Mikey showed off the hundred dollar bill he'd pocketed to the Skokie drivers. He danced on the bartop! Greed! One day the cab driver had been arrested at O'Hare cargo for not having an Interstate Commerce sticker and at the airport cop station they had Mikey for stealing a Chicago driver's load. When a detective questioned him, Mikey Israel embraced the cop and kissed him on the lips hard.

The state of the economy was hashed out among the drivers at the Swift, a desultory topic, one that pulled out all the greed and envy and the usual idiocies from the souls of the drivers (and anyone else) and put it on display. The cab driver thought to himself those old boys in Idaho and elsewhere (like the North Woods) who thought the Jews controlled the world ought to sit by the Skokie Swift sometime and listen. Some of the guys were kvetching about the income gap between the rich and the average man, who couldn't get ahead. Solly Zimmer said something funny. The cab driver loved to sit with old Sol. He wasn't the only one who felt so, and Solly had his regulars. One was a creative director at a big advertising agency downtown, who used to hire him to drive him around for weeks on end while he was on one of his drinking binges. Old Sol had never been in an airplane and the advertising man hired an airplane just to take him for a ride. Solly had told about it at the Swift next day. At one point in the drivers' animated conversation how the wealthy were taking more and not leaving any for the little guy, old Solly had asked in his scratchy voice, "Wid all my problems, I should worry about the *rich?*"

That had struck him so funny. It was greed put Rita in the trouble she was in tonight. She had said if he took this ride for her it would bring them the money they needed to head for the North Woods. Hell, they didn't need money for that! The bag on the backseat was nothing but a big package of greed—all the world's problems were caused by greed, and even those who were not themselves greedy were made miserable by the greed of others.

He drove the dayshift for Red Top Cab. One morning when he showed up at Howard Street and Chicago Avenue for the start of his shift, his car was not ready. He walked up to see why. Inside, the windshield was splashed with a trickle of blood. The nightman had been held up at the Davis Street elevated station and shot in the back of the head. He lived, but walked with a limp.

Greed. But sometimes when you were on the wrong track you just had to keep going down it until the moment came when you could switch tracks for the right one. It was all he could see and he must have faith, he told himself. Somewhere along here had to be the Rendezvous bar. He couldn't quite remember. The road had turned dark, with the kinds of businesses that closed up at night and turned off their lights. It was not a neighborhood of surprises, at least not big ones, and if there was any larceny in its soul, it was definitely petit larceny. Waukegan Road, in one of the joints on it, yes, it was just the halfconscious, lowpulse setting for a nice fat bag of coke to change hands and nobody the wiser or could care less anyway. He was tempted to feel at ease. The dire sensation that oppressed the cab driver was of the concealing commonplace. At the Rendezvous, would he meet only plain Mr. Rodriguez, who would take the package and spring him from this nightmare?

He sped up eager for it to be over. Dread had reached the ironbound intensity to cage him in his car if he didn't come across the place soon. The insane ordinariness glimpsed through the windshield's black crystal might burst like the skin of something rotten, revealing a paralyzing inability to picture himself in these events. He might not be able to make himself get out of the car. Like the eye of the night, the club's blue neon legend sought his own, *The Rendezvous.*

In the window more blue neon sketched the figures of a man and woman locked in a blue embrace, attracting silver moths. He swung in discreetly to a parking space in the narrow strip. Next door was a bowling alley, the Strike King Lanes. Somebody came out the glass door, a glimpse of a redandsilver-shirted crowd, clatter of pins falling to applause. A whole world was suggested to the cab driver, a night. First the cheerful activity in the lanes, then rest, romance in the dim blue Rendezvous, a life from which he was cruelly cut off, like a messenger from a burnedout evil star. A voice whispered to him insistently to call Rita at Luminati's restaurant at once and warn her about the cop. Why hadn't he thought of this before? He should have done it already. Could he get through to her in that booth? He looked about for a pay phone in the littered entrance to the Rendezvous Lounge.

But there wasn't one. It was a problem, more than he could handle. He was moving toward the crowded bar in a trance to get it over with. His eyes, used to picking out passengers in the clubs, searching for trouble signs, found the bartender's and locked into them. She was a tall blonde wearing a T-shirt that said "Meet Me at the Rendezvous" and a pair of tight jeans high on her waist. "Cab," he said, *"Rodriguez."* His and her (cold, no nonsense) eyes went down the patrons at the bar one by one, to a small dark man nodding over the wet formica, whose eyes flicked up through lank black strands of hair. The cab driver walked out.

After close breaths of airconditioned stale beer and cigarette fumes, the recovered night was fresh and open as a huge purple flower. Then it closed hard. A brown package of cocaine waited on the backseat. The muffled friendly hum from the bowling alley flattened out to something broken and deranged. He got in his car and waited, just like he'd waited for many rides before. Mr. Rodriguez came unhurriedly through the door. He spotted his cab and paused to light a cigarette. Above the glow in his hands his eyes peered warily left and right. He was wearing an orange rayon shirt that hung loose over his belt. In the blue light from the stylized couple in the Rendezvous' window, his brown skin looked purple.

"Go," he said under his breath, getting in.

"Right," said the cab driver amiably, his voice cracking. "Anywhere particular?"

No reply. A puff of smoke was expelled past his ear. Mr. Rodriguez touched his shoulder and pointed. They headed toward the city, down Waukegan, taking the Caldwell branch, entering a stretch of forest preserve. The cab driver had a hunch Mr. Rodriguez might appreciate the few minutes' lampless seclusion this route would afford. Correct. Behind him a discreet rustling began, like a rat stirring, the squeak of a knife on the heavy paper, just like the cop's, and finally the whisper of the plastic infill being removed. This time it heartened him. The ordeal was close to being over. One thing, in the woods' shadows, all the black tape and coffee grounds had to've been less offensive, maybe.

"Go," repeated Mr. Rodriguez softly.

On one side, the darkened homes floated past, only an occasional window lit by a frugal populace. On the other, the Caldwell Woods extended south and west some precise distance described in the city's ordinances. It was a part of the city's band of renowned forest preserves, recreation for a fortunate citizenry provided by beneficent and farseeing forefathers. But a rampant, brambly woods it was, riddled with unmarked paths to the river, full of squirrels, not just the furry kind.

He had picked up a strange ride here one time. The guy had been standing at the weedy curbside, leaning on crutches, with the woods at his back, a big white cast on one leg. A homeless bum with a broken leg! Naturally he had stopped and picked him up, the sort of load other drivers would speed up to pass by. He had to park and almost carry the guy inside the cab who could not walk almost. He felt sorry for him, but before the ride was over he would find the dude had a thick wad of cash and a .38 special in that leg cast of his.

The "bum" had waved the day's *Sun Times* at him, showing him on the back page a feature about how a boy had caught a piranha in the Humboldt Park lagoon yesterday. He wanted to see for himself, he said, and they took a ride to the near Southside to Humboldt Park to investigate this. He wanted to find the boy and hear the story firsthand, he said. He had let him out at the park and helped him to a bench, where the "bum" had assured him he would be fine. He was going to wait and get the full story. He had pulled out a big roll and peeled off the fare and a twenty dollar tip for helping him, along with an ironic grin, noting the cab driver's surprise. "You're a nice guy," he said. "Take care. There are piranhas in the lagoon." The cab driver had asked him again if he was really going to be fine, and that was when the guy had pulled out the .38 and remarked that he supposed he would be.

Out of sight of the busy streets, away from the picnic grounds, hobo camps sprang up for a night in the forest preserves. "The homeless"—as if those dudes wanted homes. The cab driver pictured their indolent even desperate freedom with a pang like the worst homesickness. That fellow with the quick grin and the broken leg cast hiding inside it a thousand dollars and a gun had had a freedom and mobility he envied right now. Your best judgment about people might turn out different.

"Kennedy!"

Mr. Rodriguez wanted him to take the Caldwell ramp onto the Kennedy Expressway picked out ahead in the cab's lights.

"Hey, I got an appointment, I got another ride," said the cab driver without conviction. He realized he had been anticipating Mr. Rodriguez returning to the Rendezvous.

"Go!"

"Hey, I'll drop ya where ya can catch a city cab. You'll get a better rate."

Mr. Rodriguez muttered in Spanish under his breath. He gave up and pulled onto the Expressway, pushing down his fear with the reasonable observation that he could have known it wasn't going to go down without a hitch. Even run of the mill deliveries didn't. Liquor store runs got screwed up. You could imagine with a big sack of drugs. The night air kept seeming to get hotter.

The anguish was going to be prolonged a little longer. The superheated air rushed in the open windows. People were always changing their minds or wanting more. That was the cab business. He ought to look at it from the guy's point of view. Maybe he didn't know one thing around here but the Rendezvous Lounge. He was not from this part of town. Naturally he wanted to beat it out of here and get home. It wasn't likely a guy like this had a driver's license. With resignation, the cab driver flicked on the meter.

Doing sixty down the freeway helped. It would be over soon at this speed. The hum of the tires was soothing. Probably after all these paranoid changes, the dude, whose business was dope, not fucking with poor cab drivers, would lay on him the usual generous Spanish tip. Half the time the Spanish didn't know where the hell they were going let alone how to get there. It was a foreign city to them yet.

One night, a guy, a busboy, had come out of the kitchen of one of the fancy restaurants on Milwaukee Road in Wheeling, said, "Wayne." Meaning on the Northside of the city, twenty-five miles away, that Wayne! No cross street, no number on Wayne either, just Wayne. Didn't seem to know any other English word. Could've been John Wayne. Or Wayne Gacy. When they got there they had to just cruise down it, also Clark, then back again because Wayne breaks up considerably. They drove along, the guy in back not recognizing anything, saying, "No, no, no," like Mr. Rodriguez saying, "Go." Halfway downtown and back. In the end the meter had read eighty-five dollars, when the guy had finally given up and just got out to walk. In all conscience the cab driver had knocked it down to forty-five but he'd been cruising around for an hour and a half. The guy who still didn't know where he was but wanted to get out anyway had accepted the reduction without expression, paid him, then given him a five dollar tip, a noble gesture. Fifty bucks. What did bus boys make? But the Spanish were of that race that appreciated cab rides. He loved them for it. The whole concept like a time warp, a cab ride, like to the big hacienda or something special, one got that feeling, they were poor, dignified, and a cab ride was some deal. The cab driver had always liked the Spanish very much.

"Where ya goin exactly?" he called out to the hood Rodriguez in the back seat in a friendly way trying to mend fences a little, make the ride more pleasant. His voice sounded like it came out of the oil sump somewhere.

"Go," said Mr. Rodriguez firmly, bringing his hand over the seat and making a shooing motion. The Spanish always were bad at directions. Maybe it was the language barrier, but try as he might he couldn't warm up to this particular guy.

"Go! Go!" The man grabbed his shoulder hard.

"Jesus, go, yeah, go where?" He had to look back to see that Mr. Rodriguez was signaling to take the Ogden Avenue exit, which they had just passed. People treated cab drivers all the same, crooks were no different, waiting till it was too late to give directions. He made a right turn across lanes and drove back to it on the shoulder. In spite of his surly mood, Mr. Rodriguez smiled at the audacity. He laughed approvingly, and said, "Yes."

They found themselves at a redlight at Ogden Avenue. Then, the light green, Mr. Rodriguez reached over to point them straight across busy Ogden, not to turn, as would have seemed natural. They continued on ragged Racine Avenue, which appeared to deadend immediately ahead. It didn't, but plunged in darkness, jogged right, past sad tenements.

The lights of Ogden Avenue were gone behind them. Racine descended between black windowless warehouses. A greasy hole of a viaduct yawned open like a coalmine, the headlights swallowed up in the blackness. The cab driver hit the brakes and picked his way among the potholes and chunks of asphalt. The headlights seemed to have stopped working. Fear threw a darker screen before his eyes. If a guy was going to get his brains blown out, this was a good place for it.

They bellied out of the hot depths, and over a spar. At this point the asphalt completely gave way and Racine struggled along as a dirt road through a freightyard. Even his brights were ineffectual in these sootsmeared caverns. Between dread and night, consciousness reduced to a smoking candle. The cab driver kept the car pointed forward, trundling slowly over mounds, in and out of the holes. As long as they kept moving, as long as the road didn't die against the rails or some unknown bend in the Chicago River, fear stayed in bounds.

Twice or three times, faint lights stabbed at them coming the other way, and battered old beaters passed them by. Amazingly, someone else knew this route, the backwoodsmen of the city. For a moment generations of litter and rubble were picked out barely, before being abandoned forever. With a strange pang of nostalgia the cab driver realized they could not be that far from that crazy short street he had been so happy to discover this afternoon, Governor's Parkway. The landscape of wonder had been transformed to one of fear. That was the uncanny thing about the cab business, never before in quite this brokendown primeval part of the city, then twice in one day. How near to one another dwelt pain and pleasure, fear and trust, charm and nightmare.

Then the street smoothed out and breathed again. Curbstones took up again, marking their path. Apartment houses, stores, thank God, back in civilization. A whine of traffic filled the air from below them where the Congress Expressway sent up flares against white walls like a wildly reflected firelight. They cruised across it on the overpass. Below, ugly impersonal slab of concrete, highroad of humanity! path of light! the old carbonstreaked highway sang its hypnotic song. Even Mr. Rodriguez appeared cheered up by the commotion and light, who leaned forward peering intently through the rising exhaust fumes. He was not your average Spanish guy, he knew his streets, he knew this shortcut, anyway.

They passed the University of Illinois campus, St. Frances-Cabrini Hospital, the Bulls' Stadium. Here he was at the United Center for the second time today. At Eighteenth Street Mr.

Rodriguez signaled to turn west. They were in a Spanish neighborhood, yes of course, that had been their destination, Pilsen.

At once the sidewalks were jammed with people. Illuminated signs turned the air rose and amber. Kids ran shrieking through an open fire hydrant gushing into a flooded intersection, a small lake through which the cab crept slowly not to create a wake. The cab splashed past stoops upon which young and old sat and smiled and watched the street with tolerance and interest. Latin music pulsed dramatically from upper windows and darkened doorways, washing through the open cab windows in waves of passion. The young blades held up traffic in doubleparked hotrods, sweet senoritas made poetry in motion on the sidewalks in skintight glitter jeans. The cab driver stole a glance into the rear view mirror, where Mr. Rodriguez's eyes gleamed festively, his lips curved upward in a smile like home.

In spite of circumstances the romance of the Latin night stole even into the cab driver's heart. Fear was allayed by the vivid throngs out playing on the summer's night. As it was for most gringo Chicagoans, Pilsen (named by a different generation) was foreign territory for the cab driver. The newcomers had found a few cracks to survive in. The storefronts sported garish handlettered signs, dingy south of the border fiesta touches, fluttering pennants, movie posters, strings of peppers. It was all intriguing and lush. In front of a window that made the bold claim SUPER MERCADO, Mr. Rodriguez invited the cab driver to stop. Thank heaven, they'd arrived home.

But he didn't make any move to pay. Mr. Rodriguez leaned far forward, creating intimacy. The cab driver could feel his breath on his neck. It was an awkward moment begging interpretation.

What the hell, he thought, always ready to indulge the customer a little more until the bill was paid, maybe the guy had to go inside for money, this often happened. If he asked, he'd say sure. His heart came back from its Latin fling. He glanced once more in the mirror and saw something sinister had again crept into Mr. Rodriguez's warm eyes and spreading smile.

"You . . . me . . . come . . ."

He'd taken the guy all the way home. What more could possibly be wanted of him? To kill the witness? Nawww! He wasn't paranoid. Maybe Mr. Rodriguez wished him to come inside for a festive occasion, snort a little coke? When a deal like this went down, there was some partying to follow, you could believe it. Maybe it had to be considered in the light of some Spanish notion of dignity, hospitality, or correctness. No doubt. Did Mr. Rodriguez wish to say a real thank-you and invite him for celebrations? Coming from poor countries as they did, the Spanish appreciated their cab drivers as jaded Chicagoans never would or could. He loved them for it.

The cab driver had a flash, reflective, objective, and totally irrelevant, how much Americans were going to miss, not understanding other cultures, never learning Spanish, as they never would learn. He was the same.

Mr. Rodriguez trailed his arms over the seat, and began picking through the cab driver's things. For the cab driver, the poignant note of Spanish culture faded rapidly.

"Hey!" He pulled some photographs out of Mr. Rodriguez's hands, and pointed at the meter. "Twenty-five bucks!"

Mr. Rodriguez gazed at the meter with about as much concern as if it had been a clock telling the time in an unknown city halfway across the globe. *"Come . . . me!"* he insisted, pertinently, flicking the cab driver's shoulder. He seemed to be waiting for him to shut off the motor and get out.

He stopped looking at the meter like it was an indecipherable artifact from space and smiled more closely, staring at the cab driver's ear. He reached out and gripped the cab driver's wrist firmly. His smile widened to a loony grin. His hot breath was so close he could have bitten the cab driver's ear without moving his mouth. The cab driver yanked his wrist free. The guy had turned into a jerk ride, a nuisance load, insisting on being a welcoming committee, and inviting him in. Every cab driver got crazies like this from time to time, who wanted to buy you drinks and dinner. Mr. Rodriguez didn't have enough English to see the cab driver meant him well and meant it when he said he couldn't linger, and meant no insult by it. Far from it!

"Good luck! Enjoy! I gotta get back to work though."

Something was wrong. He might as well face it. He couldn't imagine what it was though. Not enough in the bag? The trapped gloom of the old street pressed in on him. Sagging, sinking, misshapen survivor, battleground of wave after wave of immigrant races, it mocked his hope of an easy departure back to the north.

Mr. Rodriguez got out of the car and walked around to streetside and opened the cab driver's door. He invited him with a gesture, and waited for him to respond. Mr. Rodriguez gave himself a self-justifying squeeze of the crotch, leaving a white handprint.

"I don't know," said the cab driver, "I'm just a cab driver." His eyes blankly flicked Mr. Rodriguez's. "Forget the money. I was just supposed to give you that package. That in itself is my reward," he added dryly.

His sense of humor had taken him as far as it would go. He cranked the wheel hard—Mr. Rodriguez grabbed the wheel. They fought for control. He was going to drag him down the street if he hung on. But he had parked too well. He saw the knife swing through the air toward his ear and reached out a hand to block it.

The Cadillac slammed into the car in front of it and the tires spun. Mr. Rodriguez stuck the blade under the cab driver's collar and played around with it there. It felt extremely sharp like it would go through his flesh like butter. A warm trickle of blood started down his chest mixing in the rivulets of his sweat.

They stood almost touching each other in the street. Mr. Rodriguez smelled sourly of beer. When the cab driver shifted slightly, Mr. Rodriguez followed as in a mirror. The razor gleamed in the watery light of the street, floating bellyhigh. A streetful of voices rose and fell. In a secondstory window across from the Super Mercado a woman's silhouette disappeared. The light went out. The brick tenements exuded the heat they'd absorbed all day.

For a sicksweet instant, drawing him far away, the cab driver tasted Rita's lips on his own. He pried with his tongue into the gap between her teeth, a place to hide. He was more vividly with her than when they'd kissed in front of the restaurant. What had they done with her by now? He'd never called her to tell her that there was a cop outside the restaurant waiting and watching. It was hard to guess who was worse for Rita's health, that cop, or the old man she was with.

His own health wasn't that great at the moment. It was easier to fear for Rita. He wanted to think of her and of nothing else. He found it hard to acknowledge Rodriguez or even look at him. He resisted reality, looking down. The brown wrapping and the plastic

192

inner liner lay mangled in the street. A halo of white powder had spread out where Rodriguez had ground his foot in it.

He remembered the bodyguard staring into the tall grass after the Fist, not going after him, then retreating to the restaurant. It wasn't that a hundred grand meant nothing to his boss, but it wasn't worth getting shot for, was it? That was a lot of dough to say good-bye to.

But he figured they would not lose it. It was Rita's problem to get the money back from Bobby, or the cocaine from some hoods, and they thought she would. It was *her* deal that had suddenly gone weird and it was *her* ass that would get tore up if she didn't fix it. They might even kill her, she might believe. She was banking on their conception of her as smalltime, unconnected, nobody, dumb, weak, and torturable, in their grip past thinking otherwise. He knew from personal experience this morning in Jackie's how she could give even a stranger that sort of impression, let alone guys who abused her. They had let her go at once. She would have to go straighten things and bring it back to them. That was what the man and his boy would be figuring. They would have had no choice but let her go, how else would they get their drugs or money back? They never thought twice about it. It was a lot of dough. And that would've been her plan.

It looked like it was working. Both cabs that had been parked in front of the restaurant had gone missing. The fat man must think he owned her, after what he was accustomed to doing to her, thought he knew everything about her, and could let her loose to do his bidding. Having fastened ropes around her body, he thought he had her soul in chains too. What she would face, if she failed to get his money back, only she knew and that man. He had her tied to him by invisible psycho wires, didn't he, so he thought? Right now she'd be circling out around to retrieve her getaway nut from under the hood of the stalled Lincoln. She'd be long gone.

"Where an when, Fist?" asked the cop idly, as if thinking aloud rather than really asking.

"Shee-it!"

"I ain playin. I was playin in that field, but now I ain playin no more."

"I be lookin at the floorboard, cool nigger wanna know where, when, probly why an wherefore. Lemme up from down here first, Pageant!"

"Ya remember my Daddy? Useta say, 'Things get worse.' Praise the Lord!"

It didn't matter. Words were slippery. He didn't need the Fist to tell him where she was headed, where the two of them had set up for the meet. Because they weren't meeting. In a few minutes he'd have her in his sights again. It didn't matter what the Fist and Rita had dreamed up because he'd be doing their dreaming for them from now on. What bothered him was how he'd get the fat man, because by acing him out as she had she had let him out, too.

"He be dealin, ya know that, I guess," cranked out the Fist hopefully, as if reading his mind, sensing control shifting out from under him if he didn't start giving up a little. The cop knew something, or had guessed something, he could tell.

"He be the man, but you caint guess on what scale, copper. Ya better stake out his ass. I was gonna cop but the count was too short. I hadda hat. Ya too late. Ya caint fuck with nobody for what they *thought* about doin! I can tell you all about him, Shooter. I'm clean, an you know it. By luck I ain hold *nothin*, less American money aint legal no more."

"Ya hold your dick all you hold, Fist, an ya can't reach that at the moment."

A few hundred yards before Fox Glove Road ran into the Laboratory Drive, the stop sign a red berry in a yellow mist, a doe bolted out of the scrub woods and froze in his lights. The seized tires let out their almost human shriek as the car came to a stop a few feet before her. Her eyes shone pink and blank as the buttons on a furry deer toy. The cop couldn't remember if he'd ever seen a wild deer before. He didn't know as he was seeing one now. The creature had the weird and perfect grace of a vision or a dream. Tan flanks, fluffy cottontail, and pricked ears were so pretty and clean they couldn't be real. The polished black hooves, barely clinging to the asphalt, might as well take it straight up in the air from here, in a climb out of dreams no less fantastic than the leap that had brought it across the drainage ditch to stand face to face with himself and force him to hit the brakes.

He had seen yellow warning signs at several places along the road, with stylized black silhouettes of leaping deer authored by the same bureaucratic hand that produced those gingerbreadman restroom designations. Their unconscious effect had been to persuade him that there could be no such animal around, certainly none such as he was seeing right now. The shock of it thus all the greater, in confrontation with the wild being, he felt in the presence of a Power whose resources of Beauty filled him with awe. Lost and confounded in the act of seeing, he was as frozen in place as the deer was. Man and animal beheld each other. All else was forgotten, momentarily, as if this meeting with the graceful creature had been foreordained. Finally, after a minute, he blew his horn, but it didn't budge.

He found himself in a staring contest he might lose. Transfixed by the headlights, the deer gave no promise of moving. The perfected tangle of its limbs looked as unlikely to carry it forward as its roots of moving a tree. Did his own eyes stand out like distant red planets just like the deer's? Unable to take his eyes from the deer's, he put the car in reverse, backed up thirty feet, and started to go around it. The deer took three quick steps and froze dead in his lights blocking him again. He wondered with stupefying horror if he might have to bump it gently, or plain run it down to get past. The eyes of the deer generated a secret light of their own, like a man's steadfastly refusing to talk. They delivered him their message just the same of profound difference. The night that had been understood and grown familiar became real and strange.

A hard gleam at the corner, coming from the direction of the Labs, a car approaching slowly ran the stop sign turning onto Fox Glove. The equal intensity of light from the opposite side released the deer and it leapt nimbly into the woods. The cop started his car forward, his hands trembling on the wheel. The oncoming vehicle cut its brights and he savagely flicked on his own. He knew who it would be. He saw the crown of the cab's toplight and pulled down the visor in front of his face in case his brights didn't blind them. The cab's highbeams came back on to stay, too. The cop had a glimpse of the professor squinting angrily, turning his red face to curse him, Rita sunk down in shadow in back, as they passed. How glad he was to see her! How dear she was.

He realized he'd been counting on the Checker driven by the brother from Chicago. The Checker brother he could have dealt with. He could have pulled them over and sent the dude on his way. But the professor might try anything. He might've moved too fast for her to think if it had been the Checker, but the professor was a problem. He was almost as bad as number 17 as far as being unpredictable went.

Cab drivers were cantankerous unpredictable motherfuckers, weren't they? Rita might have already done some talking to the professor and got his nose wide open as the Cadillac's, and they might make a run for it. Rita and the bag she had with her were the whole game, they were all he had now, his most precious possessions. He must not let them get away from him. She was going to help him put that bag on the fat man. She was going to help him bring him in and his boy and Bobby as well, tonight.

She might get so scared she'd rip open the package to the wind and let it sift out in the breeze. Even if it was her passport out of town. She might be scared of jail worse than anything.

Yes she was smart and brave and given two seconds might do it. He must let them go by in the darkness for a moment and not get too close. The professor might have recognized him. They didn't need to see his lights behind them. The cop coasted through the stop sign, rounded the corner, and when he was hidden by the cornfields braked to a stop fifty yards up the Labs Drive. He turned off his lights and motor and listened and waited in darkness a few seconds. He'd soon find them on the Tollway heading for the city.

"Goddamn, Shooter! Don do me this way!" wailed the Fist so the skin on the back of the cop's neck prickled. With the deer and all, he'd almost forgotten he was there.

"Lemme sit up, don treat me like no dog!"

The cop lit a cigarette, not offering any. He flicked on the domelight, and took another look at the money in the Fist's briefcase. He thrust in his hand and hefted several bundles, dropped all but one, thumbed its edges, did some arithmetic. Maybe eighty, a hundred grand, maybe more, give or take, in old bills. The smell of the money was a thick, dirty perfume.

The image came to him again of that bodyguard of the fat man staring after the Fist hiding in the grass in the vacant lot with their money, how he had suddenly turned around and gone back to the restaurant, as if the money wasn't everything. They were counting on Rita getting it back, but all the same, all this money, right in front of you, you could walk away from? He stared at it in the dim brown light. Well, life mattered too, but this was a lot of cash. Or— the imponderable thought formed in his mind—was it *not* a lot of cash to the bodyguard's master?

He snapped the briefcase shut and turned off the domelight. He drew deeply on his cigarette, and watched the smoke curl in the darkness tinged chemical yellow by the Labs. He fell into a reverie. He thought of his mother, for some reason, who had died before he'd entered high school. She'd never seen him play varsity ball. He was not one of those youths moved to deeds by mother's love. His father's whip hand and earnest philosophy had seen to that part of things, for she'd been gone. His Daddy'd had complete charge of him. He'd always wished she could have seen him play ball. The Fist had never met her, never known her, but he'd said she'd "laid a Pageant on his ass." A sorry ass like Bobby could never guess the beauty of his mother.

"Damn you, Fist," he said to the man on the floor behind him.

"What? Aw, Shooter."

For a second the cop was bathed once more in the quiet light that had come from his mother's eyes, the liquid light of all that was holy, if anything was holy. She'd had one green and one brown eye and the effect was uncanny beauty. He was always soothed as well as troubled by the far look in her eyes, in memory. He took for granted that as a youth he must have been soothed only, wrapped up and supported by her quiet gaze, but now he was sometimes troubled by the secret of her that would never be revealed. It seemed to him somehow that she had actively harbored a secret that he had not been old enough to learn, not that the loss of her had created one. Maybe she had seen something beautiful. He figured she had, that things of that nature were for such as her to know and see. A faith that she had was her meaning for him now. Not like his Daddy's meanings, plain and hard as calloused hands and the love of a God who expected you to work and try. To the extent he had a shred of any religion it was not his Daddy's oldtime fervent religion but the look in her eyes in memory that was a kind of fleeting glimpse of a mysterious heaven that he knew that she had seen.

He came to himself and started the car. Why was he thinking of his mother? It made him sad and happy at once, neither very useful emotions right now when cold calculation was wanted. Was it the Fist bringing back old memories, good and bad memories, to trouble him from childhood? The gang leader who had made snide remarks to Rita about the beautiful people he came from had no idea what he was talking about. Coach had been a good man too, never mind Bobby. Damn what Bobby had thought of him.

The oddest thing struck him that it was the deer, the deer's strange eyes, that had brought memories of his mother back to stir and haunt his heart.

The unholy thought made him shudder. It seemed to him an unnatural thought from which he wished to flee, the commingling of the deer and his mother. The weirdness of this made him seek companionship with even the Fist. Shaking his head to be rid of thoughts, he turned his head and spoke in a low confessional voice over his shoulder.

"You shoulda seen this damn deer, man, that just walked across the road. You shoulda seen the look she gave me, man, swear to God. I aint superstitious, but that deer looked human. I mean the look in her eyes, man, you know? Actually, damn if I ever *seen* a real deer before except in the zoo, I don't think, have you? I don't think I have. The strangest feeling I had, it could tell me a *secret,* if it could speak."

"Hawww, homeboy, don't do me like no *deer,* man. Lemme up off this here floor."

"No, you oughta seen that deer, Bobby. Had a secret, just like you. But your secret don't mean shit no more, Fist."

"Whacha wanna know?" came the querulous, disoriented wail from in back, giving the cop a start.

"Nothin no more from you, Bobby! . . . Fuckin *deer!"* muttered the cop, and turned the car, as if released, like the doe, from a mystification.

There was no mystery about Rita's physical movements, only the motions of her soul. It was just stone business for a guy like Bobby. But to him she was fascinating. When the chance was right, he'd talk to her hard and fast. Strange how he felt he had known her a long time, her soul. She wouldn't have a very trustful memory of him from this morning. How differently he felt about her now. Together they would set up the man using the Fist's money and what she was riding with now. She'd go for something like that he was sure. She had to have vengeance in her heart.

Then he'd see that she made her escape, when it was all over, unless she wanted to be with him, like she really might have this morning, but if not, with plenty loot for herself. But she might find that hard to believe yet.

Speeding, doing ninety for a while, after a few minutes, he spotted the professor's cab again a few miles down the Tollway, as he knew he would. Cruising down the big road, with the cab in view half a mile ahead, he reached for the Johnny Walker, and remembered it was gone.

Not missing a beat, he cracked open the briefcase, fingered a fifty out of one of the bundles, rolled it into a tight cylinder, and stuck it in his nose. He reached way down and fished around in the dark with his hand and finally found the packet on the floor, and clumsily shook all that remained in the glassine packet onto the back of his hand, where it made a pale, ragged scar, like a river meandering across a map of strange country. With two snorts, he hauled it home.

"Whacha doin?" snickered the Fist through swollen lips, who knew damn well.

Ah, the pure glaze of enlightenment, the lens that revealed. He saw everything about these actors, the fat man Rita would fill him in about. He'd hold her in the crook of his arm, like a child, so vulnerable she was with what she had in her purse, a bomb to blow her youth apart. He'd help her—he'd never hurt her but he couldn't let her see that yet.

"You aint got shit on me but that bag, an you blow that up yo nose, copper! You measly snifflin hypocrite!"

199

Up ahead, the obnoxious professor was swerving from side to side past cars like he was drunk, but showing no serious signs of thinking about giving a chaser the slip. A small red poppy of paranoia bloomed in the cop's heart just the same. It was too much of a coincidence when you thought of it that a partner of number 17's had pulled up in front of the restaurant just at the moment Rita had needed him. He picked up his glasses and studied the professor through them. He had his head half turned, he was yakking hard over his shoulder at Rita. He was smitten by her, like his pal "the Cadillac." They were all hoping to have a crack at her and she was using them. His impression of the professor and even all cab drivers shifted from clever punk to simple chump, the only possibilities, once again. He pulled up by a carlength.

On the back floor, the Fist hacked out a long, bubbly, bloody cough, spat, and sighed. He and Rita weren't leaving town tonight.

"Oh Jesus, have mercy," he pleaded softly, to himself. "Forgive me, Jesus!" he exclaimed after a while. No Hawaiian vacation. "Oh, oh, Rita, I'm sorry, baby. Okay, copper, here it is, les do it," he suddenly piped up in a surrendering voice.

"The Green Mill Club on north Broadway, man. You aint got nothin on me but green American money, no matter how you lie. You can have her, muhfucker! She be loaded! But she aint who you want, okay? You want that *man,* an I can tell you all about him."

The cop was paying him as much mind as a man in a boat a fish on a stringer. The moaned club name made no more sense to him than if the Fist had suddenly decided to impart the secret of his favorite ribs sauce. It might have made sense if being interracially mixed on the Northside of town would have been just the right cover. Rita and the Fist would have been seen and not seen. They could have walked in topless. People, white liberals and black liberals alike, would have politely or genuinely not noticed, and they could have exchanged all the dope and stolen money in the world. The cop had a preference for Southside bars where blacks were not treated with kid gloves, for the simple reason they were the whole clientele, and where a mixed couple would draw honest, healthy stares. In the liberal jazz joints, they had computer devices that mixed you a weak drink under the cash register. The liberal was the one who smiled at you while the computers did the ripoff, the cop thought absently and maliciously as the cocaine in his brain did a downward swirl. Bobby's news might have made sense—if they weren't already south of Lawrence Avenue.

"That club near Lawrence, aint it?"

"About."

"Fist, there aint no *north* Broadway. If there was, there'd be a south Broadway, an there aint no such a thing," he mused. "Only Broadway. Maybe what you mean at the north end a Broadway." Cocaine had him rambling a bit, he noticed. He kept his eye dead on the cab crest of the professor.

"Yeah, that so?" said Bobby, conversationally, interested. "Oh, yeah, then," he remarked in an agreeable, hopeful tone. "Well, at that club, wherever, that where she be."

"If ya aint lie, she do an end run around your ass!"

"I'm the fuckin goalpost!"

"Yeah, she must don't dig the split. We aint goin to no Broadway. We past Lawrence, we south a Addison already. "

"Shit, she don't know what to do with it by herself."

"She think you strongarm her ass."

"You lyin muhfucker. Where we really at? She don't think that, do she? Jesus, what the world come to."

"I got her in my lights, man. She right ahead a me in a cab an we *headed south*, man. When she git where she goin, I'm gonna snatch her ass an say I got the two a ya makin the switch. Tell me why I can't do that, Fist. What she hold, an your briefcase a money, it aint like this morning in Jackie's, Bobby."

The Fist stalled for a while by coughing several times, long and liquid. He brought it up and tasted it and thought it through and added up the score. "Blood, Shooter, I'm coughin *blood.*"

"Hey, where is she *goin?"*

"I don't know where she think she goin, Shooter."

He spat on the floor a juicy flourish, came to an end of thinking, and decided it was time to talk for all he was worth.

"Okay. . . . Okay. Listen up. The man's game clear in South America, man, him an they turn over together like cute dice, baby, they operation in the millions, baby, ya got no idea how his shit come down. His game so long ya can't imagine what I sayin, Shooter. Ya think I be tellin ya a story, don't ya, basketball player? I know. The shit in a hospital, can ya dig it? Hid in a pile a powders like trees in a forest. Dig? The way it come in so beautiful from

201

Ecuador someplace with like shipments a lifesavin materials an shit, don nobody touch nothin, man. That shit got a U.S. government stamp of approval. It has a *license* on it. I know the hospital where he load, basketball player, an I know when he do it. "

The cop's pulse, loaded down with chemicals like a barge on a river, some evil South American waterway, lunged thunderously. Could he have stumbled on a major source? He hadn't dared to let his thoughts go so far. Something in the Fist's voice told him the man was not entirely falsifying things, if maybe trying to sound like he knew more than he did. The road before his eyes blanked out in a vision of what might be within his grasp. A closeup of high stacks of white cartons, imprinted with scientific specifications, glowing in the sun on a dock of a medical plant in a tropical country somewhere. Brown men loading shipments of vital medicines, more various than they knew. Stamps of committal, tax paid, a "STAT" delivery, pharmaceutical connection beyond reproach, protected on all sides by unimpeachable international conventions, which might arrive without inspection at a hundred destinations. Not a hospital, the Fist was misinformed, or holding his last card close. A laboratory warehouse in a far Northwest Chicago suburb.

In a wave of cokedup clarity, the cop saw that the man wouldn't leave a breadandbutter deal to a woman who played victim for him. If it had been hers to make, and now to clean up after, could it amount to much in his scheme of things? The Fist might be telling it straight. A hundred grand not the centerpiece! Chumpchange! Again he saw the bodyguard turn back to the restaurant. The road came back, black and clear. The vision of the vast smuggling network came and went, and all he had was a shifty gangbanger from his youth in chains behind him, the funny money at his right hand, smallchange, and a shivering, hungry excitement for a new tomorrow like nothing he'd known before stirring in his soul. In searching images like long combers on a night beach, his thoughts reached as far as they would, took what they could grasp, and receded with the stealth of drugrunners, leaving a glitter trail. He had one idea. Keep Rita before him. She would help him get to the fat man tonight. They would bring him down together.

Just west of the Loop, they pulled off on Eighteenth Street. The cab with Rita inside drifted into Pilsen. "Spanishtown, Fist, we with the Mexican boys, motherfucker! Rodriguez, yeah."

"Rodriguez, shit! What you know about Pepe?"

They pushed through crowds in the street. Music was in the air. Kids played in a hydrant that almost soaked him through the window. The white Cadillac, Bull's-eye cab number 17, suddenly showed up in the professor's headlights.

Here's where they had sent him. That poor, sorry 17. All suspicion that the cab driver was any other than a sucker caught up in the dangerous webs of others left the cop, who slid into the shadows under a broken streetlamp no more than three carlengths behind the two white cabs parked almost together. A completely novel sensation, something nearly akin to fellow-feeling for a cab driver, confused him. This was no time to go soft in the head. The stark fear he felt was for Rita.

She'd sent him here with that killer decoy, and now she had followed after him, for what? To see him dead? To commit suicide herself? As if echoing the cop's thoughts, Bobby from the floorboards mumbled, "That the *last* place she should be at. She wanna die? Pepe Rodriguez? That where we at?"

What was the professor up to? He got out, leaving Rita in his car doubleparked just behind number 17. He walked around the Cadillac glancing inside. For *what,* he (and Rita too) wondered. They couldn't know he had stashed his whole week's groceries with Wisconsin this morning, who had been riding around with them all day. Reassured they were still there, Armchair headed straight for the doorway Rita had pointed out to find his friend.

It came to the cop with uneasy irony that he must have sent the cab driver to the very spot she'd known where to find him. But what was she up to? See some Mexican hoods about what? It didn't make sense. She'd brought the professor driver for some reason. Wait a second, she cared about cab driver 17? She'd thought better of the fatal errand she had sent him on? She'd come down here to try to *save him?* While this disturbed him in a way he didn't understand, if it was so, she had heart, and it bode well for his plan to make her see how they could set up the man who was selling drugs to wreck kids' souls, if she had that much wild heart.

"Look like she got a heart, Bobby, after all she been through."

"If we on Eighteenth Street she done lost her mind."

"Naw, that cab driver she has taken pity on is all I can think. Because she don't need to come down here for no baby powder."

"Cab driver? If I see that crazy mutha! Copper, if we aint on Broadway, I caint help ya, but it aint her ya want no way, I tol ya."

"We really sposeta be up Broadway, huh, Fist?"

"She aint follow the plan."

"Look like Rita all heart to me. Cause this don't make sense."

"She drown in her stupid heart, why she let that muhfucker do her like he do, why I was helpin her escape."

"You were?"

She had put herself in danger coming to find some hoods she had doublecrossed with a bag of talcum powder. Was she going to apologize? The cop shook his head at the realization that she cared for that skinny punk of a no-account cab driver, because there was no other explanation. If she went in some door around here they would cut her throat for fun and every reason. A nobody like her they would toss in the dumpster in the alley even if she gave them back what she'd stolen from them. They would never forgive the indignity of opening that bag and finding nothing but bath powder. The horror of that and the shame you could not make Mexicans to forget, no matter what amends you made. He'd thought she was bad and bold, but she was full of love, really, by the look of it, or else he didn't know what was happening. If she got out of the cab and took one step he'd hit her running, lift her to his shoulder, and trust her to hang onto that purse of hers for dear life.

"Open up!" shouted Armchair. He tried to peer through the darkened front window. He banged on the door with his fist with all his might, shouting, "You got my friend in there? *Open up!*"

Nothing happened.

"Hey in there! You got a cab driver in there?" yelled Armchair. "Open up! I know he's in there. I see his cab right here in front!"

His idea of cab drivers took another querulous turn from conviction of their existential foolishness and/or diabolical cleverness to something completely new, he hardly knew what. Not that he liked them any better. On the street side of the car, Rita climbed out and fell straight onto her hands and knees. This was so astonishing he forgot about the professor, and never even thought to get out and grab her, which had been his intention. She crawled on all fours on the street around to and opened the driver's door of the Cadillac. This was dumbfounding and had the momentary effect of paralyzing him. The interior light in the Cadillac came on.

Across the street the lights of a store and the apartment directly above it went off, then on again, almost simultaneously. Somewhere down the street a door was flung open, and the muffled salsa music grew hard and bright.

"Listen, I know important people in this town!" yelled Armchair. "I've called a federal judge. He's my uncle. You can't hold that man in there! He's a college graduate!"

The door of the grocery store opened, and Armchair barged— or he was pulled—in.

The dim interior light of the Cadillac had gone out. Rita, who had disappeared from view crawling around the front of the car, stood up. The cop laughed under his breath, seeing it coming. Maybe she was getting adept at it by now. The hood rose on by now practiced hands. You wouldn't have thought those slender arms held the strength. Into the engine compartment of number 17 the Cadillac cab she stuffed the real package.

The cop laughed from deep down at her bold opportunism. He finally understood. Joy rose up in him savoring this moment before the kill. He recognized all these people's games, and could move on them as he wished. Poised above them, seeing all, their lives and purposes drifted to him like a kind of food. Not that he would tangle with those hoods in there. Maybe he'd give them Bobby. That'd be better than busting him. The fat man he would move on later tonight, when he knew more. For Rita, he felt only kinship, love, and admiration. Yes he loved her. He would save her. If she started for the storefront, that would be it. He'd grab her, and she'd be free of all this.

Instead she ran the other way across the street on her wobbling highheels and disappeared into the mouth of an alley before he could move. Everything she did amazed him. He might have his hands full if they came out after her. He touched his gun under his arm. She hovered there amidst the empty spirit bottle debris of old bad dreams and the aftersmell of mad backalley desire. She wouldn't stray far from her white treasure, pearl with a well-known price. Or did it seem the mystery of mysteries, burned pure at last, by bolts of terror straight from hell and the transforming courage she'd always known she had?

Two evil-looking guys came out the door the professor had disappeared into and began searching the cabs. One found a sack of groceries in the front seat of the Cadillac, peered into it and pulled out a few cans, and tossed the rest as far as he could into the street. They sprang the trunk lids, found nothing of interest in the Cadillac's, and pulled out from Armchair's trunk some of his junk. Exclaiming to each other while clothes, old shoes, books, even pots and pans, a rolledup rug, golfclubs, a picture in a frame and a couple of tires without rims went through their hands, they had not expected this quantity and assortment of items in the trunk of a cab. The sheer scale of their investigations seemed to overwhelm them. They began to swear and to comment derisively, and it made the cop laugh, causing the Fist to shift apprehensively. The hoods scowled at each other. They quit without finishing. They forgot about the Cadillac, let alone pop its hood. What with Armchair's amazing various cache of goods in his taxicab, not having found what they were looking for, or anything of value of any sort, they appeared defeated by it, and left everything lying in the street, and the doors and trunks of the cabs wide open, and went back inside. The cop, remembering the professor's evil genius, now indirectly playing out in such dire circumstances, marveled.

Shooter Teagarden, laughing under his breath, wryly delighted, suddenly grimaced, thinking. He lowered his head, clinging to the shadows. The pleasures of this watch, the thrills of anticipation, developed a shadow of their own as perversely he was reminded that his routine would not have brought him to this high point. Had he tipped off his superiors what he was into, they would have brought in others, called him home, and he never would have had such a good time. Maybe he would have been rewarded for his initiative, and maybe he would have been reprimanded for dodging procedure. He would not be having this amount of fun. At best he would have had to share it.

The truth was even worse, wasn't it? Always it was. This rich excitement would not be equaled again in the ordinary course of things. Not even if he brought it off the way he was dreaming it would go down. Even if he got the man, and them all tonight, it might be like this morning in Jackie's when he had realized that it would not be enough. It would be over then, and back to the soulless routine. Might get a commendation, but his troubles would return, they would not have been resolved or banished by success. His old weariness and dissatisfaction with his life he could taste already waiting to creep through his door again, mysterious midnight of his soul. No more fun like this any more! From this peak, he would fall back into the regular desultory order of things. The freedom he had right now he wanted never to end!

An idea leapt into his head with all the unexpected charm and outlandish grace of that deer leaping into the road in front of his surprised eyes standing on its black hooves. He stared at it and it stared back at him fervently and instantly commanded all his attention like the red eyes of the deer had. He didn't any more recognize it from his experience than he had the deer, and it fixated him with the same shining, compelling, never seen before, almost holy force. It was strange and familiar at once, like the deer, as if he must have seen this new wild creature before surely, but he hadn't.

It would be a way to ride the wave, leap from crest to crest freely, keep the power and excitement growing. It couldn't have been more astonishing, and it couldn't have been more obvious and real. He'd go up, and not down again. He'd jump straight from the dirty street through the beautiful trees into the flying clouds. A wild logic, like that of the Power that created the deer, had found its way into his soul. Here was his chance.

He would help Rita. If she was willing. She'd be his good luck charm on the road out of town as he would be hers. She had that something about her, that spunk. Whatever she thought she was doing down here in Mexicantown, he was sure she was a strong one when all was said and done. She would understand him. All he had to do was think of everything he'd seen her do today. She represented the intention against long odds toward freedom, something he understood to his core. She was his inspiration.

He felt about her as he felt about himself. It occurred to him that that deer on the road had been an omen, a sign that a secret was about to be revealed to him, this daring plan that had suddenly come to him. The shape of his own amazing escape made itself clear to him now, in the shadow of her misbegotten own.

Just like that another vision, a very amusing one, formed in his mind as the inevitable corollary of his genius. He saw the Fist walking jaybird naked through the dark countryside somewhere way out from the Labs out there in the cornfields, and he laughed.

It would give him the time he needed to develop his idea and carry out his and Rita's escape. He chuckled some more and considered the righteousness of it. He couldn't leave him down here in Spanishtown to tell them who had their money, he couldn't let him go, he was dangerous, and he was deadweight now. Those cornfields would be the place for Bobby.

"Fist, ya know where ya was by that restaurant, what town?"

"Yeah? Shit, no."

"What towns aroun there?"

"What ones?"

"Damn, I don know myself."

He searched around for the map of Greenshores, and flung it open. Flicked on the dome light. "Greenshores, Round Lake, Gray's Lake . . . all like that, near in Wisconsin."

"Naww . . ."

"Ya know that Gray's Lake?"

"Fuck."

"Where the real gray folks live, Fist, ya know, farmers, big dudes on tractors an shit, chawin snuff, cats with little whitey spectacles down on their nose in front a the general store, big gray beards downta their waist, packin shotguns an huntin knives an godamighty. Gray boys, man."

The Fist gagged and spat.

"Aint shit."

"Hey, I'ma cut ya loose. Not in town with them farmers, don't worry."

"Yeah?"

"In the cornfield."

"No, Shooter, no, shit."

"Bout five miles down the last gray road."

"Fuck, man, don't do it."

"Gonna hafta keep your pretty jacket, though."

"Whacha wanna know else, Shooter?"

"Gotta take your pants, shoes, everything."

"Ya wanna know bout that man's operation, right?"

"Gonna let ya keep your shoes maybe."

"Fu-u-u-u-ck."

"Naw, caint let ya keep your shoes neither. Nothin."

"Aw, fuck, man!"

"Bobby, I think I gotta take a knee. I gotta shoot off one a your kneecaps, man, cuz ya run too fast. Sorry if it hurt. Just one knee, boy. You still got the other'n. I gotta do it. You can limp. Cuz I need a few hours."

It was such an amusing necessity and he laughed again hard. The Fist began laughing, defeatedly, too, and then the cop some more. It was a strange duet of bitter laughter, with the cop's gloating tone cut by something effectively sinister, and the beaten man's pitiful titters touched by a despairing falsetto note of inexplicable hope. They laughed like boys, exhausted by fighting, or even lovers, exhausted by loving, who keep on beyond limit.

In the alley she breathed almost easily again. It suited her to be hiding in an alley. The abandoned ugliness and deadend stillness met its welcoming echo of nothing and nobody in her. She knew herself hidden in an alley, deserved to be here, and was almost free. Every piece of falsely gleaming tin and glass found its reflection in her fearful, hopeful soul. The stench of urine, the full garbage bins, made her blink and gag, and that felt right. Things could only get much better, or much worse, for one crouching for her life in an alley. She rejoiced to have found Wisconsin, or his cab anyway.

If she got Wisconsin out of this predicament she had landed him in, she might make it yet. But if something happened to him in there through her fault, she might lose heart and not make it after all. Anyway, it was up to the bookreader cab driver friend of his now. What luck to have jumped in his cab, of all the cabs up there, a friend of Wisconsin's to help her. How good to her God was to have arranged that. She believed in her luck, no matter how bad things got, because her luck was all she had.

She pressed her back into the protective shadow of a grimy window casement. It was ancient, buckled and weathered, caked with filth and cobwebs, and so deeply recessed in the brick she felt almost hidden, though she wasn't by a long shot. The brick walls of her cave gave off the day's storedup heat. She could see the white cabs parked side by side. Wisconsin's had been left at a weird angle, pointing into the street. When she saw it and her worst fears had been confirmed, a great wave of self-loathing had washed over her, but at the next moment, gladness, because she had found him. She'd been hoping against hope that his cab would not be here, and he would have had the sense to disappear and save himself and forget about her. But she was so damn glad to see his car.

It had freed her, for a moment. She should have been savoring her freedom from the moment they had let her go and she and the bookreader had raced to fetch the package out of J.A.'s Lincoln. But not with Wisconsin in trouble. Under the weight of fear and shame, the sight of Wisconsin's car though in danger was wonderful.

No one could ever know what freedom meant but her. The slaves, probably, as she was a slave. That was one reason she liked black people, even that sorry cop this morning, Bobby's so-called boyhood friend, that dirty mean guy, who had uncovered her scars, and even squeezed them. Even him, she had liked for a moment, or at least, understood. She knew what it was like to be a slave.

Being in an alley was nothing, she had been in far worse than an alley. It was an improvement and it was nice to be alone, even in an alley. Nothing left to lose in an alley, and that was a kind of freedom, as Janis Joplin sang it. She had nearly forgotten this salutary feeling of aloneness like the shattering sense of life itself fresh and new, every memory of it almost wiped clean off the slate of her soul after two years in thrall to J.A. and MacDougal.

She'd had no choice but to hide the cocaine in Wisconsin's motor a moment ago. She couldn't just walk around with something like that on her here. If they found it on her, they might kill her, a nobody like her, and him too. At the same time truly it was her commitment to their dream of escaping together to the North Woods tonight. All she had done so far was increase his danger if those guys inside came out and found it in his car. He'd been in danger from the moment he had met her, but he hadn't known it. To think so made her start to weep. When they escaped this scene together tonight, when he came out of that storefront where the bookreader was right now talking to the Mexicans, then the $100 K of cocaine would ride with them, and it would be their ticket to freedom. She wiped her eyes with both hands.

What did the driver who was delivering it have to do with it? Everything—how their minds worked. They might be torturing him right now. Bobby had explained it to her, an afterthought, when he'd heard her plan, not that he cared what happened to some cab driver. That the guy who brought it would not know all about it would make no sense to them, although that would have been perfectly logical to an American. They rode around in cabs all the time, didn't have any way else to get around, and they thought cab drivers knew things. In their culture a cab driver usually was the owner/possessor of a car and that made him somebody. Wisconsin had a Cadillac of all makes of car to have, they would have checked that out. A cab driver was the man to them in a way that was inconceivable to Americanos. It might be his doom.

It was Bobby's idea to rip these guys off, not hers, but she'd gone along with it. She had been escaping from J.A. not these guys. But she obviously couldn't give them their drugs. She'd have nothing at all then but get murdered. She meant to trade it with Bobby for his money later on Broadway. To somebody who knew what to do with it, it was worth a lot more than $100 K. It was her ticket to ride but not if they found it in the cab motor. They might kill all of them, even the poor bookreader.

Bobby was out there someplace with all that money, he was probably at the Green Mill on Broadway by now expecting her. It was getting late. How long would he wait? Bobby was going to Honolulu. When she had asked him why Hawaii, he had said, no, Honolulu, he had always loved the sound of that name. She didn't think he even knew Honolulu was in Hawaii, when he first mentioned it to her. He would wait until closing time for her, she was sure, he was that right a guy. She and Wisconsin would stop and make the switch. The coke was worth a great deal more than the money in that briefcase to a guy like Bobby who knew how to cut it. Bobby had a cool and interesting conversation, no matter

211

what that cop thought about his old friend. She'd only just met him, but she thought Bobby had a big heart. She wondered how he'd react when she told him she wasn't going with him to Honolulu. He'd understand.

She squeezed herself more deeply into the dirty cave of the window casement. Even if she'd had the sense to hide it, at the first pain she would scream out where it was if they got her, and that would be hell for her and Wisconsin both, and it would not save them. She really believed his crazy pal was going to get him out somehow. She'd never met anybody like that bookreader cab driver and the ride down here had given her hope. He was a graduate of the University of Chicago he claimed and knew several important judges in town, so he said. She kind of doubted all that, but there was something unpredictable seeming and even outrageous about the bookreader dude that had created faith during the ride. He was in there explaining the score to them right now, about the important politicians he knew and how he had told the cab dispatcher to call the cops after ten minutes if he didn't come out with Wisconsin. Ten minutes was almost past.

A whole bag of poison and self-revulsion was ready to spill down on her head and paralyze her again if something happened to them. She prayed it wouldn't. Wisconsin had had a dirty trick played on him. It wasn't her fault. But of course it was. How was she to know that J.A. would not let her go out with the package and talk to him, and would send MacDougal instead? J.A. had smelled a rat, no way he didn't. But he was unprepared for Bobby just up and strolling out the front door with his briefcase. That had caught him by surprise. In her heart she knew she was the guilty party.

Opposite the dark alley Wisconsin's cab gleamed vaguely, life abandoned and motion cut off. The thought that he had actually driven to meet that Rodriguez and had handed some hoods a box of talcum powder made her gnash her teeth wildly and bite her lips till they bled. She cried out softly wishing it weren't so. And now she'd hidden the real bag in his car too, hadn't she, somebody she trusted and maybe even loved. But if she walked in and gave it to them, they would kill them all. It would pay for their North Woods vacation and much more, when they met up with Bobby.

All the way down here, the bookreader guy who claimed to be his best friend had tried to talk her out of the ride and into going someplace for a drink with him instead. She'd had to keep his hopes up, or else he might have dumped her out. The first thing she'd done as soon as she'd gotten in the cab sitting in front of Luminati's before they'd taken off for the Labs was to ask him to call number 17 on his radio. Her voice had cracked.

"Say, see if number 17 will answer."

"The Cadillac? You know him? He's a friend of mine."

"Yes, I know him. I'm supposed to call him and meet him."

"Listen, are there any papers on the floor there by you?"

"What?" She didn't know what he was talking about, or that he asked all his fares that, as he was the possessor of important documents for the novel he was writing, and didn't want to lose anything, or it could be he just liked to put his passengers on. She said no, and then the dispatcher said number 17 did not respond. She knew very well what that meant and she felt a lump grow in her throat. He was at a club or a movie, the bookreader had insisted, squinting at her in the mirror. Her emotion filled the cab. At the Labs he was obviously intrigued by her opening the hood of the Lincoln and fishing something out. Something strange was up, and something was going on with the Cadillac.

When she'd said she wanted to head down to the city, he had responded that he "didn't like long rides," strange for a cab driver. But she'd said that's where she wanted to go because "number 17" was down there. They started for the Tollway but he immediately began asking her to go on a date with him. He seemed to forget all about his friend. He'd kept up an outrageous patter about all he knew and who he knew in Chicago, trying to impress her, everything he saw out the window reminded him of something else like he owned it, or knew the people who did. She recognized that hopeless, pathetic, and charming bravado. She'd always liked insane losers like this guy, probably because she was one too.

At one point on the ride he'd asked her, "Read any good books lately?" making her laugh in panic. What a thing to ask while they raced after Wisconsin his friend to rescue him (which the bookreader didn't entirely realize yet). She liked to read books okay but she didn't discuss personal things like that with just anyone. She instead asked him to call number 17 on the radio again, which he did with no better luck. Seventeen wasn't answering, and the dispatcher asked him not to bother him again, prompting the bookreader to assure her that he must have forgotten his date with her and was probably at a club with his girlfriend. She knew better.

He kept talking about his friendship with "the Cadillac," as if that should make him okay, at the same time he tried to persuade her that his friend was so thoughtless he had probably forgotten all about her, and gone to a movie. At about the halfway point on the ride, she explained approximately the part of the city she wanted to go, and he had said he didn't go to "that side of town" and what did she want there anyway? He suggested that instead she should go on a date with him elsewhere. She did not reply to that.

"Okay, so where exactly we going to find the Cadillac?"

"I'm not sure but I know the first place to look on Eighteenth Street, I don't know the address. I'll show you."

He took that in and was silent for a while. She hoped he was more than he seemed. There was something strange about him that gave her hope, for no reason that she could have said. If it didn't work out this time, it would prove she was meant for nothing at all.

She explained a little bit of it to him, by no means all of it at first, as she was afraid of him turning around and heading back to Greenshores. But mile after mile, as they approached the Loop exits and passed them, she let on more and more, till on 18th Street she had finally let him know they were on their way (and almost there too) to *rescue* their mutual friend, who had delivered some goods that were not what they were supposed to have been. She was afraid some bad guys were holding him for ransom, as a hostage even, that sort of thing. That Wisconsin had delivered a purposely phony bag to those killers for her she did not say.

"You say *what?*" His voice was an incredulous whisper.

"It's true, they've made a mistake."

The friendship this guy professed for "the Cadillac" seemed real in spite of him trying to hit on her, and so she'd humored him and come on to him all the way down, because he seemed insane enough and sincere enough to try something. She meant him to be in a mood to do something, to try anything, the crazier the better, as he now claimed to be prepared to do.

"They can't hold a cab driver! It makes no sense."

"Yeah, I know."

"I'll explain something to em!"

Good, she prayed. She didn't know what else she was going to try if it didn't work. They'd take the cocaine and all jump on her one after another and kill her for laughs afterward. So she'd made herself helpless and sexy and available, and told of the deadly danger "the Cadillac" was in without explaining it entirely for fear of alarming him too greatly. He added up two and two and finally reacted with silence and by getting serious. He stopped trying to explain to her that "the Cadillac" would never have gone to "this side of town," as it was apparent that he had, from what she was saying. When she finally spilled it (almost), he stopped talking and bore down on the wheel. Then they saw the Cadillac.

When he'd seen the empty Cadillac left pointed half out in the street, the bookreader (as she called the guy to herself because he had been reading a book when she got in his cab and after his question what books was she reading lately) had changed his tune angrily and finally gotten the whole truth out of her fast. He was all seriousness and excitedly shaking all over by now and wanted to know what was up for real. He could see that "the Cadillac" was in big trouble, with the cab parked cattywampus to the curbstone and abandoned that way, a crumpled front fender too.

Of course he had known something was up when he'd seen her retrieve a bag out of a black Lincoln towncar's engine compartment at the Labs, but she had just mumbled something then that he seemed to accept. It hadn't been his business, except to make her even more interesting, but it was his business now. Now she poured out to him the whole story in one agonizing breath.

"He took *what?* He did *what?* What does he care what's in a package? He's just the cab driver! He doesn't know what people give him to take. He *shoulda* known, he *shoulda not* done it, but—! He didn't put anything in that package! How *totally ridiculous!*" cried the bookreader.

That was just it! She couldn't agree more but those hoods didn't agree probably. There wasn't time to explain to him what Bobby had told her about the Mexicans' cultural ideas concerning cab drivers. It was just as well, because she could see that his outrage was just the right thing at the moment. It wasn't necessary that he should contemplate what was the Mexicans' point of view. It was better if he never considered it. He had to persuade them of *his own* American view of the situation.

He'd jumped out and banged on the door of the grocery and let out a shout about some important judge that he knew well downtown. It was more than she could have hoped for! They would never know what hit them, they would not know what to make of a character like this, she hoped. She'd been sitting on the edge of the seat holding her breath. When she'd seen Wisconsin's Cadillac on the street it had taken her breath clean away.

She'd had to move fast in case they came out after her, which they might do any minute if they beat up the bookreader and he admitted she was out here. And who could blame him if he did? She was ready to slip away fast farther up the alley if they came out looking for her.

When they'd seen a second cab driver come in on them, had it sobered them up to reality as it ought to or had the surprise of it made them start cutting and chopping both of them up with those blades of theirs? They'd been burned and certainly insulted by the bath powder in her package. J.A. had crossed her cruelly when he'd refused to let her go out to the cab driver with the bag, and had sent MacDougal instead. J.A. just saw through her, didn't he? He was counting on her knowledge of that to make her come back to him probably. He'd smelled a rat from the beginning but it hadn't worried him, had it, because he knew her all too well. He was waiting for her to fall apart like a sap even now and bring it home.

With a sudden retching sob, and tears starting in her eyes again, she wondered if he might be right. What would it be like if the cab drivers never came out again and she had to go back for real? She wouldn't be able to go on alone without Wisconsin.

She made herself ready to slip farther up the alley to just where she could barely still see his cab. But what if they never came out again? They might kill Wisconsin and his friend just for the hell of it, and split. She might be standing in front of an empty grocery store with two dead bodies in it. Whew, heavy, heavy. She might let herself go back down, if anything like that happened, never leave the city, go back to J.A., beaten. She would not have the heart to go and find Bobby. She had a whole bag of poison ready for herself, didn't she? Always ready to pour down on her own head. Her fate to use or be used, in spite of good intentions. Look what she had done to Wisconsin! She prayed to Mary. Whatever J.A. was he wasn't some Mexican gangbangers.

The door of the grocery opened, and hope fired that it might be Wisconsin but, flame of despair, two of the Mexican gang guys came out, not the cab drivers. Hood friends of Rodriguez. She didn't remember them. It looked like the worst, and she took several steps up the alley catching her breath. They didn't look for her over this way. She paused, ready to run up the alley. They went straight to the cabs and began to search them. Christ, now she had done it, hadn't she? She cursed herself and at the same time prayed fervently to Jesus, Mary, and the Holy Father not to let them look in the motor compartment and find the bag where she had had no choice but to hide it. And they didn't. Her prayers availed. They appeared rushed, overwhelmed, and apparently they thought they had no time to be thorough, and didn't tear off the hubcaps, rip out the seats, or even open the hoods of the cars, probably because Wisconsin's pal the bookreader had convinced them they had ten minutes before the cab dispatcher called the cops. They looked in the Cadillac and went through a bag throwing everything in the gutter. They opened the bookreader's trunk and pulled out pictures, pots and pans, golf clubs, tires. It was like a magic trick that there could be so much stuff in one guy's trunk. They spent a minute examining the contents with disbelief and stood there at a loss. It was too much for them. They stared wonderingly at all his junk and appeared almost as if convinced by it of the cab drivers' innocence, she believed. When they suddenly went back inside the store, she breathed in violent gasps and clutched the dirty wall.

Wisconsin, she understood at this moment, she was in love with, a guy she had met this morning, charming, an outsider, her kind. They were two peas from a pod, her mother would have said, that foolish bitch. But it was true. She loved him and had used him calculatedly. Oh God, she had, though it wasn't her fault. Pity, love, fear, and guilt raged through her sweeping all her thoughts away in a flood of black anguish far worse than love.

She ran off one Hail Mary after another, throwing in appeals to the other, Mary Magdalene, the repentant whore. She wasn't sure how high up she could be heard. No, she had better admit it, if her prayers were to avail, she'd always strangely confused the Mother of Christ with the one who had washed His feet, from whom he had cast seven devils, as if they were sisters or something. It might be blasphemous but she couldn't pray hypocritically. Ex–shady lady,

217

Shining One, could they be the same friend? Who was the saint for cab drivers? If only she'd known she'd have thrown in a prayer directly for Wisconsin and the bookreader.

A hand whapped over her mouth and an arm reached around her and held her breasts tight. She couldn't see her assailant. He pinned her arms. Another boy came grinning out of the shadows, bare-chested, with his T-shirt rolled up and hanging out of his back pocket, and yanked up her skirt, and stuck his hand in her panties. After exploring a while, he held the finger in front of his friend's nose, and they both laughed wryly. Even in an alley, there was still something to be lost. She prayed that when they saw the marks on her body, they wouldn't laugh at her or hurt her.

Across the street, far away beyond the thin bodies of the boys holding her and playing with her, the grocery door burst open and like a mysterious and yet a prayed-for fact disgorged Wisconsin, plunging into the street, blinking his eyes at the sad street's amber, the sneaking slumlight pouring down on him like rich cream after captivity, followed by his pal the bookreader with a drained look of terror and outrage on his face, who at once began to run, taking Wisconsin's elbow and shoving him forward so hard they both half stumbled in a rush to their cars. *Don't leave me here!* she wished.

Wisconsin's messedup blonde hair stuck out like a holy halo, as far as Rita was concerned. God had heard her, or Mary had, and all was not quite lost, was it? There was hope for her, for escape, for her love. In a spasm she fended off the boys with an instinctive violent thrashing of her elbows and a soaring spirit. One of them jumped back having caught an elbow in the throat, then following

218

her eyes and seeing what she saw covered her mouth with his hand, while the other pinned her arms again and pushed her into the shadows, squeezing the sores on her wrists, as if reminding her of them was his intention. His arms and hands were slick and stinking with sweat. Hopeful and determined as she was, he was too mean and strong. It struck her like a wrong miracle that the same evil could course through bodies so different, J.A.'s silver corpulent one, and this stubby brown barrio boy's. A terse conversation drifted from the street into the alley.

"Where is she, Armchair!"

"Good riddance! Cadillac, *let's get outa here!*"

"What she say about me, Armchair?"

"She said 'go fuck!'—Let's get *outa here,* man!" He caught sight of his groceries and possessions strewn in the street and threw a few things into his trunk fast, leaving most of them in the street.

The cab driver's eyes wandered to the mouth of the alley. A fascination was compelling him toward the alley, like a dark cave in which a treasure lies hidden.

"Man, what're ya doin, Cadillac! I always knew you were a philosopher, they always get the screwballs!" Armchair flew into his car at a speed never before equaled by his languorous body and raced his engine inadvertently as he stomped the pedal before getting it in gear.

Two punks ran out of the alley and skyrocketed up the street, all hightop sneakers, no shirts, whose rolledup T-shirts flew from their back pockets, flags of no account. The cab driver gazed after them and saw Rita walking toward him with a tremulous smile. For a second he wanted to run after the boys and kill somebody.

Beyond the sordid experience blurred by her tears of fear and rage, the sparkling blue of a northern lake had spread itself out in Rita's vision. The poet was wrong who compared the million points of light to diamonds or any earthly treasure. They were more precious, breath, soul, the guiding mysterious light. Red Cloud Lake, Water Lily Lake, the names came singing out of memory, hokey, beautiful, and common. She wanted someplace smack out of that gold and blue past, where she could float awhile, good as dead, a knottypine cabin on a lost little lake, under white birches, under a neonblue Hamm's Beersign softly glimmering in the warm summer night, the fishermen and vacationers and children and mothers passing under so happily and enjoying their time away from the city, just like the old place her father had taken them to lightyears away from the extremes of sinful wealth and wicked poverty she'd known since he'd died and her mother had heartsickened.

A fish jumped from the shining waters. She giggled in enjoyment of her own cornball imagination. Hope made its move in her heart, bold and clean as a North Woods sunrise. She grinned, one pearly snaggled tooth sending out a crooked sunbeam to a cab driver heading straight toward her. The Hamm's Beer jingle played joyously in her ears, "From the land of skyblue wa-a-aters, wa-a-aters, comes the beer refreshing . . . beer refreshing!"

She had to go *somewhere,* didn't she? She would wind up with *somebody,* wouldn't she? Why not this ordinary guy, cab driver of all things, space cadet, who had shown up in the nick of time, who didn't take no for an answer, who was walking toward her now, who was a little bit happy, for Christ sake, whom she'd managed to rescue, with the help of his friend. She had talked the bookreader into coming down here, she had done that, no matter what insulting things he had to say about her now. That she had been at least partly responsible for springing him loose, that he was in the street before her now, smiling at her happily, made him belong to her. If he could look happy at this moment, he would be happy always. Happiness, what a rare thing to find in a person. Out of some mold her angels had approved long ago, who had not given up on her completely, or their souls had met someplace long ago, she'd been familiar with his body after one glance, now she'd done something to save him even if she was the one who'd gotten him in trouble, and she was bound to him by it. She'd done one right thing! Even her high handedness stuffing the bag of cocaine into his engine compartment was going to turn out right in that case, if he'd still have her after he found out . . . and after the moment came when he saw her scars.

"Your friend might be right about me," she said.

"We're here," he said smiling.

At the mouth of the alley they embraced, and kissed, broke it off, afraid of dissolving under each other's touch. Wisconsin's shirtfront was wet with blood and sticky where her hand lingered. Her suit, which had been yanked and pulled on all evening, hung unevenly on her, wilted and grimy from the window casement.

What she had suffered from the boys in the alley, what he had emerged from in the backroom, her sense of his having sacrificed greatly for her, and guilt and wonder about it, his understanding of what he had endured to find her, who miraculously stood before him exactly as she had promised him she would, his reward, all of it keyed them to each other at the highest pitch till the street itself disappeared in their emotion. The violence in the air, the danger if they didn't get out of here immediately, pushed back like wild animals by the fire of their love, they searched each other's eyes. No more than ten seconds had elapsed since they'd reached each other's side but it could have been an hour, a night.

Something came to Rita that her mother had said to her once, that damn drunken bitch. "When love comes, don't fight it," her mother had said. It showed even a damn drunken bitch, like a broken clock, could be right once.

"We ready to rock an roll?" he smiled.

"Yes, honey!" But they would make one stop on Broadway to find Bobby. She said only, meant only, *"Yes!"*

His ears drank down the word as if it had eight reverberating syllables that kept coming to the last electric pulse. Such a wonderful, mysterious word, *yes.*

Armchair's tires had screamed past them. Now it was over, this business was extremely alarming. The gangsters in there were going to have second thoughts any moment. He'd done his part and now his friend wanted to be alone with her in the middle of this city hell hole. That centerfold, mindblowing, dopesmuggling, sly wiseass broad had nearly taken his own head off with her charms. Duty to friendship was done. Each man to his poison!

Out of the corner of his eye the cab driver saw Armchair's car blow past with something like love. Armchair had burst into the backroom of the grocery like a talking windmill. He'd made them see the folly of holding a cab driver. According to Armchair, not only did the dispatcher have the address with instructions to call the cops in ten minutes, but certain higher-ups at City Hall had already been contacted including a named judge. Those cats had never stood a chance against Armchair's bullshit. Could it have been because they suspected he hadn't called the cops, that he didn't know anyone at City Hall, was not friends with a federal judge as he claimed, nor had he graduated from college as he boasted, but had showed up there talking plain sense to them anyway?

There was always something believable about Armchair because of not in spite of his outrageousness. Outlandishly, by extremes, he created a sober atmosphere and brought men back to reason. Armchair's one-man show calmed them down, restored them to themselves, functioned as a human lightning rod draining the voltage from the room. They had looked at each other, thought better of it, and shoved the crazy cab drivers out the door as no-accounts, as if they were escaping from *them.* Armchair had the same effect everywhere.

One of the Mexicans stepped casually through the doorway into the street, smoking, and stared at the cab driver and Rita embracing in the mouth of the alley. He did a doubletake and froze for one full second. Recognizing Rita he dropped his cigarette and his mouth opened blackly to howl. Wisconsin took Rita in his arms, ran for the car, threw her into the front seat. The Cadillac's bumper was stuck up under the car's bumper he'd crashed into. He had to floor it in reverse to rip free and careened into the car behind. The Mexican had stuck his head in the door yelling for the others. In the mirror Rodriguez burst through the doorway and shoved the guy's arm as two shots rang out hitting nothing.

He ducked, pushed Rita's head down, and accelerated, not looking where he was going or what he might run over. He always had liked the Spanish. They respected a cab driver. The long car gunned forward.

The Cadillac doing fifty, through the stopsigns, through the redlights, parted the latecrowds, horn blearing. The headlights surged and fell as the latenight people jumped clear of the cruising painted Caddy. A few more blocks they'd be sailing up the Kennedy.

The stop they'd make at the Green Mill, their luck depended on it. She wasn't greedy, but she knew how it was to be helpless. It would make all the difference to their love, to have plenty of dough, be practical. She didn't mean to let little things like money trip her up ever again. She had a lot of money waiting for her on Broadway, her money, she'd earned every penny. Bobby had all that cash and she had the shit and there was some kind of a trade that had to be made for all their sakes. Maybe Bobby would be disappointed she wasn't going to Hawaii. She looked at Wisconsin imploringly.

She drew a breath, "Wisconsin, you know the Green Mill bar on Broadway? We need to stop there. It'll set us up!"

"Don't bother, Rita. Bobby waitin for ya right here."

She only intensified her beseeching look like what she had just heard could not be. Like she was begging Wisconsin to tell her the world had not cracked open again in unbelievable defeat for her one more time, had it? She didn't move or turn her head. Wisconsin did not flinch either but glared straight ahead with his glassy professional glare.

"Hang a left at the corner, please," said a deep, overly polite brownsugar voice behind him. "The guy in the backseat's always right, aint he, cab driver? Turn around and head back."

There was somebody in the backseat. There always was. Sometimes you plain forgot about them. A glance in the mirror showed him the cop's stonedout, self-satisfied mug grinning like a jack-o'-lantern, menacing, sweaty mask, a wild fleeting image glimpsed in nightwater, remembered but not recognized, known and not understood, projected from the depths of recent drowning hours through guilt and horror like deepwater closing over his head again—that he had never warned Rita about him, never made that phone call, had tried instead to forget him, had even succeeded entirely in forgetting him in the terror with the Mexicans and then excitement of finding her again. He did as he was asked and headed back the way they'd come. The guy in the backseat was always right, like he said. For the duration of the ride, anyway.

Rita was falling fast in shock, as if each hope springing up were to be cast down at once in another dizzying descent, that at this yearnedfor moment, with the road ahead finally clear, this cop had found her, whom she barely remembered, could not recognize, but knew as if by heart from some deep lost place in her soul, some doom, inescapable. Not astonishing that he had followed her so far, so long—this cop who had done his best to hurt her this morning, whom she had forgotten, that he should appear in the car with them in nightmare reality, it came at her in a toxic, sinking yet strangely assuring rush, something worse than all the worst things she could have imagined, out of nowhere and everywhere, with the touch of the blasted familiar, the ironic and fitting, yes her evil luck, the most feared thing, the expected bad luck, when all struggle could subside.

"Keep going. . . . That's right."

"You're going to get us all killed."

"I gotta get my car."

"I'll swing by an drop you off."

"Okay, keep going. . . . Now, pull over."

"Where's your car?"

"Cab driver, be cool," muttered the cop. "Take a walk, but don't get lost. I gotta talk to Rita for a few minutes. Go on, walk around the block once."

The cab driver made a contemptible move from the point of view of the cop. He leaned over to Rita and after a toughguy pause said, "I don't leave unless you tell me to, Rita."

"Do like he says!" she cried in alarm, in fury, and despair.

The cop grinned with embarrassment. It was impossible even to get irritated with the countryboy, the gesture was so hollow and feckless. The chump didn't have a clue of his position, let alone what he was carrying under his hood. It was pathetic. He was blind with love. The poor dude had kissed her wantonly in front of that grocery full of killers. As soon as he was gone, he leaned over the frontseat and making his voice sincere and mellow, said, "Rita, I'm sorry about this morning."

This was true. In the long hours affording time for reflection punctuated by the bright visions of her acts of surprising defiance and ingenuity, he had grown to regret his meanness, blindness and brutality in Jackie's.

"I—I didn't act right. I was full of my damn self, you know. I have my problems. It wasn't that I didn't dig ya. Just the opposite, I thought I would dig ya too much, I guess." This was beginning to stray from the truth slightly, but he meant it well.

Her lips parted in amazement at his tone. She looked at him for the first time. His stubbled face was weirdly streaked with dirt and sweat, and blood maybe, and what appeared to be clinging bits of grass or hay. "I don't get it," she allowed.

This cop, from this morning, on the Southside, why had he come into her life at all in the first place if not to appear again at the very moment when the path ahead lay open and clear before her, to lay waste to her most beautiful dream? Had God sent him to punish her for her sins forgotten? No, God wouldn't do that, for God was Love. At some fundamental level, where the angels did their work, if you listened, or didn't, where one's plans and hopes were really sealed and carried through, or not, she had never had a clue, had been overambitious and greedy, and just not competent, that was all, just never good enough for the freedom she pined for.

"I can't explain it. A negative mood came over me. I been so depressed lately. We all got our scars, baby."

She gave him a straightout look. "Whadaya *want?*"

"I know what you're doin. I don't want ya for it no more than for that taste in your pocketbook this morning. I want *you,* baby. I want to *help* you. Hey, ya know them masks ya were talkin about this morning, masks for fun? Let's put em on, baby! Forget this lame fool taxi driver, Rita, I got your ticket outa town. I got Bobby in my car. I got your money."

She gave him a soulsearching stare. She studied his face for the catch. He was a conniving motherfucker who was lying in wait for her soul. Something was turning over in that halfbaked cop brain of his, and she wondered with horror what it could be. What could he ever want from her, except her life, her pain?

"We can take *so much more* from that man, Rita! When I explain things to him he will pay us *so much more!*"

The cab driver, having walked as fast as he could to the corner without making it obvious he had a mission, broke into a dead run as soon as he was out of sight. He had to find a phone. There were none on the corners he was passing. He figured if he followed the music in the air, he'd come to a tavern where he'd find one.

His behavior in the cab, shouldering Rita and mouthing empty brave words, alarming her as much as it had disgusted the cop, had not been the halfassed impertinence it had seemed but a cover for several quick motions of his hands. All so dexterously done that even Rita, unfortunately, who might have drawn a little hope from it, had not understood, he had picked up a heavy rubber band from the tray of odds and ends under the dash and slipped it around the microphone to keep the transmission button keyed on and hung the mike back on its hook. With a pang at the closeness of things, he congratulated himself on his laziness not replacing the little red transmission bulb which had burned out months before. With the mike keyed on and transmitting, the receiving green went out, but the burnedout red did not light up. Incoming was silenced with the mike keyed. It looked like the radio was turned off. Even to a cop

225

familiar enough with radios, at first glance it could not be seen that the radio was keyed and transmitting, but the powerful Motorola would be carrying strongly to base even from down here, leaving the dispatcher openmouthed at what he was hearing. The tape recorder was always rolling up there. It was company policy or some kind of city ordinance that every transmission be tape recorded 24/7.

He elbowed past strollers and nightpeople, left the sidewalk and ran. Startled expressions, catcalls, followed in the wake of the sprinting gringo. Ahead, he spotted the grocery in which he'd lived out a nightmare, and the light of his hope darkened at the memory of the backroom made very small and cramped by crates and sacks of produce, in which he'd spent a terrifying hour. What a sepulchral little hole that room had been, suffocating with the cloying, acidsweet perfume of piles of fruit. It had taken a power like dreaming to latch onto it at all. He'd stumbled in, pushed by Rodriguez down a dark aisle of canned goods, been asked rapidfire questions by someone in English to which he'd been unable to respond. He crossed the dissolving black street and ran faster.

Could you be skimming across the surface of the city one minute, looking for fares and maybe even a little love, and fall through to this hellhole of a stockroom in the next? A hand had shot out and hit him under the heart. Somebody's foot had helped him down, his tailbone banging on the bitter cement, one leg kicking over a great bunch of green bananas. His eyes, rolling in his head, looked past a crowd of shiny knees at a wall stacked with softdrink cases. Bottlecaps. His old girl friend should see him now, this last funny experience he'd collected. All he lacked was his polaroid camera, to take a funny picture.

The room had been half in shadow, half in hideous over-exposure from a hanging bare bulb. It had been overpoweringly weird to be gazing up at it from a position on his back. Something like cobwebs had settled over his face and he'd swiped it away. He'd let his gaze roll to the other side, and found himself staring at a heap of round, mottled fruits in a basket, their swollen blotched skins suggesting human faces beaten beyond recognition. Recoiling from the fantasy, his whole body had jerked back as if prodded by an electric wire, something he was expecting momentarily. Mr. Rodriguez was studying him closely. His hand reached down into

226

the basket and drew out one of the fruits. A flashing knifeblade sliced it open.

"Drink?" Mr. Rodriguez squeezed the juice into his face and tossed the dripping halves onto his chest, where they'd bled juice through his shirt mixing with his blood on it. A knee had followed. The blade had come closer and closer, right into his eyes, forcing them to shut. The juicewet blade had wiped each lid in turn.

"Who *are* you, taxi?" The English speaking questioner.

"Just a cab driver."

"Cab driver see everythin. Don't miss nothin."

The Spanish always had been grateful, even admiring, cab riders. Even in his predicament he was almost touched.

"Now we gotta kill you, or blind you, one way or the other."

"Do I get my choice?"

"Sure. Who give you the bag? Do you know the girl Rita?"

"No. Not a girl. Some guys at a restaurant."

"Black guy wearin a jacket with fancy lapels? Bobby?"

"With a hairdo like a bunch a snakes? Bobby, maybe. I heard them call him that. I saw him there. White guys, businessmen, gave it to me. They called the cab. They gave me the bag."

"Who has our money? Bobby still has our money? Or who?"

"I don't know anything about any money, except the fare that's owed me by Mr. Rodriguez."

"We kill all. Maybe you. Don't you see, if we lose our money, somebody got to pay. In a way, it don't matter who it will be."

"Well, I'm broke."

He had to find a phone. He tried to kid himself about knocking on the door of the Super Mercado to borrow theirs, didn't have the margin of humor, ran flat out. The blood and juice had caked under his shirt, sticking it to his chest unpleasantly. The grocery flashed by, the saddest of memories. On the next corner was a little club. No kind of sign on it, but music welcoming. He pushed inside through hombres eyeballing him coldly, paranoid that he might have seen some of them in the grocery's backroom. They had never been ready for Armchair's bullshit! Anybody who could talk the game that Armchair talked could not possibly be all bluff, and being Mexicans they had readily believed a cab driver knew important people, and yet perhaps these guys had been in the States long enough to follow his argument that a cab driver could not possibly be in the know, too. Not in spite of but because of contradictions and wild hyperbole, as usual, Armchair had defused things.

No payphone on the wall in sight. There was no bar, behind which would be a housephone, just tables scattered everywhere. "Telephone? Telephone?" He followed someone's eye, and on a table by a back hallway spied an old black dial phone of the kind you didn't even think existed any longer, and strolled toward it, a tenspot in his hand. He picked up the phone and dialed, waving the tendollar bill in the air. A small man wearing a midnightblue suit and a cowboy hat perched over his eyes removed the bill from his hand with a gracious smile—and inserted it back in his, the cab driver's, shirt pocket. The cab driver waved at a girl, "Bud!" and she brought him a bottle of Budweiser. This he would pay for anyway and tip big. He gave her a bill whose denomination no longer interested him. Again the little guy smiling at him serenely intercepted the transaction and returned his money to him discreetly. He had a long thirsty swallow, couldn't imagine why, nodding pleasantly to the smiling man, smiling to himself as if his luck must have surely changed, when into his ear the dispatcher said, "Bull's-eye!"

"Turn up the radio! What's he sayin? Lemme hear!"

"Who is this?"

"The Cadillac."

"Is that you jammin my air, Cadillac?"

"The tape recorder's rollin, aint it? Like it's spose to? Shut up an lemme listen!"

"What is this, Cadillac? What's up?"

"I owe ya dinner!"

"I got orders piling up!"

"Every night for a week."

The dispatcher gave in, and together they listened to the fantastic things that the cop was saying to Rita. "Yow!" cried the cab driver in amazement and pain. "Roll, tape recorder!" He listened to the cop's crazy shakedown plan. "Lame fool taxi driver!" cried the cab driver. "Lame fool? I'll show ya who's a lame fool, you crazy weasel!" The man in the midnightblue suit with the cowboy hat watched him with interest.

He dropped the phone and appealed to the generous gentleman in the midnightblue suit, who said, "You musta run into trouble tonight, buddy. When I seen ya run in, God tol me"—he pointed at one of his ears—"you I must help."

Scarcely comprehending, but taking the good with the bad this night, he ran, the man smiling after him indulgently, one who has helped a desperado. Nearly to his cab, he met Rita and the cop crossing the street, the disheveled detective pulling her by her arm. It was a bad moment for the cab driver, seeing Rita's eyes so cold and spacey. A moment ago they had been headed to the North Woods! Under a streetlamp the cop's caramelcolored, lopsided face lined with greasy grime seemed to bob and glow with devious, energetic purpose. His eyes were glazed and bright red. The knees of his trousers were stained and his shirtbreast was torn open. The man looked too drunk and wasted to walk a straight line, yet he was coming on with determination. It was all the cab driver could do to hold back and not confront him. He wanted to see his face when he told him he had a tape recording all ready to drop on the desk of the Chicago Crime Commission and the Chief of Police. He got a grip on himself and said nothing for now. He tried to catch Rita's eye but she was looking elsewhere. The cop ordered him to get back to his cab and follow behind his plaingreen car.

Somewhere on the way out of the city they passed an Uncle Remus Chicken Shack. The cop gagged on the aroma of frying bird flesh. In his soul he shuddered at his people's fate of making ends meet. He wasn't poor. He was looked on as a success. Yet the truth was he'd been satisfied with so little. Beyond the crowding tenements and decrepit warehouses black and shapeless as lumps of coal, the silver sky opened up above the Eisenhower Expressway wide and true. His nose encountered the warm night breeze, perfumes of freedom and the unknown. It was only himself, Shooter Teagarden, headin' outa town, but the intriguing sensation was of meeting someone new.

He plunged toward a heightened, heroic reality. The sheer numbers were the inspiration. A few thousand stars didn't make the Milky Way—but add a few thousand to a few thousand. The cash in the Fist's briefcase was nothing, hardly three years' salary. What Rita had stashed for her getaway wouldn't change your life either. But put the two together (as they had apparently planned to do), and add to it what he was going to take off the fat man, he found himself staring at more than a quarter million, maybe even half a million dollars. Maybe more. Money like that stared back and didn't blink. Your lids shut briefly against the glare. It was the craziest plan and yet the sanest idea he'd ever had in his life. The reason he liked it so much was he hadn't studied on it, but it had just appeared to him unexpectedly like a sign—like that deer in the road. The chance to leap ahead, and be a world away.

Africa, that was where he'd go. He was vague about the geography, some lush spot that was too hot and dangerous for many white tourists, and blacks were everybody. He'd see how the brothers lived over there, check out how the ancestors must have lived on the other side of the world, and have a rounder, wholer view of life. Certainly there had to be a rich but precarious government in a tropical paradise that could use a freelance police specialist, a good man like himself. He'd read about it and was certain there would be. He'd take Jackie. They'd live like princes. He had a flash of himself on a pastelcolored balcony overlooking the turquoise sea, against a backdrop of flamboyant jungle, the pretty women with baskets on their heads glancing up at him from the marketplace below. The throbbing drums and the festive dancers. The temperature always warm and the women goodnatured. He'd side with the good guys. Perhaps he'd be in a position to do something significant and help the people. Anybody who read the papers could see his skills were as much in demand as a geologist's or an oildriller's and likely far more. No nation could do without security, and security was his line of country. Anyway he'd have independence of action, could do as he damn pleased with the coin he'd be packing. And he'd take Rita with him if she'd come.

A mood of promise harked back to boyhood's boundless excitements. Some nearly extinguished flame, joys all but forgotten, illumined the road ahead. For no reason he thought of Saturdays in springtime, out of school, given leave by his Dad, gone down to Lake Michigan, fishing from the broken pilings, winter, studies, and the basketball season, too, finally over, free as a bird. The air like clover honey, the lake like bags of pearls being spilled at your feet, the silver perch had bubbled up like found money from the bluegreen rocks, along with a bottle of wine left to cool by Jackie whose pokerface had enabled him to bluff liquor store clerks. Days when there'd been nothing to do, and all the time in the world to do it, and you were sure that something special was going to happen. Days of thinking about what you were going to do with your girl that night, and when you did it, it was like holding a mystery and squeezing a dream.

He saw himself blasting into the man's office up in those towers. Rita said there was a real chance they'd catch him with a shipment in the room tonight. If they did, he was going to be rich. The man could be shook down for plenty. Beyond thinking of it, the whole million hummed tax free. Rita would go up alone, at first, with her retrieved package, that she had been sent on to bring back to the man, that or the money.

He had witnessed her soul struggle all day and he loved her for it. He *understood* her. She would tell the man she had found the cab driver before he'd delivered it or found her friends who had listened to reason and given it back to her, incidentally taking out a contract on Bobby's life. Or whatever she was going to tell him, it didn't matter. If the room was dirty, she'd signal him some way in the window at once. If not, it would be time to call in the bets and take whatever he could get. He'd go up and deliver his message, the dues the man had to pay.

If the fat man balked, if he wanted to cross wits with him, he'd tickle his balls with cold iron if that's what it took. But his hunch was they'd come to an understanding at once, and he'd open that wallsafe she had told him about. The cop's experience (and all he'd heard of this sort of business) told him it might well go down matter of factly. The more he heard about him, the man was out on a limb, ripe for the picking, and he was a shrewd one. High in the corporate tree, with the Labs the perfect cover, wouldn't he pay to avoid being accused as a drug dealer, let alone a sex freak? He'd pay his dues. A smart man like him would want to beat the heat out front, no matter how many lawyers he had on tap. If he had half the operation in place Rita and the Fist suggested, it was a straight shot, and he saw it all the way.

The truth was, he'd never even fixed a parking ticket. How many times had a gangbanger offered him a bribe? Funny, but his line had always been that it would not be worth it for a million bucks—the sort of claim people made all their lives without ever finding themselves tested by that actual figure. Yeah, Fist, Coach's boy is wising up fast, making up for lost time. He's finally leaving the funky team.

His soul, in the act of escape, responded to the drumroll of the road flying past under his tires. The trembling air seemed shot through with the blessing that goes to the bold. Heading north on the Tri-State Tollway, a glance to the side showed him the unrealized glow of the city, no more than lamplight off a mud puddle. Night watchman, son of a night watchman. Had he ever been more? From his new dark distance, he thought of his best successes with the kids, the ones he'd pried loose from the Cobras, El Rukns, and Black Stone Nation, whose feet he'd set on the straight and narrow—a job at MacDonald's. Well, with hopes of more than that. The tinstar nobility of the profession aside, that was what had mattered, more than sending the bad guys down— weaning the young ones up, away from "leaders" like the Fist, helping them stay alive. For *what?* Had it ever been *enough?* If the gangs were a chump's chance, for a black man what wasn't? Few had the chances he'd had, and what had he become? A watchman at the gate, keeping the victims in their place. A watchman for guys like the man who tortured Rita.

A cold awareness stilled these justifications. Was he feeling sorry for himself in the bargain? The truth was he saw his chance and was going to take it. His Daddy had said, "America with all her faults is still the best hope in this evil world for the black man." True enough perhaps, and an even better hope for the white man. He was through with hope. He had a half a million bucks in easy reach, maybe more—and wouldn't be needing *hope* no more.

"Reeter," groaned the Fist from the back floor. *"Reeterrr!"*

"What?" said Rita in a hollow voice after a while.

"Whachu go see Pepe for? Why you do *that* for?"

But she said nothing.

What he wanted to ask her was—was she a prisoner too, or were the two of them gaming on him as a team now? Had the cop dealt her a card already, or was she a kidnap victim like himself? He didn't have words to ask. The way she was scrunched up by the window it looked like she might be on this ride involuntarily, but half the time she always looked like that, Rita. He couldn't find the words that wouldn't have plunged her into a deeper stillness.

"Bad mistake a yourn, Reeter. . . . Pepe gon hang his ass by nails, Reeter. *Nails,* goddamit, tell him, Reeterrr!"

"I ain study no damn Pepe, or whoever," muttered the cop.

"Ya aint? Ya got family? Your Daddy dead? You don't think they find out? Got a woman? No, you better give em back their money an you get yours somehow else, copper, Shooter, boy. You don be knowin em like I do. You ready to hat for faraway places? I am, or I wouldn't be stealin from em. I was, I mean. Honolulu, or some shit like that, far, far away. Nothin hold me back, Shooter. I warn you like a homeboy for ol time sake, shit. You *oughta* know em well enough, be a cop. You got a steady woman these days? How bout *Jackie?* The little man! They *torture,* them guys, before they kill him, Jackie boy, you be knowin that, copper?"

Damn if he didn't think he was going for the chumpchange in his brief case. He'd like to explain to him the qualitative difference between what he thought of as money and a half a million dollars or even the whole mil. That kind of bread even made you invisible if you wanted. The lowlife would think, what it meant, you could buy more.

The brazen motherfucker was trying to shake his nerve. No one was going to know about his woman or the boy either, it was a recent attachment, even Jackie barely knew. Did he think he'd leave Jackie for the vultures? Jackie was more than family, he was a habit. Of course, the little man couldn't hang around Chicago. He'd be cold meat to the cops and hoods both. He could picture his deadpan expression when he told him they were on their way to Africa. Nobody going to ever find them in deepest Africa.

"Fist, so what they do to *you* when *you* steal their money? You better think on it cuz they be after you even though you ain got nary penny, ha ha ha, nary penny, no more."

233

"I tol ya, I hat to Honolulu, farther than that. I know how them boys think. I be just *me,* you know that basketball player, I aint got no friends to torture like the little man, Pageant, man. You know I don't never study no *close* friends. You different, I know, with Jackie. I know how to disappear f'real. Split the funds a teeny bit with me, Shooter, jes gimme my little piece a action, an I school you how to lose them boys."

Carefully, tenderly almost, he was keeping his thoughts away from the tallest hurdle that must be leapt over at the last. He would be leaving the Force forever. He'd be tossing away the star—hell he'd buy a bag of them! First generation cop! One of those on whose careful, successful foundation the race would climb and grow. What would the people say? Who cared what they said. Plenty despised him for working for "the man." What was the truth of it? He *did care* what they said. And cared about them. A shiny piece of metal and a certain position in life could hide all kinds of sins of omission, failures of nerve known only to the inner man. Where he was going he'd join up again at a higher level, do great good, far more good, in this mean old world, than he'd ever have a chance to in his present state, and have a far adventure, not the average kind, and wealth, wealth! They'd see, when they heard about him later. The ones who despised him would smile wisely.

But a hard lump in the pit of his stomach made him know that ahead lay a final testing, for if he'd been bred for anything it had been the Force. For a long time his father had never once articulated this wonderful dream of his for fear perhaps of overanticipating it. If he'd been secretly groomed for anything by his Dad, it had been for the Force. Were he to see him now . . . *night watchman* . . . he was going to storm the gates of the night and take the moon in his arms, not just sit by the back door of some factory, or in the cramped frontseat of a standard issue sedan, watching the sad moonlight wash the stone face of the city. Then he saw his mother's eyes, one green and one brown, which had glimpsed Beauty, and he thought that he could do anything.

Fist was mumbling incoherently again, "Reeter, why you don meet me at the Green Mill—go downtown instead? Huh?" It hardly mattered, since he hadn't met her at the Green Mill either, and in deep despair she ignored him. He was trying to maintain some human contact with the frontseat. His voice sounded hurt for he wanted some explanation of this point of whether she had not trusted him. He had meant to share equally and in fact take her to Honolulu with him. Rita didn't reply but sighed extravagantly. She did not know he had handed her over to the cop not an hour ago, and he seemed to have forgotten his betrayal also.

The cop paid him no more mind. He'd wondered about giving the Fist the chance to rap to Rita, but the alternative was to let her ride with the cab driver, and the unpredictability of a dude whose nose was as wide open as that cabby's you had to respect. He would have liked to cut the cab driver loose altogether, but it was wiser to let him carry the dope. Besides it was a pleasure terrifying him. Realistically, the fucker was a troublemaker since he was in love and should be watched. The only thing was that Rita showed signs of coming unglued and Bobby's laments weren't helping. Naturally, in her state of mind, it was too much to expect her to believe that a cop was saving her score and arranging her escape, especially after this morning in Jackie's. Later she would see how good he could be. This element of—call it gallantry—was essential to his considerations, if only because he dug her act. It was one of the things that made him right. Later she would dig it. For now it had to be enough that there was no other way for her.

His mind filled with reassurances for her, but he couldn't give them in front of the Fist. It didn't matter what the Fist heard, but part of him was a green kid with the Fist, as always. He couldn't help it. The Fist might chuckle at the wrong moment, and blow his cool. To where had she ever thought she was going with that lowlife cab driver anyway, who lived in his car? He wouldn't ask. When the moment came that she'd admit she'd been flying blind, he'd tell her that watching her performance had been his inspiration. He glanced at her out of the corner of his eye. She was sitting rigidly, her concealing languor long gone. She saw him looking at her, and smiled at him sadly and beseechingly, not bothering to hide her fear.

He'd lay more on her than she would have ever come out of this with by herself, knowing the Fist. When he'd coaxed all he needed for himself from him, he'd start on him all over again, say, "And now, really, fat man, consider it—how much you really think you owe Rita?"

He was tired of thinking. He couldn't stop his thoughts, but all reflection was to excess now. His course was laid out, and only action would solve the riddles. He was reminded again of her little philosophy about masks from this morning. Maybe he dug it, if you could substitute a line of action for a mask, a new reality created according to your bold move. All doubts silenced and resolved, life changed by *changing* it, the right mask for the moment, as she had put it. He was sure she would understand him when he could explain it to her like that, making a certain difficult move, under cover of the bravest of masks, to achieve a condition of grace, when no masks would ever be necessary again.

His eagerness to cheer her and persuade her of their next steps with this insight, to help her be brave in light of her own words this morning, and his suspicion that the cocaine in his brain might make him forget just the compelling angle he had on it before he was alone with her and free to do so, made him hate the Fist doubly for being an eavesdropper. It was an irony the man in back would not have appreciated.

The Fist had been robbed, beaten, and shackled tonight, and he knew more was on its way, and his time was coming soon. He was in "the life," and he knew how it was done. It was going to be all over for him any minute. Maybe he wouldn't see Rita ever again. He wouldn't be ridden around, an unwanted third party, as useful as your uncle on a hot date, all night. He knew this pigheaded cop from way back. He'd been a good kid, an athlete, but plenty mean and tough. Even if he had gone crazy, his promises were still good, and he'd promised him a long walk, maybe worse than that, which he would get, if he lived.

Once the Fist sensed them circling down the cloverleaf from the big road, he began pulling himself together. It'd be okay, if the guy didn't give him something extra. At every application of the brakes, and every turn in the road, a freezing convulsion passed down the Fist's body, as if each little beaten knot of fiber had a way of understanding how much more was going to be demanded of it shortly. It would be all right, if the crazy copper didn't shoot him as a warning to Pepe, take out one of his knees, like he'd said.

"Teagarden, insane muhfucker, what the hell gone wrong with you? I knew ya was goin off the fuckin deep end some day, ya so damn straight!"

236

With hallucinatory magnification of what lay before him, like an animal in its cage awaiting slaughter, the Fist felt every slowdown and change in direction through his hands and knees as though it was his last. He smelled the end coming. The cop was searching for a dark country road to drive him down, just like he'd promised him. Once, twice, a few potholes told him the road had been found. Then the wheels began to pound a washboard dirtroad. This would be it, finally. His teeth chattered in time to the bouncing floorboard on which he could no longer rest his dripping forehead. But he had to try—like using a jackhammer for a pillow—while with Houdini contortions he pulled all his cash money out of his pocket and stuck it up his asshole.

The cab driver, following thirty yards behind, wondered at the strange turn the cop had taken down a farmer's track. He flicked his brights in case they'd lost the way, but the crooked law didn't slow. From what he'd overheard him say on the cab radio, they ought to be wasting no time on their way to the Labs, and this was no shortcut. In a roundabout way it would take you back to the main road again (or to Wisconsin the other direction), but how would the guy know that? A whiff of the monstrous fear he'd known in the backroom of the Super Mercado came again.

Dull starfall from a half-clouded sky unveiled farm buildings as they passed them by, a lopsided red barn and peeling silver silo with a weatherbeaten somnolence about them at midday, deep in dreamless slumber this time of night. A dog began to bark. There were two farms on this stretch, with some fifty acres of cow pastures and scrub between them, and then after them, a half a mile of scraggly woods where the road dipping down crossed Swamp Creek. In the daytime it was peaceful and goodnatured out here, but in the middle of the night this country looked desolate and mysterious as hell even to one who knew it.

The dog quit barking after they'd traveled on, and the obliterating silence of the sleeping earth took up. They passed both farms and entered the tangled woods. The road took a bend and the land sloped down sharply toward the little bridge that crossed the creek. The cop pulled over and stopped just before they got to it.

The cab driver braked hard, the Cadillac's tires skidding in the gravel. He studied the so-called cop's silhouette for any sign of what he would do next. He thought he would anticipate the evil move this time. Something very weird was about to go down. Cops thought they could do anything to a cab driver, let alone a renegade coked-up cop. They could kill you and think they would get away with it. It was just the sort of deserted spot a bad coked-up guy from the city would think of as the end of the world.

With all the close calls he'd had tonight, if he couldn't wake up to what kind of a trip he was on by now, he'd deserve what he got. The hiss of his blood in his ears mixing with the doleful gurgle of Swamp Creek as it meandered under the bridge told him this had stopped being police business long ago and might never have been been police business. Cop or no cop, if he got out of his car and started walking toward him, he'd run his ass over. From here he'd hit him doing forty and climb over him. He'd stop long enough to grab Rita. This guy was no cop at all. He might have been once, but no longer. He was a crook and might be a killer. The car door opened, and the man stepped out. He glared back at the cab driver and began to walk toward him. The cab driver set his jaw and revved his engine, dropped the shift lever into drive. The wheels of the big car dug a hole in the gravel and climbed out smoking. He widened his eyes to aim, adjusted his angle, and then shut his eyes tight. He floored the gas pedal. He intended to obliterate him.

He opened his eyes a crack to be sure he was going to hit him and saw the guy had circled around his own car and taken a step into the brush that edged the creek. He wasn't coming for him. He was inaccessible to be run over unless you wanted to risk winding up stuck in mud. The man seemed to be taking a look around at the country. What, had he stopped to take a leak? The cop glanced over his shoulder alarmed as the cab driver hit his brakes and the Cadillac rocked back and forth in a clatter of pebbles and a cloud of dust.

The cop gave him a long steady look of disgust. He went around his plaingreen car and opened the back door and stooped down beside it and leaned far in and did something inside. He stood up again, and after a while a man crawled off the back floor and crumpled in the road under his feet. In the glare of his headlights the cab driver caught the shine of his ringlets and realized who he was. The cop stared down at him a few seconds and finally hauled back his leg and gave him a sharp kick on the side of the head to make him sit up.

"How you get so cold, Shooter?" came the lament of pain.

"You tryin to make me laugh? Stand up an strip! Get it over with Fist an be grateful if I don shoot off both your fuckin kneecaps for old time sake!"

The cop was nearly shrieking. Far from rising, the man lolled back against the fender. The cop leaned down and spoke softly to him. The cab driver couldn't hear any more. He had a hunch he wasn't reading him his Miranda rights. The cop began kneeing him in the face. More than a wish for simple justice for past wrongs was running through his mind. This was how things had to be done for rational reasons not revenge. He was getting in practice and sharpening his edge. This was an old devil, a small one, and he'd dealt with him harshly already tonight, but he was going to take him to the cleaners one more time so he'd be ready for the next devils and the ones after that he was sure were going to plague him in droves from now on. It was far from enough that he'd beaten the Fist once tonight, and he got a fresh start.

The skinpeeling the Fist's face took grinding into the dirt under the man's knee on his neck, then the helpless absorption of what felt like boulders landing on his back, the cop's big feet, all understandable, abruptly gave way to the novel sensations of being undressed. He was being turned over and over like a child. Even his shoes and socks and his drawers were ripped off, just like the Shooter had promised—if it was the Shooter any more.

How far the cop's mug had changed from the honest one of the remembered basketball player! It burned above him in the stinging air, eyes fevercharged with blood, lips and chin gleaming and dripping, a psycho grimace. The Fist was a bad boy himself, yet found this new thing shocking. It was the incredible transformation of a moral reference point (though it had been poised against him), as much as the whipping, that overcame him. The chilling vision of the "little deacon" gone mad dog crazy almost made him forget his own problems. He gave up and took it, calmed down by a force more evil than his own. That's gangster's honor. He submitted, and quit trying to delay things. He pulled his ankles out of his drawers himself and tried to keep up a little dignity even if he was stripped stark naked. He knew how to fucking die, if that's what it was. So if the story went that he walked the plank waving his damn cock in the air, he could stand up to that too.

239

At the end though, the reality of just how far out on the dirt road he was socked him a good one, and with all the larceny in his soul he cried out, "Baby, tell him kill me, don't leave me out here without no drawers, Reeter!"

"Onliest mistake I made, Bobby, was go with you to Forty-Third street this morning, Bobby!" sobbed Rita desperately and miserably, invisible in the corner of the car.

"Baby!" moaned the Fist, drawing heart. "Make the muhfucker leave me my fuckin *drawers*, baby!"

She surely did hate to see him beaten that way. But she was on a different ride now, for real, and there was no way of stopping.

The cop opened the trunk of his car, and threw the Fist's shirt, trousers, drawers, shoes and socks, and babyblue jacket next to the briefcase full of money. As he slammed the lid down with one hand, he touched the .38 under his arm with the other. He had a question to decide concerning the Fist, and he wanted to do it rationally. Should he take a knee? He needed four or five hours at most. He didn't need till the morning. But you never knew. Did he need a knee? The man wasn't going to persuade him to wait till the banks opened or anything like that. He wasn't going to get anywhere near as close to any heat as that. This was all going down in the silent night. The man was going to come up with cash on the barrelhead, cash or cocaine or both tonight, out of his safe or the shelves and cupboards of the Labs, or he was going to whip the cocksucker and make him cry. He'd ransack the joint. For something! Enough to make up the half million at least, plus something extra for Rita. He needed not even till dawn. Dawn, he'd be gone.

The Fist was clever, and would find his way out of here, pants or no pants, shoes or no shoes, drawers or no drawers, but not hardly before morning. The dude was going to be cuffed when he left him out here. He'd just as soon shoot him in the knees. It would seal his pact with himself, against his whole past, for the future. If he was going to have to persuade the man an hour from now, he might as well get in the mood right now, and start by blowing off one, at least, of Bobby's knees. After that, there would be no backing down, would there? He'd be in the right frame to deal with Rita's old man then, for sure. Plus he'd like to shoot Bobby, no lie.

He mulled it over, measured the miles, the farmhouses along this road, Bobby's desperation and ingenuity, the intangibles as he could guess them. The devils were going to be so numerous, it hardly mattered to create another, but there was no sense adding to their number the ones that came after you for overstepping—or the ones that got a new life from an oversight of yours either. From here on he'd be looking for the necessary, not the pleasurable, thing to do. He weighed things. He would have enjoyed taking one of the Fist's knees, to say nothing of his life, the champagne bottle smashed against the bow of the ship, that kind of thing, but as far as he could see now, time and place didn't actually require a knee. He was making his escape, he didn't need to indulge himself with gestures any more toward the past. He decided it might tie him to what he wanted to leave behind, too much revenge could do that. So he decided to go light. He had unhooked his handcuffs from the iron ring on the rear floor of the car and he fastened them on the Fist's wrists behind his back. It was going to be enough to leave him handcuffed out in the woods without his drawers or trousers to hear him hollering about it. He hoped he wasn't going soft. Them handcuffs were not soft.

Having checked the steel cuffs once more, he gave the Fist a running shove down the hill into the underbrush. Faster and faster as the ground dropped, the Fist ran and skipped between slender trees until he tripped on a root and somersaulted into the muddy bank of the creek. He sat there in the warm muck and waited, breathing evenly, finding himself, taking stock, listening to the motors.

He hadn't meant what he had said. He'd meant the opposite! He was glad not to die, or get a knee shot off. He stuck his toes in the musty weeds feeling very thankful and lucky. His dignity was grounded in a deeper crack than how this might seem, so let the basketball player win and leave him out here. He got to his knees with an effort, which he was so genuinely thankful to still have, to find a drier spot to wait this out and he felt up behind him. The rolled up twenties and fifties were sticking out of his ass like a fuse. It seemed like an ample fortune to him, in the circumstances, and he pushed it back in.

His thoughts clung to Rita. He sorely regretted ratting her out, especially since it hadn't softened his own fate. Why she had gone to Pepe, he did not know. Could she really have figured he was going to strongarm her like Shooter had said? Where had she got that idea? He would have done no such thing! Sad! What could she have wanted to transact with Pepe anyway? It hurt him and he couldn't figure it. Poor Rita, in a pretty pickle now with Shooter, worse in its way than with that other man. He had betrayed her, in weakness. He was a bad guy, but he wasn't a shitass punk. He'd planned to be square with her.

Fastened to the floor of the cop car he had not been able to see that she had waited hiding in the alley for a cab driver. It would not have been a minor point to him as he lay in the swamp thinking. It would have been a new thing to ponder and be comforted in knowing she was—if not good and true—at least she had not gone to Pepe. But our knowledge is ever incomplete and he didn't know. How mean of her to think that he would rob her, and to go to Pepe! It was strange to contemplate, but he was getting so mellow in his old age, everybody was passing him by in their redoubled evilness like he was stuck in traffic and they were in the fast lane. Maybe she'd told Pepe he switched the baby powder *and* stole the money! They'd be after his ass now. Yow!

Even people like Rita and the Shooter were getting coldhearteder than he ever was by far. He was a merciful optimist compared to them. When he'd met the cop this morning in Jackie's he had really meant to buy him one for old times and let bygones be bygones. All the wrongs weren't on one side. Pageant Teagarden had been an arrogant, proud motherfucker as a kid. He had been the basketball star and gone around dissing all the poor boys who did not have his athletic talent and had to live by their wits. With Rita, he'd had an understanding and a plan, sweet Rita. He'd meant her only well and to take her to the islands. Stranded in the forest by a black and evil creek how he missed her! Both of them evil motherfuckers gone crazy.

Why the copper had a cab driver tagging along behind them he didn't know. Everything had passed him by suddenly. As he was getting beat half to death he saw the big white shiny frontend of the Cadillac out of the corner of his eye at a moment when nothing could mean much to him anymore. Part of some cockamamy scheme the boy had hatched, whatever it was. He thought he needed a ride later or he was a witness that the Shooter hadn't dealt with properly yet probably. Like most people, Bobby did not really notice cab drivers unless they were needed and thought them utterly no account. That professor dude was in a class by himself, but by now he had more to worry about than treacherous cab drivers of recent memory. He could not have rightly measured the fix Rita was in missing half her story. That Rita had not had faith in him as he made it out made him sad, even though he'd snitched on her. Had he known this was not entirely so would have been such a comfort in the swamp just now, but he drew some strength from bitterness. And he needed every bit of strength, so maybe God lets us believe what we have to believe for the moment. Bitterness helped him with his guilt concerning her (and she had not gone to the Green Mill anyway), even made him forget it. That the explanation might be Rita could have gotten involved with a cab driver and had gone to Eighteenth Street to rescue him could never have remotely crossed his mind. Like most black people he did not like them, mistrusted them, assumed they were racist, knew they were thieves, and preferred not to ever think about cab drivers in any context. He never would have guessed about Wisconsin in a thousand years. He assumed she had gone to Pepe with some dangerous story, why he didn't know.

Despite disaster and all misgivings, a rush of joy came over the Fist—to be free! As if release from raw fear brought out the child in him, he jumped up with sly pleasure and pride and executed a little splashing dance step at water's edge and laughed softly. An ancient African tale flickered across consciousness like a rabbit hopping through the glade. And he wasn't complex about it and wasn't ashamed to be free anyway, even under these circumstances.

"Don't thow me in no fuckin brier patch, muhfucker!" he sang softly to himself. He laughed and laughed. "No, copper, not in no *brier patch*, muhfucker, hee hee hee!"

The sound of the departing cars was a vague drizzle of gravel soon over and lost behind a curtain of mystery. Silence took up that was far from completely unpleasant considering he had both knees and a whole self, naked though he be. It could well have been otherwise. A dog was barking in the distance. It was a riddle how he was going to buy a pair of pants off a farmer without getting chewed by that dog first, let alone how he was going to bust out of the steel cuffs. It didn't matter how long he stayed in this forest. Pepe wouldn't find him out here, now would he? That was a solace. That was one benefit to being in a swamp in the woods, for real. He couldn't go back to New York. They'd look for him there, as much as Chicago. There was surely no hurry about anything. They'd want to kill him for letting himself get robbed. They'd never see his side of it at all, such as he would have presented it to them. Anyway he had been going to rip them off, they would suspect that even if they didn't positively know it, and it didn't matter he had not succeeded. His wish was to go to Honolulu. He liked the sound of that name, and the warmth of it appealed even more just now. They would never think of that. No, Mexicans would not think of Honolulu.

He'd call Pepe as soon as he got out of here and could get to a phone and tell him what had happened, skipping certain unimportant details and adding necessary others. He'd tell him which cop had his money. That information, and the passage of a few years, might spare his life. It might buy him a little time, for the time being. No way would they ever think of Honolulu and he could bide his time down there.

He fingered his rolled up fifties and twenties for reassurance that protruded slightly out of his ass like the string on a rocket that would carry him on his way. Seemed like a fortune. He thanked God for his blessing, to be whole and free. Never mind naked and a few handcuffs! If he didn't miss his guess, and if he understood what had been said to him and what little he had been overhearing, the Shooter was on his way to make a trickass score that was going to eat his ass alive. The Shooter had turned madman and pirate. He had kidnapped a white girl and he was going to rob a vice president. His daddy should see him now, sheeee-it! Greedy, that was all, greedy insane motherfuckers. He wouldn't take the Shooter's score if a Rolls Royce and a chauffeur brought it to him down this devil road. He was trussed up naked as a Christmas turkey, and his life was worth about that much, but at least he had his sense! The Shooter was headed into funny country on a darker, lonelier road than this one, and the Shooter's Rolls was running on three wheels and a lug nut.

She thought she heard his cry, over the whizzing air. The strangeness and horror of abandoning him naked and handcuffed in the woods came starkly to her imagination. For her too, the night's terrors had just begun. Bobby was one more loser out of many and she couldn't help him now. Just when she'd been ready to fly, she'd been caught again at the last instant, a bird shot on the wing. Her head had already reached the clouds, or it had merely been in the clouds. If she'd ever been a bird, it was one whose wings had been clipped long ago. Or one of those they kept the hood on, and strings on their feet, that were trained always to come home to master. Ugly pigeon under a viaduct hopping around after peanuts. They didn't know how to fly right and neither did she. Her trajectory had been all wrong, the coke not her ticket out but only dangerous baggage, like a bird trying to fly with stupid rocks in its claws. Bobby naked in that dirty creek with handcuffs on.

This cop was no high flier, but he thought he was. He was out of his mind if he thought he was going to match wits with J.A. and catch him out. Imagine such a thing. But she'd been encouraging him to imagine just that, to save herself. Only minutes ago, she'd promised it was possible. In his sad, doomed flight, she saw mirrored her own. He wanted to use her, of course. He'd tied her to him by a forever loose strand that seemed to trail off her frayed soul, there for all the losers to swing by, a fateful noose coiled unconsciously by her flawed soul to hang herself by. Her chance was a shadow of his own, to hear him tell it, and she resented it bitterly, as if he asked her to fly away again this time with his deadweight on her behind. On the other hand, it was all she had now, this sorry crooked cop, the story was developing that way. Wisconsin was history, too. What was he going to do to Wisconsin?

"Believe in me. Wear that mask!"

"Yeah? You're goin fishin, an I'm the fuckin *bait.*"

"I'll be watchin for ya."

"Come up with me. I'm afraid."

If this cop would come up with her with his gun drawn, she might go face J.A. again, maybe.

"Come up? Okay, but what chance we got to get him with a shipment if I barge in with you? Your job to coax it out in the open on his desk. You sure you sposeta meet him back at his office an not at his house?"

"I aint spose to meet him at all!"

"I know you aint." He looked at her knowingly, admiringly. Of course she was *supposed* to meet him, having regained the cocaine from some hoods, if not from the cab driver himself, or else persuaded Bobby to hand over the money somehow. But her plan was to fly. Unthinkable that he wanted her to go back and crawl to J.A. and set him up somehow. He understood, but in her shock confronted by him back in the city she had hinted she could do exactly so, and he believed her, he was certain that she could, even if she didn't want to. Now so near to the Labs towers she couldn't imagine it, but he could.

"You don't get the picture. Sure, there's a chance, like I said. There's storage closets he'll lock me in nobody find me for a week. He's going to be surprised to see me so fast. The weird thing, I really don't think he *expects* to see me again—at all. You know? He knows some funny shit went down. You think it fooled him? Damn but I think he wrote it off and let me go. I got the weirdest feeling. Jesus, I'll be on the floor, he's gone with the bag, an you got your thumb up your ass in the elevator. Jesus, man, please don't make me go up there, there's gotta be another way!"

"That aint how you were talking before. I figured you were all right. Listen—"

"You listen. It may be my last words. I didn't figure you like this either."

"Like what?"

"Money hungry. Stupid and greedy. Take half a mine."

"I don need no pocket change."

"Take everything! The dope, the money. Let me go. Don't make me go up there."

"If I don't see ya for five minutes, I'll come up! Keep walkin past the window without bein obvious."

"Oh Jesus, take everything."

"If he aint there, we'll go to his house. We'll find him somewhere. Girl, I'm doin this for you too now. I won't leave ya hangin up there."

Like everybody else, she was willing to *settle*. As he had been always . . . till he had seen her bold move under the hood of the Lincoln . . . till he had seen that wondrous deer, with its message for him! But he knew she was better. He had seen her in action. She didn't trust him—well, why should she? He felt for Bobby's briefcase, flicked open its clasps. Without looking he pulled out maybe seven or eight grand, as much as he could grab in one hand, and stuck it in her lap, who twisted away. What the hell—he pushed the wad of bills down in her purse as far as it would go.

"There, take it! That is nothing! We'll have everything! He'll see it my way. Believe me, baby, I know how to explain it to the man!"

"Let me take up all the money. He might go for that."

He ignored that. He noticed she had taken hold of her purse and pressed it to her nevertheless.

"How ya gonna signal me, if he's dirty?"

"Jesus an Mary."

"Rita, I'll take it out of his hide. If he touch one hair on your head. I'm gonna tie his ass over the desktop."

"Oh, God. Mary, please."

"How ya gonna signal?"

"Jesus, I'll sit in the window. If I can."

"Yeah?"

"Yes, please, Mary. I sit there sometimes. I'll scooch my ass in the glass. If I get the chance. Ahh."

"Damn you girl, don't ya think I know you? What you're doin? You give me the idea!"

"I gave you? You call this an idea? This is a big mistake."

"I want to escape too!"

"You fucker. Give it to me straight! *I gotta go up!* I don't got no choice."

"Without me you got nothing—but *dead!*"

"Yeah, jail, shit."

247

"Hey, Rita. You're not goin to jail under no conditions. Okay? Forget it. Either way. Okay?"

He slumped behind the wheel, suddenly weary with dreams. She couldn't see what he saw. It was like they were back in Jackie's this morning, and she was a poor dejected thing.

"How ya gonna off the bag now without Bobby, huh? I know the buyers. I deal with em every day, but we need much more, man! Listen, after . . . ya wanna go to Africa with me, see the lions, man? They never find us over there, honey."

"Gimme a break."

"Hey, remember how your Dad took ya to see the elks? Ya wanna go to Africa, Rita? See the giraffes an lions an that?"

"Oh, *fuck,* Mary. Africa, now?"

"Lotta black folk there. Everybody almost. Why I like it. But couldn't you dig it for a while? For a vacation, I mean. We both be rich. If ya don't like it, take your money an split. Go home. Someplace new. I'm gonna see you get yours, baby. I promise. On my mother. Cross my heart, Rita. Truth, I wanna help you same as help myself. That aint no mask. That is how I feel about it. I don't know why I started to truly care about you, Rita, or why I do. I don't care what you do afterward, don't care what you think, come with me if you want my help, or go your own way if you want that freedom. My heart is pure, baby. Look, you got no idea what that fat motherfucker a yours is going to give us. Jail? You wanna see somebody who is afraid of *jail?* Afterward, you gotta go someplace, you an me both, for real. He never think of Africa. Them Mexicans neither. That is a big place!"

His old lady would hear of it though, through the grapevine. The rumors would start and in the end they would get the story, the whole story, how he had gone off to Africa with a white broad. Even the boy would hear, he cringed. He didn't care! All the masks would come down revealing the freedom that canceled out everything. He didn't care what anybody heard or thought.

The Labs towers thrust up on the horizon, cold green cliffs, a long way from sunny Africa and lions, something from a forbidden planet. The closer they got, the harder it became for her not only to picture it the way Shooter planned it but to picture it anyway at all. The queer conviction kept growing that not only would J.A. be surprised to see her, he did not *want* to see her. How embarrassing it would be, like she was really asking for it this time. Her body stiffened with intolerable anticipation. She'd sing so fast, if they called a tune. They'd see something of it in her face as soon as she opened the door. J.A.'d be looking at her in his amused way. He'd be smiling, so you come back? Then he'd hustle her through the buildings, out a secret way, and give her what she deserved. She tried to imagine what they would do to her if she pushed them this far. She indulged a tempting thought that immediately became a dead certainty. She'd cross the cop and tell J.A. the news the moment she walked in. Dissolve in a puddle, and whisper on the waves. It'd come natural. Later, she'd receive her punishment, for this, for nothing in particular, and everything in general, at levels only she and J.A. understood, but maybe not so bad if she sang fast. She could feel the guilt and self-hatred welling up inside her. Soon it would become a brimming pool ready to spill over in self-destroying voluptuousness, with a new poisonous spring to feed it, her failure to escape. J.A. would smell a rat the moment he caught sight of her, and she was sure he did already.

She couldn't go that way, could she? Could she go back that far down again? Reluctant fondness came into her for the bad cop beside her who was betting on her will to freedom. He was using her all right, and had more faith in her than she did in herself. If he wasn't playing completely straight with her, whoever did? At least he might not rip her off completely. But he did not understand what he was asking her to do, and it was her own fault for lying to him and giving him false hopes.

"Look, Shooter, baby," she pleaded one more time, but with a new, yielding note in her voice, "he figures, he already gave at the office, ya know? I mean he might not be that crazy to see me tonight, at all. Not this soon, it's suspicious, impossible, in fact. Not ever, he don't want to see me, I got this feeling. He don't buy how it went down. An I don't want to see them again as long as I live, an they'll be in my nightmares forever. He gave me a good-bye present, that's my feeling. Look, Shooter, add up Bobby's money again with what you get off the bag."

The cop's lips pressed into a bitter line. Her use of his nickname at this moment touched him obscurely, creating rage, at the very moment he could sense her giving in. It infuriated him that power in this game had suddenly shifted partly over to her, the last thing he would have anticipated. She did not understand him, how he was doing this as much for her as for himself.

"I don't believe it. He wants his money. A man like him wants his money. He definitely wants his money. Don't you want to *get him?*"

"I already got him. I stole big from him, Shooter. And I keep gettin the sneakin suspicion he knows all about it. I want to *forget* him!"

"If we take all his money that'll help you forget better."

"No it won't. I want him to forget me, too. Look what I took already, man!"

"When he comes back from the hurt I put on him, he'll never want to think of you again!"

"It might go wrong. I'm tellin ya the chance aint no good, not like I was tellin ya before we left the city, that we could catch him holdin a shipment. I lied, okay? I exaggerated. He never touches nothin. I had to tell ya that because I was afraid that ya—oh, man, why do you hate him? It aint just the money, is it, you hate him too."

"Soul to soul, baby."

"Oh Jesus," she moaned, "my soul's a big friggin mistake. My soul's never gonna let me go."

They entered the dense long cornfield marking the end of Fox Glove Road near Labs Drive, where he'd seen the deer. Before they reached the stop sign, he pulled hard over onto the shoulder with the side of the car brushing against cornstalks so the small car was half hidden. The cab came to a stop behind them after a few seconds.

"Maybe I misread ya. Showed so much spunk. Bait, huh? Weak fish happy with a little nibble."

"You don't have to go up there!"

"I never *been* up there."

"If ya had, ya wouldn't want to do it again. Come up just this one time, okay?"

"It aint enough! It don change nothin! Only one thing works now, take *a lot* more from him, baby, set you and me both up forever—or put his ass out of business! He don't want that! It aint just the money."

"Okay! I will! I'm goin up! But gimme Bobby's case of money. Like you said he wants the money, that's what he'll really want."

He gazed at her thoughtfully and considered this. She might be right, but he didn't like it. Money could vanish fast. As Bobby had put it so cleverly, money wasn't illegal. He studied her suspiciously. He admired her, but he didn't trust her. He thought he might even be halfway in love with this woman by now, and that drained all the trust from him. She had said she was ready to go up. He said nothing and waited. A minute passed.

"Okay, okay! I lose! I always lose! I'm gonna be your fuckin bait! Just don't be late jerkin your goddamn pole!"

A pale vicious fire had come into her eyes and he decided she was going to be all right. Profound strangers to each other only hours, even minutes, ago, events had conspired to bring about intimacy. The evolution of his feelings concerning Rita had progressed so dramatically from indifference to suspicion to sympathy to fascination to admiration and by now frank need of her that he was inwardly reeling. She was full of hate and stared at him hatefully, and he figured it could work.

No sooner had she put her escape plan to the test than it had taken a nightmarish hairpin turn around a bend and straight off a cliff. Maybe Mary had sent this cop to her, after all. How strange, but his need of her was plain. The last thing he could have imagined this morning, an awareness of her secret power over him grew in him, which she read in his eyes. Something like a conviction that a way out would yet shine through for her strengthened her, no matter she was going up to J.A.'s office. By the look on the cop's face, there was no stopping now.

All of his own mastery awaited the trigger of her responsive move. His own power that was growing in him depended on her faith in her own. It was intolerable and filled him with fear and love. It was time to do it and stop yakking. What was in her eyes of boldness, despair, and some sort of self-knowledge drew him. Suddenly, they seemed to wear the right masks. He took her face in his hands and held it tight. Their tongues did a number that might have been love and might have been hate.

She stared into the depths of the fields and beyond to a distant woods where she was safe. Her soul flew to the blackest reaches of the forest floor to hide. The memory of the ordinary cop she'd deceived in Jackie's this morning was gone beyond recall, replaced by an unpredictable and violent stranger she might halfway like.

"Rita!" called the cop in a voice like an axe blade falling that made her jump. He'd gone out of the car and walked back to speak to or to do something to Wisconsin. She hadn't noticed him get out of the car her mind was so fixed on what lay ahead for her. His voice seemed to come from miles away, across the farmers' fields, startling all the birds and deer. After an hour of panic so intense it might have been five minutes or an entire night, she was suddenly strangely calm. It was how she was when she accepted things. She couldn't say if it was peace or just a dumb, familiar fatalism, a wellworn mask. "Rita, come over here!" He stood by the Cadillac.

In the riot of jealousy that erupted in the cab driver's heart seeing her walk to the cop's side, devils of lost love began to loot and burn his insides. When she crossed directly in front of him without acknowledging his searching stare and was hugged and hustled by the cop into the back seat of his cab behind him, his heart jumped out into the flinty road and began to paw the gravel like a mad animal. All day the cop had had one thing or another on him. First it had been a redlight he'd supposedly run, then carrying a bag of phony powder, the dirty crook. Now he had something that "would really turn the key on him," he was now telling him. Probably it was bullshit, while he really did have something on the cop, no less than a tape recording of his plans to shake down somebody that sounded like that silverhaired executive.

The cop slammed the rear door after Rita. He gave the cab driver an intimidating and wry look as he walked past.

"Pop the hood."

"What?"

"You heard me. Pop it open."

He reached down and did it. The hood popped up. In front of the car, the cop hoisted the hood up, and after a while fished out a large brown bag.

"You carry this, cab driver? This one aint no joke, I'm sorry to say." He reached through the window and let the bag drop onto the back seat next to Rita. Her horror at this knew no bounds. She hadn't had a chance to mention it to Wisconsin and explain.

"Wisconsin, I'm sorry!" she whispered faintly from the backseat into his ear. It was too late for explanations now. The second time, too late.

"Cab driver, you got rope or tiedowns?"

252

It was too late to run him over now. He regretted he had not run him over by Swamp Creek. He'd had his chance. He had his tape recording on which could be heard all this criminal ex-cop's crazy schemes for a shakedown, but he wished he had killed him when he'd had the chance nobody the wiser. Nobody could have ever traced it to his car because they would have been gone to northern Wisconsin, where he would have had it repaired in the backwoods.

What he wished for was his handcuffs, but he'd needed them for the Fist. He bound the cab driver's hands behind his back with his own rubber tiedowns, stretching them out as tightly as he could, winding them in knots around and around the cab driver's wrists and forearms and waist. He thought about making him get into the cab's trunk, but decided to hook him to the iron ring on the back floor of his plaingreen car. He didn't want him along with him and Rita. When he had done so, the cab driver had to lie on his side half curled up. It was a very uncomfortable position the cop noted with satisfaction. The car was half hidden in the corn at the stop sign a stone's throw from the Labs towers, whose yellowgreen light filled sky like a beacon from hell.

They had been on their way together to Wisconsin. Lying on the dirty backfloor of the cop's car, he felt his guilt wash over him in a mighty wave of terror and regret at not hipping her to the cop following her before it had been too late. He had meant to call her where she waited at Luminati's before he walked into the Rendezvous Lounge but there had been no phone. He'd forgotten the cop himself. With considerable pain, stretching the cords so they bit into his flesh, he was able to strain upward and see over the edge of the window in flashes as he jerked up his head. He saw the cop, seated behind the wheel of his Cadillac cab, pulling on his own Cubs baseball cap, completing his disguise. It was too much for him, barely holding himself up with tensed stomach and neck muscles, the circulation cut off in his hands, his car and his girl stolen from him! He was unused to power games, but if this wasn't the moment, he didn't know when it would be. The evil overheard phrases rang in his ears, and he shouted them to the night.

"You gonna get *yours!* You gonna get the magic money to transform your life! You gonna steal from that executive! I got a *tape recording* an I'm going to give it to the Crime Commission and your *commander!*"

Once more the cop was troubled by an intimation that the cab driver wasn't as dumb as he looked. That camera. All those pictures. What had they really meant? Now what, a tape recorder hidden in the cab somewhere? He didn't have time to search for it. It didn't matter anymore. In a short time, all the masks would fall. It was one more demon in the air, driving him onward. The demons were unleashed now. They'd be coming at him from every direction. All that counted was his own resolve.

The cab driver was blown away to have played his hole card—and been completely ignored. He was somebody's prisoner for the second time tonight. He saw Rita's blank face swing toward him and vanish as his cab sped past him and away. In the yellowgreen light of the tower she looked deathly pale and in her eyes was horror. All he'd wanted was to take her to Wisconsin and hide her in darkness deep and natural.

Her leg brushed the bag of cocaine that was to have been her passport to freedom. It was a stone, sinking her down. How unbearably sad to leave Wisconsin tied up on the floor. She knew how he felt. How horrible and cruel it was. She could feel the bonds cut in. It felt like her own body instead of his under the constraints. How humiliating to have her dirty hand exposed before she could explain it to him. That made twice. She wanted to throw the bag out the window but Shooter would just make her go back and get it. She dutifully squeezed it down into her big purse, where it would only partly go in, sticking halfway out. She was going to take it to J.A. so they could put at least that much on him, as Shooter wished. In terror she said goodbye to Wisconsin, in her overflowing heart. She didn't think she'd see that sweet guy again.

She was with the cop now, that's what she had, she was resolved in her mind. She knew you had to play the bad card you got. That was her faith and all she knew. That was written firm as the stars in their places above, hidden behind low clouds scudding past, but there just the same, whose hazy light made the night silver, hypnotic and comforting, the familiar dull glow of a hard to read fate so inescapable you couldn't help believing its bitter wrongness had to yield to a dawn, no matter how strange..

Just ahead the starglow disappeared in the yellow haze of the towers whose threat was plain and certain. Not in control any more, once more. Her freedom hadn't lasted an hour. It wasn't just greed that was driving him, but the minimum terms of his own getaway, she thought. Who would have believed it this morning on the Southside when she'd met this cop? He was making his break just as she had. She could understand. That made two of them. So maybe it would work then. They made an evil team. It was not what she'd planned. All hope of freedom had fled, when she had almost gotten there. Having managed to escape J.A.'s compulsion, she was caught in another's mad dream. This morning she had thought to deceive a detective never imagining what phantoms of desire she would stir in his breast.

In thrall to familiar vipers she shivered and almost laughed wildly to herself. It came out as a silent twisting of her mouth in gruesome dismay. He'd think she was going crazy if he looked back at her right now. If she had to choose between J.A. and Shooter it would be the latter, because she sensed he'd suffered, not as she had obviously, but she could understand him in some way, as he did her. Had it been a black man's (or a cop's?) intuitive familiarity with her scars this morning that had showed through his disgust like a secret tear of sorrow? He knew all about her, and there was nothing to hide. He was going to *help* her! How she resented that.

They had gone through the gate, the cop playing the part of a cab driver with a fare in back. The guard had stared at him, but recognized her, and waved them through. He was speaking to her out of the side of his mouth, something at the last to give her courage. He hardly felt in control of his own voice.

The guard had peered in and grinned at her. The top of the tower loomed out of sight, and the bottom of her anguish fell out so she swooned. After her treachery, her successful escape from him, how she was going to physically walk back into J.A.'s office and face him she couldn't say. It had always been hard for her to make a decisive move let alone such an impossible one as the cop was asking of her. He was forcing her, that was how she'd make it.

She went into a kind of out-of-body state and found the move being made for her. She was being excruciatingly forced back over a bridge she'd successfully burned. She could almost sense the smoldering timbers ready to collapse about her. She'd never make it up the front steps.

But then she just got out of the cab and silently started walking for the tower door. The cop said something more to her from behind she couldn't hear. He reminded himself of Coach before the game giving a peptalk from the sideline to a player zoned out with gametime jitters. It must have been hard for Coach to just let you go play.

Going up the steps her legs felt steadier than she'd expected. That strength left her the moment she remembered what she was doing, which she did at the doorway. Pushing through the heavy glass door, her resolution, what little she'd mustered, left her, and she felt numb all over and could hardly make it through the door. She glanced back once more at him, his sweating face tinged monstrously green by the reflected Labs' light. She missed his sinister comforting presence beside her.

He stared at her steadily, urging her on wordlessly, like Coach reminding you of the gameplan with only his eyes and a signal or two. It was just the feeling he had when he sent one of his nervous and reluctant kids to a new job, too, full of hope for them. Maybe she was right and he should have gone straight up with her. Held her hand. Naw, that wouldn't do it, that wasn't the plan. It would be like Coach grabbing the ball for a layup. No score. And this game was real.

She'd never been so alone, because crushed on all sides. Through the shimmering windshield the cop appeared to be sinking under water like a troll under a bridge. Then he was gone. She felt proud of herself just getting into the lobby, without him. Well, it was a kind of bravery. Instantly she was in confusion, because it was all for nothing. All feelings had left her except weird abject fear and empty objectless exasperation. The moment of extreme loneliness she experienced in the lobby was crowded with everybody except herself. For a moment Wisconsin's face came before her and she was transported back to a dream lost yet so bright it was a nourishment in the air. It evaporated tastelessly.

Her friend Wisconsin, whom incredibly she had found and rescued, was gone from her life for good now. In the blazing airconditioned lobby she stood frozen, certain of one thing only, what Shooter wanted of her next was impossible, but she was going up to do it. He was gone behind her now, and J.A. was just ahead.

A familiar astringent chemical odor came to her nostrils, and the shadowy world she shared with J.A. sealed over her like the door of a gas chamber locking. The glass door fell closed behind her noiselessly, and her breath was squeezed out of her by her snakes and mistakes. The airconditioning droned distantly, disceetly. The next step was the bright elevator, the stroke of midnight.

There was a place beyond fear she knew well, beyond fear and just this side of insanity, and it was calm and delicious there. Perhaps that was where she was headed now. No escape necessary from that soundproof room with no doors, where every solace of the destroyed heart was abundantly available. In this private cave of the secret mind where she ate wild honey at the end of time she would hide and pray silently for herself, sad old friend she had thought she had said goodbye to. Herself beckoned. Something dark and sweet awaited at the point of surrender. For the moment she forbade it entrance to her heart. Only that little drop of faith that it should not be so sent her forward toward the elevator that would take her upward into the tower.

He barely saw the gate, the road, the cornfields. His thoughts followed Rita alone. If the man had eyes out here, he would have picked up only that Rita had arrived in a Bull's-eye cab, yeah, Bull's-eye driven by a black guy from the city. The cab entered the cornfields and he swung over, grabbed his binoculars, and picked his way through the corn to a position with a good view. It was sweaty work and he was covered in pollen and green sap. He needed to be directly in front of the window. His own car with the cab driver tied down in it was a half mile up the road.

He decided to walk through the corn a ways so as to be hidden in the corn some distance from either car. It was tough going through the resisting stalks, but he didn't notice for he thought only of her. He shoved the stalks aside and stepped over them. He glanced at his watch. Eleven minutes since he'd dropped her, not bad, though six more than the five he'd promised her it would take him to start looking for her in the window. He anxiously poked his glasses through a seam in the cornplants. He counted down from the top of the nearest tower the three floors she had said to the man's office on the corner. The window shimmered blank.

He stepped back as far as he could into the field and still see the window clearly. The yellow light of the towers fell through the black cornstalks and covered him with jagged stripes. Far above, the skies soaring as never in the city suggested that his life had already changed for good. Her fears were groundless. Nobody was going to disappear in a modern office building. It wasn't a catacombs, just a tall stack of cubes.

Time that had been spurting dragged now. Like it or not, she was in charge. The obvious that he had nothing to do but wait on her hit him like an unexpected hitch. He'd thought there'd been an end to waiting and now it began again with a vengeance. Worried that he might have mistaken the window, he swept the whole honeycomb with his glasses, back and forth, up and down. When he counted down again and looked, it was just in time to see her walk by. She moved through the bright frame casually. It must be going all right. Tossed her yellow head and was gone.

His face and hands were cut up from the march he'd taken through the cornfield, and he was drenched in sweat. The night had not cooled off any. Having seen her was a relief—the way she'd thrown back her head. He was staring through the glasses at a modern painting on the far wall of the office, a silver angel riding a blue horse in front of a forest of dayglo orange trees. The angel appeared to have no eyes. The trees were on fire. A phony, fag picture. He had the feeling that somebody who owned a painting like that couldn't be *bad*. Suddenly everything was giving him confidence. He was drawing it out of the deep fields at his back. It was falling on his head with the soft, clouded starlight. And his soul was awash with wonderful, beautiful craving. He wanted, wanted— the money, Africa, the world. He wanted to help her, too.

She came back into the window again sooner than he had expected, gazed out long and longingly, leaning on her palms and with her forehead pressed against the glass. What was she doing? It wasn't exactly the signal. What was it? Something cold and knowing ran down his spine. He took a step back into the corn and dropped the glasses on their strap in case they should glint. Behind him unknown pressure crushed a stalk, giving him a start.

Something rustled down an unseen furrow. A big rat or raccoon. Unless it was a man. He ducked and whirled, surprised by the feeling of alarm. The glasses on their cord thumped his chest. By now the man might have sent his sorry bodyguard into these shadowy fields. He became cognizant of the depths of the fields for the first time. Straightening up to his full height, he peered over the tassled amber tops of the cornplants, their dark mass below swirling under like (he supposed) the deep sea. Transfixed by the confusion and reach of what his eyes took in, gone was the illusion of having his back against a safe green wall. The acres of high corn were full of secret caves and tunnels. Vulnerability like a rat gnawed his insides. He was giving away a head shot. He crouched again low under the jungle weeds bearing bulbous fruits. Damn if corn didn't look weird as hell close up!

And loud! Now that he cocked an ear, the whole joint was going off like popcorn. Ticking, scampering, intricate muffled racket that passed for silence until you suddenly heard it. It was like somebody had turned up the volume. For the life of him, he couldn't stop the waves of nerves that were coming in, probably the cocaine fucking with his senses, that poison. Rats, big bugs, wandering the furrows, snapping sticks and pebbles clinking. The green juices slightly cooling down in the corn patch in the night. Snakes in their nests, just waking up, slithering. It gave him the creeps so bad he wanted to run. When he'd pictured his tropic exile, it was the hot exuberant city, or the bright bare beaches where no obscenely painted creatures hidden slid.

A booming *crack* and quick steps now. *Steps,* and no mistaking it. Noiselessly as a city guy was able, he went down on his knees and knuckles, smashing leaves and stalks. He pulled out his .38 and pointed it, his mouth fallen open as if to hear better through it, increase the availability of the membranes to pick up the next vibration, his eyes blinking on the dark labyrinth of corn rows. Was it a decoy? Rita in the window, the guy distracting him from behind, covering while the fat man cleaned house. Crossing him, for a fat old man who'd tortured her. She'd be crossing herself and her own best chance in the world. Softly, the blackgreen emanations of the fields around him made a sharp taste of danger and death.

Trouble came from the unforeseen quarter, the seemingly harmless that you'd taken your eye off of. *The cab driver.* That's who it was! All the crazy things he'd seen the guy do today? He was out of his mind in love with her. Country boy would see him through the corn leaves. He could sneak up vengefully on account of how he had choked him. Spotting the cab, he'd know where he was. Could he be that dementedly jealous and angry to come after him? Carelessly he'd never bothered to search the punk for a piece or a knife and had only tied him with those rubber straps, but he'd had nothing else. It was the guy's own tie-downs but about ten of them. He'd wasted his cuffs on the Fist. He didn't see how he could possibly squirm out of those coils and coils he'd bound him with.

He was on the downside of the dope was all, and he tried to take hold on himself, but intuition whispered to him not to discount it. He hadn't suspected the cab driver all day for nothing. He waited and listened, impatient for it to happen. The bright papery ticking of the corn under an imperceptible breeze was loud enough to hide the motions of ten men let alone a stealthy country boy. The green dust was so thick down here he was going to sneeze, and he clawed at the base of his nose. Somewhere to his left, a sucking chattering started up like somebody frying bacon. Frogs, or some goddamn thing, croaking. He listened for all he was worth. The cab driver, if that's who it was, might use the frog noise to advance. *Somebody* was out there, no possible doubt of that.

But nothing happened. It made him wonder if he was making it all up. He detected no more movement in the stalks, minute after minute. He was going to have to get off his knees before his legs went to sleep. He was too tired to hold this fighting posture much longer, and he had to lie down. The binoculars on their strap he peeled from his neck and set aside. He moved one knee back, then the other. He leaned forward on his hands in the furrows, straightened one leg, then the other, behind him, and stretched out flat. He caught a hillock in the midriff, but the support felt good, though it instantly squeezed all of the breath out of him. The relief at first was pure pain. His knees stung, and his toes tingled. He pressed the side of his face to the earth and breathed and tried to rest. A breeze sighed through the leaves, and he became aware of a million crickets. Their chirping swelled till they were like an electric powerplant humming in a crescendo. He glanced at his watch. Eighteen more minutes had passed in a frenzied blur.

Paranoid motherfucker! Damn shit! Throw all the booze and cocaine in the lake. But if he'd had some powder left, he'd have stuck it in both nostrils as fast as his fingers could lift it. He'd have paid fifty bucks for a double of Scotch. Hell, with the funny money he had in Fist's briefcase, he'd toss down a hundred for a taste of any kind of juice if somebody could have brought it to him. He should have saved some, but who could've told him he'd be in a cornfield this time of morning?

Getting back up on his knees, he craned his neck around and poked the glasses through a hole. Blackness was all he could see from every angle, as if it dripped from the cornleaves, and hung in clumps covering his eyes. The tower seemed to have disappeared off the edge of the earth. He couldn't even see its awful light. He leapt up in fear he had lost track of everything. He hadn't checked her window in more than a quarter of an hour. What if she was desperately signaling to him? He stood up on his toes and over the top of the corn he saw the tower but it was far away now. He had moved that far back into the corn crop. He ran forward once more and, Jesus Christ, she was back there still in the window gazing down at him! What did it mean?

Or had she just come back again? She was in the same pensive study almost like she was looking for someone. Was she just killing time and looking around? It wasn't at all a posture they had discussed. She was to sit in the glass. There must be a sill or ledge she could sit against, but not like this. He racked his brain why she was mooning around up there. What would it mean now, if she were to give the signal? Success on the desktop for him in the tower, or death before he ever left these fields? Her ass in the glass, the onset of all the wondrous things he'd been dreaming . . . would he run for it and catch a slug?

The earth creaked. Twigs splintered. Pebbles clabbered like bells. Something began to hop wildly within arm's reach to the left of him. He turned about and dove deeper that way into the corn to

261

search for it. A dancing crow, a whirlwind, corn devil! Jesus! It took off down the furrow forty miles an hour, galloping on and on out of hearing. Big jackrabbit ate something spilled out of the Labs, got real big. Damn horse or pony it sounded like. He was going crazy!

Guy could have moved a mile in that noise. Impossible to see six feet through the tangle of leaves. Somebody could be under his nose, waiting for another move to guide a shot.

The cop pressed himself against the earth once again. Left to right, up and down, he pointed his gun. He limbered his wrist. He caressed the trigger. The insects moaned and groaned. The leaves of the plants rustled against each other ceaselessly. A vehicle was coming up the road. Headlights cut a swath through the fields. A forest of plants was picked out with millions of silverblack big scrolled leaves, and all the shimmering tunnels and caverns among them. *Crash crash crash!* It sounded like more than one out there.

His hand with the gun in it leapt through the air with the blind instinct of a cornered animal. The headlights passed over him and up the road and an immense darkness descended. In dazzled blindness, he listened. The guy was coming in from the other side now. How had he gotten over there? Then he heard the footsteps making a closing circle, one after another, as soft as an Indian's. Nothing broke, no stones rattled, no fibers screamed. Earth and creeping feet meshed. Dirt squeaked at the limit of hearing, spilled down unprotestingly, soft black powder. His senses were tuned so sharply, almost to the breaking point, he lost him for a moment in the richness of the roaring silence. He was like a man in a waterfall. He'd lost his senses. He could be shot like a dog.

For a delirious instant he awaited the blow like a doomed prey. He retained sufficient self-possession only not to fire at the air. Nobody rushed him, no bullets whined his way. He awoke slightly in the depths into which his morale had crumbled, the side of his face pressed into the dirt. What was happening to him? A bat whirred and plunged overhead. Spasm of nauseating fear. He raised up, cocked an unreliable ear. Nothing but a long sigh, his own. The palebonewhiteness of a birdpecked corncob at the end of a stalk caught his eye and he jumped up and stretched for it. He peered—a big gray moth fluttered into view. Tick! Tick! It brushed the corn tops. He aimed for it. The cob flew end over end through spangled space and exploded in the foliage. New waves of silence.

Silence so overflowing with groans of the greenery, whistles down the sky, and the beating of his blood, he was going to be sent over in a wave. His fear was harder to take than any danger. He wanted his soul back, if he had to get shot for it. He began to walk.

"Hey, boy!" he croaked.

He heard him take off ahead of him, scared off, bounding through the black growth. Guy was retreating, the bold tactic had startled him, flushed him out. Gun in hand, stumbling in the furrows, the cop fended off cornleaves and fought through the stalks slowly. He offered an easy target crashing like a mowing machine, but the cab driver or the bodyguard or whoever it was must have lost his nerve and had taken off running.

He began to whoop, broke into a run, too, slashed by the knife edged fibrous leaves, twisted his ankle on a clod, hopping. Up ahead the cab driver loped faster and faster. Farmboy, he jumped easily from ridge to ridge, you could hear him plain as day! The cop doubled over, leaned on his hands on his knees, gasping for breath, drenched in his stinging sweat. He'd never catch him. He drew rasping breaths, and listened to the other blasting through the stalks, the explosions carrying vividly.

It didn't seem to get any farther away or rather it seemed to start over again from one spot, before diminishing in a disorderly way, as if the guy were jumping back and forth kicking everything around him. Seemed like a herd of animals was surrounding him. The whole fleet of Bull's-eye drivers. He wondered if he was manufacturing these awful impressions from inside himself out of the ocean of terrible sensations that swam through his own cokedup brain. And as this suspicion hit him, and sunk in with a certainty, the thudding and crunching abruptly and completely stopped. A lifeless, peopleless quietude reverberated to the now clouded stars and back, as if he'd stepped off into a hole in solitary space, where there'd be no familiar down or up, here or there, anymore. The background "silence" noisily mocked him. It was only a cornfield—but green monkeys and orange parrots chattered and laughed at him from the jungle trees. He was alone with madness clawing at him. He pointed his .38 helplessly and dropped it to his side. He wiped the sweat and dust from his face with the back of his sleeve. If the cab driver had come at him with a gun pointed at his head, he would have embraced him.

Deeper into the fields he plodded on, paused and listened, his skin prickling down his back. The guy was hiding, waiting for him out there. His heart was stampeding, driving blood and chemicals through his body. The way it was slapping his rib cage, his heart seemed a feature of the world outside, apart from him, out of control, like everything else. Despairing confusion brought an unaccustomed moisture to his eyes, and in a rage he took off again and began to run flat out.

His burst of speed carried him out of the corn into some scrub woods and before he could stop himself down into a rocky ravine that had been hidden by the trees. Halfway down its side he tumbled against a big rock and clung to it or he would have plunged clear to the bottom. Barely picked out in the dull starlight that reached down into the pit stood many deer, seven, eight, more, he couldn't count them all. They hesitated in a secondlong frieze.

For a moment, heads turned, the beautiful creatures stared sidelong at him with their solemn eyes which he would have sworn contained secret knowledge. Seemingly they would have told him something in a chorus if they only could have made themselves understood. Then they leapt, all together, but in file, up the farther side of the ravine and one by one vanished into the trees. They fled from him, and on and on they ran. As soon as they were gone out of his sight, but for the crashing of their hooves that kept on for many seconds, he would have doubted that he'd really seen them.

Rita huddled in the rising elevator assaulted by grotesque, defeated visions of herself dancing in the dull silver walls, closing in on her from all sides, grayfaced, missing a tooth, without eyes, with a smashed nose, her hair streaked down, a victim of vile tortures, a beatendown, brokenup version of herself, inhabitant of a familiar cell, wearing a prison uniform even, she thought. These melted looking fragments of her person at the corners of her eyes were crazy, nightmarish, and sadly comforting, suggesting the end of hope and volition, the peace of a familiar hell. She had been sent up here to take a directly backward step, to try an impossible con on J.A., who would smell it the moment she walked in. The elevator was like a jail cell where she might wind up yet if that Shooter decided to come down plain cold cop.

When the doors opened on J.A.'s floor, she just stood there and let them close again. She couldn't bring herself to step out. She was glued to the wall. The capsule hung motionless in space. Inside the elevator with its warped mirror walls, she could hide for the moment. It was like standing in her steamedup bathroom on Astor Street after soaking too long, late for an appointment with J.A., disoriented by drugs and luxury, paralyzed by too much cocaine, coffee, cognac, and hot water. She could hide just another moment, then another. Sometimes J.A. had found her like that, when she hadn't shown up someplace, in the early hours, plain starving, and nearly drowned.

It was like staking her last fifty that day at Arlington, when J.A. had come up and first spoken to her, smiling and spinning his game, while the horses ran. Torn between winners and losers, wholly unequipped to tell the difference really, not knowing one end of a horse from the other, if she were charitable with herself looking back on it, out here on a sunny afternoon with some vague notion what was classy on a sunny afternoon, a high school dropout, a loser ever since, in her own eyes, sensing only excitement and glamour then, and some attractive danger in the man, her young life had hung in the balance, and her soul had tarried painfully on the knife edge, listening wonderingly to his promises, and why wouldn't they be true . . . as if the sweetest decision were no decision, and the only freedom not to make a move, knowing she would say yes to him . . . still safe as long as the horses ran.

The world was full of dark corners, sudden revulsions and revelations, unpleasant necessities and grim realities she'd found out, and it cost a lot to survive in it, to say nothing of living halfway well, and she'd never had a wornout dime. He'd been her luck, and if it had turned out to be some strange luck sometimes, what did you expect for nothing? If it had been a bad bet, and she'd been losing ever since, she couldn't get out of the game. She was tied to him, with interest. He was her security, all that she knew. She had no words for her condition, in fact, as she sank in it. Had she stayed in school she might have had some metaphors, but she was almost illiterate. She was a sharecropper of the soul and body, a white slave kidnapped downriver, even if her chains were made of rope and her bonds were in her head. She appeared not even of age. He was old enough to be her father, more like her grandfather. She took his word about things. She was tied to him, as to authority, tied down like a sheik's tent in a sandstorm, awaiting the finishing touch of his ritual, by which he raised the tenor of the proceedings from compulsion to mad dream, the application to her face and head of one or another from his diverse collection of masks.

It would be the cat, this morning. Sipping coffee from a fine china cup in one trembling hand, he made an adjustment of the furry mask with the other. Gazing out of it, she could see her black nose and long whiskers. Part of her wondered how she had ever gotten herself into something this crazy, and another part of her had come to think of it as normal, at least normal for her. So there she was. Nothing to be done about her life today. Not till another day, for all good resolutions had unraveled. . . .

The elevator door opened with a mechanical hiss and in stepped a blue uniformed maintenance man rolling a tall mop and bucket, startled to find her just standing there inside. The way she looked at him made him lower his gaze at once. Wide-eyed, he smiled in alarm at the floor to hide his embarrassment and reached out blindly to press a button and they went down a floor, where he rushed out of the elevator the moment the door opened.

The prison walls stared back at her and she saw her masked, distorted self in the mirror walls of the Lab elevator which hung motionless in space near the top of the tower in the silence of the night. She was just as unable as she always had been to make the next move. The door did not close. Finally, she pressed the "close" button, just to hide again, but after a moment, she pressed J.A.'s floor number determinedly, and up she rose. This time, when she arrived, keenly felt necessity and the wish not to be found by somebody else inside the elevator drove her out of her cocoon into the empty blazing hallway. Having emerged she did not change into a butterfly, however, but remained an ugly naked grub. Why was it so bright? So bright and chemical yellow in the silent night. She'd never been in the Labs this late at night before. Was every floor always lit up like this in the night? What a waste of electricity. The lurid brilliance spotlighted her paltriness, stupidity, and pain. . . .

When the whole crosshatched arrangement was complete, he stepped back like a spider admiring its web or a demented Boy Scout his unmerited handiwork. Approaching her he took a pinch of her flesh in both hands till she cried out. He stepped out of the bedroom, closed and locked the bedroom door, walked down the stairs and out the front door. Wait a minute, where the hell was he going? They had been up all night and driven out here before dawn. After a moment the motor of the Lincoln flared up like a flame exploding over her whole naked skin, slowly fading, going around a corner to searing silence. Hey, this was not part of the game! At least he always kept her company. Aw, he must be going to the convenience store for milk or Dunkin' Donuts for breakfast, he'd be back soon. She hadn't had a chance to ask.

It was really frightening that he was not here in the house. All the lights were off and the dawn was not breaking. She missed him as the prisoner hearkens to the footfalls of the jailer. The cat mask itched. She was uncomfortable as could be. The cords cut into her flesh. She wagged her collared neck back and forth, and the little bell tinkled. Tears welled up and rolled down. Here she was again, believe it or not. The first gleams of dawn finally exploded at the window promising a terrifying light. She was so alone in her terror. It had been a long night, and she fell thankfully sound asleep.

When she awoke, the room was bright and hot and she was lying in pools of her sweat and, though she couldn't see it, where the cords had cut her flesh, some blood. He had forgotten to turn on the air conditioning when they came in this morning. That must mean he would return soon. She couldn't see the bedside clock but it must be getting on to highnoon. The window stood ajar on whose sill a half-full glass of cognac boiled in flame. He had put it there after giving her just one sip. That's how he did, never letting her drink much, because he didn't like how she acted drunk. Things came out and she said things loudly. He had seemed to forget the glass carelessly on the sill, but she thought he'd done it on purpose for her to look at. He kept it in sight as a reward for her quiescence, and he rarely rewarded her. No breeze came in the window. No sounds of neighbors. At long intervals, a car passed in the street. The ropes were too tight this time. . . .

When she thought about it, she was more afraid of Shooter than of J.A., but when she stopped thinking, she was more afraid of J.A., whom she was heading for, so walking like a zombie, she started and stopped again every three steps, then thinking about it more, moved a few steps on. In this manner she made her way, and it was going to take her all night like this. She moaned softly to herself with her lips closed some phrases to the effect that this was not at all a good plan as she shuffled on. The floor was freshly waxed and gleamed like yellow ice. A yellow sign on a black tripod had been set out by the cleaning crew warning in bold black lettering WET FLOOR! WATCH YOUR STEP! Yes, the floor was wet and slippery. She felt she would slip on the floor and keep falling forever, slide down the corridor, down all the stairs, and out the door, like a rat flushed out by a hose.

The institutional smell of wax was the end of dreams but maybe the terminal point for this unbearable anxiety also if she could take just a few more steps. Every now and again she seemed to wake to herself and then she prayed to Mary. Anyway in a minute it would all be over. She approached an endpoint with the walls of the hallway converging on her, the walls closing in at the point where J.A.'s office door would appear just around the corner. No matter how hard she thought, she could no longer picture any sequence of events from now on that would end up in freedom and joy but only abject doom and slavery once more, or worse. She couldn't imagine what would be worse but there would be something. It was going to be seriously humiliating to see J.A. now. She took a few more steps, listening to the sharp click of her heels, and stopped about forty feet from J.A.'s corner suite. She pulled her handkerchief from her bag and held it over her mouth. She listened for Mary's voice which she knew would be very quiet. One way or another, with the evil man up here, or the evil man below, stuck between the two of them, all was lost. Somebody was walking behind her. Only Mary could save her now. Mary, is it you? . . .

He'd taken a chance—she could scream. But she never would. She didn't want to be found like this by strangers, and then she had a hunch that true fear might strike if she ever really screamed for help and none came. Anyway he never left her for long like this. He'd be back any moment. She'd never scream even if she was dying, it would be beyond shameful and embarrassing to be found tied up nude in a cat mask. If there were any neighbors around here, she'd never seen any, maybe because she and J.A. usually wound up here before dawn. On a warm day like today you'd think some of them would be puttering around their gardens or lounging on their patios, but she couldn't hear any.

She was trying to remember some happiness of late risings from satin sheets, evenings in the best bars and restaurants in the city. It eluded her, in favor of a soulshaking nostalgia for a hokey scene, sitting in a funky wooden rowboat with her father on the glittering blackblue waters of a dime-a-dozen Wisconsin lake, poles in hand, sharing a worm. She wept remembering, tears streaming as freely as summer rain. Why did such a memory with its common high freedom attack her in her present evil condition? For that's what it felt like, no comfort such a happy recollection, just the opposite, a soul destroying mocking assault from within. What became of the good things? Why did they always go away? Even her first days, heck, months, hanging out with J.A., had been nothing but pleasure and good times, nothing like this business with the masses of rope and goofy masks that had somehow stolen over her.

She forgot herself in lightfilled sorrow at a childhood paradise freely given by the Creator, just as freely taken away, as her father had been taken away from her. But how in hell had she ever allowed herself to wind up like *this!* The cat! Misery and shame swept over her so complete, diving into every corner of her being, and shaking every last resistance, it uncovered hope of redemption. That what had existed most intensely at one sundrenched moment of girlhood might appear again in eternal bliss! She could not even exclude J.A. from this promise. She was full of pity, enough for everybody. She seemed to glimpse him in the transcendent throng, deviously commanding silverhead overweight from too much good Chicago restaurant fare, a round white shadow among the other luminous forms, certainly not a good man, no, but not bad anymore, just himself, escaped from it all, too.

The cords sliced into her as if they were shrinking, making her know that no miracle would come today but in wishes and flashes

269

only in her mind, most painful light that scourged. But he might show up the next minute. He'd never left and driven away so long like this before. The cat mask no longer itched and stung but presented her with a gross deformity of her skull to get used to. The last thing she felt like was a cat, for she seemed to be underwater. She seemed to have metamorphosed into a blue eel or a seasnake, nothing as nice as a cat. The afternoon progressed.

What if he didn't come back all day, *all night,* or something? What if something happened to him? What if he *never* came back? What would she do if she woke up tomorrow still in this thing, almost dead? Naked, immobile, masked, lost and disoriented, panic hit her and convulsed her body in shivering waves. This was the moment of extremity when God appears and His loving presence replaces the so-called "reality." She calmed down because He was with her and would bring her through. There was nothing else now but Him. Even though she didn't deserve it, she knew that He would deliver her from the "terror by night . . . the destruction that wasteth at noonday," even if it was all her fault. It was His time, now.

The bitter loneliness of a little girl being punished for some mysterious sin had long fled, without answer or solace, a stage in her soul's descent. She was just *working* now, physically struggling with each minute—"building time" as the prisoners say. The whitewalled bedroom at the zenith of the day had radiated like the inside of an electric bulb, a melting globe of frosted glass, the drapes waving like filaments. Now the light was fading to a brilliant amber glow, but the late afternoon heat kept rising. She was so hot she was cold, hot or cold, she couldn't say. She was a body in traction, her thoughts coming of their own accord in fragments and snatches, hinting of a coming unsupportable chaos. . . .

Somebody was coming up behind her. She froze, then forced herself to walk again as if casually. If it was J.A. or MacDougal, they'd know at a glance. She had lost her sullen pout. She covered her confusion by pawing into her bag. The fat brown parcel stuffed partway into it obscured all other contents. The touch of the heavy paper under her fingernails sent her stomach reeling. It was the original package entrusted to her by J.A. early this afternoon, the price of her freedom still within her grasp, infinitely far beyond it in reality. At the moment it was the plain evidence of her deceit.

It had been her ticket to ride and the last thing she had ever conceived of was coming back with it in her cold and sweaty hands. She pushed it guiltily as far into her handbag as possible, but it stuck out as big as a loaf of fresh bread—with streaks of grease on it from where she'd jammed it against the firewalls of two different engines.

She realized that she still had her handkerchief in her hand and pretended it was what she had been looking for. She retched and coughed into her handkerchief which she held over her whole face. She was hiding in full view in her handkerchief like an ostrich, she thought with a miserable smirk. Why did it make her tremble as if J.A. would not be pleased to get it back? Sure, he'd be glad to get it back, of course. He'd forgive her. He was rich and he knew all the scores and could be indulgent. He wasn't threatened by any lowlife cop for he was clean as a whistle. He had it all under control, and would be kind. She lifted her head and braved a smile at another Mexican janitor in a blue uniform, who smiled shyly back as he passed. She'd just throw herself on J.A.'s mercy.

The human contact again brought her to her senses, and in the vivid interval before she reached J.A.'s office door, Shooter's resolve came brightly again to guide her, offer the certainty of escape if she could keep her act together just a little while longer. It seemed possible, even likely they'd carry it off, as he'd explained it. They'd go to Africa and hide out, what the hell. See the giraffes and stuff. She reached with all her spirit for her brazen attitude, at least the mask. The momentary illusion of strength vanished in a pearly gleam of the indirect lighting off the door of J.A.'s suite. She stood before it, wavering, teetering, hand outstretched to knock. She had been going to shove open the door in her brash manner, then it occurred to her to discreetly rap. She had no more bones than an oyster, and here came the forks. She could barely bring herself to touch the door with shaking fingers let alone strike it. She reached out a curled up small blue claw....

Outside it was a supersuburban late Sunday afternoon without neighbors. It occurred to her that though she knew the name of the town, Greenshores, and that it was vaguely far west and north of the city, she'd never taken a bearing from a map or a cab driver, and knew no more where it really was than dawn's grim shadows streaking past the windshield of J.A.'s Lincoln, or haphazard and nervous pictures of old farms and new corporations from the window of a crazily circling taxi. She'd never given a fuck where his house was, frankly, on White Horse Lane or whatever it was called, but suddenly this lack of knowledge instilled a dropping awe. She was in the suburbs of nightmare reaching to gray infinity without rhyme or reason, suburbs effacing the hills and filling up the valleys, with phantoms for people, no end in sight.

Behind the catface the tears welled up. A bottomless grief opened wide and swallowed her. Bad as this was, her entire life was what was sordid and horrifying, everything she knew. She did not ask God to help her escape, but *promised* God that she *would* escape. Soon. When her chance came, she would get out of here for good, and her chance would come soon. This was her plan. This determination came to her lips in a whisper, as it often did.

She wanted to pee so bad and the pain of holding it in was unbearable and she was going to let go. The burnt yellow minutes crept past without report, the fiery light mounting in empty crescendo, exploding in a blinding conflagration in the horrible windows, receding in purple embers, magnificently glowing, meanly dying, and, finally, desire, hope, tears dried up, starry, silent night on the steppes of the trackless city opened out, deepened in the abyss of new homes. She was beyond loneliness, beyond sorrow, beyond finding, only hanging on barely in a trance to life without wishing to do so, her soul a black pit in whose watery depths cold smoke swirled, the last spark quenched.

Into sweet and oblivious depths, she sank, in confusing currents, muddy, and blue. Turquoise seas lapped over her at the edge of a thousand foot drop. A mermaid dove over the reef, trailing silver bubbles, played with fishes. Sharks gaped halloweenteeth but didn't yet bite. Jellyfish didn't yet sting. Electric eels whistled down her spine and vanished through holes the color of pennies at the bottom of a wishing well. Her soul impossibly promised land. Giant leatherbacked crabs stared at her through eyes at the ends of stalks waving fingers of guilt. She swam through bloodred surfs, her heart full of improbable hope.

It must be midnight. She prayed to Mary for death, which she conceived as resurrection as the humblest, meanest angel. She was a tiny wisp of unknowing babe, wide-eyed and helpless. Except how evil and injured. She would scrub the toilets of purgatory, if

God would only change this life of hers. In her despair, she found the doubtful notion that God had planned something like this for her, and clung to it, knowing it would take the worst to change her. God couldn't have dreamed *this* up, it was her own damned fault. What in life could be worth anything after this, she thought, but simple *freedom?* But what was freedom, anyway, would she even know it if she found it? It might be a state of mind or condition of the soul to which she was a stranger. She might never get it, if she wasn't capable of recognizing it and really didn't know what it was, if she got there. Although she could not believe her pain could get any worse or her heart sink any lower, with these reflections, she felt the elevator she was on about to slip its cable to nowhere.

Nonetheless, her prayers brought her a profound sleep, she had no idea how long.

When she awoke and stared as if for the first time at the trap she was in, she went insane. She might have been a butterfly waking up from the collector's ether with pins through its wings. There was nothing to do but instinctively, violently, forlornly flap. She worked her wrists and ankles fitfully, and back and forth she wagged her catmasked head, as the early morning hours writhed past. Her skin puffed up red parted and gaped where her neck and forearms strained most forcefully against the sharp ropes, which, moistened by her sweat, had shrunk ever tighter and hardened in the night air and now became sodden with her flowing blood. Like a small animal with a valuable pelt in a steel trap, she didn't reason about it, but fought persistently against her cruel bonds, and did not feel the blood seep out....

"J.A., it's me, honey!" she whispered in a cracking voice of surrender and tap-tapped her fingernails ever so lightly on his office door. Her breast rose and fell like something slimy respirating under a rock. Clearing her throat, "J.A., it's *me!*" she insisted importunately, cringing, pathetic tears brimming.

She had entirely forgotten Shooter the cop below and his plan by now. She was bending at the door like a frail reed in a storm and begging to be let in to come home out of the rain. The terrifying question of J.A.'s reaction to her when he saw her come back with the goods became the limits of her world and it was mystery and misery enough. No way he wouldn't have smelled a rat, hadn't smelled one days ago. Imagine him sitting there in Luminati's restaurant making stupid small talk with Bobby! How much of her game had he already guessed? How shameless and transparent it struck her now, when she had come back. Maybe it had been amusing to him to observe her pretense of shock when Bobby ran, listen to her protests and promises that she would find him and get the money, or bring the parcel of cocaine back, seeing through her game all the while. Even J.A. at his insanest when he was pinning a new mask on her wasn't that dumb. The game was so outrageous and silly it made her grin like an errant child, made her laugh out loud and shiver, standing on one foot then the other before his door.

The intuition she had had in Luminati's that J.A. had written the whole deal off, had had enough of her, was letting her go (if that's what she wanted) eerily insinuated itself into her thoughts once more this time as the only possible explanation for his calmly knowing and resigned behavior when Bobby had taken off. MacDougal had jumped up and run after him, but J.A. had barely reacted. He had picked up his drink and relaxed back in the booth. At that moment she had persuaded herself that he thought MacDougal would catch Bobby, and if not, that she would straighten things out somehow. Of course, J.A. had no such confidence in either of them. He had seen through her, and he had let her go.

Or could he have been figuring she would fail one more time, and come crying back again, and here she was? That she brought the package might really surprise him. Lightning flashes went off in her brain, long and palesilver over endless troubled seas as she pondered the dread possibilities.

What if he had already said goodbye to her and truly didn't want to see her no more? When she drew the bag out of her purse, with what mask on her face, he'd know he was being set up. She had tried to explain it to Shooter but he was too far gone in his mad get-rich scheme. Never had she imagined *coming back*. It had never mattered what J.A. knew or not or intended or not because she had planned to be long gone by this time. (And J.A. himself had seen and accepted that, she again thought.) Her hands fell to her sides with the sorry, shattering conviction that she had been given her freedom (if that's what she wanted) and a ticket out—a ticket she had mislaid. That was what J.A.'s indulgence of Bobby and all her bullshit had been about, J.A. sitting there in the booth smiling cold. Sickening assurance poured over her in a voluptuous wave that J.A. had it all covered, that he understood her better than she understood herself, that he had given her up and let her walk with the bag of coke as a goingaway present. No hard feelings. Take all you need, baby. You were worth it, kid, and now it's time we moved on, if that's what you want. When he saw her walk in, he'd know she had blown the play and it was a new and dangerous game. How sad for them both for he would see through her at a glance. How stupid! He would sense the danger in an instant, not even needing the shitfaced grin she'd give him. He'd be ready for her, and he'd win. She'd be down for the count and she would sing. Whatever he wanted to know! Even that there was a cop out in the cornfields waiting for her signal, especially that, first thing. She'd warn him. She gave it all up and got ready to sing through her tears. . . .

By a blessed change of mood that came on her with a heaving sigh, she threw off her hysteria, stopped fighting, and somehow calmed herself again to the interminable wait. She'd been overtightly cinched up in agony and solitude for more than twenty-four hours now. She had peed on the bed but her shame could not have been greater. The night must be nearly past. But it never was. Only God was helping her maintain now, she knew. And she thanked Him in loud cries of praise. There was nothing else. Otherwise, without Him, she would have fallen apart and be raving and slobbering. It took something like this to make you understand that He was.

Dawn finally came, and after it the mild morning light, which for some must have been cheerful, but for her was like molten lead poured over her body. When she heard a car pull up in front, her blood surged for her rescuer like someone adrift on the endless sea at sight of a sail. Her throat was so parched she wondered if she could speak. She thought of all she was going to say to him. It came to her in lurid fragments. When he walked in this room she was going to scream at him and never stop screaming. How dare he leave her alone in this bondage in the house all day and all night and yet into another day? What if the maid service had showed up or someone? The motor was idling in front of the house.

He'd said they were going to Acapulco. He'd said they were going to buy a racehorse. She was going to have a car (she'd have to

275

get some driving lessons and a license). Last Christmas he'd bought her a furcoat worth five thousand bucks. She could only wear it indoors because people were against furcoats, and so was she. He'd hesitated when she'd broached the subject of a deal of her own, but given in, humoring her, as she'd known he would. She'd told Bobby to get ready. They'd set a date and now it would be soon. She couldn't afford to have him lose confidence in her now. It was her ticket out of this life and pain.

He was a handsome man of urbane charm, wealth, power, on the fat side. She saw his silvergray suit without a wrinkle, his silvergray head with no hair out of place, his eyes which did not lose their distance even when he was indulging in the most comical acts with her. Once or twice a year he brought a king's ransom of cocaine into the country, never touching the stuff, except his personal use. Parcels of it moved off disguised in shipments of antihistamines from the Labs' warehouse.

Thank God, he had come home. An entire day and night and more in the burning net. He was going to hear about it now. Oh, maybe she would go easy on him if he untied her very fast and was appalled and contrite. If she had a gun, she would blow his brains out. The motor finally cut off. She was as adept at reading sounds as the blind. It wasn't the Lincoln.

A neighbor had just pulled up and parked so early in the morning? The first neighbor! She imagined a comfortable looking man in weekend clothes, or a woman emerging from her sports car with milk and cigarettes from the White Hen, or a high school kid who'd parked his car at an awkward angle. Hell, she ought to be riding around with one like him, having fun with a kid her own age, not doing this weird stuff with J.A., whose car was not the one that had just pulled up.

It was not him after all. Her disappointment was knife sharp, but not so sharp as her fright, for *someone* was at the *frontdoor.* She heard the thick clack of the frontdoor being opened with only a faint protest of her heart. It was a sound too potentially terrifying and humiliating to be let far in. He hadn't locked the frontdoor!

They didn't even knock but just entered whoever it was. She did not acknowledge it was happening and even pretended that it wasn't. It wasn't the way J.A. came in the door, banging it against the wall sometimes. It was rather stealthy and sneaking. The

276

police? She could hope so, but they would have at least rung the bell first, or shouted something, wouldn't they? Why would the police come? The intruder was silent.

The cleaning lady? A girl friend of whom she'd been unaware? Warm red hope licked up, washed her head to toe, the friendly chance. Some sister who would . . . no, not cut her bonds, she didn't want to displease J.A. and mess up his nice ropes, and no woman could possibly untie all these strange knots. Damn, let her get a knife and cut away! A sister who would sit by her then, kill the time and maybe laugh a little together, and definitely cry while they awaited J.A.'s return. At least she could take off the stupid mask.

Although the pain at her wrists, neck, and ankles, where she was most tightly tied, was severe, it was constant and so, intermittently, forgettable. She could not see the red stains on the sheets and the congealing blood on her skin felt no different from the half-dried streams of sweat. Beyond the obvious elements of the spectacle she might have presented to an onlooker (thank God, there would surely be none until J.A. returned), of which she was acutely conscious, she could have had no idea how really shocking her appearance was by this time. And someone now on the stairs.

That motor had not been the Lincoln's and maybe she was just hearing things now and making this up. Maybe nobody had come in. She listened intently. She might be getting totally paranoid by now. She was not sure she had heard anyone come in at all.

Then, there was no mistaking the footsteps on the staircase. Somebody was coming up the stairs, coming ever closer, and it was no woman's steps lightly resounding on the polished yellow wood, but big feet, one heavy foot after the other, slow and tentative, as if exploring. She listened, her cat's whiskers trembling at attention. Those weren't his steps. It wasn't J.A.'s car, it wasn't J.A.'s feet. On the fucking stairs, coming right at her closer and closer! Whoever it was paused on the landing.

Heavy they were, and they weren't as quick and sure as his steps, fat as he was, as much as she wished and kept hoping they were. They were clunkier, at the same time uncertain. Nearer and nearer, up they came. One of the top stairs creaked very near. Whoever it was did not belong here, you could tell, but they knew how to come this far, reaching the head of the staircase. And now coming up the hallway toward her.

Somebody *looking around.* Whoever it was was only a few feet away from her now. She didn't breathe, she kept her head perfectly still, for fear the bell on her collar would sound. "J.A., please!" she silently entreated, in panic.

"J.A.?" came the subdued question like an echo. She couldn't fail to recognize the voice of his boy MacDougal! She swooned in abject fear, and trembled with gratitude that J.A. at least had sense to lock the bedroom door when she was in here. She had heard him lock it....

She tried the office door. Not locked! She peered in a crack, wiped the tears from her eyes with her fingertips and commanded the mask of the sullen scowl to appear, but it wouldn't. Then she pushed with her shoulder and was inside. Lights were blazing and the silence was so intense she could hear the electricity humming.

She stepped past the secretary's desk and gaped at the familiar, richly furnished rooms as if she'd never seen them before. J.A.'s private office was the next one. The door was half open. She was no longer even a trespasser but the merest slippery shadow. Consciousness flickered down to some primitive life form ripped out of its element on the sea floor, dripped on the carpet. She pushed the hair from her eyes, parting seagrass. In blue and gold shimmering bands of light, hope dawned unbearably, for J.A.'s office was empty as a lazy stretch of water to a fish that's jumped the net. He wasn't here! Relief washed sense clear out of her, and she awoke the little girl sent to Sister Superior's office for fighting, when for a fleeting moment the Sister's absence had meant she wasn't to be punished after all.

When her father had gone away, it had been the sun going behind a cloud forever. As long as she had waited it hadn't come out again, and so she fought a lot with the other girls. Any second the nuns would come in through the door. J.A. wasn't here, but suspicious as a knowing child she held her breath and stood on one foot then the other, awaiting. His absence was more ominous than anything. She *would be* punished.

She hovered by his big desk, felt an urge to kick its legs, before he came through the door at her. She needed a drink as badly as she ever had in her life, and with a mawkish, contemptibly cozy pang of stealing from him again, she walked over to the liquor cabinet. Hogtied, or by his side, she'd always had to fight J.A. for a drink. Probably rightly, he had always feared her getting reckless when she got too high.

Her hand reached out for a bottle of cognac. Her solitude in the deserted room played its unearthly music louder and louder. Something like invisible wings in the air batted her cheek, an angel trying to comfort her. She brushed it away, not wanting comfort now, saw herself sneaking a drink as usual, and beside herself in rage, raked all the bottles off the shelf. She yanked open the next cabinet sweeping out more bottles and a whole collection of whiskey glasses and cognac snifters. She picked two up, one in each hand, and flung them against the wall, two more, and more and more. Bottles that hadn't broken she took by their throats and smashed on the desktop one after another as if she had been christening a fleet of ships. *Bon voyage!* . . .

"J.A.!" rasped MacDougal urgently at her door. His proximity a few feet away made her shudder and shrink within herself as though she could hide beneath the mound of ropes. She felt glad her face was concealed beneath the cat mask now, for it was all that hid her. Thank God for the closed door, the locked door. It seemed to her the thinnest protection imaginable, thin as a sacramental wafer, and yet it was the most important and substantial thing in the world.

The door was behind her head to her left. She had a desperate desire to see it and confirm its stability. It was all that stood between them. But there was no slack in the rope that bound her collar to the headboard and she couldn't risk the little bell making its charming tinkle if she tried to see.

"Hey, J.A., you sleep?" MacDougal complained peevishly. "J.A.?" he muttered under his breath almost to himself, as if he was as confused as she was to find himself apparently alone in the house.

After a while, "Hey, J.A., wake up!" he implored the empty air, but was rewarded by nothing more than silence.

What did it mean? They both wondered, in their separate worlds, on different sides of the door. She hoped the keyhole wasn't large enough for him to spy through. As many hours as she'd spent in here, she couldn't remember much about the door at all. She could actually hear him breathing, just standing there. Would he hear her heart pounding?

He wasn't calling for his boss anymore. He was listening, just as she was, listening and waiting for something unknown. She heard his feet shift away, as he turned away, and then as though thinking twice about it, she heard him come close again till his toes were pressed right against the door, with him staring at it, his nose an inch away.

"Rita . . . you in there?" he whispered huskily. His lips must be almost touching the door. In some animal way, he sensed her presence on the other side. He must know something about it, too. She didn't breathe.

"Rita! . . ."

He spoke her name with knowledge and desire. What was the point not talking? It would just incite him. He might break the door down. She must speak to control him.

"Who's that?" She made her voice casual and sleepy. "J.A.?"

"No."

"MacDougal? You? Where's J.A.?"

"I was sposeta drive him to the airport."

"Airport? He went to the airport? . . . Maybe you're late."

"I'm right on time."

"He went to Dunkin' Donuts, I think. Must've changed plans. Be right back, he said."

"Yeah? . . . Hey, how ya doin in there, Rita?"

At his try at a domineering leer through the door, her laughter was genuine. In spite of her plight, their usual relation asserted itself, in spite of the sling she was in.

"Need anything, Rita?" he persisted characteristically.

"Your nose, MacDougal!" Her maliciousness shocked her.

"Rita, I got an iron bar for ya."

"Well, that is tempting."

She laughed, glad of the diversion. She was grinning from ear to ear stupidly behind the mask like the cat that got the cream. She could always get a rise out of MacDougal. She could torture *him* anyway. Tears of laughter came to her eyes. Who would have thought she would find comfort in MacDougal's pathetic banter?

"What the hell ya do in there, when he leaves ya in there?"

"I knit sweaters . . . for cold Chicago winters. I'm a princess, ya know, MacDougal. J.A. locks me up for safekeeping with balls and balls of yarn to weave."

Misery does love company. She didn't want him to go away! Damn if it wasn't passing the time. They were like kids, with J.A.'s protective presence in the air between them enforcing the rules like a strict though absent father.

"MacDougal, too bad the door is locked. But I know where the key is."

"Where is it? I'll get it!"

"Oh, I can't tell. What would J.A. say?"

"What J.A. don't know won't hurt him. Anyway he wouldn't mind sharing. You know how he feels about me."

"Sure, MacDougal, sure, honey. I know how he feels about ya."

"Listen, baby, I got things to do. I can't stand around here all day. Ya think I'm gonna have it for ya forever if I don't get a little encouragement? Where's the key?"

She laughed warmly. Whole minutes were getting killed. She was almost having fun. Anyway she was getting through a bit of her endless ordeal with a momentary diminution of the pain and oppression. It was a half hour's vacation from hell. A searing white curtain had lifted revealing this scrap of human companionship, MacDougal, of all people.

"Oh boy, you do tickle me."

"Rita, I'll give ya a thousand dollars!"

"A thousand?"

"I promise. You're worth it!"

"Well, nice of you to think so."

"I got it in my car. I'll go get it."

"Okay, I'm waiting."

"It's in the car, if you're serious."

"That's money, MacDougal, ha ha!"

"I mean it, ha ha ha! Ya don't believe me?"

They were actually laughing together. He might be kind. She even thought she detected a note of irony or self-awareness that was new to him. His desire for her was touching as it was pitiful. The threat had worn off somehow. She had the impression that she could control him even if he found her like this. If he saw her now, wasn't there a chance he'd be so shocked he'd untie her? Maybe if he felt pity she could get him to cut her free. Later she'd beg J.A.'s forgiveness for ruining his ropes. She had a scalding sermon all ready for J.A. As for herself, this was the last time.

Realizing her intolerable state and overwhelming wish for liberty were performing the wrong miracle of investing MacDougal with illusory hopeful qualities, catching herself toying with the terrifying idea of begging for his mercy, a quality she did not think he had, truly, she laughed and cried at once, all silently. Her disorientation, she realized with a lurch of her heart, was complete.

It scared her so badly to find herself chatting with MacDougal that her thoughts jumped out of her immediate quandary to her *plan*, the imminent coke deal she had put together which was going to net her far more if it came off than the split J.A. had promised, more than Bobby from New York could guess either (because she hadn't revealed her half of their plan yet). *Escape*, that's what it promised. Nobody but tortured her could know what *escape* ever meant. *Freedom*. She dwelt on it, savored it, envisioned it, coming so soon now, arrived on a pretty blue lake, wherever and whatever it would be, anywhere at all, someplace so nice. She was no longer in the solemn barewalled tortureroom in J.A.'s house in Greenshores, and she had forgotten his leering boy MacDougal.

"I got much more than that in the glove compartment an I'll give it *all* to ya! Tell me where the *key* is, Rita!"

She was brought back to her bed of shame and pain in the stifling room with a jolt. Her vulnerability was unbearable. She screamed out in anguish, "MacDougal, ya phony, ya aint got no thousand dollars! Ya aint got rent money, jerk! Ya probably don't got fifty dollars, turkey! You're lyin! All you got is crumbs J.A. drops. You aint got the dough, Joe, to ever touch *me!* An even if ya did, I'd never let ya!"

She was a victim awaiting every outrage. She was no longer able to suppress the sobs, and they rent the silence uncontrollably. But he didn't hear any sobs, just the outrage—to him. He was used to absorbing Rita's barbs and taking her condescending smiles. Two nights earlier at the Astor Street townhouse, J.A. had been partying with a couple of expensive hookers (in addition to Rita), one white and one black. He had invited the white one to attend to the needs of his sidekick, and instead she had split saying she was going out for Chinese. This in itself had been so funny, and the deeply offended look MacDougal had been unable to hide had been so deliciously pathetic, Rita had laughed openly in his face, not necessarily with ill will or contempt. It was just funny.

282

But not to him. Suddenly he couldn't understand this rampage of hers from behind the bedroom door. There was a wild note in her voice, and it struck him like out and out abuse. She was no longer joking, or laughing and luring him on, as he tended to explain her behavior to himself, but gratuitously insulting him at the top of her lungs, his employer's whore putting him down like a dog! He grabbed the doorknob and shook the door violently. He felt like rattling the sucker off its hinges to get at her. Just like that he was in the middle of the room, at the foot of her bed. The door had not been locked after all. . . .

She hesitated listening to the shrieking echoes of the broken glasses and bottles in the faint pulsations of the overhead lighting. She walked to the outer hallway door of the office suite and locked it. She returned to J.A.'s inner office, her soul rioting, and made sure everything on the floor was broken. If it wasn't she stamped on it till it was. She went to every corner of the room and swept and pulled everything off every shelf. She examined every picture before yanking it down, every figure carefully after she knocked it to the floor to be sure it broke when it fell, if not she gave it a swift kick or tore it between her hands. Pictures in frames she repeatedly kicked about the room like footballs, until she stuck her foot through them, and books whose pages she reached down to rip out she went on ripping to small pieces. She upended the lamps crushing them down on their shades again and again like driving a spear into his dirty heart.

With an ornamental knife, sharp though used by J.A. only to make lines, she gashed upholstery, lampshades, and paintings. The prized one of the blind angel on the horse, supposedly created by a famous artist, which J.A. liked to brag had cost him a bundle, she sliced to ribbons, hanging down, before jumping on it. She carved her initials on his desktop twice in huge jagged letters.

A golf trophy on an end table she grabbed by its clubswinging torso and hurled through a glass case that housed curios from J.A.'s travels—ceramic black horse and cowboy rider with silver spurs from Ecuador, porcelain white tiger from China, a collection of giant blue seashells (he'd told her were quite rare) from the islands. Every last thing in the room she meant to break to little pieces. She reached in past the shards of the cabinet's glass for the golf trophy she'd thrown through it where it had stuck and now used it like a hammer to make finally sure every ornament and idol was smashed to bits. . . .

"Jesus Christ! Look at ya! Jesus!"

Her position in his eyes hit her like a bucket of ice water on her naked skin in the hot white room. "Untie me! Untie me an ya can do anything ya want to me!"

Their eyes met, hers from behind the mask with pink nose, black whiskers, sharp furry ears, bell tinkling—his bugging out of his head. For an instant they both struggled with the possible meaning of J.A.'s oversight.

"Looks like I can do anything I want already, Rita." He laughed crazily, and walked around her. "Why, you're bleeding, girl! What a scene. Damn, you put me down, an this is what it is!"

"Please, MacDougal! You have the power. Use it kindly." This improbably made his face fall, and he seemed to ponder things for a moment.

"MacDougal," she whispered, "I been here all fuckin day an night. I'm hurtin bad, man."

"Yeah? I can see. Blood, too. It aint my fault. I didn't tie you up. How'd you get yourself in this situation?"

"I'll give *you* a thousand dollars!"

"Ha ha! Shit! The day you give me a thousand bucks."

"I have a thousand dollars, unlike you, an I'll give it to you."

"Well, I can't help you. I would if I could . . . but this is J.A.'s business. . . ."

He sat down heavily beside her and studied the cat mask as if its details fascinated him.

"Look at me MacDougal! Look at me!"

"Don't worry, I'm lookin, Rita!"

But although she was naked, all he could look at was the mask as if out of modesty, or perhaps the blood and horror disconcerted him. He touched the mask with a finger. It had slipped down a little and he straightened it on her nose. It was not a full mask, but left her mouth uncovered. He grinned. "A fuckin cat!" He put his hand on her.

"When the cat's away the little mice play," she mumbled wearily but viciously.

"Ya oughta go to the dentist for that tooth a yours, Rita."

"Untie me, please, MacDougal."

284

"I told you, I can't. You're a mess, man. Rita. Pretend I'm the dentist."

"Ya know what J.A. will do to ya if he walks in here right now and finds you in here?"

"Yeah, nothin. Anyway I'll hear his car. Ya think he'll care? If he does this to you?"

"Yeah? Ya think he's weird or somethin?"

They both knew full well J.A. was very wealthy and could be dangerous.

"You're the one that's weird if ya ask me."

Behind the catface the tears soundlessly flowed. The material of the mask no longer absorbed them and they trickled from her cheeks. She closed her eyes very tight. A grief opened in her in which the scene dissolved. Bad as this was, her life was terrifyingly worse. From some distant place, she prayed fervently for them all, MacDougal, even J.A. She did not ask God to help her escape, but *promised* God that she *would* escape, again, finally stop selling her soul for the lush and pampered existence whose true nature came into focus when J.A. exacted his stupid price for it.

After some time she recovered herself to her immediate circumstances, opened her eyes, and was surprised to realize MacDougal was just standing at the foot of the bed, doing nothing, an agonized pensive expression on his face, which now turned to infinite contempt. . . .

At last she turned to J.A.'s massive desk, spilled out its drawers, and ripped up papers and photos, some of herself, she was astonished to see, masked, and weird as could be. So he kept them in his desk! You wouldn't know it was her really, and she hoped it wasn't. No one could possibly know since her face was masked. Seeing the photos added nothing to her understanding of herself or her fate, but made her very cold inside, as if she had failed God. *She'd escape now!* It was somebody else, she hoped, but supposed it must be her. It was the her she was tearing to little pieces and dropping behind her as she fled.

Jumping left and right, back and forth again wildly, to beat on things with the trophy over and over and make sure to grind all the pieces underfoot, she tripped on something in the debris piling up and suddenly went over on her high heels, banged her head on the corner of the desk and blacked out for a few seconds. She found herself reading undersurfaces strangely magnified and distorted, like objects glimpsed at the bottom of a swimming pool she had fallen into and was drowning in. Disoriented and in throbbing pain she was unable to catch a breath.

But the tower was floating through space, the tower no more than an illusory gold web spun from J.A.'s lust and greed. The room with her in it seemed in orbit toward some black star. The walls were dissolving and she would be thrown out to drift lost in space. Threatened, he'd run away and withdrawn his vital support, and all clung waveringly to thin air. The room surged and shook under her prostrate body. She was sure the tower was going to collapse. The vertiginous promise of an elevator drop straight to nowhere sang in a wind that built from the heart of J.A.'s absence. Where would she go from here? As if the builder had cheated on materials like a dishonest coke dealer the windows were thin as films and might pop out or dissolve and suck her out in midair. The danger of falling to earth from up here sang searingly, silently, though the windows were sealed for the airconditioning. She apprehended the tower as a lonely cliff from which she'd never be able to climb down, but she might fall. She fought her dreamy dizziness and dragged herself up onto her knees by the ledge of one window and forced herself to stare down at what threatened her.

The world was down there for her to escape to. She touched her hot forehead and stared at a trickle of blood on her fingers. She pressed her smarting head to the windowglass feeling its smoothness and coolness. Reassuringly it also felt thick and heavy against her skin. Her apprehension changed to being caged in, sealed in. She remembered Shooter out there too far away in the night for her to help now. Far, far below, the cop was lost in the black and silver fields. She felt so sorry for him and wished she could signal him in some way to console him. She would like him to know that he would never get what he wished for but that it was all right just the same.

Wrapping herself in her arms tightly to keep pieces of herself from spinning off into the disorder of the room, she tried again to contemplate her next move, arriving at a point of inner darkness so intense it threatened to blow out her mind like a candle. All the wreckage and debris began to twitch and turn over at her feet as if it were coming alive. It was moving over itself like a bed of maggots, some of the maggots flipping up into the air, cold and slimy. She sat on the window ledge and drew up her legs beside her—till she remembered it would have been her signal to Shooter to come up, an eventuality she wanted to postpone forever.

Jumping away at once, she fell down on J.A.'s leather couch, which she'd slashed, the stuffing coming out, and drew up her legs under her again away from the writhing floor. She swooned, and curled up, covering her head with her arms, overcome by a desire to sleep, sleep amidst danger. Shattered things below her feet moved and grated against each other in a deadly whine of everything breaking apart for good, the last grinding, wailing note, when the sorrow would become absolute and final.

Was this how it was going to be when he cut the last tie? World new and wide, gone unearthly strange. Into the ghostly ravine he stared, from which the last beautiful deer had leapt, clamoring up its sides, leaving an empty barren and a profound silence as their hoofbeats diminished behind the leafy veil of the scrabbly woods. How sad that they had run from him so fast, before he could have fully understood them. But he thought that he had understood well enough. He glimpsed in the pit the deer had led him into the weird, chartless realm he'd doomed himself to roam out in.

The loneliness of it hit him like no balmy breeze scented with palm and clove, but a howling sandstorm off a shifting desert. What if he got to Africa and couldn't dig it? How had he conned himself into thinking he wanted to leave the States? Chicago, for that matter? Which he would have to do if he pulled this thing off. Leave everything he'd known for a B-movie adventure. Never come back. Somebody who cut short his vacations to get back to the routine. When had the normal life begun to bend and change elusively? How had he gotten to this terrifying, precarious *here?*

What if Jackie didn't want to go? Refused, when there was no turning back? He'd never consulted with him, there hadn't been a chance. But he was always taking Jackie for granted. What if Jackie didn't dig a trip to Africa, and he couldn't persuade him, and he had to leave him behind? Dead meat! He couldn't dig it without Jackie. Even if he came along, make no mistake, it would never be the same. He was seeing everything in a different light. Those niggers over there would smell him out, an American with a bad conscience. They'd always have something on him, even if he owned them. Life itself would have something on him. The false note once played would reverberate on and on forever. He had made a wrong move. He saw with clairvoyant clarity that this emptiness and fear might never end.

Broad is the way . . . he heard his Dad's voice.

He had the astonished raw sense of having sold himself something hollow and fraudulent. Without warning the bottom had dropped out of his enthusiasm. What had happened to his certainty he would shake down a dealer before this night was over and be superrich and carefree? The idea came to him to turn himself around and find his way home. It would be a mighty endeavor by now. He felt harshly chastened, but even more relieved. His knee hurt and he wondered if he could move to climb out of this gully. He became afraid. His wrist was bruised or even felt broken. He examined it without result. The crystal of his watch was smashed.

However he had come to this, the path had forked many times and he was a long way out. Tracing that path back in reverse would be an act of faith. Holding onto the big rock he had fallen against, he squinted back up the side of the steep ravine. It looked like the side of a mountain to him, curtained in mists. Cornplants like undulating tropical grasses loomed overhead reminding him how far from the straight and narrow into deep places he had wandered. All of a sudden he saw his position through the eyes of his father. How tawdry, shameful and cheap. You cheat, you betrayer of trust! He was so lost! But then—how wonderful—his father's voice came to his ears as of old, uplifting, encouraging, judicious, and mild.

288

"One step at a time!"

It was a tone as you'd talk to a child in. He laughed out loud, madly, a sob in his throat. It was just the sort of corny old thing his father would have said, had always said. How welcome it was! He couldn't remember if the old man had ever said exactly such a thing as that, or on what occasion, but he probably had at one time or another. It fit now. How good to hear it again. He had always been full of the old timey wisdom, the kind of thing that had used to drive him to despair as a kid. Right now it was just the thing. How else was he to climb back out of this ditch and back to a normal life that was unimaginably far away—as far away as Africa? One step at a time. That would be what would do it.

He laughed manically at his condition, to stifle fear of the effort ahead, pushing stalks out of his way endlessly after he climbed out of this hole. He took a step upward, and halted. Then another, fighting to keep his balance, and not roll back down the side. It was only a few feet more, and even if he did fall, it would mean a bruise or two, not the oblivion which sang at the edges of his mind. He had escaped by no virtue of his own some hellish exile. The deer it seemed to him had warned him off in time. His perception was wholly that dreamlike one of struggling to come in from some numbing extremity, and being stuck there, threatening to crumble beneath his feet and suck him over.

He studied his cracked watch, as if it could help him, and found it had stopped. Time yawned and gulped like a snake swallowing a rat, bulging, slow. The slanted, rough ground undulated beneath his feet ready to drop him to a crazier, sicker level. *"Things get worse,"* reminded his father, bolstering his will. He stared behind him into the no-man's land between fields and forest. It seemed like the ends of the earth, farther off than Africa, and he hadn't even left Chicagoland.

At last on his hands and knees he clambered onto level ground. He rested, panting, cornstalks whispering over his back. And now, as far as the corn went, he was back in the corn all right. He began to laugh at himself dementedly. Now he was confused and directionless. The corn grew a foot over his head. He got to his feet and began to walk listlessly, unsure of his direction. The joy of being on level ground was brief. The corn leaves sliced at him with their dusty tentacles, razor fingers grasping and cutting him. It was the monotonous humid jungle into which he would have sunk without a trace, with nothing real to hold onto.

No wonder the old men like his Daddy had their guiding wisdoms to show them their way through. Had he never developed any of his own? Streetwise, he'd thought he had, but it seemed he hadn't. He had nothing ready of his own on hand for this here now. He felt blind though he had his eyes to see. Then he thought he had his Dad with him nearby, for he'd heard his voice. In a break in the vegetation he gazed at the Lab tower, huge and yellowgreen on the fields' horizon, a terrible beacon. There was his light all right, a macabre luster, like a lighthouse on the rocky coast guiding the slave ships in.

Evil star! What he had been about to do, steal from master. House nigger, purloin some small items. He had been made for something far, far better! He was a true man, none of this. He'd gone wrong there for a minute, that was all.

There was a momentum to his plans he wasn't sure how he'd turn around. It wasn't going to be easy. Half-forgotten devils, the cab driver's tape recording, if he hadn't been bluffing, the Fist's briefcase full of some hoods' money. He'd need his help to return it to the Mexicans. Or Bobby could keep it for all he cared, if he wanted to. Was he going to have to scour the country roads for nude Bobby to give him back his money and clothes? He had no idea where he'd left him. He didn't know the territory. He might never find his way out of this cornfield. Maybe the cab driver would help him find him. Oh, the cab driver, he must free him too.

Rita was in the tower in God knew what circumstances, in desperate trouble, maybe. He'd done it to her. What a money dream to give up, which he'd had in his grasp, and could still reach out and take at this moment. He'd sent her back to hell for it.

Things get worse! said his Dad. All he wanted was to get his old life back which he had not valued. Rita was helpless, in danger, into which he had pushed her without a thought.

Perhaps nothing of outer circumstances had altered during the mad interlude while he'd chased shadows through the fields. A quarter million, maybe the whole mil. Life of overarching freedoms, Africa, the world, to let all that slip away into the night.

Maybe she was signaling him right now in despair! He must get back to the tower. Bizarre—he shouldn't take the money? He shouldn't take her with him on a beautiful safari? It had seemed so much fun and so right, too. But he had come to a roadblock inside himself, big as a house, solid as a rock, far more substantial than the Lab tower shining against the sky with its unreal light for the slave ships to come by. A bright signal, telling him *WRONG WAY,* like a highway sign, go back, go home, before you crash.

All he had to do was go up there, reach out, and close his fingers over the fat man's neck. Guys did things like that every day, took the cash, and became happy, didn't they? Why couldn't he take the money? Naw, man, it didn't feel like anymore.

As lost as he had felt this past hour, there must be profound levels of lostness he had not yet even glimpsed that awaited one like him, who had at last been chastened. Wishedfor escape from his stupid problems had inspired in him a sorryass dream of ten cent glory back in the homeland, the ludicrous desire to go to Africa and set up with some tinhorn thirdclass dictator.

It came to him that lynchings had taken place here. He played his mental game and knew they had. The earth under his feet was red and running with the blood of his people, mixed with the sweat and bitter tears of the anonymous Slave Centuries in the killing fields. Sure, in Illinois. Burnings alive, anonymous grief and slaughter. Every day in the city gangbangers continued the white man's dirty genocide, too, murdering each other and innocent bystanders in the funhouse mirrors mistaking each other for the enemy, and he could only hope to slow them down. Whom they didn't kill some of his own white brothers on the Force would make up for. He had to warn his boys and keep them from joining in the madness. He had nearly run out on them when they needed him.

The ancestors had not kept their faith in the deep lost fields of Slavery for such an outcome. Could he have thought to abrogate their unimaginable sacrifice in the sacred abyss of fathomless servitude to the American pharaoh by making a run with their money, saving his own skin? It was *their* money he'd have been stealing! By what lucky fate of timing of his birth was he free, through no effort of his own, when they had languished lifetimes and generations doing forced labor, with no glimmer of light or hope save dim faith that only the living God could have bequeathed them? The cross they had borne he had taken lightly. One of Moses's band, he had run back to beg flesh from pharaoh.

Unknown heroes, angels, had struggled blind through hell for centuries for what he had been handed on the Force to keep for them. They had survived with incorruptible spirit though drunk on bitter gall so he could be a man, a citizen, a police officer with the star. You could so easily be tempted by the sense of life as all-corrupt, corroded, and rigged. There were choices. As if he could have fashioned his individual salvation in service to some bought out loosechange Goldcoast princeling, such a shallow selfish read on life. He had work to do for his salvation now.

He had caught himself on the edge of the pit, and the nightmare was not over. The Labs towers shone in the night like an evil constellation by which the slavers had oriented themselves in the long crossing for the Americas. Their terrible light shone bitterly on. He had been drawn to it like one of the birds that circled their spires endlessly. Like fire to the moth, the lurid light of a true midnight of the soul had compelled him.

One step at a time. He had the truest star to guide him.

He had his life to win back. A man had to know who he was. First, he had to rescue Rita and help her onward. What was he waiting for? The man might be laughing at him up there—where he might never find him or her. It came to him how presumptuous he had been to think he could catch the fat man dirty up there, a competent evil man like that. Rita had never bought his plan, he had forced her to go up there. Her signal might never come.

He finally came to the end of the fields at the edge of the road, and stared up at the tower. He searched for the office window. But before he could find it, something else claimed his attention, something moving in the depths of the shadows up the road at the corner of his eye. He thought it was the leering deer returning, and peered to see them, and cowered with fear before those knowing, supernatural creatures.

A big man's dim form slowly stepped into the light. He studied it, hypnotized. A big man in a shiny black suit and a starched white shirtfront. He stared in horror. It was his Daddy, in his Sunday dress clothes, silhouetted against the glowing tower light, come back to him. He was chewing and sucking on something like a drumstick held in both hands. His shirtfront, white as a dove's, was bloodsmeared. He reared back and threw. The thing came sailing through the air straight at him, a human remnant, a *kneejoint,* dripping blood and trailing sinews. He ducked and groaned, a violent dizziness knocked him to his knees, and he was bombarded over and over again by the blasphemous image. He tried to be sick. Tried to pray. He had almost shot Bobby before pushing him down in that creek. How close he'd come to doing that! He had really wanted to do it. Whoa, his Dad was eating Bobby's kneejoint!

If he had kneecapped Bobby and left him bleeding and dying in the ditch, would that have given him the devil's own strength to do the same to the fat man up in the tower and push ahead with his sordid plans to go to Africa, rich, to his doom? Would that have not sealed his fate? He was supremely grateful that he did not have the poor buzzard on his conscience. He put his arms over his head and wept under the eyes of his father. He had come that close to maiming and even murdering the homeboy. Something hard inside him gave way at last.

His Dad placed his hands under his arms and helped him rise. There was no blood on his Dad's breast, no way. The bloody image was of his own doing. His Dad was clean and upstanding. He knew nothing of Bobby or his knee, that's for sure. He was here with him, as he always had been, insignificant, a nobody, principled and firm, lowly but invincible, warm and strong.

Pacing the road's edge, poking with his bruised hands by now conversant with the sharp green life bristling and swooning around him, his trembling fingers located his abandoned fieldglasses. He parted the last of the cornplants and raised the glasses. The tower rose in a sheet of flame before him, a gleaming crematorium. A wave of heat from it blasted him.

He found the window and saw Rita dart past, radiant as a bird on the wing. Quick she was gone. The painting again, but not as he'd seen it before. All ripped in tatters. Orange trees, burning. A blue horse, on a ride to nowhere. On its back a blind angel with little red scars where its eyes should be. The trip was to hell, like his Daddy had threatened.

It was suddenly easy to imagine her disappearing in the wall of light like a bird into the sun, the blinded lost angel in the painting. Mad anguish rushed in. What if they had taken her somewhere and she was gone already? Just a nothing, a little streetsign they had used enough. His whole purpose and meaning, what little there was left of it, was to save Rita, whom he had sent up there. It came to him in a rush of dizzying pain as if there would be no end of the things he had mistaken.

The light in the window was suddenly blocked off. At first he couldn't make out what he was seeing in wavering gold and shadow. It looked like a blownup photograph of a cut-in-half apple, luscious and ripe. Then he realized it was what he had been waiting for, her signal, her ass in the glass—her bare ass. She stopped shaking it at him, pulled her skirt back down, and vanished, leaving the empty window shining out upon him blank and despairing. He began to run. His impulse carried him across the drainage ditch and two hundred feet up the Labs' entranceway before it hit him that what she'd meant by it probably wasn't a call for his help.

The bump on her head from when she'd fallen and it had struck the desk throbbed painfully, a reminder of something important. She burrowed more deeply into the slashed leather cushions, in a chill airconditioned sweat. The hopedfor escape with Wisconsin came back to her with sick regret, the hurt surprise in the cab driver's eyes when she had caved in before the cop, and then when he had pulled the bag of poison out from under the hood of the cab before she'd had a chance to explain. She couldn't think what it was she needed to remember, and slept again, for a moment.

A taste of piney woods, in showers of artificial yellow light, a painting of a beautiful forest with a knife stuck through it. Through the forest sped a cab, on its bumper a tourist sticker put out by the chamber of commerce illumined by the moonlight, USE OR BE USED. The violent music began again. The room began to turn over on itself as if she were inside a cement mixer or a meat grinder. With all her might she clung to the picture of the green woods in a little cabin in a glade, then a jolt of love or poison hit her soul, and she woke tumultuously from sleep.

What had become of her fine solitary readiness to escape at all costs? Drugs and money were negotiable for any future and she had both. White and green, like pure pigments, they could paint any picture. The allure had been of cutting all strings, to float with the wind and see what brand new might happen. *Freedom!* All she wanted right now was to forget about it all and sleep. She forced herself to sit up and confront her situation. J.A. had let her go and it was time to get going! Wisconsin tied up in the squad car couldn't help her any more, and she didn't see how she could help him either, any more than she could help Bobby naked out there in the swamp, nor a sad cop in the fields who was waiting for her signal. She had the bunch of money he'd stuck in her purse and she had the bag of coke. She looked about her at the fine mess she had made of the office. She was free to go by now, wasn't she?

She could still *walk*, couldn't she? She saw herself heading away from the towers through the fields, through black meadows and up the edge of the road and far away until dawn broke. It would be a charming hike through realms of honeybees and wildflowers this morning. She laughed madly—naked as Bobby, almost, she'd be. The fields and forests shone and sparkled in her mind's eye like a lyrical rough sea wide and deep enough to conceal you, that you could sail out upon, which would hide and succor you.

She'd probably get lost and just drown, with her luck. The potential freedom and strength in this vision was an unbearable weight needing release. Time to do it and find out! She sat straight up and her head cleared a bit. Her mood shifted, and her old spirit of adventure suddenly lifted her off the couch, and a grin split her lips, showing a charming gap between her front teeth if anyone had been there to see it. She didn't need companions anymore. She would walk, on her own hind legs, which God had given her.

Not on these heels though. She had some tennis togs in one of the closets. J.A. had bought her a white tennis outfit, made her take lessons. He didn't come near the court with his bulk, but he liked to make the scene at his country club, have drinks on the sidelines, do business, meet new ladies. She'd never learned to play much, but she always won a point or two from sheer distraction in her opponent caused by her short skirt that showed her fine legs, or they let her win, because some dude was thinking how much he'd like to steal her for an hour from J.A. She reached in the closet and touched the white skirt and top on a hanger. Silly costume. She found the tennis sneakers on the floor, barely worn. Who would have ever thought they were going to save her—walk with her to freedom?

Tennis shoes in hand, she drifted to the window and for a long moment stared down at the open fields as at protective arms ready to embrace her—or jaws to swallow her whole. Again she cooled her forehead against the glass. She tried to guess where Shooter the cop was hidden. She'd leave by the back door, via the loading docks where the trucks backed in and parked. He wouldn't know a thing about finding his way back there, would he? It was past time to get out of here. If J.A. came in now, it would be the disaster of her life. Or Shooter could come running up here any second now ready to tie J.A. to a table or whatever he had in mind. The ludicrousness of that, pleasant as it was to contemplate, made her laugh out loud grimly at the longshot that had been the cop's scheme. What would he do when he found her alone up here, with no pot of gold for him, after all? Might be plain cold cop again, disappointed, in need of some victim to save his day. Ah hell, maybe not, he wasn't a bad guy, and he'd believed in her. A pang of guilt surprised her, that she was skipping out on Shooter. He'd been using her, like all of them. Why the hell should she feel bad for *him?*

He was counting on her, had shown faith in her, yes, faith, in her. A sigh on her lips turned into an angry groan of impatience. He too had his profound and troubled dreams! What a note! Time to forget all the losers! She turned around to the window, hauled up her skirt, pulled down her panties, stuck out her bare ass and gave him his signal!

Back into the silver timecapsule with its funhouse walls, down the tower she plunged. She had to move her ass now. Poking out her nose, she saw seagreen walls of the tallceilinged stockrooms. She took off down a submarine passage, pushed open the door to a gangway, flew up a short stairs to the loading docks. Into their maw, cavernous and antiseptic, holding monstrous stacks of white cartons shrinkwrapped in plastic on pallets, she found her way

WISCONSIN

with her nose in the air showing disdain for all witnesses. Loud voices and the rumbling of a motor caught her short, and she composed herself and walked casually past the spotlit offices of nightshift guards and shipping clerks. Not much action going on this time of night but one long 18-wheeler backed up to dockside motor rumbling. Buried six feet deep in medicines and hospital supplies, a few dozen kilos of J.A.'s cocaine inside a case of anti-coagulants might be starting a journey to Detroit or St. Louis.

Two guys unloading boxes off a forklift leered at her inquisitively as she strode close by. She hoped she looked like one of the young executives who made an aggressive style of sneakers with business attire. Nobody messed with her. She clambered down the steel ladder. The night was still so oppressively hot. It seemed to swallow her. Beyond the big gray-and-red rumpend of the trailer, a no-man's land in a molten silver mist opened on the black fields. Slipping past the truck with its great longdistance wheels and mudcaked undercarriage, she felt her pitifulness and vulnerability to full measure. Escape on foot lost its ideal trappings, and the long, arduous tramp, life and death struggle ahead of her, jarred her soul to the quick. Yikes! She peered ahead into what looked like endless darkness. She squared her shoulders, and kept moving, feeling as obvious as a scarecrow in a cornfield. She had a feeling that back on the docks they were staring after her.

Over the black uneven road, strewn with big clods of hard dried clay and greasy threatening unrecognizable forms, her white tennis sneakers glowed ineffectually like little rabbity cotton puffs. The empty spaces before her overwhelmed her, threatened to drown, not hide her. A pragmatic realistic undeniable fear seeped in through cracks in her spirit she couldn't hold out against. She could feel it spread into her hands, her bones, a physical terror, the kind that had always overwhelmed her plans. The vision of lush meadows which would draw her to their breast was a lost memory in the dire and scratchy intimations of the real, dirty, dusty hike up the hot littered highway it was going to be until she caught a lift. What a night it was going to be. She banged her shinbone on a stray piece of iron rod sticking out in the road, rusty axle looked like, nearly sprawled, and laced the night with a strong oaths. She covered her mouth with her hand and wiped the tears from her eyes. Some fool might run out of the stockroom to help her. It felt

297

like she might have drawn blood. The tennis shoes were so flimsy, meant for a lady's game, not a trek through this back territory, and her legs were bare and sensitive. The stinging pain shot clear up to her thigh, and her heart fell with queasy anguish. For a few paces, she walked with a shivering limp, until the sharpness of it subsided to a dull throb. Why was it always like this for her? Weren't the right way and the easy way ever one for her?

For a moment she thought of Wisconsin tied to the floor of the cop's car. She wanted to go and untie him so they could flee together and her inability to imagine herself doing so made her sob aloud as she trudged onward. No, no, that was sadly over, she sobbed. It would just be to deliver herself to Shooter the cop again. Wisconsin by now was a pleasant dream she could hardly remember, a casualty of a reality she was finally gaining on. The cop would be thinking the same way and was probably back there with Wisconsin already, waiting for her to show up.

She moved ahead as fast as she could and still keep it casual. Just taking a breather or getting her exercise, she hoped it looked like to eyes still on her from the loading dock. Right, at three in the morning! Had it been lunch hour, an observer might have concluded this was how she took her exercise, a turn around the grounds, except for the fateful big bag she was carrying with nobody knew what odds and ends in it. Her big purse, stuffed with a brown parcel, slapped her hip jauntily and desperately. The loaders certainly must have wondered what she was up to climbing down the ladder at this hour. No telling what they thought, she didn't care. She was free now. She was on her way. She drew strength and reclaimed her soul more with every step.

There were no parking lots, except one for the truck trailers, no outbuildings, picnic tables, nothing of a civilian sort out here along the truck track, only a gate and guardshack at the end of it, then the desolate fields. A glance over her shoulder showed the lonely black and orange glow of the docks receding, no human silhouette standing out against their distant fire. She had made it!

A quarter mile ahead, the silhouettes of a low gate, the small guardshack, and a big shed pushed up black humps against the glimmering sky, marking the truck exit to Labs Road. The dark lump of a parked car beside them alarmed her when its headlights suddenly came on. The guard's car of course! It hadn't occurred to her there would be a guard out this way at night, but of course, some sleepy guy, or who could say? Maybe some suspicious, alert guard guy to badger her, arrest her, molest her probably, and they'd discover the mess in J.A.'s office. The car's motor revved.

Her mind began coming up with things to say to a guard, who shouldn't have been there this time of night in her scheme of things, but who of course in reality was always there. Each gambit she thought to try on him she rejected as too lame or too provocative. She wanted to run away but there was nothing to do and nowhere to run now but forward to meet him resolutely.

The dark gate, the solitude of the fields ahead, and scruffy woods beyond them drew her forward by a sinister persuasion, the con game of the universe on her she hoped it might not be just this one time. She clutched her slight hopes tight to her breast just the same and felt she would just keep walking till they stopped her or she wearily went under. The formless black road closed around her luminous white feet like the first small waves of an ocean to drown in. It was a different ordeal, seeming to bear no relation to any other, but her exhaustion and despair were all too familiar. Only her tiny hopes were new, the resilient kind that come to you when everything is over, call them last hopes, the kind God gave you. It was not her vision of a tramp to freedom through the warm fields when inspired for a moment she'd looked down on this scene from on high in the tower window. This was the real ordeal. She bit her lip almost to bleeding and kept to her springy stride with a will. It was now or never for her. She got ready to face down the guard.

The car that had been revving its motor by the gate lunged toward her, its headlights rising through white mists to blind her. What the heck, why were they coming for her? Couldn't they just wait till she walked up to them? She stepped back, hands raised to block the oncoming lights, dripping greasy phosphorescence. She was weird and tiny, gray and grainyskinned, about to be nabbed by the Labs' security force. Oh, she must look a fright too with her forehead bleeding and her shin scraped and her suit no longer crisp. She sought forlornly for her air of authority around here as J.A.'s girlfriend, the words that wouldn't make her out a victim, words she didn't know.

As the car loomed up, she saw she could turn it into the lucky break she needed. She'd find a way to coax a lift out of some lonely security fellow to the bus station or someplace. This was how she would get away unseen! Damn a walk in the woods. She'd get him to take her to the train station or probably the Hilton hotel for a cab, at least. Here he came—she steeled herself, got a grip, looked sexy, and cleared her brain for inspiration. A few plain words, and he'd be her meat. She stuck out a hip, opened her jacket, and let loose her finest toothy grin. The seductive words burst forth freely, her reward for getting up off that couch. She pulled back her jacket and thrust out her breasts. She grinned and flashed the gap in her teeth and put mayhem and victimhood in her eyes and the words sang through her ready with their near professional promise of helplessness and raw pleasure.

She figured she had him hunted down and trapped already. Then she saw the cab's crest. It wasn't a guard, it was a Chicago cop. He had come around back here waiting for her. He had outfoxed her one more time. He'd known she would run out the back. How could she have thought he wouldn't? How dumb of her not to know he would. He was a cop, wasn't he?

She'd been misjudging him since the moment she'd met him. The first thing he would have checked out was the backroad to this place. He had followed her since this morning, caught up with her at Luminati's, and even tracked her down on 18th Street. How could she have deceived herself that he wouldn't find her again now? She shouldn't have showed him that moon up there, beaming down royally at him to taunt him that she was running for it and meant to lose his ass. The cab rolled forward till it was right beside her, her eyes refusing to adjust to the shadows inside as it came.

"Rita, get in!"

She took a step back instead and stopped dumb as a statue in the glare. In amazement, then wonder, she peered past the dazzle of the headlights. It seemed she would stand there lost in thought forever. He had to reach out and draw her inside. It was being pulled out of a pit to warmth and safety when she'd lost all hope. It was too far to climb out of, to come back to, to remember.

There was such horror and despair to get past. The machinery of their escape was in motion before she could emerge from blank astonishment. She hunched against a blast of impossible ecstasy as the cab made an easy circle. Neither broke the awed silence. The cab driver nodded casually at the guard and they were gone into the road. In the indecipherable luck everything was so strange, in its miraculous turn to goodness in answer to a prayer she had never dared to pray. On a surge of joy she finally believed and her resistance gave way.

"How could you know I'd come out in back?" she gasped. It wasn't what she wanted to say.

"How did you know I'd be there at the back gate?" he said.

She refrained from an honest answer to that. Her confusion grew into a feeling of wordless grace. She had nearly forgotten the cab driver in her nightmare ordeal while never ceasing entirely to cherish a notion of him in the dream they had momentarily had together. But she had relinquished beyond redeeming all practical hope of their escape so that his face had ceased to come before her. Here he was again. It proved their souls were in communion beyond time and space, and they were meant to be together. She leaned her elbow against the dashboard so she could gaze into his eyes while he drove, and he could see her face and the road.

After everything, they were finally on their way again, on the unlikeliest trip, which each had harbored open and secret hopes for, counting themselves crazy for believing, it seemed so long ago, starcrossed lovers who had presumed to wish for so much, who knew so little, whose plans had been violently interrupted, who had lost everything, and found it, and been found, again.

To the North Woods—once again! Laughter, warm and world creating, burst from both their unknown throats, a shared joy that was almost agony, as appalling longedfor recognition broke upon them simultaneously like a sleepless hungover dawn, a new hope so irrational and pure it hurt, telling them they had come together, however they had done it, whoever they were by now, and however they were to make good their escape at last.

A lastditch faith had taken the cab driver to the back of the towers. He felt he was emerging into sweet air and clear meaning from a blind underpass, one which, though he'd chosen to enter it, was beyond the wishes let alone powers of anybody to have merely chosen. Why it was turning out right he didn't know, but it was, and he'd never doubted that it would, for no reason he could name in this world.

Had the cop ever driven a cab or limo, he might have been familiar with the almost limitless elasticity of those rubber tiedowns, if you had strength enough to stretch them out. Had he never noticed the nearly vertical trunklids of the liveries at O'Hare Airport gaping with boxes and bags held down by only those useful flexible straps? The cab driver had worked his way loose from his bonds, hardly to go after the cop in the cornfields, as Shooter paranoically had imagined. Knowing it would come, his wrists raw and almost bleeding, after nearly an hour he had struggled to his freedom. He'd thought about ripping out the copcar's spark wires and throwing them in the field, but decided not to. Pointless. He only wanted to forget the man, who had nearly taken Rita from him. He'd walked to his own car, by some sixth sense knowing about where it would be, or by the straight line to anywhere that takes a man true to what is his own. A magnet held an extra ignition key inside one of the Caddy's wheelwells.

Rita, falling into his arms, rubbing her cheek against his, had the idea an angel had brought it about. It was the approved of next step, the right road to salvation. Here was a man whom she had loved and despaired of, to whom she was happily beholden by various dubious moves of her own, somebody she didn't deserve, a nice guy, who would actually help her, as she'd help him, and they would not mix poison with their nurture.

"You always show up just when I need ya. It must be a sign." She threw her arms around his head. "All the trouble I caused you. I thought ya woulda put me down," she whispered in his ear.

"I could've kicked myself for not telling ya about that cop. I should've called you as soon as he stopped me, before I gave the package to Rodriguez."

It was more than she could bear to hear that name and remember the chance she'd taken and the near loss it recalled, and she opened her mouth to blurt something wildly true that she did not know yet, and clamped her lips over his mouth instead, as if her tongue could transmit truth that escaped her guilty mind in all her searching for it, without words not yet to be spoken or trusted, could seal all outstanding accounts, and lick things clean.

Having trepidatiously walked up the dirt road a quarter mile thinking to assay the possibilities of the nearest farmhouse, Bobby had been discouraged by the intermittent barking of the dog warning of his approach. His nerve had failed, or perhaps wisdom intervened. He'd never had his drawers in a knot like this before, in fact, *no drawers 't'all.* His appearance naked and in handcuffs might dismay the most Christian farmer, if it was his luck to find such a one, even if awoken by shouts of "Two hundred dollars! I got two hundred dollars fer ya!" which was the style in which he had planned to announce himself. Particularly in the middle of the night, he might get shot. It would be best to wait for daybreak—if then. He had retreated back down into the low ground beside Swamp Creek where in the little glade into which he had earlier been flung he felt oddly secure, if hardly comfortable, for it was a very warm night. He was able to keep his thoughts together, not to panic, and to believe that he would see the night through. But his condition was pretty stark and awful, especially the handcuffs.

He wondered at himself going back to exactly this unwelcoming low spot, but being near the farm buildings had only felt like danger and trouble, and it is a peculiar thing, but sometimes the last place he has been, no matter how poor it may be, feels like home, to a roving man. The prick of the occasional mosquito he inured himself to, since he couldn't brush it away. It was not much to bear, comparatively speaking. There really weren't that many mosquitoes, strangely, as if this desolate spot under the bridge were too hopeless even for bugs.

He felt familiar with these old woods. His people were from the country, anyhow. Maybe that is where he would head after this, to the piney woods of southwest Georgia. You could hide down there from the likes of Pepe or the cops. Or it would be someplace new he'd never thought of that God would show him.

Things would look different tomorrow in the light. He dropped to the ground and invited his mind but there wasn't much. Sitting with his shoulder against a tree, occasionally laughing pitifully to himself, but muttering significantly, "Don' thow me in no fuckin brier patch, muhfucker, ha ha ha," now and again, and congratulating himself on still having both his knees, remembering mad dog Pageant Teagarden, how it could have been much worse, nearly shedding a tear of fright and self-pity, he heard running feet.

Running feet! He heard it in fear and trembling that something new and bad would come again, but it could be *help*, couldn't it? He kept still and listened intently.

People thought they were silent but the woods were full of sounds if you ever listened. He imagined for an instant he'd been hearing things in the ticking forest but the footfalls grew louder, *pat, pat, pat, PAT, PAT, PAT. . . .*

Who could be running up this deserted road in the middle of the night? They were nearly upon him, or his part of the road, heading toward the bridge. Maybe it was someone else in straits too, running for his life, and they would be friends.

He rose and, stepping deftly over the forest debris, hid himself behind a roadside bush. Peeping out, he waited for the riddle to solve itself and the running person to appear through the mists. Actually it sounded like more than one, and there was a peculiar jingling.

Around the bend came a jogger wearing pink shorts and an irridescent skintight tanktop, a dog trailing behind her.

Just as the jogger and her dog passed by him, Bobby in his numbed confusion understood it was his moment to act, and he thrust out his head through the bullrushes, hiding his naked self with leaves, and not knowing what to say or how to say it, cried, "Don't be frightened, maam! It's only ol Bre'er Rabbit here! Only ol Bre'er Rabbit! Please help!" And he grinned as ingratiatingly as he knew how and waved entreatingly while keeping his naked body below the neck hidden behind the scratchy brambles.

The force of her shock caused the jogger to trip, and as she nearly sprawled on the ground, she craned her neck wildly to look around. "Oh fuck, you scared me!" she screamed. Thinking his luck had turned, Bobby walked forth. Then, one more look at him and she stopped being a jogger and became a sprinter and ran up the road as fast as her legs could take her, and her dog careened in joy. She ran faster than she ever had in her jogging life. She would have set a record for the women's hundred.

Bobby in the road mulled over the sorry state of human relations. In the Bible how often women and others helped poor wayfarers in desperate circumstances like himself. The woman at the well who gave Christ a drink of water and the good Samaritan who bound up the wounds of a stranger and all. He remembered these stories dimly from his childhood. No African American youth escapes the influence of the Bible entirely, even one on an early career path to becoming a gangster. An elderly aunt who had had nominal charge of him after his mother had gone to prison had taken Bobby to Sunday School on several occasions, and he had listened to the stories he heard there. His thoughts turned to God.

The jogger and her dog had gone around a bend in the road. Later, had she stopped and helped him, he would have sent her thousands in remembrance. It was partly his fault, as his thought process was nearly paralyzed by his nakedness, and he hadn't found the right words to approach her with. In the Bible the people in the stories often had a good conversation. He forgave her but he would rather have sent her thousands.

Maybe dawn approached if people were jogging, although he didn't think that much time had passed. He went back to the side of the creek and waited for the sun to rise. It might be the sun to rise was what it'd take to inspire in him a plan. The farmer would be able to deal with it in the morning, maybe. People's natural fears subsided in the day. He'd walk straight up, and they'd have to do something for him. He wasn't wanted for anything lately, and he'd tell some kind of story, a wad of money stuck out in his hand.

An unearthly timelessness began to abide in the shadowy forsaken glade. The terrible creek burbled inexorably past. The air finally lost a bit of its sullen heat, but not much. No breeze stirred. Instead of lightening, the night deepened. He was thirsty. The wait became long. The cuffs chewed into his sore wrists when he moved.

He contemplated his condition. It was not promising. It became hard to bear. He lay on his side and stared through the intertwined branches at a velvet black starless patch of sky, at what he prayed was the darkness before a dawn. "Jesus, he'p me!" he muttered.

What he had was to go to the end of this hallway, to the corner office on this floor on this side of the tower, if his calculations were correct, and ascertain that Rita was gone, as he knew that she would be, and did not need his help, which he also knew. He knew very well she did not want his help, and that she would no longer be in the man's office suite. But he had to be sure. He was doing this for himself, not her.

Only to the end of the corridor, but it was a long walk. His footfalls echoed weirdly in the empty and forlorn tower. Rita had taken this walk an hour ago.

"If you leave the path, each step back be a thousand miles!" He heard the beloved voice. He thought that his father was near.

The door was wide open. He walked through it past a well-ordered secretary's station to a big inner office and braced himself in the doorframe with both hands and stared at the carnage as after a hurricane.

Broken glass sparkled like rare jewels heaped and scattered all over the floor. A tall floorlamp stood upside down on its accordioned white shade, cabinets rested against one another ripped from the wall, shelves were swept clean. Chairs with their upholstery gashed out, objets d'art stamped on and kicked to the corners, the painting of the angel on a horse hanging down in torn strips—everything the man owned was sliced up or broken to bits.

He couldn't take a step without his foot crunching in her created chaos. A translucent flame sprang up from everything.

Some tornup photographs, amidst the spilled contents of a desk drawer, arrested his eye. He had an eye for what was wrong in any scene. They held him. They reminded him of the cab driver's pictures on the cab's front seat, had she torn them. And why would she? With a shudder, he doubted it. He'd thought it was him in the fields but it was only the deer. The poor lovesick guy, who was still tied up in his car, probably another colossal error in judgment he was going to have to fix somehow, could not have been involved in anything like this. He gazed down at the pieces of the tornup photos at his feet with a sickening hollow dread.

He didn't want to see it, but at last he knelt and slowly arranged the pieces with a kind of care, like assembling a known or not difficult to figure out puzzle, the reddened, splayed, bound arms and legs, the weird animal and fanciful masks, like Disney creations gone rabid and mad. He'd known it without ever picturing it like this or wanting to. He came to the one of the executioner's victim in the black hood. He got off his knees and went to the window, unaccustomed tears in his eyes.

He thought of her when he had finally realized her spunk and courage, when he'd seen her fumbling with the heavy hood of the Lincoln in the parking lot this afternoon, preparing her escape, that wonderful moment when she had at last slammed the heavy hood down. He had understood her then. He had been her secret accomplice at that triumphant moment.

He stared out the window into the night at the dead stars and dirty towns. A silence prevailed in the torn apart office suite like the end of the world, with all the tears shed and dried up. He hoped Rita was traveling fast. He wondered what she had pulled out of the hat this time, and how she was traveling. He saw her again walking out of Jackie's joint this morning without a word or a look, so lost, so seemingly without light, such a pitiful thing. He had watched her hail a cab and almost let her go then, and now he'd have to.

His own life, the routine life of the street, grueling, petty, violent, racist, monotonous, malignant, and sometimes redeeming, raked him with frank longing. Man, he wanted a drink. He went over and poked with his foot in a mashed cabinet which had apparently been a liquor cabinet. Broken bottles lay about underneath. He searched around with his toe. Sure enough, happily not every one of them had shattered when she'd swept them off the shelf and tossed things onto them, and in the rubble, of all lovely things, was a new fifth of J&B, still whole. It peeped out like cheerfulness itself from the mess. He pulled it out and confronted it with a feeling of common, ordinary blessing.

He righted a chair and sat down at the man's disfigured desk and almost had a drink. Looking at the deep scratches she'd made on the desktop he raised the bottle to her. Then he found himself staring at the bottle for a long time. The strange idea came to him that the last thing he needed was another drink. The run through the woods, the race up the tower to this violent desolation, had left him drained and sober. He had the feeling he was seeing things with clarity. He did not want to lose this feeling and decided not to drink more.

He had two guys tied up out there, one in handcuffs naked as a squirrel in the woods, the other wound in rubber tiedowns in the back of his car. He was going to have to go out there and rescue them both. Bobby'd had a deal with her, maybe he'd been going to help her too. Perhaps Bobby and even the cab driver had been better friends to her than he had. The strange thought hit him that the cab driver had been trying to help her, too. This made him suddenly conceive of the cab driver as an actual person, as a human being, you might even say, someone who could be in love, who could be unselfish. He remembered how he'd sent him to his fate with a bag of talcum powder for some gangsters. He had damn near almost plugged Bobby too. He shuddered at all he had done. His thoughts moved with unwonted fellow-feeling.

The right path had become such a routine to him that he had lost it. How precious the ordinary progress, the righteous habit. As he gazed about him at Rita's inspired act of destruction, a mighty self-liberating gesture as it must be, so vivid he found himself being pulled along after her, into a higher air, something that had coiled noose tight in him relaxed. An unexpected lightness of spirit rose in him, the witness. Presently he strolled through the room, on his way out, kicking things like a boy let loose in a junkyard. Yes, it seemed to him a wounded heart might almost heal after a piece of work like this.

"Go, baby!" he murmured.

308

Bobby heard a car approaching. It drew him to his feet in a paroxysm of weary will and he decided he would throw himself under its wheels and beg for mercy from its occupants, shouting, "Two hundred dollars! Help me please! I been kidnapped and left for dead! Two hundred dollars fer ya!" He couldn't think of any better to say. The direct approach, mentioning money, would be best. His lips twitched anticipating his cry.

Let them call the cops. He had plenty of stories always ready. He started forward through the trees to run directly in front of it, but as here came the car around the curve, at the last moment acute apprehension at his nakedness in handcuffs, an oppressive memory of the jogger's shocked reaction, and sheer numbness that had set in with the wait made him falter. He was never going to get out of here!

He was going to have to deal with it before he passed out and perished, and he was beside himself with regret when he thought he saw a cab speed by. A cab out in these woods! Now that was what cabs were for, to rescue strays like himself, and a cab driver would have known the meaning of two hundred dollars if nobody else would, the thiefs, the goniffs. Too fast it was gone! He caught a glimpse of the toplight like a little crown on the roof, saw the big bull's-eye on its door. One of the local cabs, the dude would have probably sped up and passed him by, when he saw not only a black guy but handcuffed and *buck nekkid!* With his luck it would have been that professor cat anyway.

At least he had missed that guy. In this way he consoled himself and felt better, as much as Armchair often helped people out in his peculiar way, even by recalling him, the mere thought of him, gratitude for a near miss of him.

Then through a gap in the trees he saw it was that big old Cadillac cab that had been following them at this very spot when Shooter had thrown him in the woods. While taking an unholy beating in the road he had seen the big frontend of the white Cadillac out of the corner of his eye. Why was that wrong cab come back here? It was an evil sign and he was glad he hadn't tried to stop that cab either.

But in the last instant he couldn't believe what he saw. He must be losing it—he had seen Rita in the frontseat driving the cab! Well, he must be on the edge of total exhaustion at death's door. Her face was transfixed and pale and blessed like an angel's flying through space. Just as the cab with Rita driving it vanished past him forever, something flew out of its window and whizzed in an arc like love itself over the brambles and through the limbs of the trees to thump softly to the ground no more than forty feet from where he languished, as if dropped from heaven.

His senses fastened firmly on the spot on the forest floor from which the heartening *thump* had come. Crooning to himself now, he poked around in the warm moss and roots with his bare toes. He knew what he was feeling for. If her appearance on the scene driving a taxicab was a shock, what she had cast his way could be no mystery. He had been waiting for his luck to change for years and years, and this was it, in his extremity. His toe struck the bag of cocaine, the real one. Dear Rita!

He looked about him and marked the peculiar shape of the nearest tree, which looked like a woman with her two arms outstretched in fright, or to embrace you, he wasn't sure which. He sat down against it. He thought he might die here and he imagined how, just like in the movies, he would meet his end while the gold lay at his feet. He curled into a ball at the foot of the woman-shaped tree. A man who had had his life and his knees saved from an insane policeman on a rampage by an Uncle Remus ruse and a bag of whitegold flung almost on his head by a passing angel owed

310

something serious in return to his Creator, he knew, but what was the question. Surely God would keep him alive to figure it out. He wouldn't let him die now in the middle of the story. In the movies that happened, but only to godless men.

He would do good with it and help the needy! He'd be honorable and generous with good fortune. He thought of friends whom he might help. His friends and the needy were mostly the same thing. He was very thirsty and his wrists were killing him. He hoped he wasn't thinking these fine thoughts just to impress God into removing the cuffs and getting him some trousers.

His eyes didn't leave the road but he could feel her eyes asking something of him. He didn't know what it was. Whatever it was, it would be all right with him.

It would be all right, whatever they did, she knew. Such a strange, rich freedom between two people was certainly new in her experience. Wisconsin's presence, to be sitting beside him again, left her happily floating, as if anything were possible now, and she really didn't know what could be coming next, but it would be good. He had his own thoughts, and she wondered what they were.

"A penny for your thoughts."

"They're worth a penny! I don't have any thoughts except of you, Rita. *We're on our way!* I haven't been driving these old roads for nothin. Nothin to catch us now! We're on a road that cop don't know exists. That old man neither. We're leavin the city behind. Rita, we're gone now!"

"Don't worry about that cop," she muttered, thinking of how he had tied Wisconsin to his floorboards.

"Not any more."

"He's standing out in the damn cornfield. He wanted to take me to Africa to see the lions."

"He did?" said the cab driver, wonderingly.

Surely, with the two of them, the words *use or be used* need never apply. Good fishing was promised by a rapport like theirs. Soft, spacious days, and big, starry nights. She shivered at the memory of a profound coziness, while an Indian on the label of a beer bottle winked her a signal over the years like a magic ruby. Her father had let her sit up on the barstool next to him like a big girl. That was when she had belonged.

They had taken several turns and she no longer had the slightest idea where they were if she ever had except that they were headed by these back roads for the Wisconsin border, and thence onward far north, far past all the cities and towns to the lakes of the North Woods. They were passing through a dense woods already, dark and still, where life came from, nature's womb. Could that be water shimmering through the trees? It was like being in the North Woods already. Could she be heading toward remembered bliss at last?

Out of such fruition, the devastating notion she'd entertained earlier that J.A. had actually let her go was suddenly born anew— and whether an infant tender and mild or an inconceivable monstrous birth—this time a certain conviction. She really had been given her freedom, she now thought, when he'd put her in Wisconsin's friend's cab in front of Luminati's restaurant after Bobby had done his dash out the door. He'd done with her!

Then it could only mean, as she had feared—she thought back to the moment, tried to see into his hooded eyes—she had nearly doublecrossed herself, going back. J.A. was capable of the grand gesture, and when he made one he meant it to stick. He had been telling her goodbye, she'd been worth it, don't come back no more—take what you are taking and good luck to us all! Imagine that, cast off like a note in a bottle, after everything.

But it was for keeps, and there she'd turned up again, having been given her freedom and whatever she could take with her, had the courage to rip off. There had been nothing to fear. But she'd been very afraid. It was a poignant and terrible understanding, like having one of the horrid masks lifted from her ugly face and having one more humiliating insight into her soul's enslaved condition shoved down her craw. Even if the cop had made her do it, she had gone crawling back to him. She was glad she had smashed up his office. She wished she could have burned down the whole tower.

As if wonder followed wonder, it came to her that maybe poor greedy Shooter did wish her well, too, as he had claimed, it might be so, maybe he really did, and he never would have harmed her either. All he'd wanted was his own getaway. He would never pursue her any more now. He would let her go, too. He would have to since she was gone. Was there nothing left to flee or fear? It didn't matter because she was her own now, her own. If they had finally had to let her go, it was because she had made the first move all on her own and succeeded finally. She had made good her escape from them both, by her wits, somehow.

You didn't give somebody her freedom even if you wanted to. Someone's freedom wasn't anybody else's to give. It wasn't givable, only takeable. You took it for yourself or not at all. She might have been living in a gleaming castle made of marble, or she might be in a mud hut in Africa, even lying in the mud like Bobby in the creek right now, it didn't matter, you made your freedom out of marble or mud, whatever came to hand, whatever you had, as long as it was your hand that grasped and did it. And the proof of this was that it was never finished and you had to keep on making it every minute, or you might lose it again, she saw.

She had a long way to go before she'd ever be sure of herself as *free*. She had outfoxed her devils. But she had to keep outfoxing them. It made her fear them all the more, like looking back down into the abyss, as if they were monsters out of her own inmost dreams that could re-create themselves, shadows that belonged to her and could pop up again anywhere, anytime in the road ahead. When she thought of where she had been and where she was still coming from right now, it struck her like a hard, raking slap on the jaw how far she had to go, on her own, her own. The force of this jarring thought brought a cruel wave of clarity.

313

A pickup truck suddenly swerved blindly out in front of them from a forest track—from out of nowhere it seemed—and the cab driver had to hit his brakes.

"Hey look at the bumper!" he cried leaning forward. "Look at that—ESCAPE TO WISCONSIN! There's our sign!"

"It's a sign all right," she laughed, "a bumper sign like on half the bumpers in Chicago."

"Okay! Okay!" He laughed too, and gave her a squeeze.

Through the window soft green boughs whispered, deep waters glimmered, a polka dance played down memory lane, an Indian on a beer bottle winked at her, and the bumper sticker disappeared in the faint wash of their headlights as the pickup truck sped ahead.

The thing was there were signs that weren't meant for you.

"Wisconsin, I gotta be alone."

Rita, staring out the window at the passing blackness, covered her face with her hands. The blackness became complete. As much as she had showed herself to him a moment ago, she hid from him now, for, suddenly, she was already alone.

"What?—Alone?" exclaimed the cab driver incredulously.

"Alone, man . . . that's what I said."

"But we found each other!"

"A sign. I been thinkin about that. Ya never know about signs. I met J.A. at the race track. I thought I'd won. I thought it was a sign. It was a sign all right. I don't know what I feel. I've lost the hang of it. I been wearin masks, man, deeper down than I knew. I don't know what's a mask an what aint no more. I don't know what's *me.*"

"But why did we find each other? We're together now. We've made it, we're on our way, Rita. I'm in your corner!"

"My corner! Ho ho. It's a corner I want out of. You couldn't begin to understand what's in my corner," she said. And to herself she thought, *And when the day comes when you find out what's been in my corner . . .*

"Rita, life is a card game without rules an no limit—"

"Tell me."

"You got to have an ace. Something they can't take away. You draw the ace, you stop thinking. You leave the game a winner. You make something of it."

"I know, Wisconsin. I know it."

314

"I know you been in trouble, Rita, since the moment I laid eyes on you. I told you so. What do you think I've been doing? Don't you think I know it? You'd be surprised what I could understand and do understand. I know what feeling good is too and how to heal your soul when you finally get ready to—an we're ready! We're goin to the *North Woods.* We said so."

She stared ahead at the black road and mused to herself, *I thought I was wearing masks, but what if those were my real faces?*

"Wisconsin?" she said.

"Yes?"

"Really. I got to be alone."

"Rita, that's not how the story goes!"

"It's a different story!"

Exactly what would it all be to him, tomorrow, on the cab post, if he lost her after this? He'd come this far with her. He'd found her once, and now he'd found her again. Only to lose her now.

An old memory came to him sharply and unaccountably of an incident he had always been a little ambiguous about. He had had a call to a nice residence in the town of Libertyville, on a warm bright summer afternoon, the kind of shimmering somnolent day that seems to hold no surprises. To his astonishment the fare had not appeared through the front doorway of the prosperous home, but, throwing a suitcase out first, had jumped out through a side window. A young girl had run to the cab and asked to be taken to O'Hare Airport. This girl told him a lurid tale of emotional abuse. She was clearly underage. He had suggested to her that maybe it wasn't as bad as all that, and did she really know where she was going, and maybe she would like to go back home again. But she had been adamant, and tearfully she had begged him to keep going, which he had done. He was a cab driver. His job was to take people where they wanted to go, not question the destination. His role was to give people that freedom. Even kids, he had decided. God would take it from there. He could still see her small form heading into the terminal, hopeful and forlorn. Once again, he decided he had been right in helping the child escape.

He stopped the car in the middle of the empty road, opened the door, and got out.

"Hey," she said, "where ya goin?"

"Fishing, night fishing, or for a hike, who cares," he smiled at her. "I don't know."

"A hike? Fishing? Where are we? Take me to the bus station, Wisconsin! We're out in a field! In the middle of the night."

"I know where I am. Do you know where you are? You'll find your way. Take the car, if you have to be alone. Go on. Drive yourself wherever you want to go. The car's all yours. That's what a cab is for, to take you where you want to go. I don't want it without you in it, Rita. Wisconsin is straight ahead of you. You can take this old road right over the line and keep heading north about four hundred miles to the North Country—the one you remember— you'll get there."

If she saw it different, if she wanted a different ride, he helped people take the ride they wanted. Tomorrow his car would be a hollow shell that would mock him, without her in it. Let her be alone right now, and take the car. She was younger than he was, not as young as that kid by any means he had helped escape to the airport. He wanted her to get away from whatever troubled her here to wherever it was she wanted to get to, even if it wasn't with him. If he couldn't take her there, let his cab take her by itself. He wondered if she would do it, take the car and drive away by herself.

"Your *Cadillac?* You're a funny guy, Wisconsin."

"You're not exactly average either, Rita." He found himself smiling when he ought to be crying. "I can make a new car like this!" He snapped his fingers. "I can create one out of smoke!" That wasn't quite true.

"I think I've forgotten how to drive," she murmured. "I don't have a license. I wonder where I am."

"Nobody's going to pull a cab over. Don't run any redlights!"

"I can't leave you out in the woods. I can't take your cab."

"To you it's the woods. It's home to me."

He had tried to let her go more than once tonight, and now he'd try again. But it got harder every time. He walked a few steps away, letting her go. He was fighting the only way he knew how now. Perhaps it would shock her into staying.

While they spoke she had slid over behind the wheel, the more to keep close to him than to have taken the wheel. But now with one hand she gripped the wheel. She looked at him in the night. Through some patches of heavy wet clouds the muted starlight made everything more real and alive in its mystery than hard sunlight ever did. He was a good person, she thought, and she was not. He had knelt down on one knee in the road. She dangled a foot out the door, as she gazed at him, touching the ground he knelt on. One thing she was sure of, it would not be fair to him if she stayed. He dropped some stones from his hand, not looking at her.

The headlights washed over him when she accidentally put it in reverse and for a second couldn't find the brake. When she did, she killed the motor, and couldn't find the key. A confusion of hope, fear, weariness, and awe racketed through her. Love, when it comes, don't fight it, her mother had said. There was something she needed to know. She jumped out, pulling off her jacket as she ran to his side.

"Look at me!"

He did. In a violent gesture as though thrusting a blade into his heart she peeled her high-necked, long-sleeved blouse over her head, her arms sinking past her sudden nakedness. Whether it was the shadows, or the healing light of the night, or truly something that was not in him to see, if it was her scars she had meant him to see, no matter how he drank her in, he never did.

She got behind the wheel again and after a desperate search was able to find the key and start the engine with a trembling hand. The rigid scars on her neck must have stood out blue and obscene. He had seemed oblivious to them or at least had given no sign of seeing them. That was the last thing she had expected. She had hoped to be absolved, in his eyes, by some kind word of his, perhaps, but not that he should overlook such marks from hell entirely. But what had she expected? Far from reassuring her, it blew her mind so she wanted to get far, far away, fast. Whatever he saw when he looked at her she could never possibly be.

"Wisconsin, your *Cadillac?*" She smiled faintly at him in the night one last time.

He didn't reply but gazed steadily and calmly at her without noticing her smile.

A nice guy like him could not possibly understand a mistaken soul like hers, she thought. He was in his world. She didn't believe he was dissembling to get her to stay. But the real question was not who he thought she was, but what she thought, who she wanted to be, and she didn't know. She had to find out for herself. There wasn't anything wrong with that, was there?

"It don't feel right taking your car," she frowned at the thought of depriving him of his cab.

"You can bring it back to me sometime."

"Yeah. I don't even know where I'm at," she said softly, painfully aware of both levels of her meaning. The way she said it

318

sounded a little childish, even peevish, he thought, but at the same time it was profoundly touching.

"You haven't been there since you were a kid, really, have you? That peaceful place. That peaceful lake you want is about four hundred miles from here straight north. Go on! Good luck! You'll find your way, won't you, Rita?"

"Yes, Wisconsin. I am going to try."

Anything was possible now she had made her break, made good her escape, and defeated all her demons. But still she hesitated behind the wheel, in the big car on the deserted road.

She had no idea what would happen now, or what she was capable of. Life had almost flipped rightside up again, and she didn't know what to make of it. She was going to have to think things over and find out about them, a duty to herself and God she felt sure she had now, and which she would have shirked had she stayed with Wisconsin and let him try to solve the problem for her.

She took off faster than she intended, but she hadn't driven a car in years and she'd barely learned how to begin with. The tires spun in the dirt. For the first two hundred feet the Cadillac wandered from shoulder to shoulder.

Grit struck his legs like birdshot and a fine dust flew into his eyes as she burned away. He stood in the road and watched her go into the darkness erratically. Quickly, the taillights were no more than cigarette embers in the night.

There were certain common skills Rita had never mastered. It had been a long time since she'd tried any driving. But though her hands were sweating on the wheel, she was doing better than she'd expected and was at least keeping the big boat on the road. Tears started in her eyes but she didn't dare lift her hand from the wheel to brush them away, and down they ran and at last dripped from her chin. She silently sobbed, and retched, knowing the horror that had to come out. Even Wisconsin she could forgive for trying to put one more mask on her with his clever love. But herself? She had to *be* with herself a while.

On the curves the tires skidded in the gravel and she almost lost control. She pressed the accelerator until the big car was careening over the dirt road as fast as she could go and still hang onto the wheel. She was surprising herself by not winding up in the ditch. The speed felt wonderful, rough, and clean. So far the ride seemed true, and she felt headed in the right direction, and in her heart she honored Wisconsin in some strange true way by having taken his car, even though it seemed a crazy thing to do. The tears were drying on her crusted cheeks, stinging in her eyes.

At a sharp bend in the road the bag of cocaine slipped out of her purse and fell heavily off the seat to slap against her ankle, an insulting reminder of everything ugly she would like to leave behind. The road dipped and she suddenly thought she recognized the spot where Shooter had stripped poor Bobby naked and shoved him into the woods. Yes, there was that same narrow bridge over a dirty creek just ahead where Bobby had plunged after having been beaten senseless. This was the very place where that horror show had made her shiver to the depths of her soul as she shivered now. Was he out there yet? Must be! Naked, whipped, and chained. The big car breasted the bridge over Swamp Creek at high speed, hitting the timbers too hard, bouncing ponderously on its springs, its headlights sweeping the treetops.

When the last red glow of the taillights was snuffed out like a cigarette butt crushed in the dirt as she went around the bend, he had a bad moment. It was one thing to propose she take his car and another thing to watch her do it. He began walking aimlessly. Then he stopped dead. What had he just done? He was suddenly on foot, a strange condition. He became acutely aware he no longer had his car. He felt naked and wholly out of his element without his car. Apparently he had given away his Cadillac. It was more than a little shocking.

Then again, it was one thing to be without his car, and another to have really lost Rita. Compared to that, seeing his Cadillac go into the blackness was no more painful than one of the stones falling to the ground that he had been counting in his hand. Against losing his car, it even felt warm and good, like she was with him yet, that she was driving it. He hadn't exactly lost his car, it had entirely changed its meaning for him, even as it vanished. It had been on the verge of becoming a tin can, a fetish, a miserly remnant hoarded against the passage of beauty. It had always been a cool ride, suddenly it acquired mystery.

He stumbled on a ways. Looked at in a cold light, it was a crazy, impractical thing to have done. If it had been a ruse to get her to stay, it had backfired.

He became aware of where he was. Just past the next thick stand of trees, on the corner of an even narrower dirt crossroad, was a friend of his, an old farmer's house, who had had so many accidents and tickets the judge had yanked his license and wouldn't let him drive anymore. He took him out shopping or for a drink and dinner, someplace or other, every week or two. The first time he met him it was a ride to the courthouse. The old guy, who was over ninety, was by now the kind of ride and the kind of friend they could go a long ways not talking, just comfortable together in silence. He could dimly see a corner of the roof of the farmhouse through the trees. He was hungry, and the old man, who was an early riser, would be making breakfast soon enough.

He strode briskly toward the farmhouse now that he had a destination, which disappeared behind the black trees as he drew near. He found he was enjoying the motion, the tramp on the dark road. It revived him to move his limbs sharply, and made him feel hopeful. Suddenly he felt light. It felt good swinging along on foot. He felt almost happy in a bittersweet, resigned way. It might not last. How strange, without his ride. And Rita gone on down the road in it. He hoped she got there, wherever it was. Strangely, having given her his car made losing her bearable. Was he a fool?

Later, he would call Armchair to pick him up at the farm. He wanted to tell Armchair *this* story and see his face then. He had lost her, but he thought he had gained something after all in exchange, though maybe he was kidding himself, and it was mysterious, whatever it was. Armchair's reaction might throw unexpected light on things, as it often did, although not always. Maybe the cops would find the cab at the train station.

After ten minutes' walk, he reached the door of the old farmhouse, which was back around the side. Just reaching out to knock on the paintpeeling old screendoor with the weeds encroaching around it, he suddenly glimpsed over his shoulder slowly passing on the Swamp Creek road an alarmingly familiar plaingreen car. He hesitated with his knuckles in the air an inch from the screendoor about to rap on it. Of all the damn things, if it wasn't that miserable cop, crawling up the road in fits and starts. He turned clear around to stare. He couldn't believe he was seeing that man again he'd just escaped from. Not looking for himself, he trusted. Why would he now? He stepped back into the shadows to be on the safe side. He had wanted to take her to see the lions in Africa, she'd said. If he was still chasing Rita, he was moving too slow. She had a head of steam this time. The plaincar disappeared up the road, braking and accelerating awkwardly like he was searching for something along the roadside, his soul maybe, hunched over the wheel peering to the side into the woods. He wondered how she had gotten away from him. He hadn't thought to ask her. A wave of absolving feeling passed over him for them all, even the cop. What a night of mad desire it had been.

The motor quenched as the first rays of dawn stabbed past thick wads of dirty looking clouds resting on the treetops. A blast of heat from the whole sky heralded the sunrise. He turned back to the screendoor, but before he could knock, a shout from inside the farmhouse when the old man spied him on his doorstep stayed his hand.

"You here so early? Just in time for breakfast!" cried the old farmer giving the sagging screendoor a firm push outward. The porchlight came on, but it was not needed now.

"Good, cuz I am hungry, been up all night," he said, catching the screen on the back of his hand, smiling at his friend.

"Where's your car?" He peered around out the door.

"Never mind."

He thought of Rita speeding ahead on the road, going where only she knew. He hoped she got there. He felt a cab driver's faith she would. The people always got where they needed to go, and she would too. He was sure she would. And himself? Maybe he'd do something different than drive a cab for a while. Something new. He'd have to today anyway.

"What ya been up to, boy?"

"Breakin my rule, Pop!" He laughed. Hey, love was a catch-as-catch-can business, wasn't it? It was hard to let her go.

He walked inside the farmhouse, whose backdoor had over the years by long usage finally become its frontdoor. The original frontdoor had in fact at some point been nailed shut. The first room you entered was the kitchen.

"Gettin involved with the fares!"

He sat down at the kitchen table, and let her go.

Bobby felt the weight of blessing. He would not be selfish with good fortune. He would spend generously and give to friends. Dimly he suspected that sheer exhaustion and the cruel facts of his condition were making him sentimental and lending him noble impulses his bad habits and normal hedonism would lead him to go back on later. This possibility troubled him sincerely.

As he mulled it over, and the first glow of dawn insinuated itself through the glen, a new motor sounded its approach. This time he didn't budge. Probably just a commuter now with the dawn. They would run him over if he went out there in their rush to get to work.

"Damn traffic jam," he mumbled, nestling down in the soft rotten leaves. Let whatever come and find *him*. He had had his luck. He must find his way out of here but he wasn't thinking of just running out in the road any more until he had a firm and workable plan. He awaited the practical means of his escape in the form of some inspiration from God.

In contrast to Rita in the cab, this car seemed to be coming along at a crawl. As it came near, he gave a start as he heard a familiar voice call him by his name.

"*Bobby!* . . . *Fist!* . . . You out there somewhere, I know! I got your clothes for ya. Lemme take ya home, Bobby!"

It was the voice of a devil. He rose straight to his feet in horror, thinking to flee. If this didn't beat all, now why would he be coming back except to shoot him, for real? The car passed by at an imponderable one mile an hour. It stopped just past the bridge.

To deceive him, finish the job and kill him this time. Still, he took a tentative, stealthy step, not to flee, but to look. He heard the car roll forward again slowly. Something compelled him against his will to the roadside for a peek.

Carefully, keeping low, he peered through the brush and would have sneered as he caught sight of the Shooter's receding trunk lid except within it were his trousers, jacket, shoes, and drawers—and he was damn it naked, handcuffed, and lost near dead in the woods. The car entered a patch of the coming dawn and dustily gleamed. Then it stopped again at exactly the uprise where he had been stripped and thrown down into the brier patch.

"Bobby, I want to *help you!* I'm goin home now! You *nekkid!* Lemme take off them cuffs. . . . I'm *sorry!*"

He was sorry? He would help him? The man unbelievably sounded contrite and sincere. Damn if it didn't sound like he had regained good sense. Something must have happened to him out there. Rita had escaped him for one thing, he had seen that she had. He had lost hold of her somehow and she was gone in a cab. There was an awful ring to Shooter's cries. His plans to rob that man must have certainly gone awry.

He had been going to shoot off his knee. He might have bled to death out here. Anyways he had thrown him in the briers to suffer all night long and maybe die. Now the man who had been going to shoot him had returned to *help* him, thinking better of it? He was sorry for it? He had ranked his score, ruined his Hawaiian vacation, stolen his girl, and beaten him badly. He stood stubbornly, and finally returned to his place in the glade. Shooter wished to salve his own soul, was all. If it could be that he had had a change of heart and meant to mend his ways, well, it was his mess to clean up. Let him clean it, if he could.

Still, he was affected by his gesture, as unexpected in its way as Rita's had been, who had done him a mysterious kindness. The sun was just rising and he was already getting damn baked. *Who else would get him out of here?* He found he had somewhat forgiven him in spite of everything, somehow. But he thought better of it. Don't cast your pearls before swine, he remembered vaguely. Something had been happening to him in here, too. His ass was still intact anyway and he had almost understood something. An angel had pitched him a blessing, Rita, as he had known, all heart. He had seen far into Shooter's evil heart tonight and too far for trust.

He groaned involuntarily so loud he was afraid Shooter might have heard him from the road. He touched the roll of money slightly sticking out of his ass like a fuse of a 4th of July skyrocket able to propel him. Bitterly he thought of the degrading beatings he'd received tonight from the man. Proud of how he'd handled himself, thereby arriving in the "brier patch" instead of killed or maimed, he apprehended the reality of a long day ahead, after a long night. No, but maybe this was the last ride out! What if the man was for real?

The cuffs cut into his flesh. His nakedness stung. Inspired from moment to moment by wild desperation, swooning fear, and absolute fatigue, something in his brain gave way and he found himself at one of those fabled impasses when God alone must help. What if Shooter's apparent change of heart was that very help? For a moment he gave in to such hope.

Disgusted with his nakedness, weary and hurting, trusting God, who had so recently made an unexpected appearance in his thoughts, with the $100K bag safely hidden at the foot of the woman-shaped tree, a treasure the cop could never dream was there and which he had no intention of mentioning, that had been thrown to him by a friend whom he'd betrayed, the Fist was down low yet confident enough to take a leap of faith and run after his homeboy, shouting ancient and endearing epithets into the dawn.

But how paltry that would be! How the hell had he gotten down in this greasy swamp for real anyway? It wasn't so simple. He stepped back farther into the woods. He would stay hidden. The very impossibility of his isolated position was a rush, better than drugs, a promise. He didn't need to not be naked, didn't need to be clothed and freed of the handcuffs, didn't need to be rescued by the asshole who had put him here. He walked back into the forest, on and on, experiencing as he went a soaring freedom, like jumping off a cliff and finding you didn't fall but rose. Only God could straighten out the deeper thicket of his life.

In a devastating flash of astonishment and humiliation he realized that Bobby even in his most extreme plight would not be helped by him. Nobody would, so it seemed. He felt a chill of surprised bereavement, as if people like Bobby, Rita, and even that cab driver had lately been his friends. He was going home wild and alone as he had come out here. He hadn't helped Rita, hadn't confronted let alone arrested her old man, couldn't help Bobby, couldn't help nobody! That cab driver had unloosed himself.

Abruptly his unrequited desire to make amends reached a peak of such intensity that made him laugh grimly at himself.

He was going home. He'd need to tell a few tales at the stationhouse. Then he'd see about a boy he dearly wanted to help on a better path. He thought of the boy's mother with longing. These prospects steeled him. They'd be wondering where he'd been. What if they no longer wanted his help either? He hadn't been away that long.

It struck him remarkable how little the silver-hair dealer, the fat man, bore thinking about any more, when he had been obsessed by him an hour or two ago, as he thought he surely ought to have been. There would always be an endless supply of the salesmen of bad medicine. You had to start with the kids, blocked by the lack of an idea, never mind the odds against them, give them a worthwhile thought. If the growing might take many seasons, his people had been here many seasons, and they would be here always. Truly there was so much else he had to think of now.

The hot gleams of the dawn made him shudder once more at the terrors he had nearly sown for himself and all that he had nearly thrown away. He was shaken, but he was himself again. He had regained his clarity so, the trip down the wrong path almost seemed to have been worth it.

A spasm of love passed over him for his old enemy. He pushed a few feet through the trees, stepping over fallen limbs, but it brought back his lonesome stand in the cornfields. An echo of the midnight strangeness that had overwhelmed his soul in the ravine of the deer resounded. He could smell the mud of the creek down there below the bridge, everything rotten. The rising heat drew out the dank evil smells from the earth.

The last thing that would have occurred to him was that he would not find Bobby where he had left him or that—naked as a jaybird—he would refuse his help. When he could have helped him, he had wanted to kill him, and now that he wished to save him, he couldn't find him. He shook his head and peered into the gloom of the forest but did not glimpse Bobby or any hint of him. Still he felt him near, he was sure of it. He didn't have to talk to him to help him. He didn't need to hear him say thanks.

Having dropped his shoes and clothes in a heap, he slung the cash-crammed briefcase into the base of a tree so hard it made a ringing thud that could be heard a long way he felt certain. Then all hushed to stillness in the tangled forest as he crept out and headed home. After he had driven a few miles on his homeward journey, and emerged from the unfamiliar country roads into recognizable territory, he found himself growing cheerful for the first time in many months.

She was all alone with herself, and it was the best terror she had ever known, streaked by flashes of painful hope like summer heat lightning that promises rain. She had come to the bottom of it, and found her own existence, her very being. She heard herself breathe, felt herself—alive. She pressed her foot harder on the accelerator and the Cadillac shot forward, its hood pointing toward the sky.

Through the lowering cloudbank the last concealed stars suffused a leaden glow even as the first rays of the sun searched through pockets in the clouds, reducing the trees to ashy, dancing silhouettes. It was going to be another hot day, but she could smell the chance of rain in the heavy air that might break the heatspell Chicagoland had been going through. The dawning world newly inhabited by her very being opened in front of her through the dazzled windshield, mysterious, fresh, and beckoning, and she raced toward it passionately.

She thought of Wisconsin's last-ditch rescue of her on the road to nowhere, a nowhere only he had known she'd be. If she could have stayed with anybody, it would have been him. She gripped the Caddy's wheel with all her strength and steered ingeniously. She was sure she had done more for him by taking his car as he wanted her to than she ever could have by sticking with him and wondering what he wanted her to be. She would have been leaning on him to supply her with a sense of the ordinary, a simple fitness she must find herself.

It would have been more like it to go with a bad cop to Africa, who knew every lousy thing there was to know about her as only a cop could know. Now going to Africa to see the lions in the jungle with a stonedout maniac ex-cop would have been more like it, for one like her. They would have been drinking fools together on a mad safari through the bush. It would only have put off the reckoning.

The extreme oddness of driving, let alone a taxi, shook her. How improbable was it to be driving a taxicab in the middle of the woods on her getaway to anywhere? Well, a cab picked you up and dropped you off again at a place of your own choosing, and so it would be. Knowing Wisconsin just a little, she was sure he might have had the same generous thought. When you thought of it, it was no weirder than anything else she had done in her short, absurd existence.

Like a stud poker hand dealt out on the big table at J.A.'s Astor Street place on a Friday night, the gestures that had been made to her this night made their appeal to her once more to bet the limit as they replayed in her mind. She had called on every round, until this, the last one. It would be the last card that counted, and how you played it. She had made good her escape, and defeated all her doubts and devils. It was almost more than she could believe, but she had. In the end she had carried through her plan somehow, and she was on her way at last. It was all up to her now.

The last card had yet to be dealt.

"When you find love . . ." said her mother, close by.

No, mom, she whispered humbly, *I couldn't have borne up to it.*

Then the bigness of life, beyond everything tawdry, cruel, and familiar, opened before her. In the fields in pools of morning light, in the deep forests and unknown lakes ahead, in her soul which had begun to heal—for wounds like hers were only superficial—the bigness of life opened to her like a felicitous turn in the road, revealing a hint of all that had been hidden.